RANDOMS

DAVID LISS

Simon & Schuster Books for Young Readers
NEW YORK • LONDON • TORONTO • SYDNEY • NEW DELHI

SIMON & SCHUSTER BOOKS FOR YOUNG READERS
An imprint of Simon & Schuster Children's Publishing Division
1230 Avenue of the Americas, New York, New York 10020
SIMON & SCHUSTER BOOKS FOR YOUNG READERS is a trademark of Simon & Schuster, Inc.
For information about special discounts for bulk purchases,
please contact Simon & Schuster Special Sales at 1-866-506-1949 or
business@simonandschuster.com.
The Simon & Schuster Speakers Bureau can bring authors to your live event.
For more information or to book an event, contact the Simon & Schuster Speakers Bureau at
1-866-248-3049 or visit our website at www.simonspeakers.com.
Jacket design by Lizzy Bromley
Interior design by Hilary Zarycky
The text for this book is set in New Caledonia.
Manufactured in the United States of America
0715 FFG
2 4 6 8 10 9 7 5 3 1
Library of Congress Cataloging-in-Publication Data
Randoms / David Liss.—First edition.
pages cm
Summary: "A twelve-year-old boy is chosen to join a four-person applicant team to work toward
membership in the Confederation of United Planets, and stumbles across conspiracies resembling
science fiction he's been a fan of his entire life"—Provided by publisher.
ISBN 978-1-4814-1779-2 (hardcover)
ISBN 978-1-4814-1781-5 (eBook)
[1. Science fiction. 2. Conspiracies—Fiction.] I. Title.
PZ7.1.L57Ran 2015
[Fic]—dc23
2014026966

FIRST EDITION

For Eleanor and Simon

ACKNOWLEDGMENTS

I've been working as a professional writer for fifteen years, and I can honestly say I've never enjoyed working on a novel as much as this one. Part of that fun came from sharing early versions with test readers whose encouragement helped to get me past the doubts of radical genre-shifting. Veronica Goldbach, Sheri Holman, Sophia Hollander, John Aidan Kozlovsky, John Minton, Iris Sabrina de Andrade, and Heather Sullivan all provided astute and delightfully dorky feedback, as well as much-needed enthusiasm, during the early days of this project. I am also lucky to have benefited from the advice, brilliance, and friendship of the boldest federation of writers ever assembled: Robert Jackson Bennett, Rhodi Hawk, Joe McKinney, and Hank Schwaeble. And a special thanks to Jonathan Maberry, who badgered me into writing this book in the first place.

I am grateful, as always, for the direction provided by my agent, Liz Darhansoff. I also can't sufficiently thank the team at Simon & Schuster for their cosmic efforts in getting this book into shape. I am convinced David Gale must be the most insightful, hard-working, and dedicated editor in the business, and I feel very lucky to have benefited from his knowledge, patience, and Jedi mastery. A huge thanks goes out to Liz Kossnar, the Han Solo of editorial assistants. I am thankful and relieved the book landed with as sure-handed and thoughtful a copy editor as Karen Sherman.

This book owes much to support, love, and geeky enthusiasms of my family. My son Simon has always been ready to share my own genre obsessions, and my daughter Eleanor provided excellent age-appropriate feedback (thanks for suggesting flying saucers!). She also sat with me as I rewatched Star Trek films (not *Star Trek V*, just so we're clear). My wife, Claudia, has always been my best and most clear-headed champion. I'm lucky to be married to someone with whom I can converse in Klingon. And, finally, anyone who reads this book will understand why I must also thank my cats for always being themselves.

Part One

FIRST CONTACT

CHAPTER ONE

Tanner Hughes was in the process of smacking me in the head and making some unflattering observations about my masculinity while his girlfriend, Madison, leaned against the wall, tapping on her phone. This was the music of my humiliation—the vacuum whoosh of texts on their way out and the chime of those coming in. We were in my science classroom, and I was supposed to be taking an after-school makeup quiz. Mrs. Capelli, my teacher, had stepped out ten minutes before, telling me she was *trusting me* to conduct myself *responsibly*. I wasn't sure if retreating with my arms raised to protect my face qualified as responsible behavior.

I wasn't a total coward. Under the right conditions, I was willing to take a stand. When you traveled as much as my mom and I did, and started a new school every year, you had to be ready to face guys like Tanner Hughes, who were always on the lookout for fresh victims. That was the theory, anyhow. In practice, I wanted to keep things from escalating. I was in sixth grade, Tanner was in eighth, and he looked like maybe he had enjoyed some of his earlier grades enough to want to repeat one or two of them. He was easily six inches taller than I was and had about a twenty-pound advantage, all of it in muscle. I'd confronted my share of bullies, and I knew how to play the odds. In this case, I put my money on holding out until the teacher returned, which I hoped would be very soon.

I also wanted to believe that maybe after Tanner got in a couple of jaw-rattlers, Madison might possibly ask her boyfriend to back off. Girls were apt to become bored with felony assault. No luck there. Every time Tanner took a swipe at me, Madison sighed, like she was *OMG, so bored*, and then went back to her phone.

I'm not saying I hadn't given Tanner Hughes good reason to hate me. I had after all, shown up in *his* school, offended him with what he considered a lame haircut (I had been trying to coax my slightly limp brown hair into looking like Matt Smith's, and I was happy with the results, but I respect dissenting opinions), and, perhaps most seriously, looked at him in the hallway. In my defense, he had been standing in the part of the hallway where I was heading, and I like to look where I'm going, but still. I understood his point.

We had, in other words, pretty much irreconcilable differences. He found my existence offensive. I wanted to exist. I didn't have a lot of faith that we were going to work out a compromise.

I was considering the hopelessness of my position while also sidestepping a shove that would have knocked me into, and possibly through, the wall, when Mrs. Capelli returned to the classroom. She'd left me alone and made me promise to do nothing but finish my quiz, so I could understand how it might look bad to see me with Tanner and Madison in the room. That said, Tanner was in the middle of stamping his boot treads all over the emptied contents of my notebook, which he'd taken the time and trouble to scatter across the floor. I kind of thought the evidence might point toward me not really welcoming the company.

In a perfect world, Tanner Hughes would have been delivered over to our educational correctional machine and suffered a stern talking-to for his crimes against society and my notebook. This was not a perfect world, however. Tanner was the goalie for the school soccer team—it never hurts to have a guy the width of a garbage Dumpster standing in the way of the opponents scoring—and that team was one game away from securing a place in the middle school state playoffs. That Mrs. Capelli's son was a starting midfielder only served to bring the truth into sharper focus. After all, Tanner's version of events made perfect sense: I'd invited him into the class and demanded that a meat head with a C-minus average help me with my quiz. When he'd refused, I'd become so "spastic" that Tanner had been forced to defend himself. When Mrs. Capelli asked Madison if that was what had happened, Madison shrugged and mumbled a stirring "I guess," which would have convinced even the most hardened Tanner doubters out there.

That was how I ended up in the front office so the principal could discuss my many deficiencies with my mother.

A lot of kids cringe at the prospect of their parents being called in to the principal's office. A lot of kids are afraid of their parents. A lot of kids, I am led to believe, have crummy parents, but I was not one of them. I was not afraid of my mother. I was afraid *for* her, because the last thing she needed was more stress. My mother had recently been handed a bad diagnosis—a really bad one. Scary, terrifying, bad. Besides medicines her insurance company would not pay for, and exercises she had no time to do, what she needed most was to reduce the amount of stress in her life. Thanks to Tanner Hughes, Mrs. Capelli, the principal, the school, and the game of soccer, I had just become the source of more stress.

To look at her, you wouldn't know she had an unbelievably awful disease. She sat in the principal's office in her pantsuit, legs crossed, her brown hair up in a bun. No one else would have noticed the new and deeply etched lines around her eyes, the creases in her forehead, and the appearance of a few streaks of gray in her hair. On the other hand, I kept a running tally of how she looked from one day to the next.

"So," she said to Principal Landis, "tell me again why Zeke is in trouble and this other boy is not."

Principal Landis was not what you would call a thin man. He *was* what you would call a fat man. I understand that no one is perfect. I, for example, am both tall and thin—there are those who have referred to me as *gangly*—and I've already mentioned my controversial haircut. All of which is to say that I've been on the receiving end of personal insults. Empathy being what it is, I try to avoid making fun of how someone might look, but if the person in question is a complete jerk, then I say it's a good time to make an exception. This was one of those times. Principal? Fat.

I don't want to suggest that Mr. Landis was circus-freak heavy. He was not grotesquely fat. He was, however, hilariously fat. Every part of him was overweight. Even his ears were fat, his nose was fat, his fingers massive, blubbery loaves, and it was hard to take him seriously. Also, he was balding. There's no reason a receding hairline has to be funny. Many men wear baldness well, even make it look cool. On my principal: funny.

Mr. Landis leaned forward, his fat wrists splayed on the desk. The desk, in response, creaked. "Though he has been with us only a few months, this is not the first time Zeke has been involved in an *incident*," This last word generated air quotes with sausagey fingers.

"If by *incident*," my mother said, somehow resisting the urge to air quote back at him, "you mean that boy bullying him, then you are absolutely correct. I'd like to know why you aren't doing anything about this."

"This accusation of bullying is troubling," said Mr. Landis, now leaning back and intertwining his large fingers. "I take it very seriously."

He said this with such finality that I was tempted to rise, clap my hands together, and say, *I'm glad we got all that worked out.*

My mother wasn't buying it. "I don't see that you do take it seriously. This is the third time this semester that I've been called in to discuss Zeke's behavior, and each time his behavior, as near as I can tell, is his getting picked on."

Mr. Landis narrowed his eyes and pressed his lips together in a show of indignation. "Let me remind you that we are not here to discuss what other students may or may not have done. Zeke has not done a very good job of settling in at this school, as you are no doubt aware. I understand that your career has led you to move frequently, but that does not change the fact that Zeke has difficulty making friends, and he has antisocial interests. Together, these factors suggest the profile of a student who might present a danger to himself or others."

"Wait a minute," I said. "Are you saying that because Tanner Hughes comes into a classroom where I'm taking a quiz and messes with me, you think I'm going to show up with a gun and starting shooting up the place?"

"No one mentioned guns," Mr. Landis said, "until you did, just now. Quite honestly, I feel unsafe."

My mother stood up. "We're done here."

Mr. Landis looked up from my file. "If Zeke makes an effort to stay out of trouble, I will certainly rethink how seriously we have to take his threats against the school."

My mother stared at him for a long minute. I knew her well enough to understand that she was seriously considering making a comment that included the words "fat," "bald," or both. I also knew her well enough to understand that no matter how seriously she considered it, she wouldn't actually do it. At the time I thought it was probably the right decision, but later I would wish she had indulged.

I had no way of knowing that I was never going to set foot in that school again.

CHAPTER TWO

For the record, I did not have difficulty making friends, at least no more than you would expect from a kid in my situation—which, admittedly, produced some challenges. My mother was an environmental compliance consultant, and that meant she moved around the country helping companies keep up with changing pollution laws. Every year or so we found ourselves in a different city, something that was never easy for me, and was getting harder each time.

Starting a new school partway into the first semester of the sixth grade was particularly tough. Cliques had already been formed, and most kids were friends with people they'd known for years. Still, nerds find each other. Not because of appearances, though. I like to believe I look like your average kid. I don't wear Coke-bottle glasses or pull my pants up to my armpits. I don't spend too much time worrying about my clothes, but I dress okay. I could probably benefit from a little time lifting weights, but I'm still kind of athletic, and I'd been on the track team at my last school.

When I got to my new school, it didn't take me too long to find a group to hang out with. We RPGed, talked books, movies, and comics. We played video games, both in person and in co-op. I was not, and never had been, the loner sitting in his room, looking at pictures of automatic weapons and thinking about how *they were all going to pay*. I figured Tanner Hughes and his kind would pay by spending the rest of their lives being themselves. The kids I had problems with were their own worst enemies. They could be counted on to take revenge against themselves sooner or later.

Even so, I didn't have any epic, lifelong friends. Kirk and Spock. Data and La Forge. Han and Chewie (though that relationship always felt a little one-sided to me). Those were the kind of friendships I envied. I wanted a friend who would call me in the middle of the night and say, "I need you to go to the main bus station in Tucson, Arizona. I can't tell you why." I would hang up and then be off to Tucson, regardless of the consequences, because this would be the sort of friend who wouldn't ask me to go if he didn't need me. He would know he could count on me, and I would know I could count on him.

I didn't have friends who even came close to that level. Still, what I had was okay.

My father, Uriah Reynolds, had been a professional dork, which I guess meant dorkdom was in my blood. For years he made his living as an editor of fantasy and science-fiction novels. I used to love going through his home office, looking at the books he had lying around, thick volumes with pictures of aliens and spaceships and futuristic cities on the covers. In those days, I had a normal life. We lived in a quiet New Jersey suburb, an hour from New York City, and, in the way of little kids, I expected my life to be like that forever.

My dad went to sci-fi and comic conventions all the time, and he'd always come home with great stuff—*Star Wars* and *Star Trek* action figures, ship models, toy blasters and phasers. Whatever else he brought me, he would always try to find something related to Martian Manhunter, who was my dad's favorite superhero and so became mine: Martian Manhunter toys, mugs, key chains, posters, and snow globes. His green skin, protruding brow, and muscular chest crossed with two red bands were all as familiar to me as my own reflection. Martian Manhunter wasn't the most popular member of the Justice League, but my father was drawn to the sad nobility of the honorable survivor of a lost race.

He enjoyed his work in publishing, but he was always reaching for something more. Sometimes he would disappear into his office, typing away relentlessly on his keyboard, working on his own stories. I never thought too much about it, but then he found an agent, and his pitch for a TV show was picked up by one of the cable networks. It was a sci-fi series called *Colony Alpha*, and for a while it looked like my father's dreams were going to come true.

The network gushed enthusiasm about the show. It was going to be a huge hit, they assured him. I remember sitting on the rug in our living room, watching him pace around the house as he talked to his agent or the show's producer on the phone, excitement visible in his every movement.

Then, in the way dreams do, his dream began to unravel. There were the casting problems. A couple of feisty kids were thrown in to improve the show's appeal with young viewers. The network added a former swimsuit model whose main function was to walk around in a bodysuit and strike poses. The special effects were mind-bogglingly bad, and the talentless directors they brought in to save money made every scene feel like middle school theater. *Colony Alpha* was canceled after five weeks, the network never bothering to air the last three episodes.

My father was devastated, but he had come too close to give up. *Colony Alpha* was his dream, and he believed he could bring it to life somewhere. When an Australian TV producer contacted him about relaunching down under, my dad jumped at the chance. This, too, turned out be just another false hope. I still remember hearing the phone ring, seeing my mother at the kitchen table, her back slumped, her shoulders trembling so violently that her shirt rippled. I couldn't see her face, and she made no noise, but I knew she was crying, and I knew I was never going to see my father again.

The show's producer had been taking my father to visit some possible shooting locations. It was early in the morning, and there was no traffic on the Sydney highway. The police suspected the producer had wanted to show off, to impress my father with what his new Ferrari could do. A tire blew out, and the car rolled five times before it fell off the bridge.

That was five years ago.

In the year before he died, my father had to endure the jeers of science-fiction fans—his own people, as he put it—over what a piece of garbage he had created. He hated that fans believed that what they saw was the show he had envisioned. I think that was one of the reasons he worked so hard to find a new home for his idea.

The ironic thing is that *Colony Alpha* went on to become the poster child for quality genre shows mutilated by clueless network suits. It is often called the greatest science-fiction show that never was. There's fan fiction, lists of dream casts for a reboot. On YouTube you can watch fan films based on scenes from the original scripts. The dork blog io9 once ran a post called "Ten Ways *Colony Alpha* Changed Science Fiction."

Uriah Reynolds did become the sci-fi hero he'd always dreamed of being, but it only happened after he was dead.

Between work, dealing with her terminal disease, and taking the time to bail out her delinquent son, my mother didn't have much time to cook. Once she had rescued me from the principal's office, we stopped to pick up Chinese takeout so we could enjoy a quiet evening of sitting at the kitchen table and complaining about my life.

The previous year we had been in Albuquerque, where even in the winter it didn't get dark until pretty late. Now we were in Wilmington, Delaware, and though it wasn't yet five o'clock, the sun was already going down. I liked that, for some reason. I liked the cold and the quiet, and how our house was well lit and warm against the early December chill. It was nice and comfortable and safe, except in all the ways it wasn't. No matter how funny or lively or good-natured my mother might act, I knew nothing was ever going to be comfortable for her again.

"I'm really sorry you had to deal with that stuff today," I told her.

She put down her disposable chopsticks and leveled her gaze at me. "You've got to be kidding me, Zeke. Do you honestly think I'd be angry with you?"

"I know, but I hate that you have to take the time and put up with the stress and all that."

She smiled. She looked perfectly okay. That was the thing that made no sense to me. She looked so healthy and normal, it was hard to believe that was all going to change. Six months before, my mother had been diagnosed with amyotrophic lateral sclerosis, ALS, also called Lou Gehrig's disease. It's a degenerative neurological condition that causes gradual but catastrophic muscle failure. At some unknown point in her future, she would begin to lose the ability to control her limbs, and then, slowly, she would suffer failure in the muscles that allowed her to do things like breathe and swallow and blink. She was going to become a living corpse, trapped within her own failed body. I didn't want to think about her journey from healthy to disabled to helpless, but sometimes I couldn't think about anything else.

"Look," she said, "just promise me you'll stop threatening your principal."

We both laughed.

"If I made that joke at school, I would totally get kicked out," I said.

Now she was serious. "Do not make that joke at school."

"Mom, I'm not a complete idiot."

"You're twelve," she said. "That means you're a complete idiot at least part of the time."

Then came the knock at the door.

I got up to answer it, and when I threw the doors open, I saw two men on the front stoop. I hadn't turned on the porch light, and their dark suits made them almost invisible. They had grave expressions, stiff postures, and earpieces. They looked scary and governmental.

"I swear, we were kidding," I said. "I'm not going to threaten my principal."

The men looked at each other, then at me. "Are you Ezekiel Reynolds?" the taller one asked.

I thought he was about to arrest me, so all I could manage was a nod. I also flicked on the porch light. Just because you are scared doesn't mean you can't be polite.

"I'm Agent Jimenez, and this is Agent McTeague. May we have a word with you?"

My mother was now standing behind me. "What's this about?"

"Ma'am, we would rather not say on the front porch."

"Do you have a warrant?" My mother had just shifted into she-bear mode.

"Ma'am," said Agent Jimenez, "it isn't that kind of conversation."

"So this isn't about . . ." My mother decided not to finish that thought.

"Ezekiel's threats against his principal?" Agent Jimenez asked with death-row seriousness. Then he grinned. "No, ma'am. Your son is not in any trouble."

My mother sighed. She was clearly feeling less threatened, but she wasn't quite prepared to let the men into the house. "Look, I'm not comfortable with this, especially considering how vague you're being."

"I understand," said Agent McTeague. "We anticipated some natural reluctance on your part." He touched his earpiece and said, "We're go for Renegade."

I had no idea what that meant, but it sounded cool. I'd never been go for anything, at least not that I knew of.

The doors of one of the black cars in the driveway opened, and more people in suits came out. It was dark and I couldn't see who they were, only that several of them were standing around one person, as if protecting him. It was only when he stepped into the porch light and was standing just a couple of feet away from me that I recognized him.

"Mr. Reynolds," he said. "I hope I can have a few minutes

of your time." He spoke in his usual serious but easy tone. It was the kind of voice that let you know he was a friendly guy, but not one you wanted to mess with. I'd heard him use this tone a million times on TV.

"Um, sure," I said. "Okay. Come on in. Sir. Please."

I stood aside to let him pass, because that seemed to be the right thing to do when you receive a visit from the president of the United States.

Of America. Just so there's no confusion.

CHAPTER THREE

My mom managed not to freak out, which I considered impressive. She invited the president to sit, and he did. She offered him a beverage, and he declined. She stammered only moderately when she spoke. There were more agents in the house now, swarming around as they made sure we didn't keep any assassins lurking in the pantry or the coat closet. Some of the agents held out what looked like thick metal pens, which, they explained, allowed them to scan for listening devices. It turned out that we had none, which I probably could have told them, considering that anyone with the means to plant a listening device could not possibly care what my mother and I had to say. We tried not to worry about the fact that there were agents moving throughout the house, and more in the backyard, standing at the ready in case, I don't know, the propane grill decided to attack.

In the living room, my mom and I did our best to ignore all this. Next to the president sat an intense-looking woman with distractingly red nail polish, her coppery hair pulled back tightly and mercilessly clipped into place. She was perhaps in her midthirties, and she wore a severe pantsuit that looked almost military in its cut. She and her clothes were all sharp lines and hard angles, and her eyes were an unfeeling icy blue. She might have been pretty if she hadn't looked like she ate puppies for breakfast. The president introduced her as Nora

Price from the State Department. I had no idea what her job was, but she had the kind of scary expression that made me feel pretty sure she would trample anyone who got in the way of her doing it.

The president pressed his hands together and leaned forward. "Mrs. Reynolds, I apologize that I am going to be somewhat secretive. I've come here to ask if your son could be our guest for a few days. I can assure you he will be in absolutely no danger."

"What?" she asked, her voicing rising several octaves.

Ms. Price smiled, but it was more indulgent than warm, the kind of smile used only by people who have to work hard at appearing nonthreatening. "I can assure you this is a matter of national security."

I was starting to think that illegally downloading those episodes of *Teen Wolf* might have been a mistake. I knew the commercials told us that piracy is not a victimless crime. Even so, I wanted to believe the president had other things to worry about. "Why do you need me?" I managed to ask without my voice cracking.

"That's classified," Ms. Price said, not kindly. She seemed to have forgotten to appear nonthreatening.

"It needs to be unclassified," my mother said, "or I'm not agreeing to anything. These agents say he isn't in trouble."

"And he isn't," the president assured her, taking a much warmer tone than the State Department woman. "All I can tell you is that there is a visiting representative of, uh, shall we say, a foreign government, who has requested the honor of meeting Ezekiel. I can't say anything more, so I understand your frustration. I have two daughters myself, and I can imagine I wouldn't much care for it if someone came to me and proposed what I'm proposing to you. I can only give you my word as your president, and as a father, that your son will not be in harm's way, and that he will be doing a great service to his country."

"How long are we talking about?" my mother asked.

"Initially, two days," the president said. "It may happen that Zeke will choose to participate in a sort of foreign exchange program, and if that's the case, it will be longer. At that point, you would receive more information."

"What sort of exchange program?" she demanded. "With what country? Wait, let me guess. You can't tell me."

The president smiled, and it was genuine. I had the feeling he had already come to like my mother, as if under other circumstances the two of them could have hung out—gone bowling or whatever. "The only thing I can add is that it will be a unique experience," he told her. "I do feel very confident that your son will not regret coming with us."

I looked at the president. "Does it have to be me, or will some other kid work? Sir."

"It has to be you," the president assured me.

"Why would some ambassador even know who I am? Is this about my father's show?" American shows, even unsuccessful ones, can develop followings in foreign countries. For reasons that remain unclear to me, they went wild for *Colony Alpha* in Estonia.

"The father," Ms. Price explained to the president, "now deceased, created an unpopular television program."

Now there's a way to honor a man's life.

"It has nothing to do with that," the president said. "As to why it has to be you, I'm afraid I can't tell you at this time."

My mother took a deep breath and squared her shoulders, a sure sign she was about to say something that made her uncomfortable. "I'm sorry, but the answer is no. I'm not letting you take my son unless you give me more information."

"We don't actually have to ask you," Ms. Price said. She sat up straight, and the hard look she gave my mother was nothing short of a challenge. "This is a national security matter, and, as such, we can take him whether you like it or not. If you attempt to interfere, we can arrest you. We don't want to play it that way—"

The president held up his hand to silence her. "And we won't. Zeke is not going to be taken against his will, and no one is going to be arrested."

"So I can say no?" asked my mother.

"My plan," the president said, "is to stay here until I can convince you to say yes."

I couldn't imagine why any ambassador would want to meet me, but I also couldn't imagine going the rest of my life without finding out. How would I feel, years from now, when I remembered the time the president came asking for my help, and I sent him away?

It seemed to me that this might be a situation I could use to my mother's advantage. If I could help her, and find out why my government needed me, then everyone would be a winner.

"The thing is," I said, "if I were to go, it would be hard on my mom, and this isn't a good time for her to be under stress."

The president nodded gravely. "Yes, we are aware of her health issues."

My mother started at this. "That's none of the government's business. How, exactly, did my private health-care records—"

Ms. Price cut her off. "National security."

I spoke up before my mother decided to see what would happen if she gouged out the eyes of someone in the president's entourage. "Are you aware," I asked, "that her insurance company has been giving her a hard time about the treatments her doctor wants her to get?"

"Ezekiel!" my mother snapped. Maybe she thought this was no one else's business, or maybe she had an inkling of what I had in mind. Either way, she was unhappy.

The president raised his eyebrows like he was mildly amused. "Go on."

He was going to make me say it. "I was wondering if you might be able to smooth some things over, being, you know, the president and all. It would make me feel better to know my mom was getting the care her doctor prescribed."

The president frowned, deep in serious thought, and there was maybe a hint of the side of him you didn't want to see. After a moment's thought, he reached into his jacket pocket and pulled out his cell phone. He pressed one button. "A Mrs. Reynolds is going to be calling your office tomorrow. Have one of your people take her information and make certain her insurance company understands that you want her to receive any treatment her doctor recommends."

The president then looked at my mother. "That was the secretary of health and human services." He was typing into his phone as he spoke. "I'm sending a note to my assistant right now to provide you with her direct number. You call her, and you'll have everything you need."

My mother looked at him. She looked at me. "Thank you," she said quietly.

"Now," the president said, meeting my eye, "are you done playing hardball with the leader of the free world?"

"I haven't agreed to anything," my mother reminded him.

"Come *on*, Mom," I said. "He said I'd be in no danger."

"No danger whatsoever," the president assured her.

I knew what she was thinking. She was wondering if she would have been so reluctant if she hadn't been sick, and that was what would tip her over to my side. She hated the thought of what her illness would do to me, the kinds of responsibilities that would come my way, the experiences I might miss.

"You're sure you want to go?" she asked.

"I don't know what this is about, but I have to admit I'm pretty curious."

She gave the slightest of nods.

And because I am always thinking ahead, I turned to the severe woman, Ms. Price. "I'll also need a note excusing my absence from school. Can I get that on White House stationery?"

I quickly packed a small bag with enough clothes for two days. My mother hugged me several times and told me to call her if I got scared or if I needed to come home. I hated to leave her, and I was already plenty scared, but every time I thought about pulling the plug, my curiosity kicked in. Why, of all the people in the country, did *I* have to speak to some foreign bigwig? How could it possibly be so important that the president of the United States would drive two hours to Wilmington to press his case? I had to know what this was about.

I did not get to ride with the president, but he stopped me before I got into the backseat of a sedan. He shook my hand and thanked me for being willing to serve my country.

"I appreciate that, sir," I said, trying to act like I was not flipping out.

"I think you'll find it interesting," he said. "And Ezekiel. For the record, I respect how you stood up for your mother's interests. I know that all of this"—he waved his hands at the sedans and the agents—"must be very intimidating. You've got a lot of courage, young man."

"Thank you, sir," I said, feeling like a phony. I was sure that if the president had seen me cringing as Tanner Hughes smacked me around, he'd have found some other clueless kid to meet with the ambassador of wherever.

I rode with Agents Jimenez and McTeague, who were polite but not particularly conversational. As we pulled onto the highway and headed toward DC, I finally worked up the nerve to speak. "Do you guys know what is going on?"

Jimenez shrugged. "I am not authorized to answer that."

"You're not authorized to tell me whether or not you know?"

"I'm not even authorized to explain what I initially meant."

"What about you, Agent McTeague?" I asked the agent riding shotgun.

"I'm not authorized even to discuss my level of authorization," he said without turning around.

"Is there anything at all you can tell me?"

"I'm not authorized to answer any questions about what I can or cannot answer," Agent Jimenez said. "Except," he began, and then he just shook his head. "Wow. That's all I'm going to say. Wow." Then he cast a look at McTeague and the two of them burst out laughing.

CHAPTER FOUR

thought I was going to the White House. When the president of the United States comes by and says, "Let's hang," you figure you're heading for Oreos in the Oval Office. This turned out not to be the case. The president had dropped by to convince me and my mom I should go along with the Secret Service guys, but he had more important things to do than deal with me.

Our destination was Camp David, which was not as exciting as the White House, but it was still pretty impressive. How many people do you know who have been to Camp David? That's what I thought.

We passed through several checkpoints and drove down narrow streets dense with groves of wintry, leafless trees that looked spooky in the dark. We finally parked outside a large building that was more hunting-cabiny than I would have imagined. The agents led me inside and through rooms that looked like they had been designed by extremely wealthy pioneers, and brought me to a less rustic-looking office. The severe State Department woman, Nora Price, was sitting behind a desk waiting for me. Or rather, she was there when I entered, and proceeded to ignore me so she could work and I could watch her do it. I stood across from her while she typed away furiously on her laptop. The Secret Service agents had already retreated. Finally, without looking up, she gestured with a flick of her crimson fingernails for me to sit in one of the heavy wooden chairs.

The endless *clack clack clack* of her fingers on the keyboard didn't slow, but after about five minutes she said, "I'm sure you are wondering why you've been invited here."

"You know, I am wondering about that." The sarcasm was a sure sign of my growing impatience.

She sighed and pushed herself away from the computer. "I could explain it to you, but you would never believe me."

"Maybe you could try," I suggested. "Otherwise, I'll end up sitting and watching you type for a long time."

I was getting the impression she didn't like kids in general, or me in particular. She stared at me for a long time, as if wishing I would vanish. When I didn't, she offered one final, long-suffering sigh, stood up, and walked over to my side of the desk. I now saw she was holding a cylinder about four inches long and an inch in diameter. It appeared to be made out of some kind of dull black metal, smooth and without distinguishable features. Without asking my permission she pressed one end of it to the back of my hand. It let out a little humming noise, and a slightly warm feeling bloomed across my skin.

"What was that?" I rubbed my hand, but the warmth was already gone. It felt perfectly normal.

Ms. Price returned to her seat. "I've just injected you with nanites. Those are—"

"I know what nanites are," I said, feeling dizzy, though I didn't know if that was from the injection or the knowledge that I now had something top secret, and probably insufficiently tested, in my blood.

"Impressive," she said, though she sounded more irritated than impressed. "I didn't."

"Nanotechnology is pretty common in a lot of sci-fi," I explained.

She waved a hand to indicate that this conversation was going places she didn't much like.

"I didn't give you permission to inject me with anything," I told her. "I didn't see my mother sign a consent form."

She pressed her lips together. "You could always complain about being exposed to technology that's not supposed to exist, and which no doctor in the world will be able to detect, but I'm not sure it would get you very far."

"That's a fair point," I admitted. "What do these nanites do, exactly?"

Nanites are, in effect, machines built on the molecular level. They are still experimental as far as practical application in the real world goes, but in science fiction they can be used to augment natural human ability, increase brain function, cure diseases, impart information directly into the brain, turn skin into armor and limbs into weapons, change the shape of your body or face . . . just about anything imaginable. I'd always loved the idea—in theory. I didn't know that I loved the idea of having them in me right now, especially since I didn't know what they were up to.

"The nanites will help you to communicate," Ms. Price said, with less enthusiasm than the subject of advanced and invasive technology seemed to deserve.

This was starting to sound creepy. I didn't know that I wanted machines in my brain. "Communicate what?"

"Ezekiel, there's no way to prepare you for what I'm going to tell you, so I'm going to say it outright. For the past week, several nations of this world have been negotiating with a representative of a vast network of alien species. They are considering admitting our world, on a provisional basis, into their alliance, and the first step is for us to send four young people, chosen by the aliens, to one of their cultural hubs. Our worth as a species will be measured by the behavior of this small group. However improbably, you have been chosen to be part of this process."

I stared at her. She had to be messing with me, but this woman looked like she had no direct experience with the concept known as humor.

She shook her head in apparent sadness. "I know it is hard to believe." She pressed an intercom button on her phone. "Tell the representative we're ready for him."

I was about to ask her something, but whatever my question was, it froze in my throat, because a giraffe in a business suit had entered the room. Up to his shoulders he had the frame of a pretty normal man, but then, exploding out of the collar, were two feet of heavily muscled neck covered by short, nut-brown fur. Then there was the giraffe head, with a long snout, large ears, and two stubby protrusions sticking up from the forehead.

The suit was charcoal gray, and nicely tailored. The giraffe creature had an impeccably folded white handkerchief in the front pocket. I thought that was weird.

Technically, he was not really a giraffe. For one thing, he didn't have giraffe markings. For another, he walked on two legs and he wore a suit. Also, he spoke, which is not something you generally expect from a giraffe.

"Hello," he said. "I'm Dr. Klhkkkloplkkkuiv Roop." He stuck out his hand for me to shake.

In something of a daze, I shook. The creature had tapered

hands, with long, narrow fingers, and they were covered with the same brownish fur, but otherwise they looked a whole lot like they could be human. He also had a firm handshake and he met my eye, so, if necessary, I could trust him to sell me a used car.

"You must be Ezekiel Reynolds," he said. His accent sounded vaguely European, which surprised me. To my knowledge, giraffe men are not native to Europe.

"Yeah," I managed, and I thought I was extremely articulate under the circumstances. My neck was already hurting from this conversation. Up to the shoulders he was normal person-size, but with the neck the total package was close to about eight feet.

"I understand this is difficult for you," he said, "and I can think of nothing to make it less so. We might as well jump right in."

"Sure," I agreed. "That sounds like a plan."

The giraffe guy gestured for me to sit, and I did. He sat across from me, crossed his legs, and adjusted this tie.

"I work," he began, "for the Department of Sentient Integration, a branch of the Coalition of Central Governing Committees of the Confederation of United Planets. We are a vast alliance of species native to our section of galactic spiral. From time to time, when our selection committee has identified four qualified worlds, we recruit new species who have achieved certain cultural and technological milestones. From each species we identify four young beings who possess skills or attributes admired in our culture and request that they spend a standard year with us so we may evaluate them and determine if their culture is a good fit for our own, and if ours is a good fit for them. The honorable members of the selection committee have picked four beings from your planet, and you, Ezekiel, are one of them."

I said nothing for a long time. Ms. Price stared at me like I was an idiot, which, coincidentally, I felt like. Dr. Roop widened his big yellow eyes slightly as the clock ticked on.

Finally, I thought of something to say. "Is this a joke?" As soon as I said it, I realized this question might not suggest I was the absolute best the human race had to offer.

Ms. Price breathed in sharply through her nose, as if my question caused her pain. "Ezekiel, I assure you that the president is far too busy to play pranks on an irrelevant twelve-year-old."

I realized the joke theory was not holding up under scrutiny. For now, I was willing to run with the idea that this giraffe guy was an alien. Even so, I had some questions.

"Dr. Roop," I started.

"Please," he said, waving a furry hand. "There's no need to be so formal. Call me Klhkkkloplkkkuiv."

"Uh, no," I said. "I'm not going to do that." His name sounded like he was choking on a fish bone. "Look, I'm confused. Also freaked out, but we'll deal with confusion first. I mean, this Confederation of United Planets sounds an awful lot like the United Federation of Planets, which is from a TV show. You can see why I have a hard time buying it."

"Certainly," he said, spreading his fingers in the Vulcan salute. "*Star Trek.* I find it charming. You see, Zeke, for many decades we've known Earth to be a strong candidate for Confederation membership, and in accordance with our long-standing practice, we have used certain back channels to filter facts about the wider galaxy into your speculative narratives."

"You're telling me that sci-fi is influenced by actual fact?"

"Some of it, yes."

"And there really is a government of peaceful and benevolent aliens out there?"

"Yes," he said.

"And ships that can travel between stars without being limited by the laws of physics?"

"As you understand those laws, absolutely."

"And we're talking, and your mouth doesn't really seem suited to make words in our language, so there must be some kind of universal translator?"

"Ms. Price injected you with the appropriate nanites before our meeting. They are able to process and interpret virtually any language, spoken or written, and in most cases do so instantaneously."

"Then why do you sound like you have a French accent?"

"Dutch," Ms. Price said. "He sounds Dutch."

"On occasion, the translator will find analogues from your own linguistic experiences to help convey certain cultural inflections."

"But," I said, "it looks like you're speaking English. I could read your lips."

"It's an illusion created by the nanites. Otherwise the discontinuity between a being's words and its movements might prove jarring. The translator function will also provide equivalents of nonlinguistic noises, such as laughter and sighs. Body language you will have to work out on your own."

"Wow. Okay."

"You may also, on occasion, detect a slight delay in the translation when the system attempts to find a familiar equivalent in your language and then opts, instead, to provide explanatory wording. So, if I mention a type of food native to my planet, such as [*spiny leaves with dried fruit*], or perhaps an unfamiliar alien custom such as [*the ritualistic hair-coiffing of herd tenders*], you will notice the difference in my voice."

"Yeah," I said. "For sure." It was hard to describe, but when he said those things, the voice sounded slightly slower, and like it was vibrating, but not exactly. It was more of a feeling, and I understood that I was getting a rough equivalent, and there was a kind of mental pause and rush, like if a video playback had a glitch that caused it to slow and then hurry ahead to catch up. "That's cool. Wait, did you just get that weird sensation when I said *cool*?"

"I received a relative cultural equivalent of whatever word you used."

I couldn't get my head around all of this—not really. This dapper giraffe in a suit, who spoke with a Dutch accent, was a real alien, born on another planet full of giraffe people, who had access to incredible technology. And it was all real. "What else is out there?" I asked.

"There are too many things to list, so perhaps you could tell me what you are curious to hear about," Dr. Roop suggested amiably. He tilted his head to one side, but having just been told that that I wasn't getting any help on body language, I had no idea what it meant.

I thought for a second. "Are there, I don't know, space pirates?"

"Some. Not many." He lowered his neck in a gesture that I

felt sure meant something among his own kind. A shrug? "Our peace officers try to make piracy an unappealing option."

"Mysterious elder aliens and extinct races?"

"Oh, yes." His eyes widened.

"Teleportation?"

"Only on a subatomic level," he said. "Much of the defense technology we possess depends upon what amounts to, for all practical purposes, quantum-level teleportation. The process can be done on a larger scale, but requires vast amounts of energy, and the only way to teleport a living being is to destroy it and recreate an identical facsimile. Most beings choose not to experiment with the process."

"Yeah, I can see why. How about time travel?"

He cocked his head slightly. "I am not at liberty to discuss that subject."

That was a yes, I decided. "Can I transfer my consciousness into an avatar?"

"It can be done," he said, "but the side effects include shortness of breath and explosive diarrhea. It's much easier to simply reshape your existing body."

"What about the Force and Jedi powers? Are they real?"

"No," Dr. Roop said. "That would be silly."

Here was the deal as the giraffe guy explained it. Along with the other three humans, and representatives from three other species, I would go visit the Confederation of United Planets, and there we would be evaluated, though he was vague about the details. If, after a standard year—only a few days shorter than an Earth year—a species was deemed worthy, then the Confederation would initiate the first phase of integration. We would be given incredible new technology that would help us eliminate pollution, hunger, disease, and want.

"Dr. Roop has assured us that the nations of the Earth would maintain their local sovereignty," Ms. Price assured me. "In case you were worried about that."

I couldn't imagine why she thought I would even care, but still, good to know.

"How you order your local affairs is of little interest to the Confederation," Dr. Roop said, "as long as the various countries of your world demonstrate the values and behaviors we consider commensurate with our standards. We will give you the means to create a just and fair world, and if you are able to take advantage of what you are given, then you can advance to full participation in the Confederation. Eventually, you will be provided with the technology for interstellar travel."

Given how ready many people are to abuse power, justice and fairness seemed like a tall order. "And if we fail to achieve justice and equality?" I asked. "What then?"

"Then nothing," said the giraffe man. "We shall leave you alone and come check back in a few decades to see if you've worked out your problems. There's no downside to participating. You can only benefit."

"This end to disease you mentioned," I said. "Is that for real?"

"Oh, yes," Dr. Roop said. "We can't eliminate all minor ailments and discomforts, but chronic and deadly disease will be a thing of the past."

I couldn't help but think about that particular benefit. My mother would be cured. No more ALS. She would not have to turn into a living corpse. I realized that beyond how much I loved all of this for its own sake, I had a very personal interest in the Confederation of United Planets being impressed with the people of the Earth.

"Why young people?" I asked. "And more importantly, why me? How, of all the kids on Earth, did you come up with my name?"

Dr. Roop widened his eyes, which I began to suspect might be his species' version of a smile or a nod. "Adolescents are particularly well suited for evaluation because they are old enough and sufficiently educated to represent your world and its cultures, but not so fully developed as to be resistant to new ways and new technologies. Over time we have found that using beings your age—or the species-relevant equivalent—for this evaluation gives us the best and most accurate sense of compatibility."

"Okay," I said. "I guess I can see that. But why *me*?"

"Maybe," Ms. Price suggested, "we should tell you a little bit more about the other young people the Confederation has selected." She picked up a remote device, and a screen came down on the far side of the room and the lights dimmed. She then flicked a few keys on her keyboard, and the image of a kid about my age appeared on the screen. He was dark-skinned and thin with narrow, focused eyes like he was concentrating on something. He wore a white dress shirt with a sweater over it that had some kind of symbol on the right breast, which I figured was a private-school insignia.

"This is Charles D'Ujanga," Ms. Price said. "He's twelve, from Uganda, and remarkably gifted in both math and science. He was born in a horribly poor village, and orphaned quite young, but by incredible luck his gifts were discovered early by a UN doctor. Consequently, he's been the beneficiary of some excellent NGO aid that's allowed him to go to the best schools in his country. Given the political problems in Uganda, this is no small thing."

She hit a few keys on the keyboard and the picture of an Asian girl flashed onto the screen. She wore a martial-arts uniform and had her legs firmly planted, and her arms up, as if ready to block a punch. It was clearly an action photo, and the girl's short hair was pointed upward, as though she'd just landed after jumping. "This is Park Mi Sun. Despite her youth, she is the reigning female tae kwon do champion in South Korea."

"We are not a belligerent society," Dr. Roop explained, "but we respect the grace and discipline to be found in martial arts from many species and their cultures. Also, we are fond of Jackie Chan films."

I nodded appreciatively. "I just saw *Supercop*."

"That's a good one," Dr. Roop agreed.

Ms. Price sighed and clicked, and the image of another girl came onto the screen. This one had bronze skin, long black hair, and an oval face with sharp cheekbones, large eyes, and a dazzling smile. Her clothes suggested she was from India or Pakistan or someplace in that part of the world.

"And, finally, this is Nayana Gehlawat from Jalandhar, India. You may already know her name."

On the other hand, I might not. "Sorry."

"She's ranked the third best chess player in the world, though it's only a matter of time before she's number one," Ms. Price said. "Are you sure you haven't heard of her? There was a lot of coverage in the media last year when she shot up the ranks after beating Magnus Carlsen."

I shrugged. "I got an Xbox last year, so I was sort of distracted."

Ms. Price clicked her remote, and the screen rose and the lights came back up. "And there you have it," she said. "If you agree to go, those are going to be the only human beings you'll have contact with for the coming year. Besides me, that is." A normal person would have smiled after saying this. Ms. Price tapped her nails on her desk.

I, meanwhile, was considering the implications of what I had learned. That sinking feeling in my gut was all too familiar. Normally I'd swallow my pride and keep my head down, but that didn't seem like an option here. I had to say what was on my mind.

"Those guys are really impressive," I said. "They have all these amazing skills. Best chess player in the world? I don't have anything like that. Why am I even here?"

"Your confusion is understandable," Dr. Roop said gently. "Let me explain. The selection committee chooses from each world three beings they believe have the best chance of success in the Confederation. However, we do not want to bias the process by selecting only particular representatives who match our ideals, since it is never wise to evaluate a species based only on extraordinary individuals. Consequently, there is always a fourth being chosen at random, one picked from a somewhat contoured pool, but still a more or less blind choice."

"Somewhat contoured?" I said. "What does that mean?"

"In this case, as your species conforms to the quite popular male-female gender split, we wanted to balance things out with a second male," Dr. Roop said. "Also, because yours is the most culturally dominant nation on your world, and it had not yet been represented, we felt it was prudent to pick an American. Or a Canadian. We don't understand the difference."

"So," I said, "my name was pulled from a hat of twelve-year-old North American boys."

"Eleven to thirteen, but yes," said Dr. Roop.

"And there's nothing about me to make anyone, anywhere, think that I have a better chance of success than any other boy my age?"

"Initially, yes," Ms. Price said, looking at me through narrowed eyes, as if to suggest she had been steadily revising her estimation downward.

"And this healing technology you mentioned," I said. "What if I made helping my mother a condition of my going?"

Ms. Price rolled her eyes. *That again.*

"I wish I could offer such an incentive," Dr. Roop said. "Were it my choice, I would happily provide your mother with the aid she needs, but our laws preclude any technological or medical assistance to species that haven't gone through the evaluation."

I didn't think there was much to be gained by asking him to violate the Prime Directive. I knew what I had to do, so I stood up and looked at them both.

"I am really flattered," I said. "I can't believe what I've seen and learned here. This is, without a doubt, the most incredible day of my life. But I'm going to have to take a pass."

"What?" cried Ms. Price. "Sit down!"

"Sorry," I said. "I'm out. Can someone drive me home?"

CHAPTER FIVE

was not chickening out. Not really.

Sure, I was afraid. Terrified. I was going full coward on this. It's one thing to daydream, as we all have, about going off in a spaceship and having amazing adventures with a giraffe in a business suit, but when the dapper giraffe shows up and is ready to whisk you off to the stars, I think it's perfectly reasonable to want to crawl into the fetal position.

Even so, fear was not calling the shots. If all other things had been equal, I don't think excitement would have had any problem beating out terror. I was not about to miss out on new life and new civilizations simply because the thought of *leaving the planet* made me want to wet my pants.

I was backing out because I wasn't up to the task. My mom was dying, and she was going to die about the worst death imaginable. If the right person went and convinced the aliens that the human race was worthy, we would get advanced alien medical knowledge, and my mother would get to live. I didn't want to miss out on the time she had left, but more importantly, I couldn't risk messing things up. I would pass on the adventure of a lifetime and let someone halfway competent take my place.

Dr. Roop stood up and actually blocked my way. He looked down from his eight-foot vantage, and held out his long arms so

I couldn't pass. Apparently, he was taking no chances. "I don't think you understand."

"I understand perfectly," I said. "Dr. Roop, I really, really appreciate this offer, and you have no idea how much I want to go, but I'm not your guy. I'm completely average. I can't fight or play champion-level chess or do math or any of that stuff. I have nothing to contribute. You're better off getting someone else."

"There *is* no one else," Dr. Roop said, lowering his arms. The dramatic gesture had apparently run its course. "This is how the process works. The decision of the selection commit-tee is final, and it has to be that way."

"Trust me," said Ms. Price without bothering to look up from her computer. "They won't budge on this point."

"We've learned from experience that nations will go to war to get more of their own people in the initiate delegation," Dr. Roop explained. "The only way to make the process successful and peaceful is to render it immutable."

"So if I don't go, humanity is one man short?"

Dr. Roop cocked his head and looked at me with his big yel-low eyes, which appeared sad. "If you don't go, Zeke, humanity is out of the running. We'll try again in sixty years, but if we can't recruit the delegation selected by the committee, then there is no delegation."

I stood there, speechless.

"I know you are thinking about your mother," Dr. Roop said. "If you want her to have a chance at being cured, you must agree to participate."

That changed the scenario. I nodded and sat my butt back down. Ms. Price continued typing away on her laptop. A glance at her screen told me she was using my time of personal crisis, my moment to make a decision that would affect all of humanity, to catch up on her e-mail.

I had so many questions, I hardly even knew where to begin.

"When do we leave?"

"As soon as you are ready," said Ms. Price, looking up. "The other candidates began meeting with their governments three days ago. They have all agreed to participate. At this point, we are waiting for you."

They met three days ago. "You tried to get someone else too. That's how you know you can't change their minds."

Ms. Price did that thing that, for government employees, stood in for a smile. She blinked and pursed her lips. "We had hoped to put our best foot forward."

"But I'm the foot you're stuck with."

"We are delighted that an American citizen will be part of this delegation," she assured me.

"I can understand why you might feel inadequate," Dr. Roop said, "but random participants often become not simply a part of the team, but major contributors."

"I get it," I said, having had enough of the pep talk. I was the resident loser. That's how it was, so time to move on. "Where exactly are we going?"

"Ah," said Dr. Roop, sitting taller in his chair now that we'd moved beyond my protests. "You will be based for the year on Confederation Central, a massive space station more or less in the center of our territory, and the capital city of our civilization. It is the seat of government, home to several of our finest universities, and has some of the best museums in the galaxy. Approximately twelve million beings are aboard at any given time."

"So it's like *Babylon 5*," I said.

"Yes and no," Dr. Roop said without missing a beat. "The station was not built for the purpose it currently serves. In fact, we did not build it at all, but rather inherited it from a species of beings who lived long before us. We call them the Formers."

"So the station is like the Citadel from *Mass Effect*, and these Formers are like the Protheans?"

"Best foot forward," Miss Price said, clearly irritated by my dorking out.

Dr. Roop held up a hand. "No, no, Ms. Price. As I explained, these narratives are, in part, the result of our influence, and Zeke's familiarity with them may prove a genuine advantage." He turned to me. "I feel certain you must have noticed that my appearance is similar to a creature from your own planet. I am said to resemble a gorilla, yes?"

"Giraffe," I corrected.

"That's right. You are the one who resembles the gorilla. But you must think it rather an odd coincidence that I should so closely resemble an Earth creature."

"Yes, but given everything else that's going on, I didn't see the point in bringing it up." I had read, and been disappointed to learn, that most scientists believed any alien intelligence we might encounter would be so different that communication would likely be impossible. It was the height of self-absorption and fantasy, such theories said, to presume other planets would evolve species that were more or less the same as us. I guess they got that wrong.

"There are hundreds of planets in the Confederation, but thousands upon thousands of inhabited planets in our galaxy," Dr.

Roop said. "We believe that most, if not all, of these worlds—indeed, the systems in which the worlds are located—were partially or entirely altered by the Formers so that they could sustain life. These planets are all approximately the same size and have similar rotation cycles, atmospheres, climate types, and so on. More than that, the same seed stock of genetic material was deposited on each of these planets."

Here I could have mentioned the Preservers from *Star Trek* or the Ancients from *Stargate*. Come to think of it, I could have mentioned my father's show, *Colony Alpha*, which also featured a mysterious precursor race that had left behind valuable technology. Much of the show revolved around the two warring factions' efforts to find and understand ancient artifacts while the last of Earth's population, located on an isolated colony planet, found itself in the middle. I demonstrated wisdom and restraint by holding my tongue.

"Life develops in somewhat similar patterns on many different worlds," Dr. Roop continued. "You will see dozens of alien species on Confederation Central, a majority of them bipeds of approximately four to eight feet in height. This seems to be the direction in which the Formers wished us to evolve. You will see sentient races that look like animals from your world. On some worlds there are likely animals that look like human beings."

"Let's not belabor this point," Ms. Price said, moving her hand in a circular *let's go* motion.

"It is always a good time to learn," Dr. Roop said. "Don't you agree, Ms. Price?"

"I work for the government," she answered, "so, no, I don't agree. Let's talk logistics."

"Very well. To remain on schedule, we would like to leave in two days. By that time, you should be aboard our orbiting spacecraft. That ship will take us to rendezvous with the delegates from one of the other applying species, and then we will go to Confederation Central, where you will attempt to demonstrate your species' ability to thrive within our society."

"And how will I do that?" I asked, already sure I was going to fail miserably at whatever they wanted me to do.

"We will explain in due course. You need not concern yourself just yet."

"And can all four species become part of the Confederation," I asked, "or just one of us?"

"Sometimes all four groups succeed. Sometimes none do. You are competing against yourselves, not one another. Any other questions?"

"Yeah," I said. "How does space travel work? Most of the stuff I've read says that faster-than-light travel is impossible."

"I shall spare you the details," said Dr. Roop. "You only need to know that we travel outside relativistic space, so there are no problems with time dilation, if that was your question."

"I'm pretty sure what you're saying is beyond his concerns," Ms. Price said.

As it happens, that *was* my nerdy concern. I had a pretty good layman's understanding of this stuff. According to Einstein, as you approach the speed of light, you not only require exponentially more energy as you acquire more mass, but you also experience the flow of time differently than the universe around you. The closer you get to light speed, the more the variance between the vessel and everything else outside it, so at high speeds a trip that only takes a few months for the crew of a ship would happen over centuries for everyone else. I was glad to hear that these Confederation guys had found a way around that problem.

"And this is all safe?"

"There are risks, of course," Dr. Roop said, "but our safety record is significantly better than that of your auto travel on this planet, and superior even to your own aviation travel."

That was all good to know, but no matter how safe it was, my mother was not going to like the idea of me going off into space.

Apparently reading my mind, Ms. Price handed me a file containing an alarmingly thick document.

"What's this?" I asked.

"That," she said, "is a permission slip."

CHAPTER SIX

I spent the night in a guest room that felt like a cross between a wedding suite and a mountain-man hideout. In the morning I found a tray outside my door containing juice, some fruit, and a pastry. There was also a note telling me to come down to Ms. Price's office at exactly eleven. I was on time, because that's the kind of guy I am.

The first thing Ms. Price had me do, once she finished ignoring me for twenty minutes, was call my mother. I didn't love the idea of her being summoned to Camp David, but I supposed it was a step up from being called to the principal's office. When I spoke to her, I swore that everything was fine—better than fine—and that I really had been given an incredible opportunity. Then Ms. Price took the phone and told her a car was already on its way and she should be ready in an hour. Then she hung up on my mother.

"I suppose you'll want to meet the other children," she said.

"What, they're here?"

She nodded. "The participating nations agreed that a single location was preferable to having alien craft zipping all over the planet. Everyone was flown in on conventional aircraft last night. They'll head up to the ship later today, and you'll join them once your affairs are settled."

"Then, sure," I said. "That would be great."

She led me through a series of hallways and into what looked like a high-level meeting room. There was a long wooden table, and on one wall were multiple video screens of the sort that allow a president to keep an eye on wars as they unfold.

Inside, I also saw the other kids from the slide show. Charles D'Ujanga and Park Mi Sun were both sitting at the table, reading through thick binders. Charles wore khaki pants, a white short-sleeved dress shirt and a tie. Tae Kwon Do Girl wore jeans and a long-sleeved patterned shirt. Her hair was cut short, and though she had seemed pretty in the picture I'd seen, her scowl made her appear a little intimidating. They both looked up when I stepped into the room. Charles grinned broadly.

Then I saw Nayana Gehlawat. She wore dark jeans and a green and gold shirt that looked like material for a sari, with a matching scarf around her neck. Her hair was long and a little wild, falling into her eyes. I was also impressed by the fact that she was sitting in a chair, legs pulled under her, reading a paperback copy of *The Hitchhiker's Guide to the Galaxy*.

I wanted to go talk to her at once, but Charles was up and out of his chair, pumping my hand. "You must be Ezekiel Reynolds," he said. His voice had a clipped and precise accent. "I am Charles D'Ujanga, and I am pleased to meet you."

"Zeke," I said. "Great to meet you too."

Park Mi Sun looked up from her reading and gave me a brief nod. "Hey," she said.

"Hey," I answered to show I could be unenthusiastic too if I wanted.

Charles interrupted our brilliant exchange. "This is truly the most amazing thing, don't you agree? There is so much to do—papers to sign and meetings and arrangements—that it is easy to forget that we have met a being from another world, and we shall soon meet many more."

"Dude," I said. "Totally." He was more articulate than I was, but I appreciated that he was having the same trouble I was in getting my head around it.

"What's in those binders you guys have?" I asked.

"They are our individual governments' directives," he said. "You will not need one because a member of your government travels with you. I understand you are to follow us tomorrow."

I nodded. "Assuming I can get my mother to agree to let me go."

"I cannot imagine she would object to you having this incredible experience!" I hadn't met a lot of people who spoke with exclamation marks, but he was one of them.

"Yeah," I said, but I knew he could probably not imagine she had ALS, either.

"I hope you will excuse me." He gestured toward his binder. "I must demonstrate my understanding of my government's policy before I am cleared to depart."

"Sure," I said. I headed over to Nayana. Unlike the South Korean girl, she did not seem to have a do-not-disturb sign swinging from her psychic doorknob. As I approached, she held up the book and met my gaze. "Have you read this?" she asked. She had an extremely proper British accent, which I suspected was real and not the translator.

"Sure, like a dozen times," I said. "It's hilarious."

She tossed it onto the table. "Papa gave it to me before I left, but I find it far too silly."

By some miracle of self-control I kept myself from displaying disbelief. "It's supposed to be silly. That's why it's fun." I chose to say nothing about Douglas Adams's connection to *Doctor Who*, because this felt like the wrong way to get on her good side.

She studied me for a long moment, as though she could not quite believe what I was saying. I, on the other hand, was wondering if it was possible to spend a year with someone who didn't like *Hitchhiker's Guide*.

"Forgive me," she said, holding out her arm with her hand hanging limp like it had been detached. "I'm Nayana."

"I'm Zeke," I said, waggling the loose hand, "and of course I know who you are. You're totally famous."

"Oh, please," she said, with a dismissive wave of the hand. "You've never heard of me. Or do you follow chess?"

"Not religiously or anything," I said. "I don't, like, watch the Chess Network or whatever, but everyone knows about how you beat Magnus Carlsen last year." I figured I had it, I might as well use it. "That was pretty sweet."

"It is fine when people admire me for my skill at the game," she assured me. And what a relief it was to learn she was okay with my admiration. "That doesn't bother me in the least, but all the reporters and cameras and magazine spreads became a bit of a bore very quickly. I suppose if I were a plain Jane they wouldn't have cared, but they were all agog to stare at the beautiful chess genius." She shook her head sadly. "It's nothing but foolishness."

"Yeah, foolishness," I agreed. "For fools. And morons."

She was now squinting. I was starting to think I might have made a better impression, but I was also starting to think that it was possible to be beautiful and a chess genius *and* kind of an unpleasant person.

"Would you be a dear and fetch me a sparkling water?" She

gestured toward a sideboard, about fifteen feet away, where drinks and snacks had been set up. "I'm *terribly* thirsty."

I wanted to tell her that she should go fetch her own sparkling water, but I thought that there were only four of us, and antagonizing a third of my companions for the next year might be a bad move. She was almost certainly testing me, seeing if I would volunteer to be her servant when we left Earth. I didn't particularly want to be her personal butler, but I also didn't want to do anything to make her dislike me. My Spidey-sense told me she could put on a pretty fierce dislike.

I fetched her the water, and Park Mi Sun scowled at me as I did it. She clearly didn't think much of my butlering, so I guessed I had to make sure I won Nayana over. The idea of both of them hating me before we even left Earth was completely depressing.

When I came over with the bottle and a glass, she let out a world-weary sigh. "No lime?"

"I didn't see any."

She pressed her lips together and cocked her head. "Might I trouble you to ask for some?"

Like an idiot, I did ask, and Agent McTeague, a guy who under other circumstances was supposed to take a bullet for the president, ended up both fetching limes and thinking I was the lame-o who wanted them. When I finally had the drink prepared for Nayana, she gestured to a little table next to where she sat. "Right there is fine," she said, and picked up her binder.

I sat there in the room with the three of them reading their binders, and after five minutes I wanted to throw myself out the window. Then Ms. Price stepped into the room and told me she wanted a word.

We sat in a couple of chairs outside the meeting room. Ms. Price folded her hands and looked at me the way I'd once seen my mom look at a mouse she'd discovered in our kitchen, when she couldn't decide if she should chase it out of the house or crush it with a broom. Maybe that was a bad analogy, because Ms. Price seemed pretty solidly in the mouse-crushing camp.

"I want to talk to you about certain problems you may face once you leave Earth."

"*If* I leave Earth," I said. "My mother hasn't agreed to anything."

"She'll agree," Ms. Price said, flicking her fingers impatiently. "Your mother won't forbid you from helping all of humanity because she doesn't want to miss out on a year of baking cookies and tucking you in for night-night kisses."

"Do you have children?" I asked.

She scowled. "What do you think?"

"I think you haven't been around this many people under eighteen since you graduated from high school."

"Correct."

"I'll try not to get on your nerves," I told her, giving her my best smile. It was more polite than saying *You are both intense and super scary.*

She sighed. "I wish we had better material to work with, but you're what we've got."

"Thanks," I said. I packed up the smile and put it away.

"I've read your school records. You seem to get into a lot of trouble."

"I never cause those incidents," I told her, hating how defensive I sounded.

She flicked an indifferent hand upward. She could not trouble herself to care. "The president exerted a lot of influence to make certain the United States provided the adult permitted to accompany the delegation. We had to promise all kinds of beneficial trade deals with India and South Korea, and offer a great deal of aid to Uganda."

"Welcome aboard?" I offered.

Her facial tic suggested I was, once again, too slow to get the point. "It's also worth pointing out that the other species are not sending any sort of chaperone. Only Earth."

"Why?"

"Because the other species didn't think to ask," Ms. Price said. "And that is my point. Dr. Roop has allowed me to review certain data about the Confederation in advance of our departure, and I find some things both interesting and troubling. More than eighty percent of the member species evolved from herbivores. Almost none of the species eat primarily meat, and most of those that are omnivores eat mostly insects or other small, harmless creatures."

"What are you telling me? That I should order a hamburger before I go?"

She sighed at my failure to understand her point. "Do you know what the symbol of the Confederation is? It's a gas giant, like Jupiter. Do you know why?"

I took a moment to consider what I knew about planets of that sort. "Maybe there's a gas giant in the outer solar system of every inhabited planet," I proposed.

She squinted at me, maybe impressed, maybe suspicious. "How could you know that?"

"I'm into this stuff," I said. "Gas giants are supposed to be a possible precondition for intelligent life. The gravity pulls big stuff into the planet's orbit. If we didn't have Jupiter to protect us, the Earth would constantly be getting smashed by asteroids and comets, like the one that killed the dinosaurs."

She nodded. "Correct, and their symbol is this thing that exists to protect them, not a thing they have done to protect themselves. They're passive. They're *sheep*." Her voice grew quiet. "They are nice and orderly and calm and helpful, but they are not innovators or inventors like we are. All of their technology comes from these ancient aliens, these Formers, and they've been recycling their old technology for centuries. They have very little crime, and even less violent crime, not because they've solved those problems but because they never had them in the first place. I don't know why they asked us to apply—we're much more aggressive than most member species. So my point is that you are going to have to be on your best behavior. I'm less worried about your average intellect and lack of useful skills than I am about your adolescent rebelliousness. You need to keep it in check. No fighting, no troublemaking, no rule breaking."

"I am not a troublemaker," I said. I didn't want to tell her that I got picked on a lot, because that would sound pathetic.

"I don't care what you *were*," she said. "I only care what you will be. Understand that I will do anything to make certain Earth is accepted into the Confederation, and if your behavior becomes a problem, then I will deal with it in ways you won't like."

"I also respond well to positive reinforcement. I like Twizzlers, FYI."

She stood up. "Tone down the sarcasm. I'm not sure how it translates. Now I need to speak to the rest of the delegation, so go wander around the grounds or something until your mother arrives."

She went inside the meeting room and closed the door. She paused, just a beat, and then locked it. Whatever she had to say to the other humans, it was not for me to hear.

They made my mother sign nondisclosure agreements with serious legal consequences for violation, but I couldn't imagine they would have actually prosecuted her for speaking up. Who was going to believe her if she claimed the government was in on a scheme to send her son to Hogwarts in space? The end result was that later that afternoon I was back in Ms. Price's office with Dr. Roop and now my mother, looking utterly astonished.

My mother wasn't skeptical about what they were saying. It's easy to believe in aliens when an actual alien is making the case. The Confederation's laws prevented my mother from getting the translation nanites, so Ms. Price and I had to tell her what Dr. Roop was saying. Mostly me. Ms. Price tended to type on her laptop when other people were speaking.

Dr. Roop was a charming giraffe guy, but even he couldn't make her happy about her son heading into space for a year. Given that my mother didn't know just how many years she had left, I understood that this was hard for her. It was hard for me, too.

They let us have some time alone together in an adjoining room. My mother looked pale, and maybe a few years older than the last time I'd seen her. Her eyes were red, but she wasn't crying. Not yet. Or maybe not anymore. Or maybe both.

"I don't know if I can do this," she said. "I don't know if I can let you go. We have no idea what's out there, what they are going to ask you to do."

"They say it'll be safe," I told her, not liking the whiny tone of my voice.

"They say that, but how do we know?" She shook her head. "We don't."

Was my mother really going to refuse to let me do this? It wasn't like her to hold me back. She always encouraged me to take risks, but this was a whole new order of risk, and for her the stakes were high.

She stood up. "I'm going home. I need to think."

"They want an answer soon, Mom."

"I understand that," she said quietly. "But I can't figure anything out knowing that the giraffe man is in the next room waiting for my answer. I need time to come to terms with this."

"When do you think you'll decide?" I asked.

"I don't know!" she snapped. Then she hugged me tight, and I felt her tears against my neck. "I don't know," she said much more quietly.

Then she left.

CHAPTER SEVEN

I spent much of the rest of that day fending off Ms. Price, who wanted me to call my mother and persuade her to sign. I knew that would be a mistake. She did not respond well to bullies. I had to believe that she would make the right decision and that she simply needed the room to make it on her own.

The next day, when she returned with a large duffel bag in the back of the dark sedan, I knew she had decided to let me go.

Agent Jiminez, carrying the bag, led her into a private room where I was waiting. He set down the bag and left.

My mother hugged me. "This doesn't mean you have to go," she said when she released me. "It's your decision. What do you really want?"

We sat in two armchairs across from each other. She leaned forward and took my hand.

"I don't want to leave you alone," I told her, "but I do want to go."

"Because going off into space seems like a fun adventure or because you want to accomplish whatever tasks they give you and take all our problems away? Do you want to go for yourself, or to search for a cure for me?"

"Both," I told her, which was the truth.

She let go of my hand and leaned back. "I don't want to spend a year alone," she said. "You're all I have, Zeke, and I'm scared. I don't want to watch my days and weeks and months vanish forever. But I also know that's selfish, which is why I decided to let you do this."

I was relieved, and also a little hurt. Maybe I wanted it to be a harder decision for her. "Are you sure you can get by without me?"

"No, I'm not sure, but this is the most amazing experience you could possibly have, and I would be a monster if I took that away from you. It's also your duty to your country and to your planet—though I can't believe I just said that out loud. I won't be a selfish mother who holds on to her child despite the consequences to the world. The whole world, Zeke, is depending on you to do this, even if they don't know it, and I can't stand in your way."

I nodded.

"And there's another reason," she said. She wiped at her eyes with the tips of her fingers. "What's coming for me is going to be bad. We both know it, but what keeps me awake at night is not how bad it will be for me, but what it will be like for you. You're too young to have to deal with taking care of me, how I'm going to become." She paused to take a breath. "Maybe what you do on this space station will help me, and maybe it won't, but I can't ask you to watch me fall apart knowing you could have helped, could have at least tried to do something, but I wouldn't let you. If I do that, you will come to hate me, and that seems worse than anything."

I was feeling like I was on the verge of tears now. I knew she wouldn't mind if I cried, but I was a big-boy space adventurer now, and crying seemed like a step backward.

"What are you going to tell people?"

"They'll invent a cover story about boarding school, so you don't need to worry about that," she said, seeming to take comfort in the discussion of organizational details. "Do you want to see what I packed? There might still be time if I forgot anything important."

"I wish you hadn't had to go in my room," I said as I walked over to the duffel bag. "It's kind of a mess."

"No kidding."

I looked through the stuff quickly, and by all appearances my mother had done a fine job. She had sent me off with mostly jeans and short-sleeved shirts, but also a few long-sleeved shirts, a sweater, and my favorite Justice League T-shirt. She hadn't packed my ultracool Tenth Doctor coat but she had thrown in my ultracool *Firefly* coat and matching *Firefly* suspenders. She'd also put one of my Martian Manhunter action figures in there. She knew I would want it. It was like taking my father's memory to the stars with me.

"There's one more thing," she said, and then pressed a little cardboard box into my hand. Inside was a silver locket on a chain. I had never been much for jewelry, even less so for ladies' jewelry, but I decided if I waited patiently, I'd get an explanation.

"No, you don't have to put it on." She laughed and shook her head. "I never thought I'd have to give this to you."

"What is it?" I asked. "I've never seen you wear it—I don't think."

"No," she said, "but it's been in the family for a long time. When your great-great-grandfather went off to World War One, his mother gave it to him, with her picture and a lock of her hair. And then when your great-grandfather went to fight in the Second World War, *his* mother gave it to him, with her own picture and her own lock of hair. When your granddad went to Vietnam, he got it, with your great-grandmother's picture and hair. They all came home safe, so maybe the locket is good luck."

I opened it up. Inside was a little picture of my mom, and a little clasp of her brown hair, with a single gray hair snaking through.

"I'm not going to war," I told her.

"And thank God for that, but you are going far away. A little extra luck can't hurt."

I nodded again. We stood and I hugged her as tightly as I could.

"Thanks, Mom," I said.

She smiled. "For what?"

"For letting me go," I said. "For being cool about it. For raising me to be the kind of kid who could be randomly selected by aliens to spend a year on a space station."

She shook her head and then said what we had both been thinking. "Your father would be so insanely jealous of you."

I laughed. "Yeah."

"He'd be proud, too. But also jealous. I'm just proud."

"I haven't done anything yet."

"You will. I know you will." And then she went over to the table where the release form had been left. She picked up the pen and signed with a trembling hand. I tried to think about what this trip might do for her, not what it would do *to* her.

After we'd said our last good-byes, Agent Jiminez drove me, Ms. Price, and Dr. Roop across Camp David. Of the difficulties

Dr. Roop had in getting comfortable in the back of the car, the less said the better. We passed several checkpoints but were waved through each one. The windows of the car were tinted, and the soldiers never once glanced at the car's interior. I guess they'd been told to see nothing. At last we drove into a hangar, and that was where I saw my first real spaceship.

It was dull gray, with no markings, and sort of rectangular and boxy in the way of TV sci-fi shuttles, but it had two protruding engines toward the back and some truncated shuttle-type wings on the side, no doubt for in-atmosphere flight. The whole thing was about as large as a school bus and, to be honest, about as sleek. I understood it was designed to be functional, not impressive, simply a practical tool for getting from here to there. To me, it was unimaginably beautiful.

Dr. Roop boarded up a ramp and through an opening of double doors as soon as we arrived, but Ms. Price asked me to remain outside for a moment. She then proceeded to ignore me, sending out some last minute e-mails from her phone while I stood there like an idiot, moving my duffel bag from hand to hand for something to do.

After about three tedious minutes, a black car pulled up, and the president emerged. He walked over to me and shook my hand.

"Zeke, I can't thank you enough for representing our nation and our world. I know you will do your very best for us."

"Thank you, Mr. President," I said, suddenly feeling like I was heading off on a suicide mission. I reminded myself I was not. Hopefully.

"This is one of the most important moments in the history of the planet and the country," the president said. "I wish you didn't have to make this journey in secret, but if you succeed, you will be a hero to billions."

"I just don't want to blow it for everyone," I said, then winced at my words. It was probably not how you spoke to the president.

He laughed. "That was how I felt my first day in office. Actually, it's how I feel every day in office. I think the people who worry about blowing it end up getting the job done. The ones who are sure they're the right person for the job end up making a mess of everything."

"Thank you, sir," I said.

"I've made my office available to your mother," he said. "If she needs anything while you're gone, we'll take care of it."

I let out a sigh of relief. "I can't tell you how much I appreciate that."

"It's the least we can do for you. She'll have the best care possible while you're away. And you'll be in good hands as well. Ms. Price will do an excellent job."

"Thank you, sir," she said.

He shook both our hands again. "Good luck," he said. Then he broke into a huge grin. "You are the luckiest people alive," he told us, and then walked back to his car.

Ms. Price impatiently jabbed a finger toward the shuttle. That was her special way of telling me it was time to get on an alien craft, depart the planet of my birth, and leave everyone I knew and loved behind.

Despite the shuttle's buslike size, the interior portion was more like a minivan. I had to imagine that the bulk of it went to machinery and engines. Dr. Roop sat near the navigational controls, which were numerous: switches and levers and screens and buttons. There were flashing readouts and rolling streams of data. I guessed I was copilot, because Dr. Roop invited me to sit beside him. Ms. Price sat three rows back, to better ignore us while she read through more papers. I presumed her phone was about to lose reception.

There were no windows, glass possibly being a bad idea for a vehicle that traveled through the vacuum of space, but there were high-resolution video screens in the front and back, and on the sides, that acted as windows. I sat looking forward, and though I knew there was ten feet of shuttle on the other side of the screen, it sure looked like I was peering through glass.

"The other kids are on the ship already?" I asked.

"Yes," he said. "I took them up yesterday."

For some reason, I didn't like that they'd had a whole day on the spaceship without me, but I pushed the thought aside. "You do know how to drive this thing, right?" I asked Dr. Roop.

"For a simple trip like this, the navigational computer will handle the controls," he said.

"But what if something goes wrong? Shouldn't there be a pilot on board?"

"Things don't go wrong," he assured me. "But even if, however improbably, something were to happen, the shuttle can be controlled from the main ship, and in an emergency I am able to operate it."

I didn't love the idea of being flown around by a computer, but I knew I had to do things the Confederation way. You don't get to be a galaxy-spanning civilization without knowing what you are doing. Or so I told myself.

"It will take about fifteen minutes to reach the ship,"

Dr. Roop said. "The navigational computer provides a very smooth ride."

Everything was happening so quickly, I'd hardly had time to think about it. Now I was suddenly absolutely terrified. I was on a space shuttle of alien design, about to leave Earth and board a starship. This was nuts. I thought I might vomit or pass out or both.

"I have seen enough of human physiology to tell you are anxious," Dr. Roop said, "but I assure you there is no need for fear. You could not be safer. Now give me your hand."

I did. He took out one of the cylinders that Ms. Price had used to inject me with nanites, and he pressed it to the back of my hand.

"Sedative?" I asked.

"Certainly not. These are more nanites."

"For what?"

Suddenly my vision grew fuzzy, but only for a second. I blinked a few times, and the blurring was gone, but things were now just a little different. Dr. Roop had a vague, transparent number floating above his head—a reddish 34. In the lower left of my own vision, I saw a number 1 and below that 0000/1000. The numbers were translucent and easy to ignore entirely, but when I made an effort to see them, they came into sharp focus.

"Uh, what's going on?" I asked. "I'm seeing numbers."

"That's your heads-up display," Dr. Roop said.

"You're joking." I had an HUD now?

"I'm quite serious."

"Okay," I said, trying to figure the rest out. "What do the numbers mean, and why do you have one floating over your head? Ms. Price doesn't."

"Ms. Price is not wired into the Confederation system of personal growth and expansion. You and your fellow delegates are. You asked before how your species' compatibility with the Confederation would be evaluated. In our culture, we believe that learning, striving, expanding your abilities, curiosity, wisdom—all of these things have merit. From the Formers, our great progenitors, we have inherited a system whereby an individual's achievements are recognized and so become the basis for further improvements. The nanites in your system have already quantified your attributes in numerous categories, and they are also capable of measuring how well your actions and accomplishments move you toward achieving certain kinds of goals valued across the Confederation. These successes, based on their complexity and difficulty, are represented as a numerical value. There are certain set values, and when they are reached, you are rewarded by having abilities of your choice augmented through nanotechnology."

I took a moment to process all of this. "So the zeroes are my experience points," I said. "The one thousand is how many points I will need to . . . level up?"

"Correct," he said.

"And when I level up I get . . . skill points I can use?"

"Correct again," he said. "We have the technology to increase our abilities in ways that exceed our biological limitations, but in order to prevent this technology from being abused, those augmentations must be earned through accomplishments that benefit all of society."

"I can't believe this!" I shouted. "It's like I'm living in a video game! I am going to level up. And so you're, like, a level-thirty-four diplomat?"

"There is no class system, if that is what you are implying, but there are specialization tracks. When we get to the ship, you'll have time to inspect the skill tree, and you can decide how you want to proceed. It's an important choice, because all augmentations are final."

"How do I gain experience? And what kind of skills are we talking about exactly?"

"There will be numerous opportunities on the station to advance. You'll quickly learn how to pursue tasks that accumulate experience points. And that is how your delegation will be rated. At the end of your time with us, if your team has amassed a total of eighty levels, then you will move on to phase-one integration into the Confederation."

"So, twenty levels apiece."

"It doesn't matter how they're distributed as long as the total is eighty. Keep in mind, the more you advance, the harder it is to obtain each successive milestone. The first few levels can be achieved in days, or even hours, but the number of required points increases with each level. It can take some beings a decade to move from level thirty to level thirty-one."

Whatever fear I felt vanished as I considered the prospect of leveling, of gaining nanotech-augmented skills.

Then the shuttle began to move, and the fear came back. There was a thrumming noise and a series of vibrations, and then the sense of levitating, and then the feeling that we were going a zillion miles an hour, and that my stomach hadn't come along for the ride.

Through the front viewscreen, I watched as we hurtled toward the sky. Then I turned around and understood just how quickly we were moving. We were pulling out of the hangar and heading upward, and then the Earth fell behind us like a pebble fired from a slingshot. Literally seconds after we began to ascend, we were in space, by which I mean outer space. I was now a spaceman. An astronaut. At the very least a kid hitching a ride with aliens.

I was not, however, floating. It really felt no different from being in an airplane. Artificial gravity? It sure seemed like it.

And the stars! Imagine the clearest, most vivid night sky you have ever seen—the kind you can only find far away from city lights. Now imagine it a hundred times more vivid, with a thousand times more stars—stars almost as thick as the black behind them. Stars of every color, from pinpricks to big, glowing globs. Behind them hung the viscous soup of the Milky Way, bright and brilliant and real.

Dr. Roop interrupted my awe to hand me a black, shiny rectangular thing about eight inches long and five inches wide. "What's this?"

"Your data bracelet," he said. "It wraps around the wrist of your nondominant hand." He tapped at his own bracelet, and a viewscreen hovered before us, showing an exterior image of our shuttle's departure. He tapped at a few icons, and a keyboard appeared out of thin air, hovering just before him, in an ergonomically perfect position. It was translucent, made out of what appeared to be blue energy, but it was also real. I reached out and touched it, and it was solid. Not hard, but somehow physical. It responded to my touch, and I could feel a rubbery resistance with the tips of my fingers. Each stroke made a tapping sound, like it was a real keyboard.

He tapped a few more keys and sped up the image, slowed

it down, stopped the frame. Then he tapped some keys and another screen came up, listing a queue of messages. He sent that away and called up another menu, this one of a series of documents. "This device links you to the wider sphere of Confederation knowledge, and will enable you to communicate, conduct research, keep up with current events, access entertainments, whatever you wish."

He then tapped at an icon, and the keyboard and screen simply vanished. "You'll discover its many properties and uses over the next year." He gently set my bracelet on my wrist, and the two ends banded together, tightly and seamlessly but in no way uncomfortably. He then walked me through the meaning of the most basic icons on it, showing me how to remove it, activate communications, search for data, and so on.

"In the upper right-hand corner of your heads-up display," he said, "you'll find a menu that includes a few tutorials. I suggest you run through the instructions for the data bracelet when you have some quiet time. Generally, we frown on direct cognitive data integration, since we value the learning process, but we make an exception for the data bracelet, since it's the key to navigating Confederation culture."

I checked my HUD and found I could pull down menus just by looking at them. And then, when I wasn't using the HUD, it vanished.

There were so many more questions I wanted to ask, but then the shuttle banked sharply, and when I looked at the viewscreen, I was filled with a sense of wonder. There, before us, against the backdrop of black and stars was an actual interstellar spaceship.

It was really just the shuttle on a larger scale—a huge rectangle, though rounded at the corners, with a pair of massive engines affixed to each side, one at the end and another toward the middle. There were no windows, but the outer hull was made of dark metal, the same near black as the nanite injector. Only the lights, affixed at various intervals, and the yellow glow of the engines made it stand out against space.

"Wow," I said. "That's it. That's our starship!" I sounded like a total dork, but I was beyond caring. I was in space, looking at a starship that would take me light years from Earth. I wished my dad could see this.

"That is the *Dependable*," Dr. Roop said.

"What a ridiculous name!" I blurted out.

"Zeke," Ms. Price cautioned me from the back.

"He may speak if he wishes," Dr. Roop said. "However, I must admit I don't understand your grievance. Do you not think dependability a worthwhile trait?"

"Sure," I said. "For a washing machine, not a spaceship."

"Then what, in your opinion, is a good ship name?"

I was about to say *Enterprise*, but then I thought about it and I realized that it was, in fact, a pretty boring name. You don't notice how boring it is because it's always been the name of the most awesome starship ever. So what else? The *Normandy*? That's just a place in France. The *Millennium Falcon*? It sounds cool, but what exactly does it mean? Do you really want to name your ship after a thousand-year-old bird?

I rooted around in my memory and dug something up from the larger *Star Trek* universe: Captain Sisko's ship. "The *Defiant*," I said. "That's a good name."

"I can understand that, under certain circumstances, defiance is an honorable trait, but under others, isn't it undesirable?"

"I guess."

"And isn't dependability always good?"

"Yeah, but that's not the point. What about"—and now I was just making things up—"the *Victorious*. Something like that?"

"That suggests belligerence." Dr. Roop said. "It's better never to have to fight than to name your ships in anticipation of winning."

"Maybe it's a translation issue," I conceded. "It might sound better in your language." What I was really thinking about was Ms. Price's little lecture outside the library. The Confederation was made up largely of nonaggressive species. Giving ships names that celebrated victories might sound horribly unpleasant to them. Maybe I should be glad it wasn't the *Cud Chewer*.

I looked at the ship again as we approached. I saw doors opening on the side—a shuttle bay—encased by a blue energy field. My heart hammered and my stomach flipped. It was a beautiful ship, full of aliens who traveled across the stars, and I was about to go on board.

"You know what," I said. "I changed my mind. I think *Dependable* is a great name."

It looked to me like the Confederation of United Planets took its new recruits seriously, because the captain of the *Dependable* was waiting in the shuttle bay to greet us, along with several members of her crew. They all wore black uniforms with maroon trim, each with a gas-giant symbol on one sleeve. These six creatures who lined up to greet us represented a wide variety of forms, from one that looked like a giant stick insect to another that was sort of like an otter with a beak. One was almost human in appearance, but with bright orange skin and—this was even more surprising than the rest of it—weird cranial ridges along his head, like they have on science-fiction shows that want to create aliens on a budget. Go figure.

Captain Qwlessl's appearance at first struck me as a little silly. She was about as tall as I was, but about half again as wide as a human of her height. She had yellowish-brown hide that looked pachyderm tough, and her hands were huge and meaty. Her eyes stuck out on protuberances almost as extreme as a hammerhead shark's. Then there was the short elephant-like trunk that served not as a nose, but as a mouth. She raised it and spoke to me, and I saw that it contained a series of broad teeth, flat and short. "Welcome aboard." The translator made her voice sound slightly high, but confident and also strangely soothing. I knew at once that she was of middle years, confident, and probably generally cheerful. The number 43 hovering above her head told me that she had been around for a while and done some impressive things.

Though the captain might have looked like a cross between Admiral Ackbar and Garindan, the informant in Mos Eisley who squeaks Luke's location to the imperial forces, there was a seriousness to her that belied her strange appearance. Her eyes had a sadness in them, as though she had seen things in her travels she wished she could forget. Or, alternatively, she could have just been an alien with gigantic eyes. I had no way of knowing.

"Thank you for having me on your ship," I said cautiously, not knowing if I should look at her trunk or her eyes or what. I ended up just looking away.

She raised her trunk slightly. "This is the third time I've done the recruit run," she told me. "I know some members of the Confederation can look strange to those unfamiliar with galactic diversity. You don't have to pretend that it's easy or comfortable, and I promise you no one on my ship will be offended if you stare a couple of seconds too long. During this voyage, you should take advantage of the opportunity to acclimate yourself to life within the Confederation. Besides, your appearance is rather odd in my view."

"Everyone says that about me," I ventured.

She laughed or made a noise the translator told me was laughing. The captain then walked over to Dr. Roop and pressed her trunk to his cheek. She was kissing him!

"Klhkkkloplkkkuiv," she said softly. "Always a treat."

He kissed her on the cheek in return. "Yes, it is."

You'd think a giraffe guy flirting with a hammerheaded and betrunked alien would be gross, but there was actually something very sweet about them. It was somehow comforting to know these two liked each other.

Dr. Roop introduced the captain to Ms. Price. He then offered to show our chaperone to her quarters.

"I'll show Mr. Reynolds to his," the captain said.

I followed her somewhat slow and lumbering steps out to a bland metallic corridor lit by what looked shockingly like fluorescent lights. The spaces weren't as big and airy and bright as on the *Enterprise*, but they weren't as cramped and dim as in a submarine, either. Everything was unadorned and functional without being bleak.

"I presume Dr. Roop told you we are making a stop on the way to Confederation Central," the captain said. "We're picking up the members of the Ganari delegation."

"He told me," I said, though the words came out sounding mechanical. My brain simply could not process everything.

"It's nice to have different groups of initiates on board," the captain was saying. "You get to know each other. I prefer when I can deliver all four species, but unfortunately, the applying planets are too far apart this time."

"It must be a pain for you to chauffeur around a bunch of primitive species," I managed.

"Making contact with new species is exciting. The Ganari, whom we'll be meeting in about two days, are an avian species, which is unusual in the Confederation. I'm looking forward to getting a chance to talk with them."

We now went through a door that led to a stairwell, and we went down two levels to emerge in a nearly identical hall. I decided I needed to stop flipping out. I was here. I had decided to go, and now I was going. I might as well enjoy it. "If the trip takes two days, would it be possible to get a tour of the ship en route?" I asked.

She studied me with her hammerhead eyes. "Are you interested in air or water ships on your own world?"

"Not really, but I am interested in spaceships."

"I would be delighted to show you around," she said. "Just promise that if I go into too much detail, you'll stop me."

"That won't be a problem," I said. "I'd love to see how things work, what your crew does, and how you travel through space. As much as you or your crew have time to show me."

She jabbed in my direction with her trunk. "You I'm going to like. I can see that already. After your breakfast tomorrow morning, come up to the bridge, and we'll start your tour there. We operate on a Confederation-standard twenty-six-hour day here, so meet me at about 0800. You can check the time on your data bracelet."

"I'll be there!" I said, maybe a little too enthusiastically, but I decided I deserved an honest nerd-out. I was going to see the real functioning bridge of an alien spaceship.

She stopped in front of a door. Unlike on science-fiction shows, this wasn't an electric door that opened with a satisfying and futuristic hiss. It had a grip handle and folded open like an airplane bathroom door. "These are your quarters, room four-twenty-one. The door has already been biometrically matched to you, so only you can gain access."

I opened the door and looked inside. It was small but serviceable with a cot, a desk built into the wall, and a swivel chair bolted to the floor. On the wall above the desk sat a viewscreen—clearly not an actual porthole—which provided a view of the Earth below.

"I've made sure you all have quarters with species-appropriate latrines," she said, gesturing to a small door in the corner.

"That's the way I like it."

"Across the hall," the captain said, "is a common room. We like to provide a space where each species can bond, though of course you can also invite the Ganari to join you once they are on board. Additionally, you may socialize with any of the crew who are off duty. Your data bracelet is automatically linked to the ship's communication network, so it can provide you with a map or directions if you get lost. It is not possible to gain access to any sections that are off-limits, so feel free to explore."

"That sounds great," I said. I looked at her weird, alien features and felt a strange affection for this creature who did not know me at all and who was making such a concerted effort to make me feel comfortable. "You clearly like your job," I said.

She snorted. "Captaining an interstellar ship is about the

best thing I could imagine doing with my life, but some tasks are better than others." She patted me on the shoulder. "This is one of the good ones. Now, I must return to the bridge. There's a visitor's mess at the end of the hall that will accommodate your species, and you'll find mealtimes via your data bracelet."

"Got it. Thanks." I was secretly hoping she would invite me to dinner, but instead she clumsily shook my hand, perhaps having read about the custom, and left me in my room.

I set down my bag and sat on the bed for a moment. Then I began to go through the tutorial for the data bracelet, which I figured I'd need to understand to survive. I opened up the HUD, found the tutorial, and started it. There was no voice and no instructions; a kind of understanding washed over me. It was like getting kung fu uploaded into your head in *The Matrix*. I didn't know how to use the data bracelet, and then I did.

I was so overwhelmed by it all, I didn't really feel social. I wanted to lie on my bed and stare at the ceiling or look at the Earth through my fake porthole. On the other hand, I didn't want to seem unfriendly. My fellow humans were across the hall, and getting to know them seemed like the smart move. They had already been hanging out together for days, and that made me a little uneasy. Moving around like I did always made me the odd man out at school, and I didn't want that to happen again. I told myself I was worrying about nothing. The four of us were arriving from different places and we were all pretty much equal. I was going to be one of them, the human team, starting on the exact same footing they were.

I walked across the hall into the common room, which consisted of a thin metal table and a series of metal chairs bolted to the floor. The three of them were sitting at a table, and they all had their data bracelets off their wrists and spread out. Charles had summoned a keyboard and was typing away furiously. Park was reading from a wall of projected text. Nayana was examining a three-dimensional display of an alien board game, involving different-sized cubes, and seemed to be puzzling out a strategy. The three of them looked up briefly, and then, as if on cue, they looked away as if I were nothing of any interest.

I stood there for a moment, frozen, unsure how to act. There were some crazy-looking aliens walking around this ship, but there was no mistaking me for anything but what I was. There had to be some explanation, I thought. It couldn't be what it looked like, because if it was, it meant that they were giving me the cold shoulder.

"Hey, guys," I said. "Zeke Reynolds, of the planet Earth. I come in peace."

Charles D'Ujanga's voice was unmistakably cool, a far cry from the enthusiastic kid he'd been back at Camp David. "We recollect you, Zeke."

"Yeah," I said slowly. "Good to see you again too, Charles. Likewise, Nayana. Park."

The Asian girl glowered at me. "I'm Mi Sun. Park is my family name. In Korea they come first. Not everything is like it is in the United States. You might want to keep that in mind since we're going to an entirely different part of the galaxy."

"If you do not mind," Charles said, without looking up this time, "we are rather busy."

There wasn't any misunderstanding them now. They were giving me the ultra-icy shoulder. I was standing there, holding my metaphorical lunch tray, with no place to sit.

"Uh, what gives? I am part of Team Humanity, and we're all

in this together, so I'm not sure why you're treating me like the turd in the punch bowl."

Nayana scowled, finding the expression kind of gross, but I thought it was kind of gross too. We all agreed it was in bad taste. Wasn't that grounds for bonding? Apparently not.

Charles stood up and faced me. "It is not my wish to hurt your feelings, but you are indeed, as you so colorfully said, the turd in the punch bowl. You may not like it, but it is so."

"What are you talking about?" I asked. "I'm one of you."

"No, you are a *random*." He gestured toward the hovering text display coming off his data bracelet. "We have been doing research while you were delaying our departure. Historically, applicants that ostracize the random member of their group score much higher than those who attempt equal participation. In fact, if we exclude you from all group activities, our chances of success increase by almost seventy-two percent. You will, no doubt, gain some levels on your own, but we will gain many more if we don't have you to limit our potential. The data support this, and certainly what we see before us right now only further cements the case."

At first I didn't know what he meant, and then I saw it. Hovering above his head was a faint number. Five. He had already risen to level five. Nayana and Mi Sun were both level four. I was level one with a total of zero experience points.

They'd had a full day to get a jump on me, but even so, I felt humiliated, exposed, like in one of those dreams when you realize you're not wearing any pants.

"Don't you think you ought to get to know me before you judge me?" I asked.

"No," Charles said. "We are following the numbers, and the

numbers do not lie. We wish to make the best possible impression on these aliens, and that, I'm afraid, means we must keep our distance from you."

For the most part, my dad loved the movie *Star Trek: First Contact*. His only real gripe was with the end, when Zefram Cochrane operates his warp drive and attracts the attention of the Vulcan explorers. The aliens land, and humanity has its first encounter with a starfaring species, an experience that will change the future of the human race and, indeed, the galaxy. Besides the fact that it is impossible to see James Cromwell's Cochrane as the same character who appeared in the original series episode "Metamorphosis," my dad always hated how Cochrane conducted himself with the visiting and somewhat judgey aliens. He's meeting beings from another world, acting as an ambassador for humanity, hopefully beginning an exchange of technology and ideas and culture, and what does he do? He gets drunk and dances around to some—let's be honest here—second-rate rockabilly. Roy Orbison? Give me a break. "If you ever meet aliens," my dad said, "I hope you'll represent us a little better than that."

Now, here I was, meeting aliens, but *I* wasn't the problem. My fellow humans were.

"How do you think this is going to make us look?" I asked. "Do you think the Confederation wants selfish grinders or people who know how to cooperate?"

"The *beings* who followed this system succeeded in the past," Mi Sun said. "Clearly it didn't hurt their chances. It won't hurt ours."

"That is unfair!" Once again I was the outsider, late to the party, on the fringes. I hadn't asked to join the human delegation, but I'd been selected, and I should be part of the group.

"It is not about fairness," Charles said, his voice icy. "You are American. If we fail, you go back to your life of luxury and ease. You know nothing of the poverty and want in my country. Going to school for me is like winning the lottery for you. Every day in Uganda people die from illnesses easily treated in the United States. People starve. People are killed in pointless wars. Children are pressed into battle. You cannot understand what the prospect of plenty and justice means to us, and I'm not about to risk all of that so your feelings aren't hurt."

"You don't know anything about me," I said. "You don't know what I'm fighting for."

"Your mother. Yes, Ms. Price told us," Charles said. "I know you want to gain the levels for her. I understand that. If you want the cure for her, then stay out of our way and let us succeed. You will only drag us down."

I stood there, silent, not knowing what to say, feeling like it would be admitting defeat if I walked away, but not knowing what else I could do.

Nayana looked up from her projected board game. "For example, you're keeping us from our work right now. We're trying to hit level eight before we arrive at Confederation Central. That is considered the hallmark of excellence."

She looked down, and I stood there, realizing that none of them were going to make eye contact with me again. And so, humiliated, I walked out and into my own room, where I curled up into a ball and tried really hard not to give in to despair and homesickness.

CHAPTER EIGHT

couldn't decide if I should go to dinner. I didn't want to face the other kids, and I guess I was secretly hoping that one of them would come knock on my door and apologize. It never happened. Instead, I lay on my bed, looking at the faux porthole while we broke orbit and headed to wherever the Ganari homeworld was. At first I felt pathetic, but as I watched the Moon and then Mars pass by, the wonder of it all made me momentarily forget how miserable my first day in space had been.

Then an automated voice came over a speaker system. "Prepare to exit standard space."

I was trying to decide how exactly you prepare for something like that when there was a flash of light—but in my mind, not on the screen. I experienced an instant of vertigo in which I felt I was falling and flying and tumbling even though I hadn't moved an inch. Up and down were reversed, and I felt pressure as if my entire body were being squeezed down to the size of an egg, but also erupting out of my skin. The sensation was weird and vivid but only lasted a fraction of a second. Meanwhile, the wall screen didn't turn off so much as vanish. Where there had been a simulation of a porthole seconds before, now there was a blank wall. We were in hyperspace or whatever it was, which meant that I was one of the first human beings ever to exceed the speed of light. I wanted so much to talk about it with *someone*—

to toast this incredible achievement with intergalactic colas—but here I was, alone in my room.

Soon after, I heard the door to the common room open and the others talking and laughing and, worst of all, whispering. I lay there trying to decide which would be worse: seeing them in the mess hall or going without food. I decided to go without food.

What would I do if I were at home, feeling lousy about my life? I laughed as I thought about it. Maybe I'd talk to my mom, but most likely I'd reach for some sci-fi to distract me. Now here I was, living the dream. I wouldn't say the dream stank, but it was certainly stinkier than I had hoped.

I activated my data bracelet and began to search for games. Maybe I could take my mind off my woes with a little cool high-tech diversion. These Confederation guys could build starships, run rings around the laws of physics, and construct machines that allowed me to speak to creatures from another world. Their computer games would *have* to be immersive and thrilling. I had visions of being transported to realistic environments, swinging my +3 battle-axe of doom, the sights and sounds and maybe even smells of the game world so vivid they were indistinguishable from reality.

As it turns out, being part of an advanced civilization does not guarantee that your games won't be pathetic. I figured out pretty quickly that I was hooked into the ship's network, so maybe that was why there wasn't much to choose from, but even so, I was unimpressed. There were a bunch of basic board and peg and stone and token games—the cultural equivalents of chess from a few dozen different worlds. I saw the one with cubes that Nayana had been playing—Strategic Adumbrations—and though the text assured me it was one of the most popular games in the Confederation, it looked dry as dust to me. It was all about deep strategy, thinking multiple moves ahead, and that felt more like work than fun.

I found a few slightly more compelling things, including a game based on the idea of spreading galactic culture to other worlds, and the mechanics were actually kind of similar to Settlers of Catan. There was a game using tiles that had the strange title of Approximate Results from Endeavors. Each tile had a monetary value or was worth points, or could perform actions, which made it kind of like Dominion. There was also a dueling element, which reminded me of Magic: The Gathering. I spent about an hour playing against the computer, and then I went onto the shared network and played against someone with the code name Ystip for another hour or two. There was a chat function, but I felt too shy to activate it, so I never talked to this Ystip. Even so, I learned a few things about the game from him or her or it. After we'd played for another two hours, I went to sleep. A late night of gaming, just like home.

The next morning I woke up early—a side effect of the longer day, I supposed. I was hungry from having skipped dinner the night before, and I wanted to avoid the self-impressed trio, so I threw on some clothes and went in search of breakfast. Using my data bracelet to guide me, I found the guest mess, a small room where they'd set out food with which we were already familiar: some canned fruit and bread and cheeses. It was nothing exciting, but it was edible. I had the feeling they were going to great lengths to accommodate Earth tastes, and I hoped when we got to Confederation Central there would still be food that looked like, well, food. I wolfed down a muffin and canned peaches and some OJ, and then got out of there before I ran into anyone who might be inclined to exclude me.

Just before 0800, I followed the directions from my data bracelet, which projected a translucent yellow path onto my HUD, and headed out to meet the captain. I made my way to a stairwell and up three flights. Then I stepped out onto the bridge, where I did some primitive-planet gaping-in-wonder.

It didn't look exactly like the bridge of a science-fiction ship, but it was awfully close, maybe a little less *Enterprise* and a little more *Space Battleship Yamato*. Captain Qwlessl sat in a chair in the center of the room. A table contained a variety of instruments and screens, which she fussed with perpetually. About ten feet in front of her was a series of consoles at which sat four aliens, and there were more workstations all along the walls. On the bulkhead directly across from the captain was a massive front screen depicting the forward view of the ship, and all around it were dozens of smaller screens showing various alternate views of machinery inside and outside the vessel, scrolls of texts, numerical readouts, and graphical displays.

"Good morning, Mr. Reynolds," the captain said. "How do you like our ship?"

"It's pretty great," I said, absolutely meaning it.

"I like to think we don't do too badly," she said, raising her trunk. Almost certainly a smile, I decided.

Some of the aliens looked at me or pointed ocular orbs or waved sensory stalks in my general direction. I wanted to think I was being paranoid, but there was no getting around it. I heard the word "random" whispered several times.

The captain turned to look at me. "Where would you like to begin?"

What exactly was my most pressing question? I decided to start with the basics. "How do we travel faster than light?"

She rose from her chair and walked me over to where an earthworm with limbs had a station. "Mr. Zehkl, would you care to explain to our guest about our propulsion systems?"

"Sure thing," he said. His eyestalks jiggled distractingly when he spoke. "You understand the basic problem of approaching light speed in normal space?"

I told him I did, though my understanding was, I had no doubt, limited by his standards.

"We have conventional engines that allow us to accelerate to somewhere in the range of one quarter light speed, though warnings go off like crazy once we hit velocities that risk incurring time-dilation effects. For interstellar travel, the physics is quite complicated, and there is some debate about whether we move at all or if we actually stay still while the universe moves around us. But we use technology that essentially allows us to punch holes in space-time and then navigate through the apertures we create. Right now we're not technically in the universe, and we're not really moving faster than light, so we're safe from the effects of extreme speed."

"So you create wormholes?"

His eyestalks stopped jiggling and met my gaze, and he pressed one hand to his wormy body, an evident gesture of confusion. "*Worm* holes?"

"Like passageways in space?" I tried again.

He thought about this for a moment, or perhaps his translator was compensating for the idea of worms, which might have struck close to home. "I think so, yes. We call it tunneling. You enter an opening, and then you come out at the determined location. It's not quite instantaneous, but this ship can traverse nearly sixty light years in the course of a standard day."

"Very concise, Mr. Zehkl," the captain said, taking me by the arm and moving me away from his station. "He used to spend an hour saying basically the same thing. He'd actually explain the equations to anyone who was polite enough not to walk away."

"Ma'am, the equations are interesting," Zehkl called as we walked away.

The tour continued, and I spoke briefly to Wimlo, the stick insect communications officer, and then we went to the helm station, which was operated by a giant otter with a sharp and hooked beak.

"Ms. Ystip," the captain said, "can you explain the basic functioning of the helm to Mr. Reynolds?"

"Maybe," the creature said, in a high and distinctly feminine voice, "if he promises me a rematch in Approximate Results from Endeavors."

"That was you?" I couldn't suppress a smile.

"It was me," she said. "You're good for a beginner. If you'd like, you can meet me in the officers' lounge after 2200 and we'll play a few rounds."

"I'd love that!" The humans didn't much like me, but the beaked otter thought I was okay.

After Ystip gave me a quick rundown of how the helm works, we moved to the weapons console. Sitting there was a short and squat being with large black eyes that had no irises. A decidedly hoglike snout protruded ungracefully from its face, and it had a pair of menacing tusks on either side. It was covered with tough gray hide, and thick ropy hair, like dreadlocks, hung from its head.

"Mr. Urch," the captain said, "please show our guest how the weapons station works."

"Do you use weapons often?" I asked. "I thought the Confederation was peaceful."

"We are," the captain said, "but not everyone else is."

Urch rose from his seat and gestured toward it. He was the same height as I was, but broad and muscular, and he held himself like he was struggling against the urge to commit unspeakable acts of violence. "Sit," he said with a grunt.

It seemed like doing what he said was a good idea. I sat.

"Let me show you a simulation." He pressed a few buttons on his display console, and a grid appeared, green against a black background. The outlines of two enemy ships manifested. On the right side of the panel were multiple weapons sources, while data about distance, shielding, speed, and posturing of the hostile craft scrolled on the left.

"Many ship functions are automated," he said, "but in combat, all targeting and weapons discharge must be handled by a sentient."

"The computer can't do it more accurately?"

"No," he snapped as though the question offended him. "It is standard ship design to vent radiation exhaust, which distorts an enemy's sensor readings. There is no known way to compensate. Targeting must be done by cruder means. It's not a task for all beings. To operate the weapons, you need a steady hand and a fierce heart."

One of the enemy ships turned and fired some sort of weapon at us. The left side of the screen relayed information on damage. "Here is an enemy ship. It will destroy us if we do not fight back," Urch said with a grunt. "You tap on the ship to target a particular sector." He placed a long, clawed, and strangely delicate finger on the ship, which immediately enlarged and broke down into a dozen hexagons each marked with data like LIFE SUPPORT or ENGINES or COMMAND. He tapped ENGINES. "You then choose your weapon—the phased particle beam, or PPB; the dark-matter missile; or the plasma lance." He tapped the PPB button; then, when the word COMMIT appeared on screen, he tapped that. A mock beam fired at the ship, and there was a simulated explosion on the screen. The ship was crippled.

"No offense," I said, "but that looks kind of easy."

"We're in teaching mode," he snorted. "Real combat is fast and chaotic and messy. Achieving a weapons lock is challenging. Do you want to try a more lifelike simulation?"

"Sure," I said.

He pressed a few more buttons. "See what you can do, random."

The screen cleared for a moment and then blinked back to life. Three enemy vessels appeared on the screen, and they were all turning to fire at me. It was, in fact, fast and chaotic and messy. Damage reports scrolled down the side of the screen faster than I could read them. The ship itself moved constantly, and when I reached out to touch it, it was already gone. I tried again, this time anticipating its movement and targeting its weapons systems. I then considered the relative merits of my three weapon choices, but since I had no knowledge of what each did, I wasn't sure which way I wanted to go. While I tried to make up my mind, the screen informed me that I had been destroyed.

"Not so easy," Urch said with a grunt.

"Can I try again?" I asked.

"I see you like to lose," Urch told me.

I did not actually like to lose. However, I started to feel like I understood the system a little better. The setup reminded me of a much more complicated and unforgiving version of the minigames you sometimes find in sci-fi action or role-playing games. I'm not saying that playing video games somehow trained me for real space combat the way it did in the classic film *The Last Starfighter*, but I didn't feel entirely lost.

When the simulation began, I focused immediately on the weapons system of the first ship and fired at it with the PPB, which missed. I still didn't know what the difference between the weapons was, but I knew this one worked, and that was good enough for now. The ship flittered around my screen, making it difficult to get a weapons lock, but I saw a pattern to the movement after a moment, and the third time I tried, I was able to jump in an instant before it shifted position. I obtained a lock and fired the PPB and then immediately targeted the weapons systems of the two other ships. It took a few tries, but I was able to cripple their offensive capabilities before my ship took too much damage. Then I quickly fired at the life-support systems of each ship.

The computer informed me that the enemy forces were requesting terms of surrender. I looked up at Urch and grinned. "Easy," I said.

He grunted.

The captain looked at the monitor. "Not bad, Mr. Reynolds. The computer gives you a sixty-seven percent efficiency rating. What is your rating, Mr. Urch?"

He scowled at me. "In actual combat situations I am rated sixty-four percent. It is a greater challenge when there are lives depending on you."

Realizing I had just possibly made an enemy of a crazed boar creature who had claws on his fingers and whose main function on this ship was to kill people, I thought it might be a good idea to retrench. I rose and held up my hands in surrender. "I know you're right. Anyhow, that was just beginner's luck."

He locked his diabolical black eyes on my far less diabolical green ones. "Luck," he said, "runs out."

The captain led me away before I could make any more enemies and mess up my situation on the ship any worse than I already had.

We toured the rest of the ship, and if it proved less interesting, it was still great to get a better sense of where things were and how they worked. I dragged things on as long as possible because I didn't want to have to go back to my bunk and lie there with nothing to do except avoid the other humans—and now the angry weapons officer. The captain was obviously busy, but when she dropped me off at my door, she eyed me with concern, if I interpreted her hammerhead expression correctly.

"If you like, you can come back tomorrow when we pick up the Ganari. It won't be exciting, but you will get to see bridge officers engage in their duties as we drop into, and then out of, relativistic space. Learning how starships work has its advantages, if you know what I mean."

I did not know what she meant, and she must have understood my blank expression.

"Take a look at your experience points," she said.

I made an effort to see the readout in the bottom left of my HUD, and there it was. It now read 1014/1000. My tour had earned enough points for me to level up.

I broke into a grin. "Nice. I'll be there tomorrow."

She put one of her heavy hands on my shoulder and locked on to my face with her huge, wide-set eyes. "I know the randoms can be made to feel isolated," she said. "Trust me when I tell you that you don't have to be limited by the others in your delegation. You will find many opportunities to contribute."

I found Dr. Roop in the observation lounge, a room toward the back of the ship that had a large wall, where, I supposed, a large window would appear when we returned to normal space. Dr. Roop had set aside his Earthly business suit and now wore a pants-and-shirt-and-jacket combination of strange angles and contours, but it was, in its own alien way, quite dapper. The suit was dark olive green and the shirt red. He had a handkerchief in the jacket pocket. Everywhere he went, Dr. Roop remained a natty dresser.

He was typing away furiously on a blue keyboard projected by his data bracelet, and he showed every indication of being busy, but he looked up when I entered. "What can I do for you, Zeke?"

"I leveled up," I told him. "I need to know what I do now."

"Congratulations." He cleared a space for me to sit by him. "If you concentrate your gaze at those numbers you'll gain access to the leveling process. Pick the skill you want, and focus on it to select it. But before you do any of that, you're going to want to use your bracelet to study the skill tree and decide how, precisely, you want to advance."

"Where can I look at the skill tree?"

"When you go to level up, it will pull up the skill tree automatically, but we can take a look right here." He clicked a few keys on his keyboard and a 3-D projection of a flow chart began to hover between us.

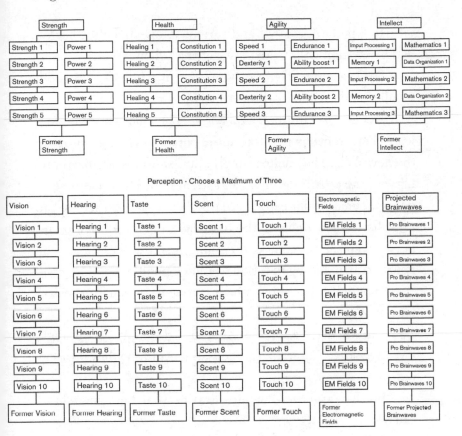

I stared at this in confusion. "I'm not sure what all this means."

"It is rather straightforward," he said. "If you choose strength, the nanites will make alternations to your overall musculature, and you will become stronger. If you choose to augment your hearing, you will hear more clearly and across a wider range. You can ask the system to overlay suggestions for specific career paths—for example, if you wanted to move toward a career in starship operations, you could see how best to level."

He typed a few keys, and various intellect, agility, health, and perception skills were now glowing yellow.

"So, I become, like, a cyborg? Part machine?" I was both terrified and excited by this prospect.

"Not at all," Dr. Roop explained. "The changes are biological. There remains no mechanical superstructure to prop up the new skills. The nanites simply alter your muscle fiber, optic nerves, synaptic firing rates, and so on in order to increase, if only marginally, your capacity in whichever skill you select. You must have some ability in the first place, of course. The members of your species cannot, for example, sense electromagnetic fields, so augmenting that skill would be pointless."

I nodded. "Just how much stronger or smarter will I become?"

"You will likely not feel significantly different after a single leveling, or even after ten levelings, but over time they do accumulate most remarkably."

"But how can these nanites rewrite what I am and what I can do?"

Dr. Roop widened his eyes in his giraffe smile equivalent. "We're not entirely sure how the process is effected. We only know it works."

Another example of Former technology, I thought. Another way in which the Confederation, as Ms. Price suggested, were inheritors of greatness rather than being great themselves. But was it so wrong that they were willing to take advantage of scraps left to them by the lords of handwavium? In his show, *Colony*

Alpha, my father had depicted two civilizations engaged in an arms race to acquire the remnants of a mysterious and vanished culture, but it appeared that the Confederation was merely making use of the resources they had available.

"If the nanites can improve my brain functioning, couldn't they also change who I am? Couldn't someone use the nanites to implant ideas or turn me into an assassin against my will?"

He laughed. "That, no doubt, is something you might find in one of your science-fiction tales, Zeke, but it is not how things work in the Confederation. We've been using this process for centuries, and no one has ever had their personality subverted. It is not possible. Nothing is being added to your personality or emotional makeup. You remain you, only working more efficiently."

"And what about when I go home?" I asked.

"If, in the course of your year on Confederation Central, you dedicate yourself to improving your physical condition, you will leave with more musculature than you currently possess. If you dedicate yourself to learning, you will improve your intelligence. We would not seek to take those organic improvements away from you. This is similar. You will have earned the changes you make, so they are yours. The nanites, however, will be neutralized, so you will not be able to continue to use the skill system."

Now, that was interesting. Did I want to level up in ways that would best help me here, or so that I would have advantages when I got back to Earth? Probably the first option, since if I didn't help my planet get into the Confederation, I'd just be wasting the opportunity I'd been given. Knowing that, however, didn't help me figure out what skill I should choose.

"That seems like a huge decision," I said. "Do I have to make it now?"

"No, of course not," he said. "You'll keep accumulating points, but if you don't apply skills, your level won't change. Everyone will think you are still level one. You may consider that embarrassing."

"I don't care about that," I said, though of course I did. I didn't want Charles and the rest thinking I was stuck on level one, though I also didn't want them to think level two was the best I could do.

I looked at the skill tree again and thought about those final options at the bottom. FORMER STRENGTH, FORMER INTELLECT, FORMER AGILITY. "Is it better to diversify," I asked, "or to try to max out in a single skill? I mean, what if I just want to work toward being as smart as a Former?"

"You won't reach the Former levels. It is not possible."

"Then why are they on the chart?"

Dr. Roop lowered his neck, which I began to realize meant he was feeling apologetic or uncertain. "They are theoretical maximums, not achievable goals. You can only choose the Former achievements when you have otherwise completed seven of the trees. That means you would need to be level seventy-five. And then, having reached seventy-five, you would have to level up yet again. It cannot be done. Sentient races do not live long enough."

"So no one has ever done it?"

"Not since the time of the Formers, and perhaps not even then. The greatest known level ever reached is sixty-six, and that was centuries ago. A being reaching sixty is a Confederation-wide media event. It happens only once or twice in a generation. I've never personally met anyone over level fifty-four."

The Confederation had clearly inherited this system and not

played around with it very much. "Are you telling me that with all your technology, no one has ever tweaked the system—created a god mode like in a video game—so they could max out?"

"The skill tree is one of the fundamental cornerstones of our culture. In many ways it defines who we are: beings who achieve and improve with hard work. Tampering with it would be a most serious crime."

Bring this system to Earth, I thought, and some hacker would crack it in two weeks. Half an hour after that, you could pirate Former status on the Internet. I didn't mention this, since it would not be doing me or my planet any favors. "What skill should I start with?" I asked.

"It depends on what you want to achieve," he said. "If you're not worried about how you look, it may be best to wait until you reach the station and get a better sense of what kinds of tasks you want to pursue. But don't put it off too long. Keep in mind that accumulating skills makes reaching new levels easier. Even if you can't sense your growing improvements, they make a difference. Perpetual hoarders keep their options open, but ultimately fall behind."

"Okay, I'll think about it a little more." I paused for a minute, not sure how I wanted to ask my next question. I liked Dr. Roop, and I did not want to stop liking him. I was afraid what I would hear if I pressed him on what was on my mind. Still, I had to know. "How come you didn't tell me the others were going to treat me like this?"

He sighed and lowered his neck again. He appeared genuinely sad. "I didn't know, Zeke. I certainly did not want to give them any ideas. No two species are alike, and you can never tell how things are going to go. They were resourceful enough to look up and examine past statistics, and they made their own decisions. I tried to discourage them, but I can't demand they do as I ask. Things will be better at the station."

"Why?" I asked, sounding a little testier than I had intended. "What's going to change?"

"You'll meet other beings with whom you have more in common."

It was like my mother, always telling me I'd make good friends at the next place we moved. I knew better by now. The new guy with no friends is never an attractive prospect.

"Thanks," I told him.

I stepped out of the observation lounge and into the corridor. And there I almost collided with Mr. Urch, the being from the weapons station whom I'd embarrassed in front of the captain. Like an idiot.

"It's the weapons master," he grunted as he passed me.

I hurried on, frightened, not wanting to mess things up any more than I had already. Then I stopped and turned back to him. I figured I had nothing to lose. "Mr. Urch," I called.

He turned back to me, jutting out his snout to show his tusks and his sharp teeth. "What do you want?"

I walked over to him, slowly, as my legs were not working at their absolute best. "You were being nice when you showed me how to work your station, and somehow I did okay and I know I looked like I was trying to show you up. It was a dumb thing to do, and I apologize."

He studied me for a moment and then sniffed roughly through his large nose, and I felt the heat of his exhalation on my face. "It is a mistake," he told me, showing me his teeth and moving his wild-hog muzzle closer to my face, "to read too much into the body language of a species with which you are unfamiliar."

Considering it seemed like he was about to gore me with the tusks he happened to have sticking out of his face, I sure hoped he was right. "Uh, okay. Yeah, that's probably true."

"I am a Vaaklir. We evolved from fierce predators. Species who evolved from herbivores and omnivores always, at first, mistake the body language of predator species. You, for example, think I am angry with you because you did well on the weapons console."

Perceptive *and* terrifying. A nice combination. "Aren't you?"

He grunted. "Pay attention to my words, not my teeth. No, I'm not angry. I like to see an applicant with your skill. It pleases me. And I will tell you something else. Vaaklir are new to the Confederation. Sixteen years ago, the first group of my species sent a delegation to Confederation Central, just as your species does now."

He seemed no less intimidating, but what he was saying made him less scary. Maybe this body-language thing was worth thinking about, especially since what he said suggested that in sixteen years, humans could be serving on a ship like this. *I could be serving on a ship like this.* "And now you're here? That's amazing."

"I was part of that delegation," he said, smacking his broad chest with his clenched fist. "I was the random."

I stared, not sure what to say, but I was strangely moved. This creature that looked like a crazed warthog was reaching out to me.

"So understand that rather than knock you down and use

my tusks to rip the entrails from your soft flesh, as you apparently fear, I would prefer to offer you my help."

He said it baring his teeth and looking like the former option was the one he really had his heart set on, but I believed he meant what he said. "Thanks, Mr. Urch. Really. And I'm sorry for misreading you."

"No apology required," Urch said. He opened his jaws and showed me his alarmingly sharp teeth. "I know how much there is for you to learn, and we nonherbivores have to look after one another. I've just gone off duty. If you wish, you can come with me to the crew mess and eat like a real spacefarer. Then I will take you to the simulation room. You can learn a few more tricks on the weapons console."

I broke into a grin. "That would be great."

"Look at that," he said, opening his own jaws. "You bare your teeth like a Vaaklir. I like you more already."

The crew mess was like the bar in the original *Star Wars* movie, only without the music or the attitude. A dizzying variety of creatures of various shapes and colors and morphologies stood on line or sat at tables, talking and laughing. The selection of food was also impressive, set on a long counter full of separate trays. The Formers, in all their wisdom, seemed not to have devised anything more advanced than a buffet. I stood in line with Urch and examined the overwhelming selection, not knowing what most of the dishes were, but noting that they were protected by a cosmic sneeze guard.

"I guess I don't get to use a food replicator," I said.

He burst out laughing. "Individual use of food production units! On a ship this size! You truly do know nothing."

"Wait a minute," I said. "Does that mean there are food replicators?"

"Of course," he said. "Do you think we have a pantry and cooks? But food production units are massive, which is why you will find restaurants and food vendors always clustered together on Confederation Central. We have one on this ship, and the mess officer is in charge of the daily offerings."

"Nanotechnology?" I asked.

"How else? The same way nanites can increase your abilities or heal you or even alter your appearance, if you so desire, they can fabricate atoms out of different atoms. Thus, food. Now, let's see what we have. Don't be afraid to try something new," he said as we shuffled past our options. There were piles and globs and mounds of things I could not even guess at. Other foods were more recognizable. There were noodles, though they were the color of blueberries and oily; strange kinds of oblong fruit; a tray of what were almost certainly greens, except they were bright orange. There was a lot, and I didn't know what any of it might be. I'm not a terribly fussy eater, but I still like to know, roughly, what something is made of before I put it in my mouth.

"Your HUD will alert you if you attempt to eat any substance toxic to your biochemistry. If there is no warning, it will be safe, though it might taste like excrement to you." He loaded his tray with a pool of brown slop.

"What's that?" I asked.

"Excrement," he said. "In [dried fruit] sauce."

I studied his face for signs he was joking, but since I had no idea what those signs would look like, I quickly gave up that project. "I thought your species were predators."

"Way back, sure. Excrement is a delicacy among many cultures on my world. Some suspect that we used to like to eat it directly from the bowels of our freshly caught prey, but there's no need to read too much into it. It tastes good."

I picked up something that looked like a roll. "What's this?" I asked.

"It's a different kind of excrement." When I set it down, he made a hissing noise that I soon realized was laughter. "I'm joking with you, Zeke. It is a kind of baked grain product. I know many species don't like to eat excrement." He picked up a glass of yellowish liquid. "But you do drink urine, I hope."

After dinner we went to a kind of practice room that looked a little bit like a small, cubicle-filled office and a little bit like one of those tiny game arcades they sometimes have in hotels. There was a series of divided consoles that could be made to operate like any workstation on the ship. Urch and I sat down at two adjacent cubicles, and he pressed a few buttons to lower the partition between us. He then called up his data-bracelet keyboard, which looked nothing like my default keyboard—his was spherical and contained hundreds of strange markings. The sphere rotated constantly to keep up with his typing.

"You have to synch this station to your data bracelet so your HUD can coordinate the sim," he said.

I called up my own keyboard, and he showed me what to do. It was actually fairly intuitive given what I'd already learned about operating the data bracelet.

"You'll run the weapons console, and I'll handle navigation," he said. "We could create artificial crewmen, including a captain, if you'd like, but then you would have to follow orders.

I think it is better if you learn some basics for now, so we'll assume we've been given freedom, by the captain, to proceed as we think best."

I looked at this display monitor. "So the sim will appear on this screen here?"

He opened his massive jaws and showed me his sharp teeth. Then he snorted a hearty laugh. "You'll see."

"Is that a smile?" I asked.

"An evil one," he said. Then he did it again. "Now pay attention. The PPB, the phased particle beam, is your go-to weapon of choice. You know what dark matter is?"

"Yeah, it's the mysterious stuff we can't perceive that makes up most of the universe."

"Good. You know more than I did. Just like there is dark matter, there is dark energy—extremely powerful energy we cannot see or measure. The Formers understood its secrets, and we use their technology to harness dark energy and deploy it for weapons and shielding. The dark energy causes the particle beam to phase in and out of the universe, generating power as it bursts into existence and nonexistence. The PPB is fast and flexible, and there will be more or less a limitless supply while the engines are running. Most battles will be fought without reaching for anything beyond the PPB."

"Have you been in a lot of battles?"

"No." Then he grunted in a way I could not interpret. "We're not a warship, but there are incidents."

"What sort of incidents?"

"You'll learn about it when you get to the station. Now you are learning about the weapons console. Here is the dark-matter missile, which is used much less frequently. It is a physical object that employs both dark energy and negative energy to disrupt the enemy's hull at the quantum level. This allows for maximum damage from the dark-matter detonations. The standard arsenal for a ship this size is twenty missiles, so there is a limited supply, and, depending on distance, they can take anywhere from one to four seconds from deployment until they reach the target. They're easier to avoid than the PPB, but if they hit, they tend to be battle enders. Keep in mind that these missiles are expensive and dangerous to produce, so in real-world situations, they are not deployed lightly. After you launch, regulations require that you confirm contact and assess damage before you choose to launch another."

"Okay." I nodded.

"Finally, there's the plasma lance. Unless an enemy's shielding is configured to avoid solid matter—which would make a ship vulnerable to PPB attack—this can penetrate shields and not only latch onto a hull, but become part of the hull. You use it when you are trying to capture and tow a vessel."

"Like a tractor beam?" I asked.

He made his hissing laugh noise. "Those are just in stories. In real life you lance a vessel and tow it with a cable that the plasma energy constructs out of ambient matter in space. It is generally used only on already-disabled vessels. Now, are you ready for a sim?"

"Sure," I said.

"Hold on to something," he told me, flashing another boar-like grin. Then he called up a menu on the console and used the tips of his claws to click on a few options. My data bracelet chirped and asked me if I wished to proceed with the simulation. I agreed, and almost instantly there was a bright flash of light.

Then we were on the bridge. The main screen showed a ship coming toward us, firing weapons. Lights flashed. Alarms sounded. I may have screamed.

"Let me pause this a moment," Urch said, and we were no longer on the bridge and we were no longer being pounded by enemy fire. He hissed out a laugh. "In case you haven't figured it out yet, your HUD is messing with your vision and hearing to produce a full illusion in the sim. It seems pretty realistic, doesn't it?"

My heart was hammering. "Yeah, you might have warned me."

"That would not have been as much fun. I had hoped to make you urinate with surprise, but I see your clothing is dry."

"Sorry to let you down."

"Another time," he promised. "Now, are you ready to earn some experience points?"

It wasn't quite like being on the *Star Trek* holodeck. I couldn't get up and walk around, and I couldn't interact with anything but the terminal in front of me, but it was still pretty vivid. I felt the ship vibrate when we were hit; I heard the distant boom of explosive decompression and decks collapsing. I made tactical decisions that got my ship destroyed, and later, after a few attempts, I made some tactical decisions that saved my ship. Win or lose, I got to experience an actual, realistic battle sim, and I was getting advice and feedback from a trained weapons officer. It was my idea of a good time.

After we finished and stepped into the hall, we saw Charles, Nayana, and Mi Sun walking toward us, laughing. I noticed the two girls had now also reached level five, and Charles had reached six. I felt a tightness in my gut just looking at them. They were going to be constant reminders that I didn't really belong here.

They fell silent when they saw us. Charles looked away guiltily.

Urch stepped out in front of them. "Halt!"

They stopped and glanced at one another nervously.

"This corridor is off-limits to guests not accompanied by an officer. You are aware of that, yes?"

"No, sir," said Charles, worry creeping across his face. "No one told us. I thought our data bracelets would warn us—"

"Unless you tampered with them!" Urch shouted. "If you have altered the security protocols of this ship, the captain will send you back to Earth. And that is if you're lucky. If I find out, I will send you out an airlock. You may check my record if you think I am speaking metaphorically. I have been reprimanded in the past for such actions."

Charles and Nayana cringed. Mi Sun, to her credit, stood her ground, though she looked worried. "We didn't tamper with anything. And we had no idea we were breaking any rules."

"That is unlikely," Urch snapped. "Return to your quarters at once, and know that one thousand experience points will be deducted from each of you for this outrageous violation of ship policy. Out of my sight, omnivore scum!"

They scattered at once.

I stared at Urch. "Is that true?"

"Which part?"

"Any of it?"

"No. None of it. Of course they can be here. Their data bracelets would have warned them if they had ventured anywhere inappropriate. And you can't take someone's points away. But they don't know that."

"And throwing people out the airlock?"

"That I do all the time," he said with his hissing laugh.

As we proceeded down the corridor, Urch explained that he did not enjoy games like Approximate Results from Endeavors, which he found insufficiently violent, but he walked me over to the officers' lounge and watched while Ystip and I played for about an hour using the colorful tiles, which were a little bit smaller than playing cards, and made a satisfying slap when I set them down on the table. Urch then called it a night, and Ystip and I kept going for another few rounds. I won about as often as I lost, which I thought was not too bad, and Ystip seemed impressed.

"It takes most beings much longer to understand the mechanics," she told me as we cleaned up and put away the tiles.

"We have similar games on my planet," I told her.

"It must be a very advanced world," she said wistfully.

"It has its moments." I thanked her and headed back to my cabin, now exhausted and ready for sleep. It had been a great night, maybe one of the best nights ever, and for a little while I'd forgotten just how ostracized I had become. And then I remembered, and I thought about how, despite all the friends I was making on the *Dependable*, in a few days I'd be at Confederation Central, and everyone who had made this experience enjoyable would be gone, and I'd be alone once again.

CHAPTER NINE

I came onto the bridge the next morning about fifteen minutes before we were scheduled to pop back into the universe. On TV shows, the captain tells the crew to drop out of warp or exit hyperspace, and there you go. In real life, there seemed to be a lot of planning and plotting and computing to be done as they readied to enter the Ganari system. Everyone had things to do. The various aliens were calling out numbers and coordinates, punching in information, double-checking readings.

The captain spared a moment to greet me, however. "Good morning, Mr. Reynolds. I see from the logs you've been doing some weapons training."

"Yes, ma'am," I said, feeling more than a little pleased she'd bothered to find out what I'd been up to.

"In a few years you could be serving on a ship like this one," she said.

"I'm not quite ready for that," I told her, "but I think I would love it."

The captain was about to say something else, but a message came across her screen, and she forgot about me as she tended to business.

"All systems synched," she said. "Take out us of tunnel, Ystip."

The recorded message came on, telling us to prepare to reenter normal space. A few seconds later there was a shudder, a moment of sickening dizziness, and a flash of light inside my mind as I lost all bearings and nothing felt right. Then the discomfort was gone and we were moving through normal space again. The viewscreens switched from showing a logistical illustration of our position to a visual image. There, before us, was an alien sun, glowing as bright as my own.

The Ganari system had outer gas giants just like Earth's system, and we zipped past them until we came into orbit around a planet that, at first glance, might have been my own. It was blue, with white clouds and polar caps. Only the unfamiliar shapes of the land masses below revealed that this was not my own world. I supposed this planet, like Earth, had been visited and changed and seeded by Formers. Clearly they had a design they liked.

I'd seen so much already. I'd met a dozen or more alien species. I'd been on board a spaceship and hung out with the captain and her crew, and now here was an actual planet, a world with its own creatures and history and societies. Not just a single being or a collection of beings, but a world, whose sights and sounds and smells were as varied and infinite as those of the Earth, but entirely and unimaginably different. Down there would be languages and history and traditions and ways of life no one on Earth had even considered. They would have myths and stories all their own.

The word "awesome" gets overused a lot—I, myself, have on occasion been a serious abuser—but this was awesome in the truest sense. I was filled with awe, and the crazy thing was that this planet, this sphere teeming with unique and unknowable life, was just a drop in the bucket compared to the hundreds of worlds of the Confederation, and then the thousands of worlds outside the Confederation.

I hated being a random and being ostracized by the other humans, but even if I was having the worst initiate experience possible, I knew I was lucky to be part of all this.

I watched as Wimlo informed the captain that the shuttle had launched, and then on the far side of the planet I watched it appear, at first a distant speck slowly growing closer. On board that ship would be four Ganari, one of whom was a random. Maybe I would be friends with him or her or it. Maybe I might have more in common with another random than I did with my own species.

"Captain!" Urch called out, snapping me from my thoughts. "I'm picking radiation consistent with a tunnel aperture forming, five thousand kilometers dead ahead. It's coming in between us and the shuttle."

The captain rose from her chair and jabbed her trunk at Urch. "Can you identify it?"

"Too soon to be certain, ma'am, but the distortion is consistent with Phandic signatures."

"Activate shielding," the captain said, her voice icy calm. She looked at my gaming buddy at the helm. "Ystip, get us between that aperture and the shuttle. Best speed."

I wanted to ask what was going on, but I knew better. I kept my mouth shut because it was the right thing to do and because the tension on the bridge was unmistakable and terrifying. This was an emergency, and at best I would be in the way. At worst, I'd be ordered off the bridge. Whatever a Phandic was, it was bad news. I wanted to go to my cabin and hide, but even more, I wanted to understand what was going on.

Captain Qwlessl spun to her navigation officer. "Zehkl, plot a course to send the shuttle back to the surface. Wimlo, as soon as he's done, override that shuttle's navigation system with the new course. Inform the Ganari that—"

She didn't get a chance to finish speaking because there was a flash of light on the primary viewscreen as an invisible scalpel sliced a jagged line into space. Light and clouds of what looked like mist oozed from the wound in the universe. Then the slash vanished, and a ship was suddenly there, blocking our view of the shuttle. I felt my body turn cold, as if every cell in my body knew that whatever had just shown up was bad news.

The ship was as black as space itself, almost invisible but for a series of flashing lights that illuminated its form—narrow from top to bottom, but broad across with a slight protrusion toward the top and its middle. It hovered in the void, its lights like the eyes of a wakened predator.

The alien ship was a flying saucer, but the most diabolical flying saucer imaginable.

"Get me eyes on the shuttle," the captain said. "Ystip, replot a course. Get us around that ship. Urch, prepare weapons lock, but do not fire until I give the order. Wimlo, contact the Phandic ship. Tell its captain that this planet has been placed under Confederation protection, and whatever they're thinking about doing, it's likely stupid."

The communications officer clacked its mandibles and typed out a message and then read the response, which popped up a second later. It was like galactic texting.

"Ma'am, they say this is neutral territory, that the Ganari have not signed any treaties with the Confederation."

"I was hoping they hadn't realized that," the captain said, lowering herself back to her chair. "Contact them again. See if they'll talk to us. We can't let this escalate."

More mandible clacking. Perhaps a nervous gesture. "They're declining to talk, ma'am."

We had now looped around the Phandic ship and were moving toward the shuttle.

"Ystip, if the Phands are looking for trouble, will the shuttle be safe?"

She answered without turning her beaked face to the captain. "No, ma'am. It has minimal shielding. If the Phands want it, they've got it."

"Can we lance it and bring it aboard before they can fire?"

"Distances are too great," Urch said. "We can lance, but we can't bring it in quickly enough, not if they mean to destroy it."

"Right." She considered the matter for a few seconds, twirling her trunk in a tight little circle. Then she turned to Ystip. "Plot a new course for the shuttle. Move it toward the surface for another thirty seconds, then reverse and bring it into the shuttle bay fast, the most erratic flight pattern you can safely implement. They're in for a rough ride, so have a medical team in the bay to meet them."

"Yes, ma'am." Ystip began furiously entering data into the navigation console.

Then there was a flash of light. Before the shuttle could even alter course, the Phandic ship fired. It wasn't like in the movies, where you can watch a beam travel from one ship to another. In reality, the beam moved at the speed of light. There was a flash and then another. Where once there had been a transport, now there was a ball of fire as the venting oxygen burned. Then the vacuum snuffed out the flame and there was only a sprinkling of debris that spiraled out of the center in a plume of metal and plastic.

The four Ganari applicants were dead. In a single instant,

they had been brutally murdered. I stared, hardly believing it. I felt terror and sadness and rage and a hundred other things I could hardly name. This place was supposed to be safe. They'd told us the Confederation was peaceful. Clearly, they had not told us everything.

The captain was standing again, looking grim. For a moment she waggled her trunk wildly, and her eyes became huge. Then she stopped moving and her expression seemed to darken. "Mr. Urch, how do we stand against that ship?"

"It's a [stone fist]-class cruiser, ma'am. Our PPBs won't do much to it, but our shields will hold off its weapons more or less indefinitely."

"Tunnel a comm beacon to Confederation Central," she ordered. "Call for reinforcements. Let's see if we can keep them busy until help shows up."

There was another burst of light, and then a massive rumble as we were hit by enemy fire. Lights now flashed all over the bridge. Alarms were going off—not mind-numbing claxons, but quieter beeps and dings and buzzes as consoles begged their operators for attention.

"Status!" the captain demanded.

"Damage to the lower decks," Mr. Urch said. He typed again furiously, and then looked up, alarmed. "They've found a way to boost their PPB effectiveness against our defenses. Shield strength is functioning only at forty-seven percent."

"So, we're not going to hold out indefinitely?"

"I don't think we're going to hold out for a quarter hour against what they have."

"Ystip, plot a tunnel. Let me know the instant we have aperture. Recommendations, Mr. Urch?"

Urch was busy tapping data into his console, and did not turn to face her when he spoke. "If we flee, our weapons capacity will be further diminished. To remain a threat, we should stand our ground, or advance up until the moment the aperture forms."

I found myself nodding. This was something I'd learned the previous night in the sim room. When a ship is fleeing, the ion wake of its engines disperses its PPB discharges. In other words, once you start running, you can't return fire with any real force. If we backed off, we would have no ability to fight, and until the tunnel opened, we would have nowhere to run.

My thoughts were interrupted by three more flashes, and the ship rumbled again. More distressed consoles cried out as they scrolled data and warnings and bad news.

"Direct hit to rear starboard engine," Urch said.

There were more flashes, more rumbles, more alarms. Things were happening quickly. We were being overwhelmed. Every member of the crew was busy at his or her terminal, entering commands rapidly, trying to keep ahead of the attack. Each of them appeared calm, but I felt like I could read panic on their alien faces.

"Forward port engine is off-line," Urch announced.

"We've lost tunnel capacity," Zehkl, the earthwormy tunneling expert, said, "and I don't think we can get five percent light until we effect repairs."

The captain pointed at the screen with her trunk. "Begin repairs at once, and let's use what we've got. Urch, move all shielding to forward sections. Siphon power from anything nonessential if you have to. Plot a course for the Phandic ship, Ystip. Best speed."

"Yes, ma'am," she said, her voice cool, though she clacked her beak a couple of times. "Ramming vector laid in."

The captain must have noticed my terrified expression, and she flashed me a sympathetic look. "Mr. Reynolds, energy shields can't simultaneously block physical objects and energy weapons. To avoid being destroyed when we ram them, they'll have to convert their shields, and if they do that, we can fire on them. If they don't convert shields, the impact will destroy them. It's a standoff, and they'll have no choice but to withdraw. We can't beat them in combat, so we're making combat a losing proposition."

Very nice of her to explain it to me. Even so, I saw there was a safety rail near where I was standing, and I grabbed hold of it. Hanging on was not going to save me, but it made me feel marginally less frightened.

Wimlo now looked over. "Captain, the Phandic ship is sending audio."

"Let's hear it."

A calm voice came from over the speaker. "Confederation vessel, we do not wish to destroy you. Surrender, and your crew will not be harmed. Refuse, and you are of no use to us."

"Commander Phandic vessel," the captain replied, "you know we won't do that. This is pointless."

"The point is your surrender," the Phandic captain said.

The captain jabbed her trunk at Wimlo, indicating an end to communication.

"Sublight navigation is now functional, but slow," Zehkl said. "We can tunnel in seven minutes."

"Plot tunnel and be ready to enter the moment we achieve aperture," the captain said, "but I don't think they have seven minutes of restraint in them. We're alone out here, hopelessly outgunned and without enough time to escape. Mr. Urch, give me your tactical read of the situation."

"If we are buying time," Urch said, "we should keep our weapons fire to a minimum. If they think we can't fight, they will move more slowly."

The captain nodded. "I agree. Escalating conflict is not a winning option," she said. "Hold fire until I say otherwise. But Wimlo, send another beacon. We won't get reinforcements in time, and I want the registration of that ship noted."

If I understood the captain correctly, she was now talking about what was going to happen after we were destroyed.

It looked like the Phandic flying saucer of death was determined to make that happen. There were more flashes of light, more rumbles. Urch called out damage reports and hull breaches, but the concentrated shielding seemed to be keeping us alive, if just barely. And, for the record, we were still moving to ram the enemy ship. Urch scowled, and his hands twitched, but he did not touch the weapons console. I could see he was itching to fire, but the captain had agreed with his own assessment. Still, if we were going to be destroyed, I knew he would want to get in a few shots first.

I watched on the screen as the enemy grew larger and more menacing, as they fired on us and we shook like a plane going through turbulence. I understood that there was a good chance we were going to die. Maybe it was a certainty. We were either going to be destroyed by the enemy or destroyed when we crashed into the enemy. The only chance we had was that the ship would realize it had nothing to gain and back off. It showed no sign of doing that.

Then there were a dozen or more flashes in quick succession. The ship rocked. Lights flickered. I heard the distant rumble of explosions. Unlike on TV shows, no consoles exploded, but I watched as several dimmed and more than half extinguished entirely. All around me the officers of the *Dependable* tapped furiously at screens and keyboards, trying to bring their stations back to life, but the bridge was now cast in a gloomy twilight.

"Shielding is fluctuating," Urch said. "Damage reports from all decks."

"Stabilize defenses," the captain said, her voice steady. "Restraint doesn't seem to be working. I didn't want this, but I won't make it easy on them. See what you can do to dissuade them, Mr. Urch, and if you have a clear shot for a dark-matter missile, take it."

Urch bared his teeth as he fired off several PPB bursts. The Phandic ship returned fire, and then things, which were really bad, got a whole lot worse.

As if someone had pulled a switch, gravity was gone. My stomach dropped out, and the concepts of up and down were distant and fond memories. This didn't feel like the disorientation of leaving relativistic space. This was something far more physical and unpleasant. I felt like I was falling, plummeting; not vomiting took all my concentration. Whatever means the ship used to generate gravity had been damaged or destroyed, and if I hadn't been holding on to the railing already, I would have gone flying the instant the gravity failed.

Then, seconds after I became weightless, we were spinning wildly, as the *Dependable* lost stabilizers and went cascading through space. Anything not tied down was thrown by the powerful force of the ship's mad gyration. The captain, in mid-order, was cast out of her chair. Everyone on the bridge was hurled from their stations. Everyone but me, still clinging to my rail. I heard cries of frustration as the officers tried to right themselves, tried to make it back to their consoles, but between the lack of gravity and the spinning of the ship, it was impossible to find a destination. There were cries of pain. Blood floated in thick globs in the weightlessness. Someone's tooth sailed past me.

Then the ship came under control, and the gravity returned, but not in that order. The gravity was half a second ahead of the stabilizers, so when the ship suddenly righted, nearly everyone went flying through the air like popcorn in a popper—some hitting the walls, some the floor, some the ceiling, some one another in midair. When everything became still, the bridge officers were cast about like battered toys. I struck the wall hard, and my arm was jerked painfully, but I was not seriously hurt.

The captain was trying to get up as she clutched a clearly broken arm. Urch had been hurled halfway across the bridge, and now lay terrifyingly still. Ystip seemed to have broken her leg, but she had dragged herself back to her console and reestablished our course to collide with the enemy ship. She was, I realized, the only being on the bridge capable of resuming her station. A few others were moving, slowly, but the crew had been almost entirely neutralized.

I looked again at Urch, motionless. I looked at his weapons console. I looked at the captain, who was typing into her data-bracelet keyboard using her one good hand.

"Trying to get backup crew, but there are injuries all over the ship." She glanced up at me. "Until a replacement arrives, I need you to operate weapons, Mr. Reynolds."

I stood still, staring at her, understanding what she had

just told me but not believing it. I couldn't do what she asked. There was no way. I wasn't a trained weapons officer. I'd noodled around in the sim for a couple of hours, but that was it. She could not seriously want me to do this. I told myself that, but I knew it wasn't true. She needed me to step up for the simple reason that there was no one else.

I swallowed and ran for the console.

I tapped the screen and quickly got an image of the enemy ship, but it was moving fast, engaging in countermeasures that made a lock-on difficult. Identifying the engines or any other specific system was harder, so much harder, than it had been in the simulation. This wasn't like what I'd practiced, which had been challenging but possible. This was so much more complicated. Our ship was moving. The enemy was moving. There were flashing lights and indicators demanding my attention. Text scrolled endlessly. We were about to be blown up, and I was powerless to do anything about it. The chair might as well have been empty for all the good my sitting in it did us.

The Phandic captain's voice came over the speakers again. "Confederation ship, you are severely damaged and significantly outmatched. Surrender and your lives will be spared."

I was desperately trying to get a lock on something, anything, but it was impossible to nail down. Every time I thought I had a target in my sights, it slipped away. The ship moved across the screen too quickly. My head hammered; my hands shook. This wasn't possible. I was not good enough. Maybe brilliant Charles, or strategic Nayana, or agile Mi Sun could have done it, but I was just a random.

I wanted to tell Captain Qwlessl that she'd made a mistake, she needed to find someone else, but I knew there was no time.

I had to make it work. I had to, or we were all going to die. I took in a deep breath, and I tried to make myself believe I was not at the weapons station, and this was not life or death. I was playing a game. This was the newest, most vivid version of Halo, and here I was in the most intense vehicle sequence ever created. It was just a game, I said. I did okay at games. I sometimes won the tough levels without having to save and start over. When I played, sometimes I liked to pretend that it was real, that it counted. Now it *was* real, and I needed to pretend it was just for fun.

I almost had their life-support system locked, but then it was gone. I was blowing this. Failing miserably. They were going to destroy us without me even firing a single shot.

I remembered all the little tricks Urch had taught me to compensate for the movement of two ships, and I honed in on my target—the engines. I failed, and then I failed again, and I failed a third time, but on the fourth try I got a lock. I fired off a volley of PPB blasts, and my console told me I had scored a direct hit on the target. There were three satisfying flashes against the saucer's hull. I pumped my fist in satisfaction and checked the readout. I had done only superficial damage.

In my limited combat experience, I'd figured out a few things about this enemy. They had better weapons, but we were supposed to have better shields. There was apparently a rock-paper-scissors balance of power between the Confederation and the Phandics or Phands or whatever they were. This time they'd come out with a stronger rock, and that's why we were taking this beating; they had improved their weapons, and we were defending ourselves with old shields, this battle could only end one way.

The one chance we had to survive or avoid capture was to

try something they didn't expect. I had to throw away the rule book and do something entirely unexpected. It was time to go James Kirk on them.

The old one. Not the new one.

Here's my problem with the *Star Trek* reboot. I enjoy those movies, don't get me wrong. They're a blast, and I know my dad would have liked them too. I don't have any problem with them tinkering with core ideas about the franchise. In fact, I love that the new movies take place in an alternative timeline so you can keep the old continuity without making the new one a slave to it. Brilliant.

My problem is with Kirk's new attitude. The old Kirk would break the rules, but only when the rules stood in the way of the principles the Federation was sworn to uphold. He believed in the Prime Directive, but he would throw it out the airlock if obeying it meant people would suffer or die, because, at its core, the Prime Directive was meant to preserve life. Old Kirk is a tough guy, but a completely moral tough guy. New Kirk, on the other hand, seems to get a charge out of breaking rules and risking lives. Tell him not to do something, and he'll do it, if only for the pleasure of being a maverick. You can explain it away, I guess. This Kirk is younger than the first Kirk was when we first met him. This Kirk grew up without a father. I suppose it makes sense that he would be more reckless, but half the time he comes across as nothing more than a troublemaker, the sort of clown the original Kirk would have declared a menace.

I was about to break some rules, but in the old Kirk tradition. I was not getting a thrill out of doing what I'd been told not to do. I wanted to get out of the situation alive because I was on a spaceship, going to a space station, and I could not accept the injustice of dying now. I refused to let my mother fall victim to her disease because these flying-saucer bullies wanted to flex their muscles. I believed the Phandic ship was wrong and we were right, and following the rules was not going to save us.

I looked up at the viewscreen and saw the Phandic ship hovering before us. That thrill of fear coursed through me, and I willed it away. I looked down at the screen and scored another lock, again on the engines, and I did not hesitate. I would not. The speakers were on, and the Phandic voice was telling us to surrender and prepare for boarding. The alarms and beeps and buzzes of the consoles were thrumming in my ears. The bridge smelled of blood and sweat. I had a chance, and I took it.

Urch had explained that the rules required I fire only one dark-matter missile at a time, and after each firing assess the extent of the damage. Okay, that was fine if you weren't about to be destroyed. I wasn't interested in finding out how well the evil aliens could dodge my missiles, especially since they would almost certainly know the Confederation rules. They would be counting on them.

They weren't counting on me. I fired five dark-matter missiles, one after another, and my console assured me each of them was locked, but they were all on different points of the saucer. My hope was that if they tried to dodge one, they would just be setting themselves up for a more direct hit from another.

As soon as those five were away, I locked in another set and released five more missiles. I had just unleashed half our arsenal at the enemy, and in case that didn't give them something to think about in the seconds between launch and impact, I peppered them with as many PPB bursts as I could fire. I didn't even care if I had a lock. I just wanted to scare them. I just wanted to do something.

"History," I shouted, paraphrasing alternate-timeline Picard, "will remember the name *Dependable*!"

I kept firing and firing and waiting for them to return the favor and blow us to pieces. I fired again, and they did not answer. Instead I saw pinpricks of light on the saucer's hull as the first of the missiles struck. Then another. Then more than I could count, because the ship was enveloped in a cloud of fire as the hull of the saucer cracked open and the oxygen was sucked out. I checked my console. Four of the missiles had gone wide, but the other six had smacked against the Phandic ship like a blast of dark-matter shotgun pellets. The saucer shuddered, and small explosions burst from one extreme edge of the hull, as though the ship burped fire. Then the entire hull began to glow, as heat spread out from the initial explosion, red then white, and the screen was filled with light as the enemy vessel burst into a tiny nova. The flash lasted only an instant; then the hot debris quickly cooled and vanished against the black backdrop of the void.

I had destroyed a spaceship.

CHAPTER TEN

Ahush fell over the bridge as everyone who was still conscious came to understand that we were not going to die. The flow of time seemed to change for me, switching from a direct drive forward to a weird staccato as reality stopped and started. The captain was by my side, patting me on the back with her good arm. Urch was now on his feet, looking absolutely terrible with a crushed nose, a gash across his face, and apparently a head wound—his thick locks were dripping with blood—but he was alive.

He took one of his huge hands and wiped it down his face, and then shook off the excess blood. "You blew the excrement out of that ship," he told me.

I nodded. I wasn't quite ready for speech.

How many beings had I just killed? It wasn't a video game. It wasn't pretend. Were dozens dead? Hundreds? They were all gone because of what I had done. They had been trying to kill us, and that counted for something. It counted for a lot, but it was still unbelievable.

"Thirty seconds to tunnel aperture," Ystip called.

"Enter tunnel as soon as possible," the captain said, relief unmistakable in her voice. "Best speed to Confederation Central. I want to see damage reports and repair estimates as soon as they're available. Get health teams up here and deploy them to all decks. I want every being on board accounted for within ten minutes. No one is dying in a dark corner on my ship. I want to see a prioritized repair schedule as soon as possible. And Mr. Reynolds, thank you for saving our lives, but it is time for civilians to clear the bridge."

"Yes, ma'am," I said. It was just as well, because I needed to go back to my bunk and seriously decompress, but not literally, because this was a spaceship, and we had almost done exactly that.

Several hours later my data bracelet chirped, and I received a text message informing me that the captain had called a meeting and my attendance was required. My HUD projected a yellow translucent path that led me to a conference room whose main features were a massive banner with the Confederation gas-giant symbol and an oval table around which already sat Captain Qwlessl, Dr. Roop, Ms. Price, Urch, and the three other human applicants. Urch, I saw, was now fully healed, as was the captain. Dr. Roop had sent a message to our delegation informing us that no one among us had serious injuries other than Mi Sun, who had broken her collarbone, but she showed no sign of having been hurt now. Clearly, the Confederation had some powerful medical mojo.

I liked that no one had been permanently harmed. I did not like that they had all arrived before me. It made me feel like I was either an afterthought or the subject of the meeting. I didn't know which would be worse. I took the only empty chair, between Urch and Dr. Roop.

"First of all," the captain began, "I want to apologize to our guests for the rough ride. Obviously, the enemy attack was unexpected, but failures of gravity and stabilizers, even in combat, are extraordinarily rare. Unfortunately, as you experienced, they are not impossible. That said, we have the finest safety protocols known to exist, and despite the damage this ship took, we suffered no loss of life or critical injuries."

That was good news. And impressive.

"I've exchanged several beacons with Confederation command," the captain continued.

"Hold on," I said. "How can you do that? It's going to take us hours to get to the station, so how are you trading beacons?"

"Comm beacons are constructed of photons, which travel much more rapidly than matter," the captain said, though her voice suggested she didn't think this was a particularly good time for a lesson. "They tunnel at about thirty times the speed a ship can."

I nodded. "Sorry."

"Your interest is commendable, and it will serve you well," she said, "but I'm afraid we have more pressing concerns right now. There is a great deal of unhappiness about what happened on the bridge during our encounter with the Phandic ship. Several governmental councils are displeased that a member of an applicant species participated in the conflict, and they are troubled by how the battle resolved."

"How it resolved," I repeated. "Do you mean that I destroyed that ship?"

"Yes," she said, her voice flat.

"Given the alternative," Urch volunteered, "I'm not sure I share that opinion."

"I agree, Mr. Urch," the captain said. "Mr. Reynolds performed to the best of his ability, and he likely saved the *Dependable* and the lives of all on board. That the Phandic ship had hostile intentions is beyond doubt. We witnessed the destruction of our shuttle and the murder of the Ganari delegation. Nevertheless, there are concerns."

"What exactly are these concerns?" I asked, though I had a pretty good idea.

"You deployed ten dark-matter missiles, launched consecutively, against the Phandic ship. Command thinks that was excessive."

I looked around the table, trying to get a sense of just how serious this was. "Is it a matter of expense?"

"Not as such," the captain said. "Military supplies should never be squandered, but it is more a concern about your aggression."

Dr. Roop cleared his considerable throat. "Zeke, did you seek to destroy the Phandic ship, or were you merely trying to disable it?"

I had that queasy feeling I get when I've messed up and been caught, but I still wasn't sure what I had done wrong. We had been in battle, fighting to survive, and I'd fought. Wasn't that what I was supposed to do?

"I just didn't want us to get killed," I said. "And I didn't want us to get killed because I wasn't able to do what I'd been asked to do. The captain needed me to stop that ship, and I did what I thought would work best. I figured I had one chance to get it right, and I took it."

The more I spoke, the more confident I felt. Of course I had done the right thing. There had been nothing else to do. Politicians liked to get attention—I knew that. They could say what they liked, but the facts spoke for themselves. To demonstrate my confidence, I leaned back in my chair and steepled my fingers. "As Captain Benjamin Sisko once said, 'Fortune favors the bold.'"

Nayana coughed politely. "Actually, I think it was Virgil. It's from *The Aeneid*."

More quietly, Mi Sun said, "Moron."

I noticed Nayana was smiling at me. It wasn't the full-wattage, supernova smile of a girl trying to get me to fetch her sparkling water, but it was still pretty compelling. Maybe some girls like it when you keep them from dying in the cold vacuum of space.

The captain was rolling her trunk in little circles, in a way I suspected meant she was mulling over my bit of *Star Trek* wisdom. "Fortune certainly favored us today."

"Here's what the detractors will say," Urch told me. "One missile might have stopped the attack but allowed some of the Phands on the ship to reach life pods. There could have been survivors whom we might have questioned."

"Life is not measured in military terms," the captain said. "It has its own value. But yes, understanding why they chose to attack the Ganari would have been of some use to us."

"I didn't know any of that," I said, now becoming frustrated.

The captain raised one of her heavy hands. "I understand, Mr. Reynolds. Frankly, I think the committees do as well. I also think, if I may speak bluntly, that there are some on those committees who will choose to interpret things otherwise."

"I see," said Dr. Roop. "It's like that, is it?"

"It is," she agreed.

Ms. Price dusted off one of the sleeves of her business suit. She adjusted a wayward strand that had broken ranks from her military-grade bun. "It's like what, precisely?"

"It might be helpful to know something about how the

Confederation operates," Dr. Roop said. "In the same way that many of your nations have ruling bodies made up of individual beings, we have bodies made up of groups. There are trillions of sentients in the Confederation, and so there are thousands of elected officials, and these are organized into governing committees, each with its small area of oversight. Inevitably, there are those who seek more power, and they seek that power through calling into question the actions of other committees or government offices. The question of which species to initiate is often politically charged, and this time more than ever because of certain . . . unfortunate circumstances."

"Usually the selection committee participates in the initiation of new species," the captain explained. "They would also decide what to do in an emergency, such as a delegation being murdered or a member of a delegation violating our treaty with the Phandic Empire."

"Violating a treaty!" I said, maybe louder than I should have. "They attacked us. They killed the Ganari, who were just like us—just a bunch of kids who were ready to go on an adventure, and now they're dead. Their families are grieving because their kids were murdered in cold blood. I don't see how there are any fine lines here."

"I agree with you, Zeke," the captain said, "but there are politicians who have to deal with the fact that our treaty forbids the use of excessive force against a vessel without providing sufficient opportunity for civilians and nonessential personnel to evacuate. There are those who are already claiming you are guilty of war crimes."

"Maybe the best thing to do would be to send him back," Ms. Price suggested, her voice suddenly a little jaunty. "A new random should be easy to acquire on short notice. As long as we stick to the original parameters, and choose an American, then no one can have any objections. My government already has a short list of viable candidates."

"I have no objection to this proposal," Charles said.

Thanks for the contribution, Chuck. I glowered at him, and at least he had the good grace to turn away.

"In an ideal situation, the selection committee would pick a new group from the Ganari," Dr. Roop said, "presuming they are still willing to participate. They might also review Zeke's status. The situation is not ideal, however."

"A ship conveying all five members of the committee went missing six standard months ago," the captain explained to the humans. "The members are presumed dead, and there has not yet been an election to replace them."

"So we're stuck with him?" Mi Sun asked. "I mean, look at him. He's a war criminal, *and* he's still at level one."

I'd been so distracted that I hadn't checked my heads-up display since the attack. I looked at it now. It read 2965830/1000. I surreptitiously checked the chart on my data bracelet. I had almost three million experience points, and I could now level up to eleven, more than double what Mi Sun had. Her scorn about my level wasn't going to bother me. The business about me being a war criminal was another matter.

"Why weren't we told about the Phandic Empire?" I asked. "Dr. Roop, you told us that the Confederation was a peaceful place. You never mentioned that these guys in flying saucers are kicking your butts all over the galaxy."

"Do not be disrespectful," Charles said.

"Bite me, Chuck," I said. "You don't get experience points

for being a suck-up." I looked at Urch. He shook his head and bared his teeth in approval. "It would have been useful," I continued, "to know that the Confederation is involved in a war with guys who significantly outmatch you."

"It's not exactly a war," said Dr. Roop. "It is more like an ideological disagreement—with weapons."

"The Confederation and the Phandic Empire have been clashing for centuries," the captain said. "Usually the conflicts take place in peripheral locations, and things rarely escalate to violence."

"Let me guess," I said, my stomach twisting as I spoke. This conflict sounded suddenly familiar to me, and I knew where I had heard of it before. "The Confederation and the Phands fight primarily over access to Former artifacts."

All the aliens were now staring at me. "How did you know that?" Urch asked.

"Because this whole thing is like *Colony Alpha*, that's how."

"Give the stupid TV shows a rest," Mi Sun said.

I didn't respond in the way she deserved. I didn't tell her that *Colony Alpha* was not stupid. Some of the elements were spot on. It was my father's show, even if he had stumbled upon these truths by blind luck. In that story, a lone human colony found itself in the middle of a war between benevolent aliens, who were clearly losing, and evil, imperial aliens, who were on the cusp of victory. In order to survive, the humans had to side with the bad guys, and the show asked a lot of tough moral questions—or at least it was supposed to before the rewrites.

"The Confederation and the Phandic Empire have learned to live with each other," Dr. Roop explained. "Conflicts arise, but usually they are resolved quickly and without much bloodshed.

Unfortunately, the attack today is part of a recent pattern of Phandic escalation."

"And some are already afraid that Mr. Reynolds's destruction of the Phandic vessel will further antagonize them," the captain said.

"Next time," Urch said to me, "you should show them how nice you are by letting them destroy you."

"We do have treaties dictating the rules of engagement," the captain said, raising her voice slightly, "but in my view, as Mr. Reynolds was unaware of them, and because his world was not a signatory to them, he is not bound by them. The Phands will not see it that way, but the councils will have to."

Ms. Price sighed. "Look, this may be uncomfortable, but I'm here to represent the best interests of my world. I'm not here to make friends."

Snarky-retort restraint. Check.

She turned to me. "Zeke, you're a nice guy. We all like you, and I suppose it's possible we are alive because of you, but you've become a liability to this mission, to Earth's chances of joining the Confederation, and very possibly to the Confederation itself. I think it would be in everyone's best interest if you were to resign from the delegation. I know that's not the way things are usually done, but surely under the circumstances we can make an exception."

"Thank you for sharing your opinion, Ms. Price," the captain said. "However, we have already made it clear that what you suggest is not an option. Dr. Roop tells me you made such inquiries before you left Earth."

"That was before this happened," Ms. Price said.

"The situation remains the same. We cannot alter the delegation without the approval of the selection committee, and that august body currently does not exist. My orders are to tunnel to Confederation Central at our best speed. We're not returning Zeke to Earth. This meeting is not to determine a course of action; it is simply to inform you of the circumstances."

"I see," said Ms. Price.

"And it relieves me to learn that you are not trying to make friends," the captain said, locking her hammerhead eyes on Ms. Price, "because no one likes you."

Outside the conference room, Ms. Price and the other humans hurried out. I guess after having tried to throw me under the space bus, they didn't want to stick around for the small talk. The captain gave me a sympathetic pat on the shoulder and then headed for the bridge. I stood there with Urch and Dr. Roop.

"This situation stinks of vomit," Urch said.

"It does," Dr. Roop agreed.

"Am I in trouble?" I asked. "I didn't *want* to kill anyone on that ship."

"I understand," Dr. Roop said. "But unfortunately, there are people who are going to use the incident to gain power. The captain will support you, and so will I. And I will speak to the members of your delegation. They need to support you as well. In public at least."

"Thanks," I said.

He began to walk away, but then turned back. "What are you now, really? Level nine?"

"Eleven," I said.

His eyes grew wide. "That is impressive," he said. "No one

has ever reached eleven before arriving at the station before. But maybe you should hold off on letting the others know how far you've advanced. You don't want to make yourself conspicuous."

Urch hissed his menacing laughter, and I understood the humor all too well. It was a bit late for that.

I had only just returned to my bunk, and was sitting on the bed, staring at the wall, when there was a knock on my door. Spaceship quarters did not appear to have doorbells. I opened it and saw Captain Qwlessl standing outside.

"May I come in?"

I stood aside to let her in and she closed the door behind her. Her huge form seemed silly in my cabin, but she appeared unselfconscious. She lowered herself onto my single chair, and I sat on the bed. When I looked up at her, I saw the dim number above her head was now 44.

I gestured toward her number. "Congratulations."

She waggled her trunk. "At my age leveling is less significant than it used to be. And the new level comes at too high a price."

"I suppose it does," I agreed.

"I wanted to talk to you more about what happened today."

"Are you angry with me?"

"For saving my ship and the crew?" she asked. "Hardly. But you are now caught up in a political mess, so there are things you ought to know—things I could not say in that meeting."

"Who are the Phands?" I asked, before she could say anything I didn't want to hear. "Why did they kill those Ganari?"

She moved her trunk in little circles as she spoke. "Like

the Confederation, their empire consists of many worlds and contains many species, but the highest levels of government are open only to one species, the Phands. They have reached out to the stars and explored, expanded, exploited, and, I fear, exterminated."

I've enjoyed my share of 4X games, but I thought it best not to bring that up just now.

"Like the beings of the Confederation, the Phands have built on, and expanded upon, Former technology and designs, though they have put their creative endeavors into develop-ing weaponry, while we have concentrated on shielding and sensors. It is our first priority in any engagement that one of our ships must never fall into enemy hands, just as they have similar orders. If we could duplicate their weapons or if they could understand our sensors and shielding, one side would dominate the other in a matter of weeks. We would liberate their conquered worlds, or they would exterminate us and take Confederation Central for themselves. It is the most sophisti-cated functioning example of Former tech known to exist, and they would do anything to possess it."

"But they cracked your shielding," I said. "Does that mean the Confederation is in serious trouble?"

"No," she said. "This happens once or twice a decade. We improve and they improve. The data from that attack will be analyzed closely, and adjustments will be made to all shielding. It was a temporary advantage and won't change much."

"If this were a one-time advantage, wouldn't they save it for a more important battle?"

"That is a very good question," she said. "Maybe they thought we wouldn't survive and be able to transmit our data to the Confederation, but that isn't a satisfying answer. The truth is, all evidence points to this having been a top-priority mission for them."

Great. Killing us was the top of their list.

"Zeke," the captain said, her voice now unmistakably serious, "they had us. In another few minutes they would have lanced the *Dependable*. I could never willingly let them capture a Confederation ship. If it had been in my power, I would have destroyed this vessel first, but there weren't enough of the bridge crew conscious to activate the destruct mechanism. So you must understand that at the very least you saved our lives, but you may have also saved the entire Confederation."

I stared at her. I didn't feel like a hero, and I didn't particularly want to be told I was one, but I did relish her point: that I had not done anything wrong.

"I just didn't want us to get killed," I said.

"I know that, Zeke. The fact that we almost lost the war can't become public knowledge, but it was important to me that you hear it. The appropriate councils will know the truth, I know the truth, and though he lacks the clearance, I told Klhkkkloplkkkuiv. Dr. Roop."

There was something about how she said his name. "Are you two . . . ?" I waved my hand in the air.

"Why?" she asked. "Do you think he's too young for me?"

"I think he's kind of tall for you."

She laughed. "I like tall beings." Then, more seriously, "I trust him, and you should too. I don't know that you can trust anyone else, so please be careful when you get to the station."

I bit back my fear and my sadness, because there was something else I had to know. I didn't want to know, and I could have just tried to forget it, but I somehow knew the answer would catch up to me, and I'd rather hear it when I was braced than have it take me by surprise.

"How many?" I asked. "How many were on that ship?"

"I can't say for certain," she said, her voice filled with genuine sadness, though I did not know if it was for the Phands or for me. "A [*stone fist*]-class Phandic saucer has a standard complement of thirty to thirty-five."

I nodded. I had killed between thirty and thirty-five beings. Now I knew.

"Did you want to kill them?" she asked. "Do their deaths give you pleasure?"

I shook my head. "No," I whispered in case my gesture did not translate. "But I didn't follow the rules, did I? If Urch had done what I did, would he be in trouble?"

"He is a trained officer," she said. "He is bound by the regulations. I chose to put you at that weapons console, and if anyone is going to answer for what happened today, it will be me."

"I can't ask you to do that," I said.

"It's not about doing you a favor. It is the truth. I had no choice but to do what I did, and I don't regret it. Neither should you. Learn from what happened, but don't condemn yourself for doing the best you could."

She stood up now, and when I stood, she put a hand on my shoulder. "I had a son, Zeke, in the exploration services. He was lost while investigating a possible Former outpost. We think it was a Phandic raid, but we couldn't be certain."

I had imagined more than a hint of sadness in those huge and widely spaced eyes. Now I knew why. "I'm sorry," I told her. There was nothing else to say. I knew a thing or two about loss, and I hoped that would come across.

"Forgive me if I'm mothering you a little. You remind me of him. You don't exactly look like him, but there's something there." She wrapped her thick arms around me and took me into a massive hug. Her body was hard—it was like hugging a piece of furniture—but her touch was gentle, and she smelled like leather and cinnamon.

When she let me go, she said, "I hope you don't mind."

"I don't mind at all," I said, feeling a little teary. The captain's affection made me think about my mother, and how she must be suffering now, not knowing what was happening to me, dealing with the fact that she would not hear from me for a year.

"I have a lot to attend to, but if you need anything, message me."

I nodded.

She opened my door and stepped out into the hall. "'Fortune favors the bold,'" she said. "For your sake, I hope you're right. For the Confederation's, I pray you're wrong."

I awoke just before six in the morning, ship's time, to the now-recognizable lurching sensation of emerging from a tunnel. As soon as we returned to regular space, my viewscreen reappeared on the wall, composing itself out of what had looked like ordinary plastic seconds before. I sat up quickly and got my first look at the capital of the Confederation.

The station orbited a gas giant, much like Saturn with its rings and multiple moons—I counted five currently visible, which meant there were likely more on the far side. The planet was stunning: a mix of deep blues and brilliant reds and ominous grays swirled in clouds of mysterious gases. It was unspeakably beautiful, and the only thing that could have made me look away was the station itself.

It was a massive disk, silver and glowing with lights; on the top a clear dome arose over more than three quarters of the surface. Though we were at a great distance, I could see buildings inside the dome, whole neighborhoods separated by a complex rail system or huge clumps of vegetation and artificial bodies of water. Above it all hovered actual cloud formations. On the fringes were huge patches of what looked like forests, mountains, and deserts. I was expecting *Babylon 5* or *Deep Space Nine*, but this was something else entirely—this was a continent in space, and at its center a massive city.

As we drew closer, I was struck by the sight of the ships in orbit, several of them significantly larger than the *Dependable*. Urch had been right about that. The size and design of them left no doubt that these were battleships, and they appeared far more suited to take on one of those monstrous Phandic flying saucers than we had been.

Many of the ships were blackened and scarred and broken, like they had seen combat. The ugly welts and scars and burns implied they'd been the losers. Maybe the fact that the ships had survived spoke to their success, and maybe they'd come to the station for repairs, but looking at that collection of blasted and hobbled vessels made me worry that I'd antagonized the winning side in a nasty war.

Only after I'd spent more than an hour staring out the window did I notice that there was a message waiting for me on my data bracelet. I opened up the communications queue and then tagged the only thing in my inbox. It displayed about a foot and a half before my eyes in blue letters against a white holographic projection.

> The rest of the delegation does not want me to speak to you, and I understand, and agree with, their reasons. Nevertheless, you saved our lives, and it would be wrong not to thank you for your courage. I will forever be grateful, but please don't indicate we've been in contact in front of the others.
>
> Nayana Gehlawat

It was a good thing she'd signed off with her last name. Otherwise I'd have had no idea which Nayana had sent this.

I snorted a laugh as I thought about what a lame thank-you it was. I also thought that, compared to the other humans traveling with me, she was a real class act.

Dr. Roop contacted me through my data bracelet to tell me to pack my bag and report to the shuttle bay in half an hour. When I arrived, the other humans were already there. The captain and some of the crew, including Urch and Ystip, had also arrived to see us off.

Urch jutted out his jaw and showed me his teeth. "Show no mercy to your enemies."

"I'll feast on their bowels," I told him. "Metaphorically."

"Probably best that way."

The captain wrapped her arms around me, gave me a hug, and then pressed the tip of her trunk to my cheek. "Be careful," she said. And then, perhaps thinking she didn't want to freak me out too much, "I know you will do well."

"Will I see you again?" I asked.

"I come by the station three or four times a year. I promise to visit next time I'm here."

We then climbed onto the shuttle and headed over to Confederation Central to begin our careers as initiates. Crazy as it seemed, we had not yet even started.

Part Two
LET THE WOOKIEE WIN

CHAPTER ELEVEN

The public knows about you," Dr. Roop told me on the shuttle to the station, "and you may get some attention from data collectors from various news outputs. I arranged that they wouldn't find out when we're getting in, so they won't swarm you right away. Just be ready in case word has leaked."

I nodded, guessing that "data collectors" were something like reporters. If so, I hoped he had been as good at deceiving the media as he thought, since having to explain myself to the entire Confederation was just about the last thing I wanted to do.

We sat in anticipatory silence. Once or twice I thought Nayana was looking at me, but when I checked, she was turning away. Did I even want her to be my friend? The warmest and most human thing she had ever done was secretly thank me for saving her, but she couldn't bring herself to speak to me in public. Maybe Nayana was merely spoiled and confused. Maybe she would come around. Waiting for that to happen, however, seemed pathetic, though maybe less pathetic than spending the next year on a space station without friends.

The shuttle had landed in something like an airport, and we took a sleek, eel-shaped commuter train to reach some kind of hub, and then another train to another hub, and then one last train. I braced myself for reporters with intergalactic notepads to come running up to us, shouting out questions, but whatever it was that Dr. Roop had done to fool the media, it had worked. No one paid us any attention. We must have looked strange to the locals, but I soon realized that unusual appearances were the norm on Confederation Central. The station was full of a huge variety of beings: some species that I had already seen, but many more that were entirely new, and many unlike anything I had ever imagined—quadrupeds and hexapeds and octopeds. There were beings ten feet tall, and some that came up only to my knees. There were beings that looked like gas clouds or huddled blobs of flowing water. Yet, for all the variety, the majority were bipeds, about human height, who looked like animals or combinations of animals I knew. We made our way through all this, receiving hardly a second glance from most of the beings we saw.

The space station was nothing like what I'd expected. It was like another planet. The air smelled of food and strange spices; the noises were of crowds and vehicles, not the humming and echo of metal in vacuum. I looked up and, beyond the clouds, I saw the system's sun, pale and glistening, and past that, bleached by daylight, the ringed gas giant looming near the horizon.

Even with all I'd seen over the past few days, I still marveled at the station. There were huge buildings, taller than any skyscraper I'd ever seen, spiraling up toward the clear dome. Some of these were cylinders, others arches or shaped like lightning bolts or branching out like trees. Aircraft and shuttles of all shapes and configurations zipped between them, and trains wound through the skies like serpents. There were plants and fountains and waterfalls. A circulation system kept the air breezy and fresh, and the light felt bright and natural.

Dr. Roop had arranged for private transport—a rectangular box that seemed to have no driver and resembled a smaller version of the shuttle, but with windows. We rode above the city, cruising over a massive park full of alien vegetation. We then touched down just outside some sort of government compound, gated and set off from other buildings. A bull-headed—literally!—peace officer in a black uniform checked Dr. Roop's credentials, and we were admitted onto the property, which looked to me like a college campus. The buildings were smaller than most we'd seen in the city, the majority of them constructed from pale blue sports drink–colored bricks. It was pleasant and strangely comfortable with its wide open lawns and statues.

"This area, within the gates, is the Council Center," Dr. Roop explained as we walked up to a building made of pale green stones. It appeared to be about twenty feet high. "This is the seat of government for the station and the entire Confederation. Tens of thousands of government workers pass through here every day. It can be quite hectic, but you'll figure your way around. This building," he said, gesturing to a squat, five-story structure, "is where you will spend most of your time. It contains your quarters, most of your training facilities, my administrative offices, and your classrooms."

"Then we are to keep up with our studies?" Charles asked.

"Not the studies you pursued on your home world," Dr. Roop said. "We will meet every morning for a few hours to discuss Confederation history and current events, and also to help guide your progress through the coming year. Other than that, your time is your own. You may leave the compound if you like, though there is a strict 2400 curfew. Public transportation is both free and easy to access, and the city is entirely open to you except for certain sections that have fallen into disrepair. And, needless to say, you should avoid the undeveloped regions outside the city itself."

"What happens if we go there by mistake?" I asked.

"You won't," Dr. Roop assured me. "You must be at least level thirty to enter those sections. But have no fear, those areas represent only a tiny portion of the station. You will have more than enough to explore in the open areas, and to make that exploration more enjoyable, you will be given a spending allowance, accessed through your data bracelet, of one hundred credits per ten-day cycle, which should prove more than sufficient for meals, though you can also eat without paying in any of the compound cafeterias. Feel free also to spend your currency on entertainment, clothes, and whatever diversions you decide to seek out."

We had now entered the lobby, which was large and, like everywhere else on the station, bustling with activity. There were high ceilings, walls with scrolling text and video screens, and countless beings hurrying from one location to the next. "The station operates on a standard twenty-six-hour day, which is the average day length for Confederation members' home-worlds. I understand it is a bit longer than what you're used to, but you will quickly adjust. Your data bracelets automatically reset to local time, which is now almost 1300, our noon. After I show you to your rooms, I will give you a quick overview of the city, and then you can explore for the rest of the day. We begin class at 0800 tomorrow morning."

Dr. Roop led us to a series of elevators, which we shared with a pair of slime creatures and their ill-behaved slime children, who fixed their eyes (I think) on us during the length of the ride. We came out into a corridor that felt curiously like the hallway of a hotel. "There are no keys," Dr. Roop said. "Like on the ship, each room has been biometrically adjusted to you. Only the residents can gain access."

He gestured toward one room, which was for Ms. Price. Next to that was the room to be shared by Nayana and Mi Sun. Then we came to the room Charles and I were to share. We were roomies.

"Hooray," I may have accidentally said aloud.

"I do not wish to share a room either," Charles said to Ms. Price.

She rolled her eyes and shrugged as if to say, *Find yourself another space station.* Charles looked at me, sighed, and opened the door.

"Set your things down," Dr. Roop said, "and then we can do a quick explanation of the city." I walked into the room, which had two beds, a dresser, a bathroom designed pretty well for beings of our general shape and bathroom needs, and not a whole lot else. When I went back to the main room, Charles had taken the bed closest to the door.

"I choose this one," he said.

"You don't want to ask if I have a preference?"

"I am nearly level seven," he said, his voice clipped. "I believe that means I outrank you."

I was tempted to cash in my skill points just to shut him up, but I didn't really care which bed I had, so I let it go.

"Fine," I said. I put my bag down on the bed, and was about to walk out, but I decided there was something I had to do first. I unzipped my duffel and rooted around until I found my Martian Manhunter action figure.

I supposed after everything that had happened, I shouldn't have been too surprised that I missed home so much. It had been me and my mother against everyone else for so long, and now here I was, literally light years away, and we couldn't be there for each other. It would have been easier if there had been some way to call her, to find out how she was and to let her know I was okay. Instead I was on my own, with no friends, and already in trouble.

I didn't even know anymore if I still missed my dad. I remembered him, and I remembered watching movies and playing catch and going on road trips with him, but he'd been dead for five years. When you're seven years old, you know if you like someone or not, but you don't really *know* a person, not the way you can when you're older. I wished I could have known him that way, but even if he was just a distant memory now, he was still the one person I most wanted to talk to about the things I'd already seen and hoped to see. I couldn't do that, but I felt like the fact that I had survived the alien attack, that the other humans and Dr. Roop and the friends I'd made on the *Dependable* were still alive and free, was because I had learned a few things about how starships worked. That meant we were all still alive because of my father, because of the enthusiasms he had passed on to me.

To honor him, I placed the Martian Manhunter action figure on my desk, standing stoic and unyielding. In some small and silly way, it felt like a small, green version of my father watching over me. Next to the action figure, I put the little cardboard box with the locket my mother had given me to remember those I'd left behind.

I looked up and realized Charles was staring at me. "Dr.

Roop is waiting for us. It hardly seems the time to be playing with toys."

"It's something my father gave me," I said quietly. So he would feel completely rotten, I added, "Before he died."

"I apologize." Charles lowered his gaze. "I've brought mementos of my family as well."

Charles was an orphan, and I knew people who had lived hard lives sometimes acted out. Maybe it was time to put our past problems behind us.

I closed the distance between us and held out my hand. "Look, Charles, I get that you want us all to do well, but given everything that's happened, maybe it's time to start over."

He shook his head and put his own hands in his pockets. "I have no wish to hurt your feelings," he said. "Nevertheless, it is in the best interest of our planet that we not be friends. The others and I discussed this after the incident at Ganar, and this was our conclusion."

I was still standing there, hand out like an idiot, when Charles walked out of the room.

Dr. Roop's overview of Confederation Central, it became clear, was only going to give us the most basic sense of the station. I had the feeling it would take months, maybe years, to really get to know a place this enormous and varied. Dr. Roop focused instead on teaching us how to find our way around and what to do if we got lost. He let us know where the major shopping and eating districts were, where we could find parks and exercise facilities, what sections were closed off because of disrepair. Finally, he showed us the room where we would meet the next day for our first class.

"Enjoy your explorations," he said. "Discovery is part of the process. And I shall see you all at 0800."

Nayana wrapped one arm around Charles's shoulder and one around Mi Sun's. I heard her whisper something to the others, and then she looked back at me, but I distinctly heard Mi Sun say no, and then the three of them headed toward the main entrance of the compound.

Dr. Roop turned to me. "I need to meet with representatives of several government committees. They may want to talk to you, so don't go too far."

"Where would I go?"

I supposed I shouldn't have felt so sorry for myself, but everyone I liked was back on the *Dependable*, and now I was alone on this space station with no friends. I should probably have taken the time to get to know the city, maybe grab something to eat, but I was feeling intimidated, and the idea of venturing alone into the vastness of Confederation Central, with its aliens and unfamiliar customs, intimidated me. In the end I went back to my room, figuring I should enjoy a little time without Charles around. I told myself I'd use the data bracelet to figure out a place to go get something to eat, but I knew I was kidding myself. I was probably going to lie down on the bed, like I did my first night on the *Dependable*, maybe try to play some Approximate Results from Endeavors online, and likely go to sleep hungry.

When I walked through the door to the room, I immediately sensed that something was wrong. It was the inexplicable tingle you get when you're being watched. I told myself I should run, but I didn't want to feel like an idiot. The room was dark but not completely so, and I felt certain there was someone in there, waiting for me.

And then I saw it, coming out of the shadows, tall and muscular and reptilian, with two yellow eyes, featureless and without mercy, trained on me. This creature, I knew without a hint of doubt, had come to kill me.

My father loved the original *Star Trek* series episode "Arena," in which a group of persnickety aliens called the Metrons force Captain Kirk to resolve his grievances with the hostile Gorn by fighting mano a mano on a desert planet. This thing in my room was a real-life version of a Gorn, a lizard man, an upright Komodo dragon, a predator chiseled by a million years of evolution to be a killing machine. Like the Gorn, this being wore a sort of sleeveless tunic that went halfway down its muscled thighs and broad tail. Its arms also looked powerful, but long and supple, with protruding veins. On *Star Trek*, the Gorn captain is intimidating and ruthless, but—and this is largely a consequence of him actually being a guy in a rubber suit—he is also absurdly slow. He can pick up a massive boulder with which to crush Kirk's skull, but you could have a pizza delivered in the time it takes him to bring the boulder down.

I only had to look at the lizard creature in my room to know it wasn't slow. Its athletic build and its tensed posture suggested speed and strength and the ability to strike with deadly precision. It crouched slightly, and I had no doubt it could cross the fifteen feet between us in a single, deadly leap. It looked at me with its blank predator gaze, and its narrow forked tongue tasted the air. My heart thundered in my chest. Did I dare call for help? By the time I moved for my data bracelet, it would be too late. If it launched forward, I would be dead in seconds.

"Afternoon, mate," it said, moving toward me, its gait rolling and confident. I noticed it had long and flat feet, wider than a human's, and it wore open sandals that revealed its narrow toes. Could it run fast in those? I didn't want to find out. Then I looked up and noticed the number above its head—a six. It was new here. It had to be one of the initiates.

The translator rendered its voice male and, for some reason, in a working-class London accent. As he came closer, the creature tapped his data bracelet, and two holographic images came up, side by side: me and Charles. He looked at the images, then at me, then the images and at me again, as if trying to figure out which one I was. His tongue tasted the air and his yellow eyes squinted slightly. "You're Ezekiel, yeah?"

I swallowed hard. "Zeke, actually," I managed. My heart was slowing down a little, because, in spite of my alarm, I was starting to think this lizard was maybe a little too social for an alien assassin.

He balled both his hands into celebratory fists. "Right, then. I'm Steve Ku Ri, with the Ish-hi delegation—the random, which makes us mates, I reckon."

I stared at the cockney lizard, trying to take this all in. I had processed that he wasn't going to kill me, so I was catching up, but maybe not so quickly. "Your name is Steve?"

"That's right. What of it?"

I rubbed my forehead. This was too much, too fast. "Well," I said, trying to figure out how to explain to a lizard man why I thought his name was funny. "It's a name among my people. Sort of a bland name, actually. It's not really what I'd expect from an, uh, Ish-hi."

He cocked his head thoughtfully. "It's a fairly ordinary

combination of consonants with a single vowel. There're hundreds of worlds with Steves on them, I should think."

"Could be," I agreed, trying to figure out how to avoid offending this alien any further.

"Probably more Steves than Zekes."

"Probably." I took a step back.

He flicked his tongue in the air, as if trying to sense something. "Are you all right? You're not a bit slow now, are you? And I'm getting a bit of fear off you. Didn't mean to startle you."

"It's okay," I said. "I just wasn't expecting to find anyone in my room."

"Well, that's understandable, given that they're biometrically sealed against intruders and all that. I'm glad to hear you're not dim. With a random, anything is possible. You could be mental, for all I know. But I heard about you taking care of that Phandic ship, so I figured you knew what you're about."

I'd made the same mistake with Urch, and here I was doing it with another alien, one who had reached out to me in friendship. I'd assumed that because he looked scary, he must be scary. Steve hadn't done anything to make me afraid of him. Except breaking into my room, but that only meant he was a troublemaker, not a bad guy. It seemed worth noting that in an early draft of *Star Wars*, George Lucas had Han Solo as a lizard man, and there was something of the intergalactic smuggler in this reptile.

"So how *did* you get in here?" I asked, deciding to press the point. Maybe he didn't want to kill me, but I still didn't know how he'd found his way into my locked room.

"Yeah, sorry about that," he said, lowering his gaze in apparent embarrassment. "That was Tamret. She doesn't much care for locks, and she thought it would be good fun to wait for you inside, so she"—he sort of shrugged here—"bypassed it, I guess you'd say. Seems like she's good at that sort of thing. Then she got tired of waiting and headed out to find a place for us to get a bite to eat. Left me here to bring you along when you showed up."

Was I always going to be one step behind with this guy? "Who's Tamret?"

"She's the random from the Rarel delegation. She's like you."

"Like me?"

He nodded. Apparently they nodded on his world. That was convenient. "You know—all mammalian and such. Not a particularly patient mammal, either. It's the self-regulating blood temperature, I expect. Makes you twitchy. Anyhow, she'll be waiting for us, so time to get a move on."

What else was I going to do? Sit around, play some games, and wait for Charles to come home smelling of good times and social aptitude?

"Sure," I said. "Let's go meet Tamret."

We took a public train that crossed through one of the plazas toward a busy commercial district. Confederation Central had moved to its night cycle, and I hurried to keep up with Steve as he pushed his way through the crowded and brightly lit streets. The buildings glowed with vibrant colors. Holographic billboards floated in the sky, three-dimensional advertisements for products and places and entertainments. A simple tweak of my HUD allowed me to access audio linked to any of the images, or have more information sent to my data bracelet. I could even use the HUD to make immediate purchases. Clearly, the Confederation had not moved beyond commercialism.

Buskers churned out music, simple and staggeringly strange. The beings around us wore an endless variety of clothes, some that looked like they could have been from Earth, others that clearly could never have been from anywhere in my solar system. There were beings with mobile tattoos that moved over their bodies, or holographic accessories that flew or hovered or flashed around them. The city was like *Blade Runner*'s Los Angeles, but without the menace or the obvious poverty. We occasionally received odd stares from beings who had never seen our kinds before, but there was no hostility. We saw no homeless, nor anyone who looked poor.

At last we came to what looked like a cold and generic office building, but Steve said there was a restaurant on one of the upper floors that was supposed to be especially accommodating to beings new to the station. We wandered around until we found an elevator, which we had to ourselves.

It was glass, exposed to the outside. The city unfolded all around me, and beyond the dome loomed the mass of the great gas giant. Past that were more stars than I could count, and the brilliant swirl of the stellar gases. It was beautiful.

"I can't believe those gits killed the Ganari," Steve said, perhaps to break the awkward silence. I had not been very chatty. "That could have been any of us. There's a lot of beings saying you shouldn't have done what you did, but I'm not one of them. You gave them what they were asking for."

"Thanks, I guess."

He studied me for a long and somewhat uncomfortable moment. His tongue flashed, which I was beginning to see meant he was trying to figure something out. "Look, mate. I can feel you're a bit hesitant to trust me. The rest of your delegation treats you like a prat, yeah?"

I nodded, not really sure what a prat was, but figuring it wasn't good.

"It was like that before you took care of the Phandic ship, and I expected it doubled up after. I get that you're on your guard, but me and Tamret, we're getting it the same as you. We've been locked out by our delegations. They think if we try to help them, we'll only slow them down, but that's rubbish. So we randoms have to stick together."

"Yeah," I said. And I knew he was right. "I'm sorry I'm being so reserved. This is just a lot to take in." I wasn't really off my game so much as I was waiting for the other shoe to drop. Despite having broken into my room, Steve seemed like a pretty decent lizard guy, just like Charles had seemed eager to be friends. I didn't want to get too comfortable before he decided he was better off associating with someone else.

The elevator came to a gentle stop, and the doors slid open. I don't know what I was expecting—maybe some kind of crazy alien dance club with booming galactic house music, like in *Mass Effect*—but this was a low-key place with scattered tables mostly filled with small groups, chatting quietly. A strange sort of music wafted over the speakers—it sounded like someone had recorded a man snoring and then warped the audio, but it was interesting and soothing in a curious way.

Steve looked around. "Maybe you'll pass a few hours with us and you'll decide we're a couple of wankers. That would be fair enough, but don't judge us first. Though the thing is, once you get to know us, you're going to love us. Well, maybe not Tamret, but me for sure."

"How could I help it?" I offered, making an effort to be friendly.

Steve nodded his lizard head. "You're a quick learner." He gestured toward the bar. "There she is. That level-seven mammal over there."

I looked over to where he was pointing, and that's when I saw her. By now I should have been past surprises, past feeling the powerful and staggering blow of the wonderfully impossible, but I wasn't. She was standing near a cluster of high tables, which I imagined were for beings who did not choose to sit, or were not designed to. Tamret was not a tall girl, a few inches shorter than me, but there was no missing her.

She wore a black skirt that went most of the way down her legs and a short-sleeved lavender top. Her clothes could have almost passed as normal in any town in America, but she was clearly not an American. Tamret was covered entirely with cotton-ball white fur, short and dense, like a bulldog's, and so tightly molded to her skin that I could make out every detail in her calf muscles as she stretched out to grab something from her table. From a distance it almost seemed as though she were simply wearing white stockings. Her face was vaguely like a human's but was also undeniably catlike. She had a blunt feline nose, and a sprinkling of stubby, almost clear whiskers. From her head grew long, straight black hair, pulled back in a loose mass with a lavender scarf that matched her shirt and her huge, equally lavender eyes. Sticking up from her hair were two large, triangular, catlike ears, the same white as her fur.

Tamret was a *neko*.

CHAPTER TWELVE

I know plenty of people who never got into anime and manga, and they would have no idea what a neko is. *Nekomusume*—basically "cat girls"—appear all over Japanese popular culture. Sometimes they are just regular girls with cat ears, and sometimes they are more like cat-and-human hybrids. I didn't know much about them except that the idea derived from the *bakeneko*, a supernatural cat from Japanese folklore.

Some people—guys *and* girls—get really into the whole neko thing, decorating their rooms with posters, going in for cosplay, and all that. I'd never been one of those people, or even had an extended conversation with one, so all I knew about neko fandom was that it existed and you could go to cons and sometimes see girls dressed up like cats.

Standing by her table was a guy at least a foot and a half taller than Tamret—and that was without counting his antlers. He wore a kind of sleeveless white robe, belted in the middle, and his own short fur, light brown with dark brown spots, didn't disguise his well-muscled physique. He also had a head like a deer, or sort of like a deer. He was a deer the way Tamret was a cat. Mingling amid the antlers was a number 23, so without going by appearances, I knew he was at least a little older than we were. Maybe a lot older. You can't really tell with deer people.

"Oi!" Steve called. "Tamret!"

She looked over and waved at Steve, and then she saw me.

Her eyes went wide, and then narrowed, and then she looked away and went back to talking to the deer guy.

Steve walked over to an empty table and took a seat facing Tamret's direction. I noticed there were all kinds of chairs available to accommodate a wide variety of body types. Steve opted for something like a bench, and when he sat, he wrapped his tail around the legs so, I assumed, no one would step on it. I grabbed something like an actual chair and sat across from Steve.

Steve looked over at Tamret, and he let out a long sigh. "You big on pheromones?"

"What?" It came out a little shrill.

"Pheromones? You know, scents that give off your mood and such. They're kind of a thing, I reckon, for most mammals?"

"I don't know anything about that," I told him, searching for the quickest possible way out of this conversation. "And I'm pretty sure I don't give off any smells."

"You sure?" he asked me. He tasted the air with his tongue. "Because I'm getting something odd from you. Kind of emotional."

"I am *not* giving off any kind of emotional stink," I told him.

And because sometimes the universe likes to do this sort of thing, specifically to me, that was the exact moment Tamret appeared at our table.

"Hello, boys," she said with a broad grin. Most of her teeth were as flat as a human's, but her canines were well developed and sharp, almost like a vampire's. Still, it was a nice smile, if a lightly unnerving and dangerous one. "I'm not interrupting anything, am I? It sounded like it might be personal."

Rather than say anything stupid, I chose to blush and give my name. "Zeke Reynolds."

"I'm Tamret."

"No family names on your world?"

She shrugged. "It's bound up with caste, and kind of complicated for people outside our [*alliance of city-states*]. Tamret is good for now." She looked away for a moment and then back at me. Another smile. "We're glad you finally made it." She sat next to Steve and then fussed for a moment with her hair, unbinding it and rebinding it again.

Steve gestured with a lizard thumb toward the bar, no doubt at the deer guy. "You making friends with that bloke?"

"In his dreams," she said, rolling her big lavender eyes. "Antlers are not my thing."

I found myself feeling strangely relieved. Right away I thought there was something compelling about Tamret. The fact that she looked like a sci-fi icon, even if it wasn't one of *my* sci-fi icons, didn't hurt, but there was more to it than that. Some people give off a vibe—who knows, maybe it *is* pheromones—that makes you want them to like you. It was as simple as that. I felt a desperate need to get her to like me, but I wasn't much helping my cause, sitting there like a total dud.

"You look confused," she said to me. "You're not, you know, slow or something, are you?"

"I thought that too," Steve assured her. "Turns out he's just shy. And maybe a little slow."

"I'm not shy," I said, maybe a little too defensively, "or slow. There's just a lot to take in on my first day."

Tamret grinned with infectious charm. She had already moved on. "Oh, and sorry about breaking into your room. That wasn't entirely nice of me, I know. It's just that they told me breaking into the rooms was impossible, so I kind of felt the need to tinker with it. I wanted to see what exactly passes for one hundred percent secure around here."

"Took her three minutes to crack it," Steve said.

"It was easy," she told me, looking pleased with herself. Her short whiskers twitched when she smiled. "I didn't go through your things."

"I wouldn't let her," Steve said.

"I was curious," she admitted. "But I restrained myself."

"Because I wouldn't let her," Steve said.

"Look, am I going to be punished for every bad thing I think of but don't do?" she asked, clearly enjoying herself. "Because that could take a while."

"I'm getting that feeling." Steve turned to me. "We'll have to watch out for her, mate."

I wanted to say something funny, participate in the banter, but nothing came to mind. I wanted to be one of them, but I felt like a tongue-tied rube.

Tamret gave me a friendly nudge. "Hey, do you know how to order?"

"I have no idea," I said, but I was thrilled by the idea of her showing me. This was a topic of conversation—just what I needed.

"I love this alien technology. Okay, you tap like this." She jabbed the pad of one of her white index fingers down on the black surface of the table. The tip of a sharp claw peeked out from her fur when she made contact. Almost instantly, a menu appeared, written in small yellow script.

I tried the same thing, and immediately received a line

of text at the top of the list: *Ezekiel Reynolds. Human. Earth. Omnivore. No allergies. Minor. No stimulants or depressants.*

"I'm right peckish," Steve said.

I was hungry too, but the food was a little intimidating. Did I want [*domesticated bipedal herding animal*] with [*tubular vegetable*] sauce and [*bitter fruit*] garnish? It was, the menu informed me, a specialty of the house. Or, if I was inclined, there was [*fishlike animal*] in [*no available translation*] jelly. Yum. Another temptation was [*grain product*] with [*bulbous, spiny vegetable*], fermented [*seed pods*], and [*yellow mold*]. I admit it sounded good, but I'm a twelve-year-old kid, so in the end I went for the [*pizza*] and hoped for the best. Then I glanced at the list of drinks to make sure I wasn't ordering urine or poop juice or fermented roadkill and picked something I was assured was [*fruity*] and carbonated. I tapped what I wanted, then tapped to confirm, and a message told me that my order had been received, and the new balance of my account scrolled briefly across the screen.

"So," Tamret said, once the ordering was out of the way. She propped her elbows on the table and her chin on her folded hands. "I get that you're still taking things in, but I'm not going to put up with you being quiet, because you're kind of famous, Zeke. I want to hear about everything that happened." Her voice was light and friendly and just like a regular human girl's. Several strands of hair had broken loose from their confines, and when she leaned forward, they fell into her eyes. She absently brushed at them with one of her white hands, and when she saw me watching her, she turned away as though embarrassed.

Our drinks came, delivered by a waiter, or possibly waitress, though I'm not sure it was either. It looked like a walking bush. "Hey, guys. Got some drinks for you," the bush said. Its tone was mellow, with almost a surfer's inflection. All three glasses were different shapes: mine long and thin, Tamret's more like a bowl, Steve's narrow at the top and tapering toward the bottom. "You're, like, the new initiates, right?"

"That's right," I said.

"That's so windy," the bush said. "But don't worry, beings. I won't tell anyone you're here. You can be all private and whatever."

This bush was freaking me out with its mellow speech. I figured we had maybe thirty seconds before it called me "little dude," but instead, it wandered off.

Tamret took a sip of her drink, but her eyes were on me, staring. I realized, after a startled instant, that she was looking over my head, and I figured she was checking out my number. "You don't get experience points for destroying an attacking starship?"

"I haven't leveled yet," I said. "I haven't had the chance to figure out what I want to spend my points on."

"What level would you be if you cashed in your points?" Steve asked.

I hesitated for a moment before telling them. Then I said it. "Eleven."

Steve and Tamret looked at each other and burst out laughing. At first I thought they were laughing *at* me, that this was the moment where everything was going to fall apart. Then I realized they were laughing in appreciation.

Steve was now shaking his head. "We're not on the station an hour before the other Ish-hi call me in to tell me I'm meant to keep my distance. They don't want the random dragging them down. The Rarels pull the same stunt with Tamret. And your kind do it with you, but you're at *eleven*, mate. You broke the bloody record for new initiates, and those pillocks are telling you to shove off."

I was surprised to see it was a universal gesture, but Tamret raised her glass, and we all clinked.

"Randoms," she said, and we all repeated it, like it had become a chant or a cheer or motto.

"We're going to make them beg for our help," Tamret said. Her eyes were sparkling at the thought of competition.

"Let's give those tossers a right run for their money," Steve said.

Tamret was smiling broadly. "Should be easy. We've got me, and I'm pretty much great at everything. We've got the bane of the Phandic Empire, and"—she gestured toward Steve with her glass—"I guess we'll have to hope you're good for something."

Steve opened his mouth in what looked like a grin, and I quickly realized it was just that—a good-natured grin, but with razor-sharp teeth. "Keep talking, mammal. It will help to dull the pain of insecurity."

"I think I have that problem under control," she said.

"Hadn't noticed, love," Steve told her.

The bush now returned with our food. My [*pizza*] was an unappealing brown cone filled with a bluish substance streaked with white, all of which gave the general impression of toothpaste. That said, it smelled kind of good. Tamret had ordered a dish of what appeared to be some kind of grain and vegetables. Steve had a goldfish bowl full of yellow-and-brown-spotted ratlike creatures, which scurried around and over one another, squeaking anxiously.

"Brilliant, but can I trouble you for some [*spicy insect*] sauce?" Steve asked the bush.

"Oh sure," the bush said as it headed away. "My fault. It completely slipped my synaptic bundle."

I looked at Steve, who was busy examining the panicked contents of the bowl. He flashed his tongue toward the opening. "This looks quite nice," he said. "Smells all right, too."

"You're really going to eat those?" I asked.

He held out his hands, palms up. "It's the Ish-hi way."

"Wait a minute," I said. "How does the food production unit make living things?"

"They're not really alive," the bush waiter said as it returned with a small bowl of brownish liquid with little translucent wings and bits of insect carapace floating on top. "They're chunks of synthesized protein, but your HUD creates the illusion that they're living creatures."

Steve held one up. It wriggled in his hand as his tongue darted out. "Looks like a [*ratlike creature*] to me." The chunk of synthesized protein let out an alarmed squeak as Steve dunked it in the [*spicy insect*] sauce and then popped it in his mouth. It cried out one last time, and then all we heard was the crunching of bones.

"I think," Tamret said, "what you bring to our trio is your ability to gross everyone out."

"Don't judge other beings," the bush said as it headed away from the table. "We're all beautiful."

"These are good," Steve said, holding up another wriggling, hot sauce–covered animal. "You want one?" The protein clump bared its sharp little teeth and hissed at me.

"It's not the most disgusting thing I've seen someone eat," I said.

"Have you met any of the poop eaters?" Tamret asked me.

"I've met the poop eaters," I told her, "but I don't judge other beings."

"We're all beautiful," Tamret said, and the three of us laughed. I basked in the sensation of finally having found a group that accepted me. We were all randoms, bound together.

It also turned out that my [*pizza*] was pretty good. The blue part of the toothpaste was something not completely dissimilar to cheese, and the white part was some kind of sauce, entirely unlike tomato, but not bad in itself. The exterior was flaky, more like a pastry, and the whole thing tasted like pizza the way a banana tastes like an apple, but even so, on its own terms, it did the job. And it was alien food, which earned it points.

The three of us were talking and laughing like we'd known each other for years. And then we were interrupted.

It was the deer guy. "Hello again, Tamret."

Her ears pivoted sharply a beat before she turned her head.

He was standing by the table, looking at us, maybe deer-smiling. I don't really know. His voice was smooth and kind of breathy. "You said you were going to introduce me to your friends."

"I never said that," she told him, turning away.

"Actually, you did," he said, his voice still completely relaxed. "I know you all come from different worlds, and there are different rules, but here in the Confederation, you don't make friends by lying to people."

"I never lied," Tamret told him. "You said you wanted to meet my friends, and I responded vaguely because I could see you were pushy, and it's best not to tell pushy people *no* outright. It just makes them pushier."

"Come on," he said in the untroubled voice of a guy who expects everyone to see things his way. "Just a little chat. Where's the harm?"

"The harm is I don't want to," she told him. Her voice was firm, but she didn't bother to make eye contact. "Now go away. I'm with my friends, and you're being kind of a creep."

"I'm not a creep," he said. "I'm a data collector. For News Output Three Seventy-One, which, if you kids had been here longer, you would know is the most respected news output on the station."

"And how long would I have to be here to care?" Tamret asked.

He shook his deer head, like we were all sad and pathetic. "I'm trying to help you, let you tell your stories the way you want them told. You kids are of interest to the media, so you might as well control how you come across. You're Ezekiel Reynolds, right?" he said to me. "Let's talk about how you destroyed that Phandic ship. Was it defenseless, as people are saying? Were you hoping to kill everyone on board?"

"No comment" was the best response I could manage. I barely even made eye contact with him.

"People are saying that you are a recreational assassin on your home world," the reporter or data collector or whatever he was continued. "They say that everyone commits murder there. Is it true?"

Enough of the bashful business, I thought. I looked up and met his brown deer eyes and tried to think of something cool to say, something that would impress my new friends. "Go away."

Okay, so that could have been done better.

The deer guy sort of half shrugged. He had this whole cutesy coy thing going on that I couldn't stand. Or maybe that was just how deer guys were. "You can talk to me, or I can send some messages and fifty data collectors will come through the front door before you can even call an elevator. Whichever way you want to go, that's fine."

Steve dropped one of his rat things back into the goldfish bowl. While it tried to scurry under its remaining fellow protein clumps, Steve slowly wiped his hand on his napkin and then stood. He was considerably younger than the deer guy, and certainly shorter, even if you didn't count the antlers. For all that, he held himself like he was completely unintimidated.

"My friends made it clear they don't want to talk," Steve said. "Now you're threatening us. It's time to go."

The deer guy looked at the rats in the goldfish bowl and scrunched up his face in distaste. "A predator species. Fantastic. As far as I'm concerned, you're what's wrong with the Confederation."

"And as far as I'm concerned," Steve said, "I don't give a toss. Walk away, mate, and don't come back. And don't send any of your reporter friends looking for us. Otherwise I may just have to come looking for *you*. We've got animals that look like you on my world, and I have a feeling you just might be a little bit delicious." He flicked his tongue in the air.

The deer guy backed away without another word and hurried out of the bar.

Steve sat down, grabbed a rodent from his bowl, and gestured at Tamret with it. "That, love, is what I can do. I can scrap. You got Zeke there for long distances, but close up, I'm your bloke."

"You just threatened to *eat* that guy," I said. "And he's an adult."

"Maybe we eat adults on my world," Steve said. "Maybe we don't. He doesn't know, does he?"

"That was pretty good," Tamret said, nodding appreciatively. "I think we'll keep you."

It was also not lost on me that it had been Steve, not me, who had stood up to defend Tamret. I'd cowered in my seat. Okay, maybe not cowered, but I hadn't been all tough and reptilian Jason Statham like Steve. I'd been too intimidated by the data collector being an adult and having antlers and knowing how things worked around here. Next time, I vowed, I would take charge.

Tamret now raised her glass again. "Here's what I say. All three worlds. That's the deal. We watch each other's backs, and we all get in. The kids in our delegations may be complete jerks, but we carry them, so we *all* make it."

We clinked again.

Tamret looked at me, meeting my gaze, and then turned away like something embarrassed her. Maybe I'd been staring a little too hard.

I had the feeling she expected me to make a toast, so I raised my glass. "I've never met a Ganari. It looks like maybe I never will, but on the shuttle I watched get destroyed, there were four kids, just like us. One of them would be sitting here with us right now if he or she or it hadn't been murdered." I raised my glass a little higher. "The Ganari."

"The Ganari," they agreed in unison.

It was the best moment I'd had since leaving home. For a moment I forgot about the rejection and the danger and the terrifying brush with death. For that instant, being in outer space was exactly what I had hoped it would be.

CHAPTER THIRTEEN

I met Steve and Tamret the next morning for breakfast in one of the government-complex cafeterias, a large open space filled with important-looking beings, every one of whom made a conspicuous effort to pretend it was not looking or perceiving or pointing its sensory stalks at us. Maybe it was just me they were pretending to ignore. After all, Steve and Tamret hadn't blown anyone up.

Tamret's dark hair was a little messy, and I got the impression she was the sort of girl who had a hard time getting out of bed in the morning, but she'd managed to throw on what would have been called a summer dress on Earth. For my part, I figured I'd start things in style and wore my red classic *Trek* T-shirt with the insignia over my heart.

The less said about the things Steve ate for breakfast the better, though I will mention that the food did not want to be eaten, and Steve had to remove the stingers before he could pop the things in his mouth. And while he was happy with the selection of seemingly living goodies, I was a little more challenged. American breakfast preferences were nowhere to be found, and I found nothing like dry cereal or eggs or waffles. There were strangely shaped fruits and vegetables—as well as plants that were clearly neither—and I decided to make a point to try as many of them as my HUD would let me eat over the course of the next year. The most popular breakfast food in the

Confederation seemed to be endless styles of porridge made from grains and plants. I helped myself to a bowlful as well as a plateful of slices of blue fruit wedges streaked with yellow stripes. They were pretty but fairly mild in taste. I wasn't ever going to crave this food, but at least I wasn't going to starve.

After we ate, we headed for the classroom, which was a whole lot like an Earth classroom: chairs, a lectern, and screens for projecting data. This was my first chance to get a look at the rest of the Rarel and Ish-hi delegations, and they were as unfriendly as the rest of the human delegation. Also, to make things even more relaxed, Ms. Price would be sitting in on every session. She glared at my T-shirt but said nothing.

Tamret and Steve and I sat in the back, like the bad kids. The other humans were sitting up front. Charles, wearing a polo shirt with his private school's logo on it, looked eager to learn. Mi Sun sat quietly and remained utterly unreadable to me. Nayana had a smile plastered to her face, but it looked phony, like something she slapped on while pretending not to notice lurking photographers from *Chess Monthly*.

"They're never going to accept you, you know," Tamret said. She was running her fingers through her hair, trying unsuccessfully to tame it.

"What?" I hoped blushing didn't translate.

"Those people from your planet," Tamret said. She was now glaring at Nayana, who noticed and glared right back. Tamret accepted the challenge and kept her eyes locked until Nayana looked away. "You like that one, don't you?"

"I don't," I said quietly. "Unkindness to randoms, remember."

Tamret shook her head, like she found me deeply disappointing. "You shouldn't be so obvious."

• • •

The amazing thing about school is that you can move it from a stuffy classroom in a crumbling and moldy building into a futuristic government compound on an ancient space station, you can replace your range of usual student types with aliens, you can introduce advanced technology, and for all that, it manages to retain its essential school-like nature. You sit in a chair, you listen to a teacher, and you wish you were out of that room doing something else.

The three other Ish-hi were hard to read: Joe, the other male, and Jill and Ann, the two females. They all dressed similarly in their tail-accommodating tunics, and I had a hard time telling them apart. The truth was, I hard a hard time telling Steve from any of the rest of them at first until I made a point of memorizing subtle color patterns on his scales. I was suddenly a little more sympathetic to the trouble he'd had distinguishing me from Charles.

"What's with your names?" I asked Steve after I'd been introduced to his delegation.

"Oh, that," he said. "Yeah, single-syllable names were popular for kids our age."

"But those names are all . . ." I was floundering.

"All what?" Steve demanded, looking perhaps a bit defensive.

"Never mind," I said, deciding that I would have to accept the Ish-hi names as one of the galaxy's many mysteries.

The Rarels were easier to keep track of. Other than Tamret, they all had reddish-brown fur, and I wondered if Tamret belonged to a minority ethnic group or if there were just different fur colors like there were with house cats back home. The other Rarel girl, Thiel, was taller than Tamret and had russet hair, just a little darker than her fur, and she always wore a sour, superior expression that reminded me a little of Nayana. Tamret told me that Thiel was the daughter of one of her world's most famous [*whittlers*]. Apparently, carving shapes from wood was a huge deal in their culture, and Thiel's father was like royalty. Thiel herself was considered something of a [*whittling*] prodigy and somewhat famous, and she carried herself as though she expected everyone to be in awe of her at all times.

Then there were the two boys. Semj was smaller than the two girls, and Tamret said he was supposed to be some kind of engineering genius. He kept to himself, and almost never seemed to seek out company, but the others in his delegation consulted with him the minute there was anything in doubt. He was smart, and they respected him for it.

Ardov was taller than I was and broadly built with wide shoulders and a thick neck, like he was destined to play Rarel football. He wore a tight short-sleeved shirt and pants made out of a dark black fabric, and he had a face that was action-hero handsome, rugged and square-jawed, with high cheekbones and piercing emerald eyes. Like Mi Sun, he was a martial-arts master back on their home planet. He was also a national champion in something called War Etched in Stone, a sport in which contestants pummel each other in a pit while simultaneously solving high-level math problems. Right away I noticed that he tended to scowl at Tamret, like he found her disgusting. He caught me looking, and shot me a look like he hated me. At that point I decided to hate him right back. I figured it would save me time down the road.

Once we got started, Dr. Roop explained that the purpose

of the class was to teach us about the operations and functions of the station as well as the history of the Confederation and the larger mystery of the Formers. He stood in front of the class in one of his dark Confederation suits, arms behind his back, neck stretched high. My own neck was going to get sore from looking at him.

"Most of you have gained several levels already," he said, trying not to gaze in my direction, "but don't think it will be this easy from here on out. The first five take virtually no effort. The second five require somewhat more. Moving from ten to eleven, you will discover, takes a great deal longer."

Try blowing up a starship, I thought. *That packs the points on.*

"You will have to work hard to earn each level," he continued. "You have a year to gain a total of eighty levels per group. It is extremely challenging. Almost half of all delegations fail. Don't ever relax or rest on your laurels. No matter how close you are, do not assume you will reach eighty levels until you have them. And keep in mind that no one will try to obstruct or hinder you, but no one will help you either—no one but me. I will gladly assist your work toward your advancement, so don't hesitate to ask. I am the only ally you have, and I am everyone's ally equally."

Dr. Roop explained the best ways to go about earning experience points. We could book time in the sim rooms, learning more about starship operations. There were computer-programming rooms, which allowed us to rack up points by writing computer code. Then there was the sparring room, where we test our combat skills against either real or simulated opponents. If we were in a less-violent mood, we might visit the research facilities, where we had the chance to work on math and engineering problems. Much to my surprise and happiness, we also had the option of playing strategy games, such as Approximate Results from Endeavors. The important thing was to gain skills that would make us of use in the Confederation, but there was no clear program of study, and those individuals or groups who could not figure out how to gain points would be left behind.

Then he ended the session by assigning us about 150 pages of history to read for the next day. "Keep in mind that learning about Confederation history gets you experience."

We rose from our desks and Dr. Roop called me over. He saw that Ms. Price was eyeing us, so he kept his voice low. "No one believes you are still at level one at this point, and it's starting to draw the wrong sort of attention. Go up to about six or seven for now. Don't ever pull ahead of your classmates, though. And do it before 1600 today."

"Why, what happens then?"

"You are meeting the chief justice of the Xeno-Affairs Judicial Council," he said. "It is time to discuss the legal and political implications of your actions on the *Dependable*."

Steve and Tamret were waiting for me in the hallway. Dr. Roop hadn't said the meeting with the chief justice was a secret, and I planned to tell them, but not in front of everyone else.

"What did he want? And how do you tell him apart from her lot?" Steve pointed a scaly thumb at Tamret.

"You think we look the same as Dr. Roop?" she asked, scrunching up her face.

"It's all that fur."

"You haven't noticed that his neck is like a quarter of his body size?" Tamret asked.

Steve cocked his head as he considered this information. "Yeah," he said thoughtfully. "I reckon that's true."

While they were talking, I was watching Charles, Nayana, and Mi Sun heading in our direction. Nayana stopped, and then the other two walked on and she came back.

"May I speak to you for a moment?" she asked, and so that no one would mistake her for a nice person, she pretended not to see Steve and Tamret.

I was not about to make my only friends on the station move, so I walked twenty feet down the hall with her. "What's up?" I said, pretending that deliberate contact with a member of my species wasn't a big deal for me.

She looked down. Her cheeks darkened in what might have been a blush on a girl who, on occasion, experienced sympathetic feelings. "You received my note?"

"Yeah. Thanks?" Did I need to thank someone for thanking me?

"You couldn't trouble yourself to write back?"

"You told me not to speak to you."

"In *public*," she clarified. "It's rather rude not to write back to someone who is risking her reputation by being nice to you."

"Ah," I said, because it was the cleverest thing I could think of.

"I just," she began, and then shook her head. "I'm quite unhappy about how we have treated you. I wanted you to know that."

"Really?" This was interesting. Maybe if Nayana was beginning to soften, the others would too.

"I asked that we include you in our leveling projects, but I have been outvoted, I am sorry to say. Ms. Price was particularly adamant. I am certainly not used to my opinions being disregarded in this way," she added, like maybe this was the real point.

"Um, okay," I said, no doubt proving her faith in me was warranted.

"I do not make a habit of sticking my neck out for others." She stood there, as though she were a bellhop waiting for a tip.

"Thank you?" I ventured.

"You are most welcome," she said and then hurried off after her friends.

Now I didn't know what to think. It looked like the others weren't about to invite me back anytime soon, but Nayana appeared to want to make amends for their bad behavior. I felt myself smile. Then I saw Steve and Tamret watching me. I think I was beginning to read Steve well enough to know he had no idea what was going on. He kept tasting the air for signals. You did not have to understand Rarels well at all to get Tamret's expression as she glowered at me with her lavender eyes.

"I'm glad to see you and the ice queen are friends now," she said when I walked back over to them. She folded her arms across her chest.

"She's just trying to do the right thing," I said. "Unlike the rest of my species."

"I can see that," Tamret said. "But I can also see that I don't care."

Anything else she might have had to say was quickly forgotten because the rest of the Rarels were walking past us now. Ardov, the handsome boy, grinned at Tamret with a mean self-satisfaction I'd seen before on too many human faces. "I know you're a random, but it's an insult to our species if you hang around with these hairless freaks."

This guy was big and muscular, and I had no doubt he had smacked around his share of Rarel fanboys back on his home planet, but I was not about to keep quiet like I had with the antlered reporter. Besides, I don't like to be made to feel self-conscious for not having fur. "It's not your business who she spends time with," I said, wishing my voice hadn't chosen that particular moment to break.

"I don't think the translator is working," the girl, Thiel, said with a nasty smirk. "I'm just getting animal sounds."

"Actually, it is my business," Ardov said, not bothering to look at me. Instead he edged me out of the way so he was standing between me and Tamret. "You're making us look bad, Snowflake."

"Ugh." Thiel made a gagging face. "Let her play with those creatures. You don't want her chasing after us, do you?"

"That's a good point," Ardov said with a smug nod.

I tried to move myself back between them. "Maybe you should—" I began, but that was as far as I got. Ardov had his hand on my chest and was shoving me away. It wasn't like he was trying to knock me down. He was moving me, like I was a piece of furniture.

"Don't touch me again," he said to me. "You won't like what happens."

Before I could answer, Steve was now standing in front of me, leveling his dark eyes at Ardov. He extended one of his thin fingers and tapped Ardov's shoulder. "Touch," he said. He said it without inflection, but there was no mistaking the steel behind it.

Ardov shook his head and snorted. "The three of you are just looking for trouble, aren't you?"

"No, we aren't," Tamret said. She had her eyes cast down, like she was a servant and Ardov was her very mean employer. "We were just talking."

"Who gave you permission to talk?" Ardov asked in that mock-serious way kids like him get, like they're working so hard to pretend they have authority, they almost start to believe it.

My teeth were now grinding. Ardov was the extraterrestrial embodiment of everything I hated. I thought I'd gotten away from this kind of thing, but here was another kid who acted however he wanted and never faced any real consequences. Dealings with someone like that always started out nasty and ended up worse.

Steve's muscles visibly stiffened under his scales, like he was getting ready to fight. So far Ardov had done nothing but talk, and if Steve threw the first punch, he would be the one to get in trouble for it. I admired his guts—Ardov was much bigger than he was.

It was Thiel who saved us, though. "I'm bored and hungry," she said. "Can we go already?"

Ardov looked at Tamret. "You're coming with us, Snowflake." It wasn't a question. "You can fetch our food for us."

"No way," Thiel said. "I don't want to have to look at *that* stuff its ugly face."

"I won't let her actually eat with us," Ardov said. "Just serve us."

Thiel turned away. "I don't want it touching my food."

Ardov smiled at Tamret. "Next time, maybe."

Tamret watched them go, her lavender eyes narrow slits, her

expression unreadable—and not only because she was an alien.

"What was that about?" I asked her. "What's his problem, exactly?"

She didn't answer me. She didn't even look at me. Instead she turned to Steve. "You want to go mess with Thiel's stuff?"

Steve appeared to consider this for a moment. "That could be fun."

I sat next to Tamret on the floor. Steve was lying on Thiel's bed, rubbing his back against the blanket, which struck me as a little odd, but I was working on being less judgmental. It seemed like we all wanted to act like nothing had happened with Ardov. I knew that game all too well—the postbully intentional amnesia—and I was willing to play along.

I had been studying the skill tree on my data bracelet. Tamret was next to me, leaning in to see better. She smelled like flowers and something warm and pleasingly musty.

"I need to level up, but I don't know what skills to pick," I said.

Steve was wiggling all over the bed. "Go strength and agility," he said. "Never hurts to toughen up."

"What are you doing over there?" I finally asked him.

"I'm molting," he said. "I get all itchy, and if I need to get rid of the old scales, I might as well do it all over Tamret's prissy roommate's bed. You have a problem with that?"

"Leaving old reptile skin in Thiel's bed? I have absolutely no problem at all," I said. I looked at Tamret. "How did you spend your skill points?"

"That's private," she said, smiling like she had a secret. The Rarels were the only species I'd found so far that smiled the same way human beings did. Either I was completely misreading things, or many of their expressions were like ours.

"Come on," I said. "At least tell me how you decided."

"Maybe when I know you a little better."

I looked at the skill tree one more time and sighed. "I wish I knew what I was going to need, but since I don't, I guess I may as well follow the recommendations for the one thing I've already done and been okay at."

"What's that?" she asked.

"Starship operations," I said. I then opened up the skill tree in my HUD, and I applied points until I was at level seven.

You'd think I'd feel different. I had put points into agility, intellect, and vision, but I didn't feel any smarter or more agile, and I didn't notice if my vision had improved. The only thing I felt was apprehension as I went to my meeting with the Xeno-Affairs Judicial Council. If there were a reason to be worried, I told myself, Dr. Roop would have warned me. Presuming he knew.

I met Ms. Price and Dr. Roop in the lobby of one of the nearby government buildings. Aliens of different species rushed all around us, many of them wearing boxy suits. Dr. Roop wore one, along with a gas-giant Confederation pin on his left breast pocket, which I took as a sign of this meeting's importance. Ms. Price wore a pantsuit and had applied enough red lipstick to make her look like she'd just been drinking blood. Her hair was tied into a bun so tight I feared she would cut off the circulation in her scalp.

"What exactly is this meeting about?" I asked as we rode up

an escalator made only of translucent blue energy.

"The Xeno-Affairs Judicial Council handles all treaties with non-Confederation governments," Dr. Roop explained. "That means both the Phandic Empire and nonaligned worlds that send potential members, such as your own. You can understand why you might be of particular interest to Chief Justice Junup."

"I guess," I said. "But that doesn't tell me what this meeting is about."

"He just wants to meet you," Dr. Roop said. We'd risen up several levels, and now Dr. Roop led us down a winding corridor. We stopped, at last, in front of a door that looked completely indistinguishable from all the others.

"There is nothing to worry about," Dr. Roop told me. "However, be certain to be respectful. This is a high-ranking committee, and Junup is extremely influential. It would be wise to make a good impression on him."

"Is he on my side?" I asked, suddenly feeling nervous.

Dr. Roop looked away. "He is on the Confederation's side."

"Don't be nervous," Ms. Price said. "You're in good hands." She then opened the door and gestured for me and Dr. Roop to enter.

Inside I saw a space that looked a great deal like the conference room on the *Dependable*. On the far side of the table, standing and looking impatient, was a being I presumed must be Chief Justice Junup. I was surprised that no one had mentioned in advance that he looked a whole lot like a goat with a turtle's shell. The shell was small and tightly contoured to his body, but it was bulky enough to make wearing a shirt difficult. Instead he had a billowing cape that hung over his shoulders. Peeking out from the shell was a very goatlike head with a long snout and curling horns. He also had a beard. It would have been a more comical mix if he were not an impressive level fifty-one.

He pressed his palms to his ears, which I presumed to be some kind of goat-turtle greeting. "You know who I am," he said, his voice less goaty than I would have guessed. Actually, his voice was low and kind of snooty—if anything, he sounded strangely like Gandalf in the Lord of the Rings movies. "I know who you are. Let us not waste time with introductions and, instead, get to our business. Sit."

I chose an empty chair, and Dr. Roop and Ms. Price sat to either side of me. The Chief Justice sat across.

"Chief Justice," I began. "I wanted to let you know—"

"You are here to answer questions, not make speeches," Junup said, "I will let you know when I require a response."

"Let's do it that way," I said, trying to sound like I was neither embarrassed nor annoyed when I was, in fact, both.

Ms. Price glowered at me, and I had the sense she wanted me to stop talking.

Junup seemed oblivious to all this. "The Phandic Empire," he continued, "has petitioned for your extradition, charging you with the wanton destruction of life and property."

"That's absurd," said Dr. Roop.

"It is not absurd," the goat-turtle said in his deep voice. "The applicant may have brought us to the brink of war with the Phandic Empire. What say you, applicant?"

"I didn't bring anything to anyone," I said. "They killed the members of the Ganari delegation, and they were trying to destroy the *Dependable*."

Junup leveled his little pink eyes at me. "I have reviewed

the transcript of events. We need not recount them. It is enough for you to know that your actions have caused grave consequences."

"The Phands may not like that one of their ships was destroyed," Dr. Roop said, "but as they instigated an unprovoked attack, I'm not certain we should care how they feel."

"Regardless of how events unfolded," the chief justice answered, sounding somewhat annoyed, "the Phandic Empire states that because the incident took place outside Confederation space, and because no citizens of the Confederation were harmed, they have broken none of our laws. However, as Mr. Reynolds destroyed one of their ships, killing many of their citizens, they want him extradited to stand trial in one of their courts."

"I presume this request is not receiving any serious consideration," Dr. Roop said.

"It is the responsibility of the council to consider all diplomatic requests," the chief justice answered.

I felt something twist inside me. The possibility of turning me over to the Phands was actually on the table. I would be sent off, to prison or to be killed. I would never see home again. I would never see my mother. I'd come out here to save her. What would it do to her if I were never to come back?

The chief justice turned his goat-turtle gaze on Ms. Price. "As a representative of your world, do you have any thoughts on this matter?"

Ms. Price leaned back and folded her hands together as if gathering her thoughts. Nevertheless, I had the distinct impression she had been waiting for an opportunity to deliver her well-rehearsed lines. "The people of Earth wish to do all in our power to protect the rights and safety of its citizen," she said, her voice flat, as if reading from a script. "Nevertheless, we understand that Mr. Reynolds's actions were disagreeable within your culture, and he must be judged by your standards, not by ours. As we put the highest priority on our continued good relationship with the Confederation, the people of Earth will not object to any decision the council should reach."

I couldn't believe it. Ms. Price has just said she would not object if the Confederation sent me off to their greatest enemy.

"Dr. Roop," said the chief justice. "Your thoughts?"

Dr. Roop raised himself up in his seat, as if to emphasize his considerable height. "To be blunt, Chief Justice, I find it shameful that you are taking this demand seriously. I would never, under any circumstances, consent to an applicant under my protection being handed over to a foreign power to stand trial, but in this case I must object all the more forcefully. The Phands may say that Mr. Reynolds is a war criminal, but we know he heroically acted to save the lives of those on board the *Dependable*—and, I might add, to keep the *Dependable* itself from enemy hands. To deliver him to our enemy, simply because that enemy demands it, would be the worst sort of cowardice imaginable."

Junup glowered at Dr. Roop for a long moment and then sighed. "I appreciate your candor, Roop. At this point, I also think turning Mr. Reynolds over to the Phandic Empire is neither advantageous nor advisable. For the time being, it seems, he is to remain here."

That was mostly good news, I thought, other than that this was a decision only for *the time being*. My fate had been postponed, not decided.

The three adults began to rise, which I cleverly deduced meant the meeting was over. Without a glance back at us, Junup strode from the room, his cape billowing behind him. Ms. Price walked out, and I started to leave as well, but Dr. Roop reached out and took hold of my forearm.

"I'm sorry about all this, Zeke," he said in a whisper, lowering his neck considerably—perhaps a gesture of humility? "You're not seeing the best face of the Confederation. I hope you'll give us a chance to show you that we are better than this."

I liked that he was worried about how I saw him, not just thinking I should worry about how he and his kind saw me. He was a real class act, that Dr. Roop. "I understand."

"Please avoid speaking to data collectors, the representatives of the news outputs. To that end, and to avoid trouble in general, maybe you should stay on the government compound for the next week or two. Just until things cool down. The demands for your extradition are now going to be reported by the news outputs, and you might find yourself a little too conspicuous if you go out in public."

I didn't like it, but I nodded. There was enough new and wondrous stuff to keep me occupied here for a week, I thought.

I'd only stepped out into the hallway when I felt a tap on my shoulder. I turned around and found Ms. Price standing there.

"Well, that's a relief," she said, as though she had not just tried to sell me out.

"Really?" I snapped. "What happened to me being in good hands?"

"Oh, I didn't mean mine," she said, holding up her hands, turning them back and forth. "You don't want to be in these. I meant Dr. Roop."

"Well, now I know where I stand," I said, starting to walk off.

"Don't take things so personally," she said, stepping in front of me to block my exit.

"What would I take personally?" I asked. "That you tried to turn me over to an alien enemy who hates my guts so they can try me as a war criminal? Don't be silly."

She sighed. "I'm not the bad guy here, Zeke. My job is to ensure that Earth makes it into the Confederation. There are billions of people depending on that, including your mother. I can't trade the fate of an entire world for that of one young man. I hated having to say those things in there, but I'm here to safeguard our entire planet, not just one citizen."

I did not get the impression that she hated it at all. She had, at every possible opportunity, tried to get me tossed out of the delegation, and she was willing to send me off to prison or execution in order to succeed. I had no idea what she had against me, but I could no longer ignore the fact that Ms. Price wasn't merely a bad chaperone—she was an enemy.

"Keep up the good work," I told her, and I walked away, trying to act cool, though I would have settled for her not seeing how scared I was.

CHAPTER FOURTEEN

tried staying out of my room whenever I could, and when Charles and I were there together, and awake, we did our best to ignore each other. My efforts to smooth things over seemed only to make him more uncomfortable, and every time we avoided eye contact or passed each other without speaking, the tension grew.

I spent almost all my free time with Steve and Tamret, and the three of us avoided Ardov as best we could. Tamret didn't seem to want to talk about him, and I respected that, though I knew he must be picking on her when I wasn't around, and I wished I could do something to stop it. But Tamret seemed okay, she seemed happy, so I left it alone.

I found I could talk to the two of them in ways I'd sometimes found difficult with my friends back on Earth. I told them about my life at home, my mother's illness, my father's death, the whole thing. I showed them the mementos I'd brought from home. Steve talked about his own life, and as near as I could tell, he was from an ordinary middle-class lizard background, though I got the hint that he was something of a troublemaker among his own kind. Tamret told us virtually nothing about herself. She would listen to our stories and ask questions when Steve and I spoke of home, but she never volunteered any information, and she would twirl her hair around her index finger and look away when she understood it was a natural place in the conversation for her to reveal something. Without discussing it, Steve and I agreed not to ask. She would tell us what she wanted us to know, when she wanted us to know it.

Despite how well I got along with the other randoms, I still hoped things would thaw out between me and the rest of the humans. It was clear to me that Mi Sun and I were never going to be buds, but Charles had been friendly enough when I first met him, and Nayana clearly didn't like the way I'd been pushed out. Since our last conversation, though, she wouldn't even make eye contact with me.

Almost a week after classes had started, when we were waiting for Dr. Roop to begin the day's lecture, Tamret reached over and smacked me lightly in the head.

"What was that for?"

"Stop staring at them all the time," she told me.

"Who?" And then, because I knew exactly who she meant, I added, "I wasn't." And because I didn't even believe myself, I asked, "Was I?" And then, because I realized I sounded like a moron, I blushed.

"They're never going to accept you," she said. "They're playing the statistics, and nothing you do or say is going to get them to invite you to hang out with them, so you may as well get used to being stuck with us."

"I don't feel stuck with you," I said. "I just wish they were, I don't know, more reasonable."

"That's not going to happen," she said, "and following them around with your sad eyes isn't going to change that."

Dr. Roop now tapped the lectern several times to indicate he was ready to begin the lecture. "Much of what you do on this station, such as interacting with different beings, visiting cultural centers, simply reading archival material, will accrue small amounts of experience. Far more important, however, is the time you dedicate to activities in this compound that are specifically designed to generate experience points. No one will require you to visit these centers, so your worlds are depending on your own initiative. However, you are only allowed to spend a maximum of four hours a day in these sanctioned facilities. Some species have more endurance or greater powers of concentration, and the time limit both keeps things fair and eliminates the temptation for any being to overtax itself in the pursuit of leveling."

That day we went down to one of the basement levels, where there was a government mathematics lab. We were invited to sit at terminals and have our math skills tested. If our ability proved to be of some value to the government, problems would be presented to help hone those skills so that we could, theoretically, eventually work on high-level equations that would help unlock mysterious Former technology.

After about two hours of testing, my terminal told me that my services were not required. Math had never been my best subject, and the points I'd spent in intellect hadn't much changed that.

I wasn't initially too upset about the session ending, but I was embarrassed to discover that I was the first initiate the system had spat out. Ms. Price stood outside the math center, typing notes into her data bracelet. She watched me emerge, pinched her lips into a sour approximation of a smile, and then went back to typing. After me came Steve, who said he'd never been much good at "maths," and then Thiel, who stormed out scowling. When Tamret finally caught up with us, she had moved up to level eight, but seemed no happier for it.

"That was boring," she said. "I hope we get something more interesting tomorrow."

We were just turning away when the door slammed open and Ardov came out of the room, his ears back, his face set in a scowl. "What do you think you're doing?" he snapped at Tamret.

"Nothing," she said, looking down.

"Are you trying to make me look stupid?" he demanded.

I had already opened my mouth, but Steve put a hand on my arm. "Let me field this one, mate."

Ardov didn't even look at him. Instead he gestured to the number above his head. A seven. "You really think it's a good idea to try to show me up?" he demanded, like Tamret had actually gone out of her way to insult him.

"You don't want her to earn points for your planet?" I asked.

Ardov wouldn't look at me, either. He was still hovering over Tamret, who had her eyes cast down, not answering. I couldn't figure out why she was taking this from him. "You better watch yourself. Do you hear me?"

"I hear you," Tamret said. Her voice was quiet, but there was steel in it too.

"My room's a mess," he said. "I want it cleaned before I get back from dinner. Semj is there now. He'll let you in. You have ten minutes to get there, and you'd better do a good job." He walked off, leaving the three of us standing in uncomfortable silence.

After a moment, I said, "Why do you let him talk to you that way?"

"It's not your business," she told me. "I have to go."

"Because he ordered you?"

"I said it's not your business," Tamret snapped, and she hurried off.

I thought about going after her, but I knew it was a bad idea. *Cultures are different,* I told myself. I knew there were things going on with Tamret and Ardov that I was missing, but I also knew there was no way I was going to spend the next year with him treating her that way. I had no clue what I could do to stop it, but I was determined to think of something.

The next day we went to a physics and engineering lab, and Steve and Thiel and I, once again, all washed out early. Ms. Price typed her notes and amused herself by inventing new facial expressions to convey contempt. Tamret did well again, as did the two boys in her delegation and all the Ish-hi but Steve. I was starting to feel like a complete loser, especially since I had to watch Charles improve until he settled in smugly at level nine. The next day, I hoped, would be my chance to shine. It was time for me to get a crack at the game room.

Why would the government promote and invest in the playing of games? you might wonder. Excellent question. I wondered the same thing.

Dr. Roop explained it as we walked across the compound toward the building that held the gaming center. "Virtually all of the games played on the government network are either originally of Former design, discovered in the ruins of their cities, based on fragments of Former games or descriptions of them, or otherwise built around elements associated with the Formers. In order for a game to be on the Confederation system, and to be viable for the accumulation of experience points, it has to contain elements of Former culture."

"Can you not create your own games?" asked Charles.

Dr. Roop looked down at him and lowered his neck slightly before answering. "There is still much we do not know about the Formers. It's fair to say that what we don't know is vastly greater than what we do, and we believe that by training our minds to think as they did, we may be able to unlock some of their secrets. For you to gain experience from gaming, the specific game must be logged and recorded. Every move of every game is then analyzed by a sophisticated complex of computer programs. One game or a hundred or a thousand will tell us little, but over many decades, we have discovered patterns that have helped us to understand and unlock some of the mysteries of our progenitors."

I was expecting something like an adult and science-fictional Chuck E. Cheese's, but the gaming center was more like a gigantic day room in a retirement home—but still science-fictional. The space was cavernous and there were rows upon rows of tables, at which sat hundreds of beings playing many of the games I'd examined on my data bracelet: card games and tile games and stick games and board games. I saw the game with cubes that Nayana had been studying on the *Dependable*. I was delighted to see that there were a lot of people playing Approximate Results from Endeavors. This, I decided, was going to be a lot more fun than math and physics.

Dr. Roop showed us the tutorial sections, where we could learn any of the games, and then told us to explore and find what we liked. The only condition was that we should not play one another until we had each logged a total of twenty hours of the game we wished to play. Apparently the system did not have much to learn from analyzing contests between people who did not know what they were doing.

"This is a government facility," Dr. Roop told us, "but the games are open to the general public, so be circumspect about what you tell other beings about yourselves." He cast his gaze on me when he said this.

Each table had a fairly self-explanatory system in which a player displays a holographic icon representing the game and the number of bright blue lights equal to the number of players required. Most games were for two players, though some could accommodate, or even require, four or five or as many as seven.

I found a blue light on a table looking for someone to play Approximate Results from Endeavors. I sat down across from a being I took to be the same species as Ystip from the *Dependable*—an otter with a beak. This one was male, and much larger, with grayer fur.

"Hi," I said. "I'm Zeke. I'm pretty new at this, but I've been told I'm not too bad."

The otter being stared at me and said nothing.

"Maybe we should turn off the blue light," I suggested.

"That is not necessary." The being stood up. "I do not play games with murderers."

It walked off without looking back, and I sat there, feeling angry and ashamed and wondering what I should do, when the chair across me was filled. Once again, the form of an alien species took me totally by surprise. The woman who sat down looked like she was in her early twenties, by human standards at any rate, and given she was level twenty-five, I thought she couldn't be too old. She was largely humanoid, but with bright green skin, a slightly protruding cranial ridge, and white eyes without pupils that seemed to glow. Her hair was dark red and cut short, and there was something extremely severe about her. She wore a loose-fitting and somewhat unflattering yellow jumpsuit that made her look like she spent her time clearing up radiation leaks.

None of those things were what drew my attention. It wasn't that she looked like a green-skinned human in a weird outfit that shocked me. It was that she looked like a Martian—a DC Comics Martian. She looked, in fact, like Miss Martian, M'gann M'orzz, Martian Manhunter's niece.

"Wow," I said. "You look like Martian Manhunter's niece."

She looked at me, and her eyes narrowed, but her face remained expressionless and her voice was flat. "Either I'm having problems with my translator, or you are speaking non-sense."

"Your translator's fine," I said. I hesitated for a second, and then decided there was no point hiding. I introduced myself.

She did not react to my name except to tell me her name was Hluh Lahhluh Hlahluh Luh.

"Can I just call you Hluh?" I asked.

"Sure, I guess," she said as she began laying out the basic game tiles and appeared determined not to look me in the eye. "Whatever you want. I don't really care. Do you want to play the base set or one of the expansions?"

"I've never played the expansions," I said, excited at the prospect of trying new tiles. "Let's do that."

She took out the tiles for the Imperfectly Articulated Desires expansion, and we proceeded to play for three hours. Hluh was something of an intense gamer, so we didn't talk much, but early on she explained she was working on an advanced [degree] in gaming from one of the major local universities. Her area of research was the playing styles of non-Confederation species.

I thought that getting a degree in gaming was pretty cool, so I figured I'd stick with her and not look for another player, even if other players might have personalities.

I didn't think she was necessarily playing to win, but to watch my style. Even so, she had a bit of a competitive streak, and though she was generally a dour creature, I saw her almost smile a couple of times when she made a sudden and clever end run around one of my strategies.

"You're reasonably competent," she told me as we were making our way through what we both knew would be our last game. "I expected something a little less nuanced from the Butcher of Ganar."

I was about to make a move, but my hand froze. "Is that what they're calling me?"

"Don't you follow the news outputs?" she asked.

"No. And I didn't butcher anyone," I said. "The Phandic ship killed the Ganari. I was trying to protect our own ship."

"I have no way of knowing what happened," she said, her voice utterly calm. "I wasn't there. Maybe you could tell me about it."

Now I was starting to get suspicious. "Are you a reporter—a data collector?"

"Yes, that's correct," she said.

"I thought you were some sort of graduate student."

"That was a lie I told you to put you off your guard," she explained in her neutral voice.

"You know what?" I said. "Forget the experience from this game. I'll clean up. I'm done talking to you."

She looked in my general direction, but not really at me "I could either produce a story in which you tell your side of what happened at Ganar, or I could do a story on the Ish-hi and Rarel random delegates. It is a story I think they wouldn't want me to pursue." She set her hands on the table and leaned forward as she spoke to me.

I slapped my tiles down. "I am starting to dislike you."

"I get that a lot," she said. "I'm told I have an abrasive personality."

"Yeah," I said. "You do. What exactly are you saying about Steve and Tamret?"

She almost met my eye for a second. "You don't know? They haven't told you?" When I didn't say anything she said, "Let me tell you what they're hiding, so you can make a more informed choice."

I held up my hand. "I don't want to hear anything about my friends from you."

"Unless you want everyone to know, you are going to have to talk to me," she said. "I think it would be better if we went somewhere quiet. I can interview you and maybe consume some food. I think it will be mostly painless."

"I'm supposed to have dinner with my friends," I said.

"You mean the friends who are the subjects of a story that will expose and humiliate them?"

I didn't know what she had on them, but the thought that this weirdo might publish or post—or whatever it was—something that could hurt my friends filled me with rage. I knew at that moment that I could not allow Hluh to hurt Tamret. Or Steve. Sure, I wanted to protect my lizard pal. Of course I did, and I have no doubt that if it had been just Steve, I'd have done the same thing, but I don't think I would have felt the same urgency.

"Fine." I almost spat the word. "I'll talk to you."

"I thought you might," Hluh said. "I knew you would want to protect the Rarel. Rumor has it you two are involved in an emotional entanglement."

"A *what*?" I demanded.

"You know," she said. "That you are sweethearts."

"People are saying that?" It made me incredibly uncomfortable to realize that strangers, countless aliens, were gossiping about me, though I couldn't help but like that they believed someone as pretty as Tamret would be my girlfriend. "What else are they saying?"

Hluh shrugged. "It doesn't matter. Beings say many false things, but I thought that might be true."

"It's not," I assured her.

"You don't like her appearance?"

"Can we talk about something else?" I asked, feeling my cheeks redden.

Everyone was more or less wrapping up now. I'd earned a number of experience points, but not enough to move up to level twelve. Even so, I saw that none of the other humans had improved either, so, just to rub it in, I took two levels, moving up to nine. I added one more skill point to agility and another to intellect. The latter was a good option for the ship-operations track, but I also felt it would be useful to have my synapses firing a little quicker for my evening with Hluh.

I walked out of the gaming center with the data collector, and of course Ms. Price was not there this time. The one day I do well, she misses out. Steve and Tamret, however, were waiting outside.

"Who's your friend?" Steve asked me. "He's disturbingly green."

"She," Hluh said.

Tamret's ears jerked back, and she looked at Hluh through slitted eyes. "Possibly."

"This is Hluh," I said. "I'm going to have dinner with her."

Tamret's expression darkened for an instant, and then she scowled at me and put her hands on her hips. "We had plans. You're going to throw us over for this vegetable?"

Hluh did not seem insulted. Nor did she seem inclined to wait for an answer. She just walked toward the exit and expected me to follow. I did.

Because of Dr. Roop's warning, I had not gone outside the government compound since that first night with Steve and Tamret, but Hluh wanted to eat in her neighborhood, and I saw no real reason to object. It was nice to see a little bit more of Confederation Central. We traveled by elevated train, and it didn't take long for me to see the wisdom of Dr. Roop's decision. A tall banana-shaped being with massive compound eyes had been watching some kind of moving display of shapes and colors projected from its data bracelet, and I guess it noticed I was staring at the display, trying to figure out what it signified. It was about to say something, friendly, I suspect, when it clacked its starburst-shaped mouth in—I don't know, surprise, I guess.

"You," it said. "You are the mass murderer."

"I'm pretty sure I'm not," I said indignantly. I was about to say more when Hluh stepped in front of me.

"Many beings confuse him with the war criminal," she said. "It's a common mistake."

The being clicked at me again. "If it truly were that vile human applicant, I would be forced to wash my eye lenses, lest I be corrupted with his evil."

"Man, I'm so glad we saved you from that," I said. Then Hluh was pulling me off the train before I could say anything else. She led me to a district where all the buildings were low and had open patios. There were huge trees, with thick orange leaves the size of car doors, but they seemed to be light because they fluttered like flags. At least half the beings in the neighborhood were of the same species as Hluh, with green skin and protruding cranial ridges. It was a whole district of Martian Manhunters. What would my father have thought about this? I wondered. Many of the beings were laughing or speaking in animated tones, so it seemed safe to assume that Hluh's affect was not specific to her kind. She was just a dud.

We sat at an outdoor café where patrons ate and drank. Some strange creatures that looked like acorns with arms and legs were deriving sustenance from listening to bowls of what appeared to be carbonated water. Hluh turned her data bracelet to record, leveled her glowing white gaze at me, and said, "Tell me why you killed all those Phands."

"The Phands murdered the Ganari, and they were trying to kill us. The bridge crew were injured, and I was the only one around who could operate the weapons console, if only barely."

"But you fired ten dark-matter missiles. Does that not suggest a desire to murder?"

"It suggests," I said, "a desire not to *be* murdered—and the desire to see my friends and the crew of the *Dependable* not be murdered."

"Is your species familiar with the concept of mercy?"

And so it went. Hluh threw leading, hostile questions at me, and I answered. After a while I stopped waiting for her questions and just talked, telling her what had happened, why I had done what I did, and what I was thinking about. I figured if I was going to break Dr. Roop's rule and spill my guts, I might as well present myself as favorably as possible.

When we were done, I told her I would find my own way back to the compound.

"Thank you for speaking to me," she said. "And let me know next time you want to play Approximate Results from Endeavors. You're not terrible at it."

"Just tell me you'll keep your word—you won't write about Steve and Tamret."

"I never said I wouldn't post a story about them," she said, her voice utterly expressionless. "Just not tonight."

"But I thought if I helped you with this, you would leave them alone."

She looked genuinely puzzled. "I don't recall saying that."

I stood up, put my hands on the table, and leaned toward her. "Do not post any stories about them. Do you understand me?"

"You appear agitated. Are you feeling ill?"

"Are you really this dense?" I asked her.

She blinked a few times. "You would prefer I did not post any stories about the Ish-hi and the Rarel. Is that right?"

I may have done some hair pulling here. "Yes, Hluh. That is, in fact, right."

"What can you offer me in exchange for sparing them from hostile public scrutiny?"

So I made her an offer—an extremely stupid offer—and she accepted it.

• • •

When I got back to the room that night, Charles was lying on his bed, doing the reading assignment for the next day. He looked over at me, his eyes lingering for a second on the number 9 above my head, the same as his, but he didn't say anything.

I was too agitated from my night out to sit still. What kind of secrets could Steve and Tamret be keeping? How did Hluh know? Was it the same secret or two unrelated things? I thought about going and knocking on their doors, but demanding my friends tell me secret stuff about themselves didn't exactly seem like a good move, especially since Tamret seemed to be angry with me for going off with Hluh in the first place.

I went over to my desk, not really sure what I intended to do, but wanting to look busy so Charles wouldn't see that I was upset. As soon as I sat, I noticed that my Martian Manhunter action figure had been moved, and since I hadn't done it and we didn't have a cleaning service, it meant that Charles had been messing with my stuff. I didn't exactly want to look at the figure's green skin right then, so I decided to put it in the drawer. As I reached for it, I noticed that the cardboard box that held my mother's locket also seemed askew. When I picked it up, it felt light, so I took off the lid. The locket was gone.

Maybe if I hadn't already been on edge I would have been calmer about it, but I don't think I would have taken it in stride under any circumstances. My mother had given that locket to me. She needed me, right now, and I'd left her behind because it was the only way I could try to save her. That locket had been her way of telling me she was okay with what I was doing, and Charles had no business touching it, let alone taking it.

I would have thought he'd be watching me, knowing I had

discovered what he'd done, but he was absorbed in his reading and didn't see it coming. I grabbed him by his shirt and pulled him off the bed, so he fell on the floor. Everything that had been building up since I left Earth—being ostracized by my peers, destroying the Phandic ship, saying good-bye to my friends on the *Dependable*, being thrown to the wolves by Ms. Price, and not being able to make any sense of why Tamret tolerated Ardov—all of this boiled over in to a single act of rage.

My reputation as the Butcher of Ganar notwithstanding, I'm not a violent person. I like blowing away Covenant grunts as well as the next guy, but video games are only pretend. In real life, I don't get a charge out of hurting anyone or anything, and so once I had Charles on the floor and he was at a complete disadvantage, I wasn't sure what I wanted to do with him.

"Where's my mother's locket?" I asked, hoping he didn't notice I was slightly confused by what I'd done.

"I have no idea what you mean," he said, raising his arms to protect himself.

"What is this about? Are you mad because I'm a better gamer than you, so you took my stuff to get even with me?" I took a step back. "That locket has been in my family for like a hundred years. Maybe you didn't realize it was important, but I want it back. Now."

"I do not have it," he said, pushing himself away from me. He risked rising enough to sit on his bed. "You are lucky I do not choose to report your actions to Dr. Roop."

"That's right," I said, my fists balled as I tried to rekindle my anger. "Go tell Dr. Roop. Tell him I attacked you, and then we can tell him why."

Charles looked down as he considered this scenario. "I did

not take your things," he said, not troubling himself to raise his eyes as he spoke.

I understood how it was with him. He couldn't admit it. He was embarrassed, and my continuing to threaten him would only make him bear down, maybe throw the necklace away. I needed to give him an out. Maybe I needed to give myself one as well, because I wasn't prepared to beat a confession out of him.

"Fine," I said, heading back to my side of the room. "I'm tired. Maybe I forgot where it was. I'll look for it again in the morning."

"Perhaps," he agreed, "that is a good idea."

It took me a long time to fall asleep that night. I lay awake listening to Charles breathing the breath of someone also lying awake, maybe waiting for me to fall asleep. It was so stupid. If we were normal people, normal roommates, we would be able to talk about this, and about all the fantastic things we did and saw, but he had made his choice, and I could do nothing about it. So I lay there, wondering about my mother's health, telling myself that she would be okay. I'd get back, and she'd be just fine, and then the Confederation would provide a cure, and I would never have to worry about her being sick again.

I finally did fall asleep, and in the morning, when I opened the box, the locket was back where it belonged. That was the good news. The bad news was the message waiting for me on my data bracelet. Dr. Roop wanted to see me at once.

CHAPTER FIFTEEN

I sat in Dr. Roop's office and watched the interview that Hluh had posted on her news feed.

This is the part of the story where the naïve young hero realizes that he has been tricked by the antisocial, green-skinned reporter into saying things he didn't quite mean, which show him in a negative light and make his life far more complicated. Actually, it didn't happen like that. I wasn't at all unhappy with the interview. I thought I came across pretty much the way I had hoped I would—like someone who had been put in a bad situation and did the best he could, someone who regretted taking lives, but regretted even more the violent attack on his friends that made his actions necessary.

When it was over, Dr. Roop sighed and leaned back in his chair. "What made you think doing this was a good idea?"

"I never wanted to talk to her," I told him. As soon as he had summoned me, I'd known what we were going to discuss, and I'd already decided what to tell him. "The data collector said if I didn't do the interview, she was going to write about Tamret and Steve instead. She said she had some secret they wouldn't want to get out."

Dr. Roop leaned his neck forward and began to rub worriedly at his stubby horns. Then he looked up at me and, meeting my gaze with his big, giraffelike eyes, said, "That is not good."

"Is there really something she could use against them?"

"Yes, there is. Both of them—"

"Stop," I said. "If they have secrets, they can tell me if they want. I don't need to gossip about my friends."

"Very well." He leaned back in his chair. "Zeke, I truly wish you had not spoken to this data collector."

"I think we covered this. I didn't have a choice."

"I see." He leaned forward and held out both his hands, as if weighing invisible objects. "So here we have not wanting to embarrass your friends. And here we have the fate of a galactic civilization based on the principles of mutual respect and non-violence."

Dr. Roop was being sarcastic. That made me nervous. "I don't see how my talking to this data collector threatens the Confederation."

"You don't have to see it," he said. "I told you not to talk to anyone. I told you remaining silent was important. Why didn't you contact me when she threatened you?"

I had no answer for that. I simply hadn't thought to do so.

He closed his eyes. He looked tired. Sad. I hated that I had put him in this position. "Have I ever given you a reason not to trust me?" he asked.

"No," I said, and I meant it.

"Next time, please don't act alone. I could have protected Steve and Tamret."

"I'm sorry. You're right."

He sighed. "What's done is done. We can't change it. And to be truthful, you spoke well, and you didn't give your critics any new ammunition. I think we have neither lost nor gained, but please don't speak to any more data collectors."

I promised him I wouldn't.

"And I suppose there's no reason to keep you in the compound," he said. "The story is out, and the other data collectors will leave you alone."

I was getting ready to go when he asked me the question I'd been dreading. "How did you get her to agree not to post about Steve and Tamret in the future?"

"Yeah," I said, running a hand through the mop of my hair. "There's the tricky part. I kind of promised her I would keep talking to her, and she could post more stories about my progress over the course of the year. I probably should have mentioned that."

"Probably," Dr. Roop agreed, rubbing his horns again. "I think I need to send some messages now. You'll please excuse me?"

At breakfast, Steve seemed pretty even-tempered about the whole thing, but Tamret was not bothering to hide her irritation. Her lavender eyes had bloodshot streaks in them, and she looked like she hadn't slept, or maybe like she'd been crying. I wanted to ask her about it, but she seemed in no mood for my sympathy.

"Why are you such an idiot?" she inquired. "I can't believe you talked to her."

"It just kind of happened." I swirled my spoonlike utensil through my porridgelike food.

"What, do you have a crush on her or something?" she asked, stabbing at a piece of fruit-like food with her forklike utensil.

"No!" The question took me completely by surprise. "She has the personality of a potato." I knew I sounded ridiculous, but I felt trapped and frustrated. Even if Tamret didn't know my reasons—which she did not, because it would have felt like bragging to tell her—I was in no mood for her to give me a hard time about what I'd done to protect her.

"Then why did you talk to her?" Tamret demanded. Her voice was low, her eyes narrow, and her nostrils flared. She tensed her fingers, and the sharp tips of her claws protruded. The whole effect was extremely intimidating.

"I felt like I didn't have a choice," I said, hoping she wouldn't press the issue.

"Have you seen what they're saying about you on the news outputs?" she asked. Her small whiskers seemed to be vibrating with irritation.

"No," I said. "I mean, Hluh mentioned that it wasn't positive, but I didn't think to look."

"You are so stupid," she said, her voice a little too loud. "That creature's report was fine, but other outputs have picked up the story. They're calling you a killer, a murderer, a war criminal. Most beings in the Confederation think you should be on trial for what you did."

I gripped the side of the table. The idea that billions of beings knew who I was, and wanted me to be punished, had never really sunk in before. It made me dizzy, and Tamret was yelling in public, with beings looking on, because I wanted to protect her.

"Can you just leave me alone?" I said. "I don't butt into your business."

"I don't have any business you need to butt into," she said, her voice low and dangerous.

"What about Ardov? How come you put up with how he treats you?"

"That's not your concern," she said, jabbing a finger at me.

"There you go. It's not my concern. Just like this isn't yours."

"I don't think you can look after your own concerns," she snapped. "I think you've pretty much proved that."

"Why do you care?" I asked, maybe more loudly than I should have. "What does it matter to you? It doesn't affect your life. Dr. Roop is mad at *me*, not us. My talking to data collectors doesn't do you any harm."

"Because we're supposed to be on the same side," she said, her voice getting quieter, and more frightening for that. "We're supposed to look after each other, not go running off with data collectors and spilling our guts. By [*the third-tier revenge deity*], Zeke, maybe next time ask your friends before you're about do something that will mess up your life."

I was actually shaking with frustration. My fingers were white from the force of my table clutching. She didn't get it, and it wasn't her fault that she didn't get it, but I had become furious with her for blaming me for trying to protect her. "Can you just leave it alone?" I snapped. "Worry about yourself, and keep your hairy business out of my face."

Even as I opened my mouth, I knew I should shut up, but it felt so good not to keep everything bottled up, just like it had felt good to throw Charles on the floor. And like getting rough with Charles, once I'd stopped laying into Tamret, I didn't know what to do.

Her eyes had become moist. She set her jaw hard and rigid. "You know what? I don't feel like eating." She stood up, leveled a sad look at me, and walked away.

Steve watched her go and then turned his Komodo dragon gaze on me. "I hate to point out the obvious, but you just insulted the physical appearance of a girl from a culture with so many revenge deities they have to rank them."

I shook my head, furious with myself. "I lost it. I was so frustrated that she was giving me a hard time over what I did for *her*—for both of you. The data collector said if I didn't talk to her, she was going to write about you and Tamret."

"About *us*?" Steve sounded genuinely confused. "What about us?"

"I don't know. She offered to tell me, but I didn't want to hear it from her."

"Well, I wish you bloody well had wanted to hear it from her," he said, "because I don't know what it could be."

"You don't have any secrets?"

He thought about it for a minute. "Not really, unless you mean my run-ins with the filth."

"With the *what*?"

"The filth, mate. The plods. Bizzies. Coppers. Law enforcement, like the peace officers they have hovering about here."

"Wait a minute," I said, closing my eyes and running my hands over my face. "Are you telling me that you're some sort of criminal?"

"Well, that's putting it a big forcefully, yeah?" he said, leaning back on his stool. "I just had a few scrapes is all. From time to time I might have been inclined to take an [*automobile-like vehicle*] that wasn't precisely my own. Just for fun, mind you. Not for money."

"You're a car thief," I said. "Aren't you too young to drive?"

"I'm not going to refuse to steal something just because I'm not old enough to use it legally," he explained as though my objection were absurd. Then he suddenly looked up. "You know, that could be what she was on about. Tamret had some legal problems of her own."

The surprises just didn't stop coming. "What sort of legal problems?"

"Something to do with hacking," Steve said. "Before you arrived on the station, we got to talking, and she told me that she was in jail for unauthorized computer manipulation, or something like that, when her number got picked for the delegation, and that got her sprung." He rubbed at the back of his head. "What about you, mate? You ever been nabbed?"

I shook my head. "No way. I'm squeaky clean."

"We'll fix that," he said, but he looked worried. "Makes you wonder, doesn't it?"

"Wonder what?"

"Well, it's rather long odds that two of us would be dicey, yeah? So it makes me wonder if maybe we're not so random as they say."

I couldn't imagine why the selection committee would have deliberately chosen criminals, but it seemed like the deck had been stacked, and in ways that made no sense. I was starting to get uncomfortable.

I shook my head, not knowing how to process this new information. "Do me a favor and don't tell Tamret about all this, okay?"

"About the two of us being dicey? She already knows."

"No, about me talking to Hluh to protect you two."

He cocked his head, and this time tasted the air with his tongue. "Why not tell her?"

"I don't want her to feel like she owes me a favor or anything."

"But you want *me* to feel like I owe you a favor?"

"I didn't do it so you would owe me a favor. I did it because we're friends."

"Then why tell me and not her?" he asked. "I know you just insulted her and called her hairy, and she looked like she'd never forgive you, but I thought you two were friends."

"We are, but I don't want you to tell her," I said, feeling exasperated. "It's a mammal thing, okay? Can we leave it at that?"

Later that day, Dr. Roop took us to the computer lab to learn how to write and replicate Former code. Needless to say, this was another task at which I failed miserably. Tamret gained a level, moving up to a nine, and when I noticed that, I should have gone to speak to her. It would have been the perfect time to try to patch things up, but I couldn't bring myself to do it. How do you apologize to someone for calling her hairy when she is, in fact, covered with hair? The challenges faced by those who live among the stars are many and various.

When we were done, Dr. Roop asked me to follow him back to his office, and sitting there, waiting for us, was my green friend Hluh.

"Hi, Zeke," she said, like we were old pals.

"What's she doing here?"

Dr. Roop closed the door and sat behind his desk, gesturing for me to sit beside Hluh. "This is your mess, Zeke. I'm just trying to clean it up."

I sat down next to Hluh.

"Did you like what I posted?" she asked me.

I didn't answer. She was too clueless to hate properly, but that didn't mean I had to be friendly with her.

"I've made an offer to Ms. Lahhluh Hlahluh Luh," Dr. Roop explained. "She will continue to speak to you and follow your course through the initiation year. I can't give her unfettered access to the training facilities, but she can talk to me and to you, Zeke. In exchange, she has promised to post nothing about what she learns until after your year is completed."

This was actually a pretty good deal. "Is this agreement legally binding?" I asked. "Will she get in trouble if she violates it?"

"Citizens of the Confederation don't violate their agreements," Dr. Roop said.

"Never?"

"It is so rare, it is not worth discussing," he said. "But yes, if, unfathomably, she were to renege on her agreement and post in a way not specified by our terms, she would face serious legal charges."

"Okay, then," I said. "I agree."

"I'm so pleased," Dr. Roop said, "but I was not asking you. I was letting you know."

Hluh and I left Dr. Roop's office a few minutes later, and I stopped her in the hall. "You really won't go public with anything I say?" I asked her.

"I can't. Weren't you listening?"

"Just double-checking. Can I ask you to investigate some things for me?"

"Things to do with your attack on the Phandic ship?"

"No, with the delegates."

She shrugged. "I guess, if it's interesting to me. What do you have in mind?"

· · ·

That night I was lying on my bed, kicking myself for not having talked to Tamret earlier. She hadn't met me and Steve for dinner, and I hated the idea of her sitting alone by herself eating who-knows-where. That was what my loudest internal voice said, but the quieter voices said I was really afraid she was getting pushed around by Ardov, and putting up with it for reasons I couldn't guess.

I waited until right after curfew, and then I got up—still in my jeans and T-shirt—and went and knocked on her door. Her roommate, Thiel, answered, holding the door open only a crack. "What could you possibly want?" she asked.

"Hey, Thiel. What's new?" When the casual thing only produced a blank stare, I asked, "Is Tamret around?"

She let out a low growl, then walked into the room. "It's your [*monkey*] boy," I heard her say in a sneering voice.

Tamret stepped out into the hall and closed the door behind her. She was wearing a heavy nightgown that made her look sort of like a Victorian cat. It was powder blue, with puffy shoulders and a hem that reached down to her ankles.

"What?" she said, leaning against the wall and folding her arms against her chest.

I took a deep breath and launched into my more-or-less prepared speech. "I shouldn't have lit into you this morning. I'm under a ton of stress, and I snapped, and maybe I needed to snap, but I shouldn't have snapped at you. You were kind of asking for it, but we can leave that for now." Realizing this was all a bit incoherent, I finished with, "I'm sorry."

"Hmm," she said, her ears rotating a little more in my direction. I could tell she was softening but didn't want to let on just yet. "I guess you have to apologize when you insult one of the only two friends you've got."

I nodded. "I don't have a lot of friends on the station, but if I had a thousand friends, I'd still be here right now, saying the exact same thing."

"Yeah?" she asked. "Are you sure it's not just about your limited options?"

"I'm sure."

"Because if you don't really like me, you can just say so."

"Tamret, give me a break. You know I like you."

"Maybe," she said. "But I see the way you are always mooning after the kids in your delegation. Are you ashamed of having me as a friend?"

"What?" I shouted. "Tamret, how can you even ask me that?"

"Because that's what it looks like."

I don't know why it's sometimes so hard to be honest. Telling the truth can feel like walking against the wind in a hurricane, and right then I almost backed down, I almost allowed the gust to blow me in the other direction. I knew that if I let her go back into that room not knowing at least some of how I felt, I would regret it. I had a chance to mend the rift in our friendship forever, and as scared as I was to take it, I decided I couldn't give into the fear. Fortune favors the bold.

"I don't know why you would ever think I'm ashamed of you," I said. "Maybe there's some cross-species static, because spending time with you makes me feel, I don't know, lucky, I guess. I feel lucky to be your friend. Also a little bit afraid, but mostly lucky."

She was trying not to smile, but her lavender eyes were

wide and suddenly looked a lot less tired. "That's a pretty good answer. But are you sure I'm not too hairy for you?"

"That was a poor choice of words," I conceded. "Please don't be insulted. You don't see me getting upset that your roommate called me a monkey boy."

"You heard that?" she asked. Her tone made me think mentioning monkeys was a more serious problem than you would normally suppose.

"Don't worry about it," I said. "I came here to apologize to you, remember? I don't care what your roommate calls me."

There was that smile again. She opened the door to her room. "I'm glad you came by. I hated being angry with you and wanting to slash your face with my claws and all that."

Thus the multiple revenge deities. "Yeah, I don't want you feeling that way. Ever again."

"Good night, Zeke." She slowly closed the door, watching me until the last sliver of light in her room vanished and a soft click left me alone in the hall.

CHAPTER SIXTEEN

A s you know from last night's reading assignment," Dr. Roop said, "the ability to operate a ship—be it a short-range freighter, a mining vessel that never leaves a solar system, or a starship that tunnels across light years—is a vital skill in any interstellar culture. The shipboard simulation room is the most challenging of all your options for gaining experience points. It is difficult to learn the different functions, but if you apply yourself to this task, you will level up faster here than anywhere else."

The initiates, Dr. Roop, and Ms. Price stood in the lower level of our building. The lights were medium bright, and the halls were wide, like you might find in an underground facility that required its workers to drive trams and wear hard hats. We stood outside a set of double doors, and Dr. Roop gestured toward them dramatically. I wanted him to open them up so we could get to business. Besides the games, this was the one area in which I hoped I might do well.

Or maybe I'd do miserably. Best to prepare myself for humiliation.

The flight simulators on the *Dependable* had been in an open area with multiple stations. Here there were a series of private suites, which Dr. Roop told us we would have to reserve in order to guarantee getting time. He brought us into one of the suites, which could accommodate up to six beings, though he said teams of four were most common. He then talked everyone through the process of running a sim, explaining the most vital posts of a starship and how to assign each workstation to a particular post. Once we all had the basic hang of the operation, he told us we were going to proceed.

"We have a tradition of pitting the different initiate species against one another for the first sim, though usually there are four groups," he said, and I had the feeling he was working hard to keep his voice neutral. "It will be less of a challenge with only three, but the basic rules will be the same."

"You are all certainly competent," Ms. Price said, "but I have faith in my home planet."

"Of course," Dr. Roop continued. "Now, you'll have fifteen minutes to assign tasks and prepare yourselves. You'll go to your separate suites, which the system will synch so you are all in the same sim. You'll then be dropped at random positions within an eight-hundred-thousand-square-mile battlefield. All three ships will be identical, so there is no tactical advantage to anyone. It's a free-for-all, sentients, and, per Ms. Price's suggestion, it is a winner-take-all scenario."

"I think you'll find human beings do well under pressure," she said.

"Let me explain what this means," Dr. Roop continued. "Sims involving ship operations are the one area in which you can agree to assign the experience points earned by all participants to the winning being or team. So you'll be playing for the whole pool. Only the team that destroys its last remaining enemy will gain experience."

He waited to see if there were any questions. When no one asked anything, he said, "Lest anyone be tempted to indulge in a dark-matter-missile frenzy, we are running the sim as though you can only have a single missile loaded into your bays. Once you launch it, you can order your virtual crew to load another, but it will be approximately four minutes between launches. This sim is meant to test your tactical thinking, not who is the quickest to fire."

So saying, he left the Ish-hi where they were and led our team and the Rarel team to our own suites. Tamret and I had been back to normal since my apology the previous night, but I was still not happy to see Ardov talking quietly to her as they walked into their suite.

I followed the other humans into ours, Ms. Price glaring at us as we entered. She evidently had some personal investment in our winning. "I'll be monitoring the battle in spectator mode on my data bracelet," she told us. "Make me proud."

I was a little embarrassed to admit, even to myself, that I liked having the chance to prove my worth to her—to all of them. I hated how they had been treating me, and I didn't need to be friends with any of them, but on some basic level I wanted them to acknowledge that I brought something to our delegation. Maybe I wanted to believe that too. Maybe it was just the basic human need to belong to a group of similar beings. If I did well in the sim, I hoped it might turn things around. I wasn't about to blow it.

The first thing we had to do when we settled in our suite was determine who would take which tasks. Right now there were a bunch of generic-looking consoles with chairs in front of them, but I knew that once the sim activated, we wouldn't be able to switch posts.

"Of course I'll be captain," Nayana said. "I have the best

tactical mind. And we certainly want Zeke on weapons." She offered me a pale imitation of her best smile. "Mi Sun will handle both navigation and communications, and Charles, you take the helm. Any questions?"

Mine was about who'd died and made her Mon Mothma, but the others seemed to accept her leadership, so I guessed she had established some kind of authority within the trio. Nayana probably did have the best tactical mind, and she was giving me my props on weapons, so I kept my mouth shut.

We took our positions, and when it was time, we logged into the system and our HUDs kicked in. Then we were on the ship.

"Oh, my goodness!" Nayana shouted. "This is *amazing!*"

Our HUDs created the illusion that we were spread out across the bridge. Charles and Mi Sun were up front at helm and navigation. I was offset by about five feet at weapons. Nayana was a good ten feet behind us in her chair. When she spoke, she even sounded like she was ten feet away. "I am very impressed with this technology," said Charles from his helm position, holding out his arms and moving them around, seeing how they looked in the illusory environment.

"That's enough chatter," snapped Nayana from the captain's chair, as though she were a seasoned veteran and had not, herself, been squealing in wonder seconds before. "Mi Sun, please scan for enemy vessels."

Mi Sun worked the console for a while. Then she grinned. "I see them, Nayana."

"That's *Captain* or *ma'am* for the duration of the sim," Nayana said.

Mi Sun sighed. "I have them, *Captain.*" It came out sounding like an insult.

"On-screen!" Nayana cried with a little too much enthusiasm.

Nothing happened.

"That's you," I told Mi Sun, keeping my voice quiet.

She made a face like she'd eaten rotten cheese and then found the correct sequence on her console.

The forward screen switched perspectives, and we saw the Ish-hi and Rarel ships more or less circling each other just out of range. Nayana told Charles to advance by twenty thousand miles, and we then joined in the dance. It was the thrill of battle: three armed predators, poised to strike, coiled with deadly tension.

Except nobody did anything. We moved around one another for half an hour. None of us wanted to commit to firing, since whichever two ships were in a firefight first would be handing a tactical advantage to the third.

"We're going to be here forever," Mi Sun groaned. "This is so boring."

"Ms. Park, have you somewhere more important to be?" Nayana snapped.

"As a matter of fact I do, Captain Bligh," Mi Sun said. "I could be earning points doing math or physics right now. Even the stupid game room would be better than moving in circles all day."

"Maybe you're right," Nayana agreed, tapping the arm of her virtual captain's chair. "Can we tunnel out of normal space and pop in behind one of them, taking them by surprise?"

Apparently, she had not done last night's reading. "When a ship first emerges from tunnel," I explained, "the shields are unstable for several seconds. They would have plenty of time to get a weapons lock and destroy us."

"Right." She turned away, but then looked back, smiling. "Mi Sun, contact the Ish-hi vessel. Propose a temporary alliance. If they attack the Rarel ship, we will join in."

Mi Sun sent a text message, but we received a response over audio. "Oi, primates!" the Ish-hi captain called to us cheerily. "Steve here. Done with all this mucking about, are we?"

"How did a random become captain?" Nayana demanded.

"We drew lots for it, didn't we? It's the Ish-hi way. And we like your proposal. Lead on! We'll back you up."

Once we broke off communication, Nayana had Mi Sun contact the Rarel ship and make the same proposal. No surprise, Ardov was captaining, and his response was much like Steve's. Lead and they would follow.

"If we can get them to start firing at each other and turn their backs on us, we might be able to take them both out at once."

It was an okay plan, I thought, though it depended on the other teams both being kind of dense. Neither of them was going to go willingly into a trap.

"We need to show good faith," I said. "Otherwise they'll never make themselves vulnerable to us."

Nayana rubbed her chin in a performance of deep thought. "Helm, bring us in closer to the Ish-hi ship. As soon as we are in weapons range, Zeke, open fire, but only a few shots, and don't let too many of them hit. Once the Rarels engage, we'll move to a position behind the Rarel vessel, catching it in the middle. As soon as the Rarel ship is beyond saving, we'll fire our dark-matter missile. No doubt your friend Steve will think we mean to finish the Rarels, but that missile will be for his ship. With a little luck, we'll take them both out at once."

"Why target the Rarel ship first?" I asked.

"I don't think I should have my orders questioned on my bridge," Nayana said evenly.

"Give me a break," said Mi Sun. "Just answer his question."

"Very well, I will show you that courtesy." Nayana gestured toward the screen, where the Rarel ship was clearly visible. "I suspect Ardov is the more formidable adversary. I'd rather not have to face him, whereas your lizard friend—no offense—is a buffoon. If the Ish-hi ship should survive the initial assault, that is the better of the two options."

I knew she was underestimating Steve, but I didn't say so. Besides, I'd rather the shame of first defeat go to Ardov than to Captain Steve.

We signaled Steve again. "We will launch a few PPB bursts at you to lull Ardov into a false sense of security."

"I get you," Steve said. I could tell he was grinning. "And we'll return fire. For the sake of realism, you understand."

"Not too much realism," Nayana warned him.

"Just the right amount, love."

We informed Ardov of our plan to attack Steve and then moved in. I opened fire with PPBs, and then Ardov fired as well. Per Nayana's orders, Charles eased us back amid shots from Steve's ship, but we did not return fire. Once Steve started in on our mutual enemy, I directed all of my fire at the Rarel ship. Ardov was new to all this and didn't know how to evade. In fact, he was holding the ship at a relative stop, like a playground bully refusing to budge, and though the movement of our ship made targeting tricky, it was nowhere near as hard as hitting a ship engaging in evasive maneuvers. Even better for us, Ardov was positioned to fire on Steve, and he could not take us on without making himself vulnerable to the Ish-hi, so just like that, the Rarel ship was sandwiched between two enemies, fighting to stay alive.

Ardov must have realized his mistake, and he attempted to back away from us, but both ships matched course and velocity, so there was nowhere for him to go. I kept locking and firing on his ship, thinking of it not as them, but as him. I was firing on Ardov, imagining that self-satisfied smirk falling away, and his growing look of alarm. I was having a fine time.

"The Rarel ship's shields are starting to fail," Mi Sun reported. The data streaming across my own readings confirmed this. Ardov's ship had damage throughout its systems, most importantly in its shield generators. Its engines were barely functional, and it looked like it had multiple significant hull breaches.

"Make ready, Mr. Reynolds," Nayana said. "As soon as those shields go down, hit the Ish-hi with a missile."

Just then my data bracelet chirped with a message from Steve. *Tell your captain to save her missile. We're watching you, mate.*

I laughed. "We might want to rethink strategy. Steve just messaged me to tell you not to bother with the missile."

"You're trading intelligence with the enemy?" she demanded.

"He sent me a friendly text. I didn't answer. Don't freak out on me."

"Hold off on the missile. For now." I didn't have to see her face to know she was furious. She had her plan, and now she couldn't use it.

"Looks like the Rarel shields are completely down," Mi Sun announced.

"As soon as that ship goes," Nayana said, "the lizards are going to turn on us. Helm, prepare for evasive maneuvers. Weapons, see if you can bring yourself to fire on your alien friend."

Then the Rarel ship began to break apart, and there was a simulated flash of light. For a moment I felt a wave of terror. It was too similar to what had happened to the Phandic ship. I thought, *Oh, no! Tamret!* But I told myself it was just a sim, and I forced the feeling of panic down. It was an illusion. It was a game, but it was a realistic one—maybe a little too realistic for someone who had been in actual combat.

Nayana pumped a victory fist. "One down, one to go! Now fire PPBs at the Ish-hi before they can fire on us. Wait, what are they doing?"

I was firing at Steve's ship, which was a tricky business because they were firing at us and trying to avoid our fire while we were trying to avoid theirs. Getting any kind of a lock was like trying to hit a Frisbee with a slingshot. But I also noticed that Steve was moving in close, and moving in fast.

"Get us out of here!" Nayana cried, sounding panicked, like she forgot, in that instant, that it was a sim.

"Wait!" I called out, but Nayana waved a dismissive hand at me and again told Charles to accelerate. We began pulling away at top speed, and Steve was right behind us, firing all the while. We felt the low rumble as PPB fire chipped away at our shields. I returned fire, knowing it would do little good.

Nayana seemed to be noticing this as well. She looked at her readouts with concern. "You're hitting him, but the weapons aren't doing any damage."

"It's why I told you to wait," I said, exasperated. "The ion emissions from our engines are watering down our PPBs. Once we started running, we gave Steve the advantage."

Nayana's face darkened. She seemed to understand that she'd made a mistake—two mistakes, really. She'd given a bad order, and had then refused to listen when her crew was trying to advise her. She had just blown the sim for us. If Steve won, I could be happy for my friend, but there was no silver lining for Nayana, whose pride would take a serious beating.

I looked around the bridge. All three of the other humans looked tense and worried. They wanted to win, and they knew we were in a position that made winning almost impossible. Mi Sun kept turning around, glancing at the captain, waiting for her to come up with an idea to get us out of this. Nayana gripped the arms of her captain's chair, a bead of sweat visible on her temple.

This, I realized, was my big chance to show them my worth. I had more real space combat experience than any of them, and I'd proved I could handle the pressure. More than that, I had devised a new strategy to confound my enemies. What could I come up with now, in this strategy, to beat Steve and prove to the other Earth delegates that I was worth having around?

Then it came to me. Steve had the advantage because he was chasing us, so let's take that advantage away.

"Maybe we could turn this around on him," I said. "He's directly behind us, so let's come to a full stop and then swing around to face him. He'll be at point-blank range, and he won't be ready for us. And if he tries to retreat, the weapons advantage will be ours."

"Was that strategy in the reading?" Nayana asked, not doing

a convincing job of hiding her enthusiasm. I'd just offered her the lifeline she needed.

"No, I just thought of it," I told her. "I can't promise it will work. Turning that quickly is going to make targeting difficult for a few seconds, but with a little luck, we'll take them out."

"Let's try it." She gave Charles a moment to enter the course, and when he was ready, she gave the order. "Now!"

We decelerated rapidly while swinging around hard, and the combination felt like falling and spinning simultaneously. I tried to get a lock on my weapons console while also trying not to lose my lunch. The maneuver had seemed like a good idea in theory, but the sudden movement of our ship made achieving a lock difficult. More than that, the instant we slowed, Steve executed evasive maneuvers, which moved my efforts to lock weapons from challenging to near impossible. My hands simply couldn't move quickly enough. Every time I tried to score a hit on his ship, it was already gone. He was moving too erratically, and the increased movement of our ship only made things worse.

"I can't get a lock." I growled in frustration.

"Ish-hi ship is bearing down on us," Mi Sun reported.

I looked up. "He's going to ram us."

"Change course," Nayana said.

Charles shook his head. "There's no time. He's going to overtake us."

"Why would he do that?" Nayana demanded.

"He's trying to force us to change the energy frequency of our shields or to retreat," I told her, "which will put us at an offensive disadvantage."

"Why would we change our shield frequency?" she demanded.

"It was in the reading!" I told her, trying to stay patient.

"You don't use the same frequency for energy weapons and physical objects."

"I fell asleep before I finished the assignment," she said indignantly, "so I don't know if you're right or not."

I was busy trying to hit my target and was in no mood for long explanations. "Just trust me."

"Like I trusted you about stopping?" she asked.

Now it was my turn to blush. Okay, my plan hadn't worked out, but I'd been trying to fix her mistake. "Nayana, stop being stubborn. I know a few things about how these ships work."

"What, from watching *Star Trek*?" she demanded.

"No, they don't work the way they do on *Star Trek*," I snapped, "which you would know if you'd ever seen *Star Trek*. I know how they work here, in real life. Nayana, I want us to win. You need to listen to me."

I thought she was going to demand I call her Captain, but she let that pass. "I think you're wrong about the shields. And in any case, if he rams us, he'll be destroyed too. It will be a draw and it gets him nothing. I say call his bluff and meet him head on, but just before he gets within three hundred miles, fire the dark-matter missile. Then fastest possible retreat."

"That's a good call," I said. And it was. Nayana had made a mess of things, but she was smart, and she'd put what she knew to good use. Three hundred miles was the cutoff for safe deployment. She wanted to maximize our chances of destroying him, and give us the minimum room we'd need to escape the damage of the blast.

"Thank you, Mr. Reynolds," she said. I turned around just in time to catch it. The big smile. I guess I knew what it took to get on her good side after all.

Steve must have been anticipating that move, because just as he passed the four-hundred-mile barrier, he both sped up and radically shifted his approach. I fired the missile, but I was rushed. I knew I was way off the instant I let it go. The missile was lost.

Charles had begun to retreat the instant I fired, but Nayana's plan had depended on the enemy being destroyed. It was not, and it was gaining on us fast.

"You did that on purpose!" Nayana shouted at me.

"I'm doing the best with what we've got," I said. I sent down the order to load another missile. If we were still alive in four minutes we could weigh our options then.

Steve's ship was looming closer now. I kept firing the PPBs, but his shields were holding. He sent some covering fire in our direction, but it was mostly for show. We could hear the distant boom of impacts, but our shields absorbed them easily.

"He'll change course," she muttered. "He has to."

"He's firing his missile!" Mi Sun shouted.

"He's less than two hundred miles away," Nayana protested. "He'll destroy his own ship."

"Evade!" I shouted at Charles, but he was waiting for the order from Nayana. It never came. Our visors filled with light, and our ship was destroyed. Steve had won for his team.

When we emerged from the sim, the Ish-hi were all clapping Steve on the shoulders and talking excitedly. The Rarels were looking about as glum as my teammates.

"Nicely done, Captain," I told Steve.

"You practically handed it to him," Nayana said. Her jaw was set and her eyes were red, like she was trying not to cry.

Nayana did not like to lose, and someone had to take the blame. In Nayana's world, it was not going to be her.

My efforts to get on her good side had clearly not worked. I wanted all of them to like me, but I wasn't going to take the blame for this. "You think I purposely missed hitting him?"

"I know you were trading messages. You said as much. And stopping and turning around was simply suicide."

"I was trying to save us from your mess," I snapped.

"Sorry, mate," Steve said. "Didn't mean to make you look bad. Just going for a laugh."

"It's not your fault," I told him. "If Nayana had listened to me, we could have won it."

"So you want to blame me?" she asked. "This is the thanks I get for being nice to you?"

"Telling me you wish you didn't have to be a jerk to me doesn't count as being nice."

"Let's not be testy," said Ms. Price, walking toward us with Dr. Roop. A three-dimensional holographic projection of our combat field was hovering above her data bracelet. "I had hoped to see Earth do better, but at least we held out until the end. No winner means no losers."

"Think again," said Ann, one of the Ish-hi females. "We won."

"No you didn't," Nayana said. "You were destroyed the same time we were."

"Not true," Dr. Roop told her. "The Ish-hi ship survived three microseconds longer than yours, and it was the cause of the destruction. The terms of the contest stipulated that the winner was the one who destroyed the last remaining enemy. Even though he destroyed his own vessel, Steve's ship met those conditions."

"That's absurd," said Ms. Price. "Scrap the game and start over. Let's have a real winner."

"I'm afraid not, Ms. Price," Dr. Roop said calmly. "But the initiates can come down here and compete any time they care to book suites. They can have as many rematches as they like over the coming year. I'm very impressed, Steve. Perhaps you and I could do some sims together on another day."

"That'd be all right," Steve said, clearly pleased with himself.

"I see we've misjudged you," Jill, the other Ish-hi female, told Steve. "From now on, you may consider yourself a full member of our team."

"Cheers, love, but I don't think so." Steve walked over to where I was standing. "Next time, it will be four teams of three. The randoms against you lot, and we'll see who wins then."

Ardov glowered at Tamret. "You mishandled the helm. Don't think I'm going to forget that."

Tamret met his gaze. "I followed your orders exactly."

"If you'd followed my orders, we'd have won," Ardov said, taking a step toward Tamret.

Dr. Roop now moved toward them. "There's no harm done when everyone has learned something," he said, his voice friendly, as though he hadn't noticed any tensions.

Ardov's ears shot back, and his fur seemed to puff. For a second I thought he was going to turn on Dr. Roop. Instead he gestured to Thiel and Semj, and the three of them walked off.

CHAPTER SEVENTEEN

O ur last formal orientation for experience points was in the sparring room, and at Dr. Roop's advice, we all dressed appropriately. I had on basketball shorts, an old T-shirt, and Chuck Taylors. Mi Sun wore her white martial-arts uniform with, of course, a black belt. Charles wore a polo shirt and cotton shorts, both with the insignia from his private school back home. Nayana wore a pink tracksuit, and she looked only marginally more comfortable about all this than I did.

The sparring room was on the same basement level as the spaceflight sim suites. It looked a whole lot like a martial-arts sparring room on Earth, with padded walls and floors. It also had an attached control room from which you could watch the proceedings, but you couldn't see the control room from the sparring room. I presumed that was so that people who were fighting would not be self-conscious about audience reaction.

From inside the control room, Dr. Roop showed us how to work the console. "You can either spar with another being," he said, "or the computer can use plasma-based field technology to create an artificial partner based on your specific level of fitness. The computer will also generate a protective field, which you can set anywhere from the maximum of level ten, which makes it more or less impossible to get hurt, to level one, in which you can get hurt, and serious injury, while unlikely, remains possible.

Some beings need the threat of real consequences to be at their best. Now, who wants to go first?"

"Can I volunteer to not go at all?" I asked.

His eyes widened. "I'd like everyone to sample the process. If it is not your strongest area, you do not need to pursue excellence in this field, but you never know until you try."

"I'll go," Mi Sun said.

"Good girl," Ms. Price said, looking up from her endless note taking.

Mi Sun rewarded Ms. Price's enthusiasm by rolling her eyes.

Dr. Roop showed her how to program an artificial opponent, and she selected one that the computer gauged as being slightly superior to her. For protection, she selected level eight. "I need to feel something when I'm hit," she said. "But I don't need to feel too much."

I'd never seen Mi Sun fight before, and I had to admit I was impressed. Most of what I knew about martial arts came from Hong Kong movies, so I'd never really seen tae kwon do in action, but it was almost as much dance as fighting. Mi Sun would begin with these exaggerated postures, with her legs wide and her arms fixed, and each blow she struck or blocked looked like a choreographed movement, but she was quick and graceful and powerful, and I knew the sense of scripting was just an illusion produced by her skill. I did not much like Mi Sun, but I sure respected her. Her artificial opponent, which looked like a rectangular-headed mannequin made of blue light, was supposed to be a little bit better than she was, but it was quickly outclassed. Mi Sun lashed out with a seemingly endless stream of wide kicks. It got in a couple of glancing blows, which caused a blue shimmer of light around Mi Sun as the force field kicked in, but the opponent was defeated in less than ninety seconds. As Mi Sun emerged from the fighting room, Ms. Price looked up, flashed her most convincing artificial smile, and went back to her notes.

Ardov volunteered to go next. Like the other Rarels, he wore a loose-fitting sleeveless robe thing that was tightly cinched at the waist and flared out with skirts to his knees. On Tamret it looked great. On Ardov it looked stupid. Actually it looked intimidating, but I told myself it looked stupid because that made me feel better.

I liked Ardov even less than Mi Sun, maybe less than anyone, anywhere, and I wanted to see him fail miserably. He was good, however—fast, strong, and unpredictable. His opponent was the same sort of rectangular-headed mannequin, and it was supposed to be 25 percent more skillful than Ardov, but he defeated it in under a minute with a series of kicks, elbow jabs, and sideways punches.

Steve went next, and that was also something wholly unexpected. Ish-hi apparently didn't dress much differently for exercise than they did for everything else: He wore what appeared to be his usual tunic. He did remove his sandals, however, and then bounded into the sparring room looking every bit the predator I had thought him to be the first time I'd seen him in my room. He and his artificial opponent were almost too fast to watch as he raced across the floor and up the walls. They lashed out with arms and legs and, in Steve's case, tail. Minus the web shooters, Steve had the Spider-Man skill set, but so did his opponent, and though he put up a serious fight, Steve lost after about ten minutes. He came out breathing hard and grinning his reptilian grin. "That was right fun," he said. "I'm doing this every bloody day."

I figured I should get it over with, and it was better to go after Steve, who would make any human appear lame by comparison. I chose an opponent at my level, and maximum force field, and stepped into the fighting room, which smelled of rubber and alien sweat.

Later Dr. Roop told me I could watch a replay of my fight to learn from my mistakes, but I sincerely hope I never have to see what happened in there. My artificial opponent and I faced off in the fighting style known as spastic playground rumble. He took a swing at me; I took a swing at him. We were both good at avoiding getting hit. In fact, I was better than I thought I should be. It had to be the skill points I'd put in agility.

After we'd been fighting for about five minutes, I was starting to get tired. Most playground fights I'd seen ended pretty quickly, and five minutes of continuous swinging, dodging, and moving turned out to be exhausting work. Finally I decided to let my opponent hit me. I wasn't planning on taking a dive, but I wanted to know what getting hit would feel like. That way I could measure how close in I was willing to move. It seemed like a smart idea at the time. My opponent took a swing, and it connected with my jaw. I didn't feel pain—the plasma field protected me from the worst of the punch—but I was suddenly on my back, looking up, and my HUD told me I'd lost the match.

When I went back to the control room, I saw Mi Sun trying not to laugh. Ardov was standing next to Tamret, whispering in her ear.

She looked at me and smiled sympathetically, as if to say it was all right with her if I was the worst fighter in the galaxy. That didn't make me feel any better. When I stood next to Steve, he looked at me and cocked his head a little. "You're the distance guy. I'm for close-up."

"Yeah, but your ship beat mine yesterday," I said glumly.

"Good point, mate," he agreed.

After we had each taken a turn sparring with an artificial opponent, Ardov asked about sparring with real opponents. "I'd like to see how that works."

"That's probably a good idea," Dr. Roop said. "Any volunteers?"

Ardov pointed at me. He flashed what I was sure he thought was an affable smile, but he just looked evil to me. "Let's go, [*monkey*] boy."

"No thanks," I said, holding up my hands, trying to act like it was no big deal.

"There are shields to keep you from getting too hurt," he said. "Unless you're too much of a coward."

"Everyone already knows you're a better fighter than I am," I said, feeling my face get hot.

"Then I'll teach you a thing or two. You'll thank me later."

Ms. Price stopped typing and glared at me. "You're making our species look bad. Get in there and fight him."

I felt everything closing in on me. I was, to be honest, terrified at the idea of fighting Ardov, who I was sure had some trick in mind for making sure I got hurt, in spite of the plasma fields. The best-case scenario was that he absolutely humiliated me without actually putting me in the hospital. On the other hand, if I didn't fight him, I would look pathetic, and I would never live it down. I hated the idea of him smacking me around, but I realized that I didn't hate it as much as I hated having the other humans, and Tamret, see that I was too afraid to face Ardov. I told myself that if he managed to hurt me in spite of the safety measures, the Confederation medical technology would make sure nothing serious happened. There was nothing to do but accept the challenge.

I opened my mouth to speak, but hesitated just an instant. Tamret was staring at me, her expression pointed, like she was trying to tell me something. I knew she didn't want me to fight, and I knew she could see I had no choice. I saw something in her eyes I'd never seen before: fear.

"I'll fight him," Mi Sun said, with the enthusiasm of someone who'd just agreed to empty the dishwasher.

Ardov looked at me. "If the ⌊*monkey*⌋ boy is too afraid, then why not? You didn't seem too helpless."

I felt relief and fear in equal measures, and I kept my eyes down, not wanting to look at anyone, knowing I'd see pity on their faces. I couldn't help myself, though. I glanced up and Tamret was looking right at me, and I did not see pity. I saw relief.

Mi Sun and Ardov agreed to fight with the force field turned down to level two. Dr. Roop advised against it, but it became clear that he would not force them to do things his way, and Ardov insisted. Mi Sun merely shrugged like it didn't matter to her one way or the other.

They squared off, Ardov adopting a position with open hands, arms at shoulder level, bent at ninety degrees. He had one leg in front of the other. Mi Sun stood with her legs wide apart, her knees slightly bent, and her fists balled, her arms close to her body. And they began.

Mi Sun didn't waste any time. She launched a spinning kick

to Ardov's face, and it hit with a sharp thud. Blue plasma flashed as Ardov went reeling back. You see face kicks all the time in comic books, and sometimes in kung fu movies. In real life it's easier to see how much space the foot has to travel, but Mi Sun was fast and accurate and powerful.

"Yes!" I said.

I felt the eyes of all the other Rarels on me, including Tamret. I decided I would keep my opinions to myself.

Ardov wiped his face with the back of his hand. There was a small amount of blood dripping from his nose. He stepped in toward Mi Sun, crouched, and leaped at her. He hadn't leaped like that during his own match, and Mi Sun was caught off guard. He passed her in the air, and she lunged backward, but he reached out and managed to strike across her face with his forearm. She went down, her own nose bloody. Without the force field, that blow might have crushed her face.

"I believe I've seen enough," Dr. Roop said. He signaled the two fighters via their data bracelets. "You've both done well. Let's end this before someone gets hurt."

"It's just getting fun," Ardov said.

"I'm fine." Mi Sun's voice was troublingly distant. She was in some kind of zone, and I thought nothing anyone said was going to pull her out of it.

Ardov lashed out with another one of his flying arm sweeps, but this time Mi Sun was ready. She ducked under it and kicked Ardov in the back. He went face-first into one of the wall mats.

Mi Sun was not about to wait for him to regain his balance. She'd had a taste of his power and did not want to let him get the upper hand again. As soon as he bounced off the wall, she landed another kick to Ardov's face. He tried to move out of the way, but her bare foot still clipped his chin. She then launched a series of quick jabs to his midsection. She stood in her wide stance and lashed six times in a row. Ardov was caught in the whirlwind of her assault and could not make his body respond. He had to take it, and his face contorted with pain and rage and frustration.

I thought Mi Sun had him, and I was breathless with excitement. I was ready to buy her a victory [*pizza*], but then Ardov somehow broke out of her hold, shoving her back so hard she stumbled and fell to the mats. Without stopping to catch his breath, he crouched and leaped like no human could, striking her, as she tried to rise, with an open hand under her jaw, sending her reeling back down. The force field sparked like a blue explosion. Mi Sun crab-walked back and leaped to her feet, quick and agile as though the blow hadn't fazed her, but when she opened her mouth, I could see that her teeth were covered with blood.

"Make them stop," I said. "She's not getting enough protection."

Dr. Roop was already signaling them before I began to speak. "That's enough," he said. "I want you both to end to this."

"Not yet," Ardov said.

Mi Sun shook her head, stubbornly refusing to quit, but she didn't look right to me. Her eyes lacked focus. Her balance was off.

Even Ms. Price, who had stopped typing for once, looked on with concern.

"Why don't you raise the force-field level?" I asked.

"I can't tamper with the system once the match has begun," Dr. Roop said. "The only thing I can do is cancel the program entirely, but if they don't stop when I do that, they'll be fighting with no protection at all."

"Right," said Steve. "I'll go in there and make a convincing case for ending the match."

Steve had only taken a couple of steps toward the door when Ardov spun around and kicked Mi Sun hard in the back. His foot struck hard and flat, and Mi Sun flew into the wall, face-first, connecting with a sickening slap. I thought the padding would be enough to protect her, and after she struck, she remained standing for a beat. Then she fell to the floor. Mi Sun's jaw was slack. Her eyes fluttered momentarily and then closed.

Ardov stood with his back to us, his head down, breathing heavily. Then he turned to face the control room, his mouth open in a sickly grin. "I win."

CHAPTER EIGHTEEN

On Earth, Mi Sun likely might have died. At the very least she would have been in the hospital for months, probably never fully recovered. But as I'd seen in the aftermath of the attack on the *Dependable*, things worked differently here in the Confederation. Before Mi Sun had even hit the floor, the nanites in her system were at work to put her in stasis and stabilize her until she could reach the medical facility across the government compound. There they spent about six hours working their high-tech, largely automated magic on her. All the initiates, even Ardov, sat in the waiting room in respectful silence, the only sound the endless clacking of Ms. Price's keyboard. Finally we received word, via our bracelets, that Mi Sun would make a complete recovery. She was awake and in no pain, but it was a sign of the seriousness of her injuries that she would have to stay in the facility for forty-eight hours, after which she would be back to normal.

"I'm glad that's finally over," Ms. Price said. She made her keyboard vanish, rose, and walked out of the waiting room.

I echoed her sentiment, and maybe even felt it a little more than she did. I didn't have warm and fuzzy feelings about Mi Sun, but she was a person, if an unpleasant one, and I didn't want anything terrible to happen to her. Nothing too terrible, at least. Setbacks, sure. Embarrassment, you bet. Abject apologizing for her rotten behavior toward me? Absolutely. The bottom line was that she was a member of my team, and I didn't want

Earth to lose one of its delegates, but that was the latter logical reaction. My first emotional response was that I simply did not want someone I knew to die.

I felt a flood of relief wash over me, and it was only then that I realized that Tamret, sitting next to me, was holding my hand. It was nice—warm and comforting. Her fur was like the softest down imaginable, and I felt the cool of her finger pads underneath and just a hint of her retracted claws. Her touch seemed comforting and dangerous at the same time, and I liked the sensation. I couldn't help but wonder what it all meant.

"I thought she was dead for sure," Ardov said. "Does this mean we can't be killed here?"

Dr. Roop made no effort to hide his irritation, but still answered. "You can survive most serious injuries provided you are near a medical facility. A direct wound to the heart or a catastrophic brain injury is almost always fatal." He looked at all of us. "But I don't want anyone to take foolish chances. And no more sparring at anything under level six from now on."

"That's no fun," Ardov said with a smirk.

"You can all go back to your rooms now," Dr. Roop said. "Except you, Ardov. I want to see you in my office."

Charles and Nayana were already leaving. I let go of Tamret's hand and looked at her and Steve. "Will you guys hold on? I want to go talk to Mi Sun for a minute."

Tamret squinted at me. Her whiskers twitched. "Why? She hates you."

"It could have been me in there," I said.

Tamret lowered her eyes, and her ears rotated back. "You're right. But you're nicer than she deserves."

I wasn't just being grateful and a good teammate. I wanted

to talk to someone from my own world about something I'd been thinking about. Charles was impossible to talk to, and I didn't think Nayana would have any insights. Mi Sun was my best shot, and I hoped her near-death experience would maybe take the edge off of her.

She sat propped up on a bed in a private room, a million machines monitoring her, beeping and humming softly. There were tubes wired into her arm. It looked like a high-tech version of an Earth hospital room. For all the seriousness of her injuries, she was now awake and reading off her data bracelet. She looked at me in surprise when I came through the door.

"What are you doing here?" she asked.

"I couldn't stay away. I'm in love with you, Mi Sun. I have been since the moment we met. From my first taste of your antisocial rudeness, I've longed for your scornful gaze."

She wrinkled up her face. "Gross. You're messing with me. Aren't you?"

"I am totally messing with you," I said, sitting in a chair across from the foot of her bed.

"Way to go—trying to stress out the girl who practically died." She was almost smiling when she said it, though. I don't think I'd ever seen her smile before.

"I'll try to work on my sensitivity," I told her.

She sighed and closed her eyes. "So, what do you want? You don't have to thank me. I was just trying to keep our planet from—" She stopped herself, and her face softened. I had the feeling she'd been about to say something nasty, and then changed her mind. "If the situation had been reversed, and there was some kind of incredibly dorky thing that needed doing, I know you'd have stepped in for me."

It was the nicest thing she'd ever said to me. It was maybe the nicest thing any human being had said to me since I'd left Earth. "I would," I told her.

"Now that we've settled that, you can go." She turned away.

I was not ready to go. I took a deep breath because I knew this was not going to go well. "Did you ever read *Ender's Game*?"

"Why are you such a geek?" she asked me. "I was almost killed, and you come visit me in the hospital to ask me about a stupid science-fiction story?"

"Just hear me out," I said. "It's about this kid who—"

"I saw the movie, okay?" She rolled her eyes.

"The book is better," I told her.

"Whatever," she said. "Make a point. I'm tired."

"You remember how they have Ender playing all these games supposedly to train him to fight the enemy, but it turns out he's really been fighting them the whole time? It looks like training, but it is really the actual battle, right?"

"Yeah," she said. "What are you getting at? You don't think that's what's going on here, do you?"

"No, it can't be, but I do think we're being used, or at least trained. Everything we're doing is either to train us to fight the Phands or to help the Confederation understand Former tech, which is in the service of fighting the Phands. I'm starting to feel like humans were chosen because we're more, I don't know, violent than other species in the Confederation. Before we left Earth, Ms. Price kept talking about how they're all sheep compared to us."

"So what?" she asked. "They picked us because we have something they need to help the Confederation. I don't have a problem with that."

"The problem is that they're not being honest. Tamret and Steve and I—"

"Stop," she said. "I don't care what you and your Scooby-Doo gang get up to, but don't make me part of it. I just want to keep my head down and gain levels. You should do the same. I can't make you stop acting like an idiot, but I don't have to listen to your theories, either."

"I understand, but—"

"I said I don't want to hear it," she snapped.

I sighed and rose from my chair. "Okay, fine." I went toward the door, and then I turned back. "You really put up a fight."

She frowned. "He still won."

"He's still a jerk."

"So am I," she said.

"The universe is so vast and full of wonders that it actually contains a bigger jerk than you. Feel better." I was turning to leave again, when she called me back.

"Hey, where are Charles and Nayana?"

"They went to get food," I said.

"So you're the only one who came to visit me?"

"I guess so."

"That's pathetic," she said with a scowl. "But thanks."

"No problem." I turned back to look at her. "I have to know something, though."

"What?" she asked uneasily.

"When you talk about my Scooby-Doo gang, is that a primary reference to *Scooby Doo, Where Are You!* or a secondary reference to *Buffy the Vampire Slayer*?"

"Get out of my room," she answered.

CHAPTER NINETEEN

Steve and Tamret and I decided to—literally—take our minds off what happened to Mi Sun, and we took a train to visit the Theater of Plant Experience, a bizarre entertainment where you fed data into your HUD and got to spend half an hour as a tree or a bush or whatever vegetable you liked. It was hard to explain, but strangely relaxing. I left feeling that I'd like to be a plant again some time, but never for too long.

The theater was in what was called the Spin District, and after we left, we used our bracelets to find a restaurant nearby. Steve picked a place that offered a wide selection of living food. The selections for me were more limited, but I figured I could be a sport, and I finally ordered [*seaweed-based noodlelike substance*] in a spicy [*no translation available, but biologically compatible*] gravy. It was good. I recommend it. Tamret proved that girls from across the galaxy share certain things in common and ordered a [*salad*].

The restaurant was on a giant patio, hanging over a busy air thoroughfare, and the floor was made of a durable substance, completely transparent, so we could look down and see the lights of the passing vehicles whisking by in the darkness. It was beautiful and utterly futuristic, like the central planets in the *Firefly* universe.

Tamret was wearing a sleeveless lavender dress, and she had her hair tied up in a bun, bordered by the protuberances of her ears. She sat with her back toward the railing, and she was lit by the city lights and stars and planet and moon outside the dome. I was wearing jeans and a short-sleeved black shirt that had somehow avoiding wrinkling. I thought I was presentable, but I was under no illusion I looked as good as she did.

I was explaining to them my *Ender's Game* concerns, without making any references to *Ender's Game*, of course. I hadn't been able to shake the notion that we were being trained for something, and that whatever that something was, it probably involved fighting the Phands.

"So what are you saying?" Tamret asked. "That we're like second-class citizens being recruited as their soldiers?"

"I've been thinking about that too," Steve said as he used a tonglike utensil to grab at individual blue worms, or maybe snakes, or whatever they were, wriggling around in a bowl. He popped one in his mouth. "Been doing some reading, too. You know most of the beings here are herbivores, yeah?"

I ate my spicy noodle things. "That's old news."

"But this might not be. Most of the planets these beings come from have no carnivores at all. Not even among their animals."

This got our attention. "You're kidding," Tamret said.

Steve shook his head. "No, I double-checked. Most of these beings come from planets where no creatures eat other creatures. Confederation scientists believe that intelligent life is more likely to evolve on worlds where there are no predators."

"That's not what I learned in biology," I said. "I thought that predators promote evolution by forcing animals to adapt in order to survive."

"Sure," Steve said, "if what you want is to survive being

hunted by a predator. But when you've got all your mates being eaten all the time, there's more food for you, right? That favors traits like speed, environmental awareness, camouflage, and such. Now take away the predators. You've got more animals competing for fewer resources, so that promotes a different type of adaptation. The animals that can best exploit their environments win out over those that are less efficient, so that means intelligence, creativity, problem solving, invention, and all that. Those are traits that, on our worlds, you tend to find among predators. These herbivores are like carnivores that eat plants."

"Except they don't know how to hunt," Tamret said.

"Exactly." Steve nodded. "Now, the last time they brought in initiates, one species was a carnivore and one an omnivore. The time before that, one omnivore. Then you have to go back eight years to find one carnivore species."

"The Vaaklir," I said. Urch's species.

"Very good, mate," Steve said, clearly impressed. "Before that, almost fifty years. You see what I'm getting at? Looks like the Confederation is trying to get cozy with its dark side."

"And when you combine that with all the ways they have us train," I speculated, "it makes it pretty clear they're gearing up for war."

"I still don't see the problem," Tamret said. "There are hundreds of worlds in the Confederation. Three more isn't going to turn any kind of tide. It seems to me that they're just fine-tuning. They're tweaking their culture, but they are doing it over the long term."

"I hope you're right," I told her, "because I get the feeling that things are more focused than that."

"Let's keep our tongues scenting the air, but I don't want to worry too much, if you know what I mean. Look at this place." Steve gestured toward the cityscape and the stars beyond. "No point in looking for trouble."

"I know what you mean." Tamret looked out at the city, and a sadness crossed her face. "I hate the thought that we're going to have to leave in less than a year."

I nodded. "I miss my mom and all, but when I think about the Earth, it doesn't really feel like home anymore. This does."

Tamret met my gaze, and suddenly it felt like Steve wasn't there. It was just the two of us, and we were thinking the same thing, even if I wasn't entirely sure what that thing was. My heart was pounding, and I wanted so much to say something to her, but I didn't know what. It was like there were words I needed her to hear, but they were just outside my grasp. I felt like a moron, staring at her, but she was staring back. I thought, *Maybe I don't need any words at all. Maybe all I need is to sit here, with the stars and the shuttles and spaceships and lights of alien buildings all around us.* Maybe that was all I needed to be happy.

Then I felt a shadow cross my vision, and I turned to see someone looming over our table.

It was Ardov. Thiel stood behind him, looking bored, and Semj was by her, his expression distant, like he was doing math problems in his head. Ardov was grinning, and I knew that was never a good thing.

"Can you believe how fragile that human girl was?" he said. "They shouldn't let beings so breakable into the Confederation. Anything could happen to them at any time."

"This is too unpleasant to be a coincidence," Steve said.

I started to rise, but I felt the smooth scales of Steve's fingers on my wrist, pinning my hand to the table. I understood what he was telling me. He wasn't about to see what happened to Mi Sun happen to me. I nodded to him to show him I understood, and he let go.

"I messaged Tamret," Ardov said with unmistakable pride, "and told her to let me know where you were. I figured maybe Zeke here wants a chance to vindicate his fellow human in the sparring room. It should have been him, after all."

Why would Tamret have answered his message? And why hadn't Tamret told us about it? I couldn't figure out why she put up with him the way she did, but that was a matter for another time. For now I knew I had to make sure he didn't push us around. "I'm flattered that you like us so much you want to hang out with us," I told him, "but we're having a private conversation."

"I was talking *about* you, not *to* you," he said. "No one gave you permission to hoot, [*monkey*] boy. We're here for Tamret." He gestured with his head. "Come on, Snowflake. You've spent enough time playing with the animals. I need you to do my laundry."

I stood up. My heart was thundering, but I willed myself to be calm. Ardov was taller than I was, and stronger, and a better fighter. He'd almost killed Mi Sun in an environment designed to make injury all but impossible. I had no doubt that he could destroy me without much trouble, but I had to bet that he wouldn't be willing to risk a conflict. I did not want to have to fight him, but I'd rather end up in the hospital with no one but Mi Sun to talk to than let him put his hands on Tamret.

"We're trying to enjoy a nice dinner among friends," I said, my voice almost steady. "You've had your fun today. How about you give it a rest?"

"How about you sit back down," he said, "before I throw you over the rail. You think the nanites would save you from that?"

Steve had a pair of wiggling creatures trapped in his tongs, but he made no effort to eat them. Instead, he sampled the air with two quick flits of his thin tongue. "You could try that, I reckon, but I can taste what you're going to do before you do it—you couldn't so much as reach out to my mate here with one furry hand without me seeing it coming. Then it would be you going over the rail wondering how the nanites factor in when you hit the ground from a quarter mile up. You want to bet I'm wrong? Give it a try." He dropped the creatures in his mouth and swallowed without chewing.

Ardov grinned down at me. "You can't fight your own battles? You need your pet to do it for you?"

"Nice try," Steve said, "but we're a team. There's no you against him. It's you lot against us. You like those odds? I know I do."

Tamret now rose. "It's fine, Zeke." Her voice was quiet, soft. "I'll go with them."

"No!" I said, more loudly than I intended. "You don't have to go if you don't want to."

"She wants to be with her own kind. Don't you, Snowflake?"

"Yeah, I want to go." She didn't sound like she meant it, but she didn't sound like she didn't, either. I just couldn't read her and couldn't understand why she was letting Ardov order her around. I watched them walk away, Ardov's arm around her shoulder until they disappeared into the elevator.

"You can probably sit down now, mate," Steve said.

I sat. "What is going on with the two of them?"

"No idea," Steve said. "I don't know mammals, but I do know beings, and there's something weird there."

"I just hope she's okay," I said.

"You find out that git is messing with her, you let me know," he said, picking up some more of his worm things. "I'd like to have a good reason to break his arms. And his legs. The medical blokes will mend him when I'm finished, so no harm done."

I wanted to see if I could gently pry some information out of Tamret at breakfast the next day, but she didn't show up. I tried to act like I wasn't worried, and resigned myself to waiting until class to see her. As we approached the classroom that morning, however, we saw there was a commotion up ahead, by Dr. Roop's office. There were several beings in peace officer uniforms, and they appeared to be arguing with Dr. Roop. And then I noticed the Rarel delegation hanging around outside the door. I didn't get along with any of them, but I had to know what was happening.

"What's going on?" I asked Thiel. Semj was the least objectionable of their group, but I couldn't guarantee he would speak to me if I asked him, and after last night's generous portion of intimidation, I didn't want to so much as make eye contact with Ardov.

"Ugh," she said. "It's Tamret. Who else? She's been caught."

"Caught doing what?" I asked, not bothering to keep the alarm out of my voice.

"Hacking. I swear by [*the deity of the caste system*], she's such an embarrassment."

"Is she in real trouble?" What if she got kicked out? What if they put her in some kind of jail? I couldn't bear the thought of it.

"Could be," said Ardov, coming up behind me. He was chewing on a piece of dried meat, like jerky, and grinning like this was the best morning ever. "Though if she ruins our delegation's chances, she is in for a hard time when she gets back home."

"Good," Thiel said. "She deserves it."

"I don't think our Snowflake deserves *that*," Ardov said.

Finally Tamret came out of the room, looking embarrassed, something I had never thought possible for her. Dr. Roop had a hand on one of her shoulders, and his neck was lowered, as though this were his own shame. The peace officers left without Tamret, however, and I considered that a good sign.

"Tamret has made a mistake, and she's sorry," Dr. Roop explained to us. "We'll talk about it more at another time. Suffice it to say that between this and Ardov hurting Mi Sun, the Rarel delegation has not made the best impression."

I immediately pulled her to a quiet corner of the hallway. "What happened?"

"Calm down," she said, pulling away from my grip. "It's no big deal. I was just rooting around in the experience-points database. They found out and overreacted. It's not like I could harm them. You can't even tinker with Confederation citizens' accounts."

"That's still careless, love," Steve told her. "They don't muck about with that sort of thing."

"Maybe." She looked sullen and defiant, like she didn't much care one way or another.

"What's going to happen to you if your delegation doesn't get in?" I asked her.

Her eyes latched onto mine. There was something fearful there I didn't like. When Tamret was crazy or defiant or foolish I could handle it. I couldn't deal with seeing her afraid.

"Did someone say something?"

"Ardov kind of hinted things might be bad for you."

She shook her head, and then she gently brushed strands of lavender hair from her eyes. "That's not your business."

"I just want to know if there's anything—"

"I said it's not your business!" she shouted. Then she pushed past me and stormed down the hall toward the classroom.

"I don't think she wants to talk about it," Steve told me, watching her go.

"Thanks for decoding."

A minute later I saw Semj, the small male Rarel, walking in the hall by himself. I told Steve to head to class, and I hurried to catch up to him.

"What's up, dude," I said.

He stopped and looked up at me, his eyes an unnerving shade of pink. "They don't want me talking to aliens," he said in the uninflected tone I tended to associate with complete weirdos.

"I won't be long, then," I said. "I was just wondering if you know what the story is with Tamret. Why is she going to be in trouble if your delegation doesn't get in?"

"I don't know," he said.

Maybe he didn't know. Maybe there were a lot of things that other Rarels knew and he didn't because Semj was some kind of supersmart and socially clueless mutant. I was willing to believe that except for the fact that his pink pupils were dilating and contracting in tiny but rapid bursts, almost like a pulse. I didn't know anything about Rarel behavior, so I had no idea what it meant, but I was willing to guess it suggested he was either lying or nervous.

It was also the kind of minor detail I never would have noticed before. Maybe my enhanced vision was helping me to pick up on subtle details. Those skill points were starting to add up.

"I think you're lying," I said. "Tell me what you know about it."

"I guess it's not a secret," he said, looking at his shoes, which were wide and flat and, admittedly, kind of interesting. "Tamret and Ardov come from the same totalitarian city-state, and her place there is uncertain because she doesn't have a caste. I don't know how she ended up casteless, but she did. That means she has no political protection. If things go badly, she'll be the easiest person for them to take it out on."

Things were starting to make a little more sense. Maybe.

"I'm leaving now," Semj said. Then, being a Rarel of his word, he left.

I turned to head back into the classroom, but Ms. Price was standing directly behind me, blocking my way, hands on her hips, her red lips pursed in disapproval. I also had the distinct impression she had been listening to my conversation with Semj, which had been none of her business. I felt myself pressing my teeth together in anger.

"Can I have a minute, Zeke?"

"What?" I folded my arms and stared at her directly. I figured I had nothing to lose by letting her know how I felt.

"I know you've been spending a lot of time with the other random delegates," she said, "and I suppose I understand that, but from now on, I'd like you to keep your distance from the Rarel female. She's obviously got some serious issues, and we don't want you making any more trouble than you already have."

Making trouble. That's what she was calling it. She had already tried to get me kicked out of the delegation, and then to ship me out to the Phandic Empire. Now she wanted to keep me from spending time with Tamret. Somehow that seemed worse than the rest of it.

"I can spend my free time with anyone I like."

"Yes, I suppose you can." She blew air out of one corner of her mouth, as though she was finding this conversation tedious beyond belief. I know I was. "You can associate with criminals and misfits, but there are always consequences."

"You already tried to hand me over to the enemy," I said. "I don't think you have too many threats left."

"Zeke, you seem to want to misinterpret everything I say and do as hostile. Please try to remember that I am here to help our world, the planet we come from, which suddenly finds itself a very minor player in a complicated galaxy. You have real responsibilities now. You don't shove aside things that matter because you have a crush on some nonhuman creature."

My ears were now burning hot. "The only friends I have on this station are Steve and Tamret, and I'm not—"

"Yes, the Ish-hi is undesirable as well. I think you should also stay away from him."

"You can think what you want," I said, walking away from her. "I don't have to do what you say."

She grabbed hold of my wrist. Her grip was tight, and I could feel the points of her fingernails against my skin, and they were sharper than I would have suspected. "The president of the United States sent me here to be his voice, and the voice of our country and our world. And I am telling you to keep your distance from the other randoms. They are going to ruin their own delegations. I don't want them ruining ours."

I could get lippy with adults I didn't respect, but being outright disobedient wasn't in my nature. I'd been raised to respect my teachers and authority figures, to assume they were right, even when I didn't like what they had to say. Part of me was trying to figure out if Ms. Price could be right about all this, but I pushed that voice away. I didn't want to believe. I did not believe it. I pulled my wrist away from her.

"Dr. Roop is in charge, and he doesn't have any problem with me spending time with Steve and Tamret, so you're out of luck. You don't have any power over me."

"Not here," she agreed. "When we get back to Earth, I am going to be the only adult who will be able to report on what happened on Confederation Central. If I want to make your life, or your family's life, difficult, I can do that."

She was now threatening my mother. I stared at her icily because I could not think of anything to say.

"I'm trying to help you, Zeke. Please remember that." She turned away and left me standing in the hall.

After class Tamret avoided us for the rest of the day, but she showed up at breakfast the next morning as though nothing had happened. She was in a good mood, smiling a lot, and her eyes lingered on me as she spoke. My breakfast porridge was a little bit better than palatable. A piece of Steve's breakfast escaped and flew around the room, and we all had a good laugh.

Then Hluh sat down at our table. Eager to prove that the

jumpsuit was not a passing phase, she wore a bright pink one today that hurt my eyes if I stared at it too long. "Hey," she said. "How are things?"

Tamret glowered at me. "What's *she* doing here?"

Several government officials at a nearby table seemed to be wondering the same thing, since they were looking over at us. Hluh grabbed my wrist as though it were a piece of gardening equipment. "The human juvenile and I enjoy an inappropriate romantic entanglement," she told the beings at the next table. She looked at Steve and Tamret. "Not really," she said more quietly.

I pulled my arm away from her. "No kidding, not really. What do you want, Hluh?"

"I've got some information for you, like you asked," she said.

"Hold on," Tamret said. "You're cooperating with this freak *again*?"

"You don't have to say hurtful things," Hluh told her.

"Yes, I do, because you are a gigantic green freak. I don't know how you convinced Zeke to cooperate with you after you made him look like a moron in front of the entire galaxy—"

"I didn't look that bad," I offered, but no one was listening.

"—but I'm not going to let him humiliate himself again so you can advance your career or whatever it is you are trying to do."

"I sense that you don't like me," Hluh told her, "but Zeke has promised me his full cooperation over the coming year, and I—"

"The *year*?" Tamret exploded. "Zeke, what is wrong with you? If you don't have the common sense to know that you need to stay away from this . . . this *being*, then how can I trust you?"

There was a moment of terrible silence. Tamret was staring at me, her eyes wide, her whiskers twitching, and I could see that she wanted me to say something that would make her believe I wasn't irredeemably dim or a publicity hound or something equally awful.

Steve coughed diplomatically. "Sorry, mate. You're going to have to work out your mammal affairs on your own time, but this is starting to muck about with my breakfast." He turned to Tamret. "This data collector over here found out about me and you, love—that we'd spent some time in government housing, if you know what I mean. She told Zeke he could talk to her or she would post about us on the news outputs. He talked to Hluh to protect us."

Other than when Ardov was working his spell on her, this was the first time I'd seen Tamret speechless. She stared at me, blinking. "Why didn't you tell me?" she asked quietly.

"I didn't want you to, I don't know, feel bad about me having been in that position."

"Thank you." Her voice was barely a whisper.

"Can I talk now?" asked Hluh. "All these adolescent emotions are getting tedious."

"Wait a minute," Tamret said, as if snapping out of a trance. "I get why you talked to her the first time, but why are you still feeding information to Miss Photosynthesis here?"

I explained the deal Dr. Roop had struck, and I told her I figured I could use Hluh to find out some things that I wanted to know about as well.

"Which is why I'm here," she said. "I looked into the Ganari delegation like you asked me to. It turns out that Sessek, the Ganari random, was awaiting trial. She broke into a secure government building. Apparently, her brother was accused of a crime, and she wanted to steal evidence in order to prevent a conviction. She claimed her brother had been set up in the first place, and she may have been right—for what it's worth."

"So three of the four randoms had legal trouble," I said.

"Correct," Hluh said. "That is far outside the realm of statistical probability."

"They told me that I was selected from a 'contoured' pool of candidates," I said. "They wanted someone male, from my part of the world, and so on. Is there some reason the selection committee would try to recruit kids who had been arrested?"

"It's a good question," Hluh said. "I wanted to let you know this in person. I don't trust that your messages aren't being monitored, and I thought you should be warned."

"Warned about what?" I asked.

"If the selection committee deliberately chose you," Hluh said, "it means somebody wanted you here for a reason, and until you know what that reason is, you should probably be on your guard. It also means that the selection process was tampered with, and that amounts to all three of you being here illegally. If anyone finds out about this, you and your delegations are all finished."

I thought back to my conversation with Ms. Price. Had she wanted me to stay away from Steve and Tamret because she knew about their criminal records? I couldn't imagine how she could have found out about that, but Hluh had, which meant it wasn't impossible. Maybe socially challenged people were better at finding out secrets. The bottom line was that if Ms. Price knew about my friends, she could hurt them, and she might only be waiting for the right moment to do it.

. . .

The three of us went our separate ways after class that day. Steve wanted to spar, Tamret wanted to go to the coding facility, and I spent a couple of hours in the gaming room that afternoon, and then called it quits because I had already booked two hours in a spaceflight suite for later that night. I wanted to work on my solo piloting, which was a bit shaky, to be honest, and I noticed I earned more points when I worked on my weak areas.

When I staggered into the hall after two hours in the sim suite, it was close to curfew. I was still a bit dizzy from trying to maneuver a small mining craft through a series of increasingly dense asteroid fields, but when I saw Tamret and Ardov going into the sparring room together, I was suddenly sharp and alert. Ardov was dressed for fighting, but Tamret was not, wearing a long black skirt and a lavender tank top. I watched as he led her into the control room and then into the main sparring chamber.

Pretty girls sometimes put up with guys like Ardov treating them terribly—I had seen it happen back on Earth—but I just could not believe that Tamret liked Ardov. She would do whatever he asked, but she never seemed like she was happy to spend time with him; it was more like she had no choice but to do what he said. I knew I might have been reading into things because I wanted to believe they weren't close. The only thing I could be sure of was that their interactions gave me the creeps. All of which meant I had no choice but to spy on them.

I went into the control room to make sure she was okay. That was all I was doing. I told myself that I didn't have to know exactly why she was putting up with Ardov. It wasn't my business—she'd made that clear—but I was just being a good friend and making sure she was okay.

She was not okay. Tamret was on the mat, slowly getting to her feet. Ardov kicked her. The force field sparked blue, and Tamret let out a little grunt. Her eyes were narrow slits, glinting with anger.

"It doesn't have to be this way, Snowflake," he said. "Just tell me what you did, and fix it, and I'll leave you alone."

Tamret set her face hard and stony. She wasn't about to tell him anything.

"Be reasonable. I would hate to have to explain to Dr. Roop and the others that you asked me to spar with you. You told me you wanted to learn a thing or two." He kicked her again. She grunted. "She turned the protection down to level one, but she didn't tell me. You know what she's like. Impulsive. I didn't mean to hurt her. It was an accident."

"You'll have to kill me," Tamret said. "And I know you won't do that. You won't ruin our chances of getting into the Confederation."

He lashed out so quickly, I didn't see the windup. I heard the crack, saw the electric jolt of blue, and then Tamret was hitting the wall mats, bouncing hard. Force field or no, Tamret was going to get hurt if I didn't stop this. I checked the panel, hoping he had been exaggerating. No such luck. The force field was turned down to the lowest possible setting, and there was no way to turn up the shielding, not without turning it off entirely. I could try that, but if my timing was off, I could end up exposing Tamret to the full force of Ardov's violence.

"I don't have to kill you, Snowflake," he said. "I just have to make you wish I would. Now tell me what you did to my experience points."

"I didn't do anything. You don't need my help to be a loser. You've got that covered on your own."

Ardov struck Tamret in her face with his open palm, and she fell to the mats again. I stood there, stunned, not knowing what to do. I had to go in there and stop it, but I knew I wouldn't last thirty seconds against Ardov, and having Tamret watch me take a pounding for her wasn't going to save her. Ardov needed Tamret alive for his delegation to reach eighty levels, but he wouldn't care if I was killed. A lot of people might not care.

I sent a message to Steve. He would be able to handle Ardov. When he didn't answer after fifteen seconds, I sent another message, this one labeled urgent. Then I sent a third. No answer. Maybe he was sleeping. It was close to curfew, after all. Maybe he'd turned down his data bracelet so it wouldn't wake him. I wanted to go run to his room, bang on the door, but I didn't dare leave Tamret alone for the five minutes it would take.

Not that my being there was helping her. I stood by, helpless, while she took a swing at Ardov. The force field flickered, but he didn't even flinch. She didn't have the strength left to hurt him, even with minimal shielding.

I should go in there, I told myself. Maybe the two of us together could do something. If we teamed up, we could overwhelm him. It sounded good, and it would work in a movie, but in real life I'd just end up being a punching bag on which Ardov could show off his strength. I didn't have anything to bring to that fight. My increased intellect and agility and vision had helped me tell when Semj was lying, and these skills seemed to be making a difference in the spaceflight sims, but they wouldn't amount to much against a guy like Ardov. I'd figured out a way to save the *Dependable*, but this wasn't the same kind of problem. The sad truth was, I had no real skills other than pushing buttons.

Which, I now realized, was what I needed to save Tamret. Maybe if I could rig things properly, then I could get us both out of this without anyone getting hurt. I called up my keyboard and did a quick search. All I had to do was program my data bracelet to keep me synched with the main console in the sparring room, and Tamret and I would be safe. I hoped. It was a crazy idea and a long shot, but it was all I could think of.

My timing was going to have to be perfect, because if I got it wrong, Ardov could really hurt Tamret. He might kill her. I took a deep breath. I could do this, I told myself. This was nothing compared to the fight with the Phandic ship.

I entered in the data, synched my system with the control room's, and then went over to the door. I'd programmed my data bracelet to let me know about the cycle changes with a slight vibration, something no one else would notice. As soon as the first vibration kicked in—a long, single note—I opened the door to the sparring area.

"Hey, guys," I said, doing my best to sound oblivious. "What's going on? Anything interesting?"

Ardov had been turning on Tamret, but now he stared in disbelief. "So," he said. "Finally ready to fight me?"

"Nah," I said. "But me and Tamret had a date to get milk shakes. Well, not a date. A plan. We had a plan. And she was running late, so I figured I'd track her down."

Ardov began stomping toward me. His fists were tight balls, like sledgehammers, and I wasn't safe. Not yet. I needed to buy a few more seconds.

"You can join us, if you want. Come on, Ardov. You know what I think your problem is?" I was blundering my way through this, but the moment I spoke, I knew it was the right move. Ask him a question, and he has to pause to answer. That would give me the time I needed.

"What?"

Then I received a vibration from my data bracelet—this time three short notes. I was safe.

"Your problem is that you're a big, smelly butt. That's your problem."

He turned on me, his fist jerking back, and he slammed it directly into my face. I tried my hardest not to flinch, but I don't think I was successful. At least I did not turn away. I held still and his fist collided with the plasma field, set to the highest protection.

I'd set the sparring room program into a cycle, but in order for it to work, it had had to shut down for several seconds, which is why I'd needed to delay him. Now I hoped to get Tamret out of the room before Ardov forced me to take advantage of the next phase of the program.

I gave Tamret my hand. Her grip was warm and soft and I liked how it felt. I pulled her to her feet, and she looked at me with gratitude and relief.

"Let's get out of here," I said.

"You two aren't going anywhere." Ardov positioned himself between us and the door. "I'll keep you here as long as I need to, and I'm willing to bet there's a way to hurt you, even with the force field turned up."

"We don't actually have to be enemies," I said, figuring I had nothing to lose by trying something crazy—not hating each other. "Come on, Ardov. We could just start over."

"No." He leaned back and then seemed to lift from the floor as he launched into a flying kick aimed directly at Tamret's middle. I tried to get in front of it, but there was no time. It connected, and though the plasma field flashed blue, Tamret let out a grunt of pain.

"Thought so," he said. "Even with the field on, it still hurts where I've already kicked you."

He'd kicked her in the stomach. I felt a buzzing in my head. Ardov had hurt Tamret. I could not think of anything else. My jaw was clenched, and my own fists were balled. Somewhere, beyond the buzzing in my head, Ardov was laughing, asking me what I planned to do about it.

Then my bracelet vibrated, indicating the next phase of the cycle, and suddenly it was all clear. I had three seconds, and I used them. Ardov was in the middle of a speech about how we were too weak to stop him, too afraid, too pathetic. That's when I hit him. I took him by surprise, pummeling him once in the nose with my fist. Maybe he would have reacted faster under other circumstances, but he thought the field was set to maximum. He might even have leaned into the blow contemptuously. In any case, I made full contact, and with the field completely down, he went reeling backward.

He cried out in pain, and put both his hands to his nose.

"That hurt!" he shouted, sounding nasal. And when he turned back to face us, I saw I had bloodied him. My hand hurt too. You don't see that in the movies, but it was painful to punch someone in the nose. I shook out my fingers and turned to Ardov, hoping he'd had enough.

It would be nice if when you hurt the bully, he turned out to be a coward—just like in all those books we read when we were younger. It usually doesn't work that way, though. It didn't work that way this time. Ardov rounded on me, but I stood my ground, and with the field back on high, his blow glanced off of me with some unpleasant pressure, but nothing more.

He stared at me, his expression slack and dumb.

Tamret took my hand again. Her eyes were cast down, and she hadn't said anything, but she knew I'd come for her, that I had been there for her, and we didn't need for there to be any words.

"Turns out I've got a few moves," I said.

"You're cheating!" he declared.

"Yes, Ardov," I agreed. "I'm cheating. It's a rigged game, and only I know the rules, and if that's how I keep you from beating up on Tamret, then I feel pretty good about cheating. So how about you step aside."

Tamret was still holding my hand, and she must have felt it when my data bracelet buzzed again, because she now looked up at me. "Oh," she said. "I get it."

She then turned and launched herself into a sideways kick, moving with more agility than an Olympic gymnast. She caught Ardov full in the face with her foot, and he went reeling backward, slammed into the wall, and fell on the floor.

Tamret walked over to Ardov, who was on all fours now, his head hanging low. He raised a hand a little bit off the floor. "No more. I've had enough," he said weakly.

"I'm not so sure." She raised her foot as if to kick him again.

"I promise," he said. "I'll leave you alone."

She paused. She now had no idea, of course, if her blows would land, but I didn't think she meant to hurt him anymore. She just needed him to believe otherwise.

"How do I know you'll keep your word?"

"I swear by [*the primary goddess of revenge*]!" He was

crying now. Actual tears were matting the fur on his face.

"Those are just words, and I know words mean nothing to someone like you. But I swear if you try to hurt me again, if you try to hurt anyone I care about, next time you will die. I swear it by [*the primary goddess of revenge*], and if you aren't willing to keep your word, you know I'll keep mine."

She raised her foot again, and he flinched. Maybe that was enough for her, because she smiled and turned away. She then took my hand. "I think we're done here," she said, and led me toward the door.

Once we were in the hall, she threw her arms around me and hugged me so hard it almost hurt. I didn't mind.

When she let go, she grinned at me. "That was really, really clever."

I shrugged like it was no big deal. In fact, I was maybe the proudest I'd ever been in my life. This was better than saving the *Dependable*. I didn't have to worry about the harm I'd done. Tamret was safe, and no one was seriously hurt. This was what victory felt like.

Tamret's eyes misted over, and I realized she had begun to cry. "I'm sorry, Zeke." She choked and stammered out the words.

"Why are you sorry?" I asked. I had no idea.

"I'm sorry I kept secrets from you." She pushed me away, and just like that she was done crying. She wiped her eyes with the back of her hand and took a deep breath. "Let's go out. I need to get out of here, get some fresh air, see the city."

"It's after curfew," I said.

"I just came within a breath of being killed. I don't really care about curfew. I have no idea what a [*milkshake*] is, but I plan to get one. Do you want me to go out by myself?"

I did not.

A quick search on my data bracelet had identified this as the closest eatery that served anything like a milkshake, and it was a pretty good approximation, though the flavors tended toward root vegetables, and gelatinous chunks bobbed in the glass like icebergs. The location almost made up for the floating chunks. The restaurant was on the roof of a midsize building toward the station's center, so all around us was the city, with its buildings and lights and wonders spread out almost to the horizon. Above us, three of the gas giant's variously colored moons shone bright through the dome. There was a low, whining music playing, like mosquitoes buzzing to an irregular and unpredictable beat, and there were other tables with other couples. They were at their tables, and we were at ours, and all of Confederation Central was lit up in every direction and the stars were blazing above us and shuttles with their flashing lights darted through the sky.

Tamret's jaw was a little swollen, though the nanites were hard at work to minimize the damage. My hand, too, was already feeling better, and I was still nearly dizzy with relief. When I'd first set foot into the control room, I'd been so afraid that I would fail her, that I would have to stand by helplessly while Ardov hurt her, but instead I'd saved her with my button pushing. Now here we were, overlooking all this beauty, all this wonder. I did not imagine it was possible to be happier and more content than I felt at that moment.

"Why does he hate you so much?" I asked.

"Well, now he hates me because he thinks I've been messing

with his account and keeping him from gaining experience."

"Have you?"

She laughed and shook her head, and her hair fell forward and danced around her face. She whisked it away and looked up at me. "Don't be silly, Zeke. Of course I have."

I leaned forward. "Are you out of your mind? You are going to get yourself kicked out."

"They'd have to catch me first, so I think I'm okay. Their security amounts to a sign saying 'Please don't break our rules.'"

"I thought hacking the skill system wasn't even possible."

"For Confederation citizens," she said with a wicked smile. "For Ardov, the security was a little more lax."

"I don't believe this. Are you some kind of compulsive criminal?"

"You're talking like your chaperone, Ms. Price," Tamret said. "You know she wants me to stay away from you, right?"

"Did she tell you that?" I felt my whole body tense. Was Ms. Price going around trying to ruin my friendships behind my back?

"She said it was for the good of your planet, that I was getting in the way of your making friends with your own kind. She said that you were only friends with me and Steve because the other humans didn't want you."

"You don't believe that, do you?" My voice broke somewhat embarrassingly, but I hoped it would get lost in translation.

"Well," Tamret said airily, clearly wanting to tease me now, "I see how you look at the others in your delegation."

"Tamret!"

"Back to the story. I was talking about how I tinkered with Ardov's experience points."

I tried to put Ms. Price's meddling out of my mind. "Which you should not have been doing! They caught you before, and this is even more serious. You know how they are about the point system."

"And would you really care if they kicked me out?" she asked.

I could not answer that. Not truthfully. I couldn't let her know how much I would care. I couldn't tell her that if I hadn't been fighting for my mother's life, I would rather be kicked out myself than have to stay here without her. "Why was he harassing you? Why did you put up with him bossing you around?"

"Because he can," she said. "I don't belong to a caste, Zeke. Not anymore, and that means I have to obey the leader of the highest caste in my community. That's Ardov. According to our law, I have to do what he says, provided he doesn't tell me to hurt or degrade myself or others. If I don't obey him, I'll be arrested as soon as I get home, regardless of how well I do here. I pretended it doesn't bother me, because that was the only defense I had."

I didn't know anything about the caste system in her culture. She had never wanted to talk about it before, and I wasn't about to start asking her to explain it. I felt like I understood the main points, even if I didn't know how she had ended up in such a vulnerable position.

"And 'snowflake,' since you are so clueless, is an insult. Maybe you noticed no one else in our delegation has my coloring."

"No one else in my delegation has mine," I said.

She scrunched up her face. "I guess. Now that you mention it."

It was crazy that differences in skin color had caused so

much misery and pain on my world, yet to Tamret the range from Charles's dark brown to my sunless pink was hardly noticeable.

"Is white, uh, fur so unusual? Is it an ethnic thing?"

"No." She shook her head. "It's a recessive trait. Maybe five percent of the population is born looking like this. In some cultures we're actually considered good luck, if you can believe it." She brushed hair away from her face, but then let it fall back, obscuring her eyes. "Not my culture. We aren't treated kindly. And Ardov is from a well-connected family with a lot of relatives in the leadership caste. He considered my being part of the delegation an insult to him and his family. That's why he acted the way he did. So I pretended not to care, and the first chance I had, I messed with him by hacking his account. But it got out of hand. Which is what you saw when you were spying on me."

"I wasn't spying," I said, feeling myself blush. "When I saw you two together in the hall tonight, I had a bad feeling. I thought I should check it out."

"I know. I'm sorry I didn't talk to you about this before. I was, I don't know, embarrassed, I guess." She put a hand on mine. "I won't forget what you did for me. Anything you need. Anytime. Any reason. You name it."

"You don't have to thank me," I said, feeling my face burn. "I'm your friend."

"I know you are, and I know what it means." She took a long drink. "My father worked for the housing authority in our city-state. When I was eight, the real estate market pretty much collapsed. There were a lot of reasons, I guess—the economy and all that. I don't really understand it, but I know it wasn't any one person's fault, but they needed people to blame. One of those people was my father. He'd never done anything but serve as he had been asked to serve, but they arrested him. I still don't know if he was killed or sent to a gulag."

"I'm sorry." It was a pathetic thing to say, but there was nothing else.

"He and my mother married pretty young. And she was so in love with him." She smiled when she said this and looked off, like she was remembering something. "It was embarrassing to me, you know, to see how much they loved each other. Holding hands and kissing all the time. And when they took my father away, she couldn't accept it, you know? People who disappear like my father don't come back, not ever, but my mother wrote letters and spoke at civic meetings. I didn't know anything about how things worked, but I knew she was making a mistake. I wanted to tell her that he was gone. She couldn't get him back, and she had a daughter, a *snowflake* daughter, who needed her, but I couldn't say it, because I wanted him back too, and because I didn't want to face what I knew was true: I wasn't enough for her. If he was gone, then I wasn't reason enough for her to live."

"Tamret," I said. "You don't have to tell me this."

"Yes, I do. You need to understand." She paused for a moment, her eyes distant. "So, no surprise, they took her. When she was arrested, I became an orphan according to our laws. I lost my parents' status and caste. And because she held our housing permit, I had to leave our home. She was dead or in a gulag—I didn't know—and I had nowhere to live and nothing to eat. Children without parents don't exist, and I was a snowflake, so there was no one lower than I was. Things were going to end up very bad for me."

She was crying now, the silent tears streaming from her eyes. I took her hand and she squeezed it.

"My friends let me live with them," she said. "Some of them had parents who were sympathetic, and they were kind to me. But I couldn't stay with one family too long, because of the risk. Sometimes I had to hide in basements and closets and under floorboards when people were home. I lived that way for three years, and I knew that I was never going to be anything but a burden to the people I cared about unless I could figure out a way to change things. Little things. Secret things. I learned my way around computer systems so I could shift things around, help the people who were helping me. And when the government started cracking down on dissident kids, and some of my friends got caught in the net, I was not going to let them rot behind bars or face the silencing squads without at least trying to help them. But I got caught. My government is a lot more worried about security than they are here. Anyhow, that's why I was in prison when Dr. Roop came for us."

She wiped at her face and sniffed and seemed to will herself to stop crying. And like that, she was done. "I wouldn't still be alive without friends, so please understand that my friends are everything to me. Then I left the friends I had behind. I came here in a ship with three Rarels who hate me. I was all alone, and then I met Steve." She grinned. "When I first saw him, I thought he was a terrifying monster, and then he opened his mouth, and about ten minutes later he was like the best friend I'd ever had."

I nodded. "I know exactly what you mean."

"And then you," she said, her eyes cast downward.

"And then me."

"This is an amazing place," she said. "These Confederation types are the most wonderful creatures, but I think maybe you and your green data collector are right. We've been brought here for some reason, and I know that things aren't going to be calm forever. But I have my friends, and if you and me and Steve stick together, I think we are going to be okay."

We didn't talk on the train back to the government compound. We didn't need to say anything. We sat in our seats, swaying with the movement, looking out the window, feeling the alien and comforting warmth of each other's presence.

I walked her to her room, and we stood in the hall outside her door in the dim night-cycle light. She took both my hands in both of hers. "This was a good night," she said. "You rescued me."

"I pushed some buttons."

"You rescued me," she said again, smiling shyly, turning away just a little.

Tamret was clever and wild and a little frightening—maybe more than a little frightening. I felt like I could spend a day, a week, doing nothing but watching her, looking at her fur, her ears, her face, thinking about how it was like and unlike a human's. I was fascinated by her, and there was no point in pretending otherwise, but was that enough? Could I just like her and admire her and want to be with her without wanting to change the way things were?

Then I thought that the time was running out. We'd started with a year, but the days and weeks would slip away. What if she liked me too? Did I really want, years from now, to look back and think about what I should have done if only I hadn't been afraid to risk—what? Feelings? Discomfort? I'd destroyed a starship, and I'd defeated a bully with ten times my strength. Was I really too scared to tell a girl I liked her?

"Tamret," I said.

Her eyes locked on mine.

"Oi!" Steve shouted. He was hurrying down the hallway, cinching his bathrobe. "I just got your message, mate."

I couldn't quite keep the irritation out of my voice. "What, the one that said, 'Help! Come right now!' that I sent like three hours ago?"

"I'm a deep sleeper. It's the Ish-hi way. Everything all right, then?"

"It is now," Tamret told him. "Zeke saved me."

"I helped her out a little," I said.

"By saving me," she said.

"So," he mused, "all this waking me up was for nothing, then?"

"No, not for nothing." She now took Steve's hands in hers. Just the way she had held mine. "I'm glad you showed up. Eventually. After everything was all over. But you showed up because you're my friend."

"Right," he said. "All right, then. Looks like there's nothing left but the talking, so I'm going back to bed."

Tamret let go of Steve and opened her door. She slipped partway into the darkness. "Good night, boys."

Boys. The two of us. Equal. I was such an idiot.

I watched as she shut the door, and I thought of everything I wished I had said. I wished I had told her how I felt, though I wasn't sure that even I knew. I wanted to tell her that I was there for her. I was her friend. Anything she needed. Anytime. I wished I had told her, but I'd waited too long.

CHAPTER TWENTY

I slept little that night, replaying the fight with Ardov in my head. And going out with Tamret. That too. I felt like I was examining every word of our conversation, reading it like it was all in code and I had to decipher it. I remembered everything I said, and I cringed, thinking of a thousand ways I could have said it better, made myself seem cooler or more interesting.

Just after dawn, a knock at the door interrupted my sleeplessness. Charles was curled up on his bed, and he stirred a little. I was awake, and hoping maybe it was Tamret.

It wasn't Tamret. It was Dr. Roop.

He was fully dressed and had the gravest expression I'd ever seen on a giraffe creature. "I must speak with you."

I went back in, threw on some jeans and a T-shirt, and followed him to his office. He sat in his chair at the other side of his desk and looked at me with huge dark eyes. "Do you have something you want to tell me?"

At this point there was probably a whole lot more I didn't want to tell him, so I figured I'd play this as smoothly as possible. "Not really," I said. Very deft.

He sighed and lowered his long neck. Then he pointed in the general direction of his snout. "Do I appear to be foolish in your eyes?"

"Not as such," I said, but I was still not sure what he was

getting at. He could be talking about the incident in the sparring room or about leaving the compound after curfew. Maybe I was forgetting something. I was breaking the rules with such regularity that I was having trouble keeping up with myself.

"Ardov spent much of the night in the medical facility," Dr. Roop said. "He claims he was in the sparring room, and he set the parameters too high with the sims."

Oh, right. The cringing and wounded Ardov. I had forgotten all about him because I was too busy trying to figure out how to talk about my feelings with an alien neko.

I thought I might as well do something that wasn't entirely pathetic. I told Dr. Roop the truth. "That's not what happened."

"I *know* that is not what happened," Dr. Roop said, "because I reviewed the log images."

"What was I supposed to do?" I demanded. "Let him hurt Tamret?"

"Of course helping Tamret was the right thing to do, but I don't understand why you didn't message me. You may recall that talk we had? You were supposed to trust me."

At the time it had never occurred to me to call Dr. Roop, but now that was kind of hard to explain. "Things were kind of crazy. I needed to do something, not wait."

"I am familiar with the concept of the 'snitch,'" he said. "But Ardov was hurting another delegate. Then you left him alone, without calling for medical attention, after you knew he'd been hurt."

"Am I in trouble?"

"Right now, your infractions are the least of my problems. As for Ardov, there is no way to banish him without destroying the Rarel delegation's chances. I've had a long talk with him to make sure he understands the consequences of his actions, but he doesn't strike me as the sort of being who is overly concerned with consequences." He rubbed at his horns with one hand. "The selection committee really left me quite a mess."

"I'm sorry," I said. "You've been a good friend, and I've made your life more difficult."

"Next time, come to me with anything," he said. "I'm on your side, Zeke." He waved me off with one hand. I was halfway out the door when he said, "Oh, and please try not to break curfew again. If you don't mind."

Ardov didn't come to class that morning, but Steve and Tamret and I passed him in the hall that evening when we were heading out for dinner. The healing facility had done its work, and he showed no sign of the beating he'd taken.

He paused, looked at Tamret, and made some weird spiraling gesture with his hands. "I have treated you badly. I beg your forgiveness." There was no sign of sarcasm or hostility in his voice. Was it possible that Dr. Roop had actually scared him into reforming himself? Yes, there was a chance, but there was an even better chance that he was simply waiting for the opportunity to strike at us.

The three of us had booked time in the ship simulation suite for the next night, but when we got there, Charles, Nayana, and Mi Sun were just showing up as well. Charles, I noted, had finally risen to level ten.

"Look." Steve pointed at them. "The primates are here."

"Hey!" I said.

"You're one of the good ones," he told me.

"There's no need to be uncivil," Charles told Steve.

"We only have the suite for two hours," Mi Sun said. "Let's not waste our time bickering with the randoms."

Tamret put her hands on her waist. "Good call. You should use your time trying to learn how to operate a ship instead. For all the good it will do you."

"You cannot intimidate us," Charles said, gesturing toward the number ten floating above his head. "You enjoy name calling, but there's not one of you above level nine."

"Have you ever considered that we simply haven't leveled our points yet?" Tamret asked.

"I don't see why you would do that."

Tamret smirked, like she had a secret. "You never know."

"What I know," said Nayana, "is that the three of you are never going to catch up, so the normal delegates have to pick up the slack."

I held up my hands in a *we come in peace* gesture. "We're all just trying to do what's right for our planets," I said. "I know none of this is personal. We all want our delegations to get our eighty levels. I know you think leaving me out is the best way to do it. I don't agree, but I understand it. So how about we end hostilities?"

"He's trying to keep us out of the simulation," said Nayana. "He figures if we keep talking, we'll lose our reservation."

"He's trying to be friendly," Tamret said. "If you weren't so stuck up, you'd see that."

"Put your animal on a leash," Nayana snapped.

"Hold on," I said, stepping forward. "That's not cool."

"Then tell her to stop meowing at me." Nayana sniffed and turned up her chin.

"How about we settle our differences in the simulation room?" Mi Sun suggested. "We'll square off in a battle sequence, and we'll see who is victorious."

"What are we playing for?" Nayana asked. "This needs to be worth my while."

"Honor?" Steve suggested. "Let me know if your universal translator got that one. I know it may be a tough concept for your species."

"Steve, you do know I am one of them, right?"

"Just go with it," he said.

"You're so eager to take us on," Nayana said, "because you've got Zeke. He's the only one of you who's worth anything. You'd never dare to take us on if he came over to our side."

"We'd be down a man, wouldn't we?" Steve said.

"Then how about me and Zeke against the two of you?" Nayana proposed.

For an instant I liked the idea. It wasn't that I wanted to go up against Steve and Tamret; I had nothing to prove by taking them on, and I didn't want to beat them or be beaten by them. But suddenly Nayana wanted me on her team. I had a chance to be with my own kind, to prove once and for all that I was a valuable member of the delegation.

Then reality set in. No matter what happened, I was never going to be one of them. It was wishful thinking to believe otherwise. "No way," I said.

I looked over at Tamret. Her eyes were narrowed and her jaw was set. She had seen my moment of indecision. She had seen that I'd been tempted to throw them over and run back to my own species. "I see Ms. Price was right about you," Tamret said quietly.

"No, she wasn't," I told her. I then turned to Nayana. "Me and my friends against you and your acquaintances."

"That works for me," Nayana said. "We'll use artifact carriers. And the winner gets all the experience points. The loser gets docked an equal amount."

"Winner take all is fine," I said, "but you can't take someone else's points."

"The kitty cat knows how," Nayana sneered. "Ardov told me that she was siphoning off his points, which means she can tinker with the system. So let's play with real stakes."

"Works for me." Tamret folded her arms across her chest and glared at Nayana. "The winning team splits the points between them. The losing team gets an equal penalty."

"Forget it," I told her. "You are not doing that. You'll get caught, and then you're out of here. That doesn't help you or the Rarels. It's not worth it."

"I won't get caught," she said. "And your human friends have to promise not to tell."

"You can't trust them," I said. "We're a totally untrustworthy species."

"I guess you are," Tamret said, glaring at me, "but I'll take my chances."

"This is not necessary," Charles said. "It is dishonest, and I don't wish to see anyone get into trouble."

"I don't see why this is worth breaking the rules," Mi Sun agreed.

"We're doing it," Nayana said. "I want to put these losers in their place once and for all."

Everyone was against this except Tamret and Nayana, and yet somehow we were all going ahead with it.

. . .

We went into our suites and synched our systems, which would drop us on opposite sides of a gas giant orbited by twelve moons, which ranged in size from a large asteroid to atmosphered worlds larger than the Earth. Both teams were to be in artifact carriers—so called because they were often used to whisk Former artifacts away to safety as soon as they were discovered. These vessels were not much larger than transport shuttles, built for speed and defense. They were reasonably well armed and had powerful shielding and tunnel drives. Most importantly, they could easily be manned by three beings.

It was never in doubt that Steve would take command. He had defeated Nayana before, and we were counting on him to do it again. He also took the helm position. I was on his right, operating the weapons console. Tamret, on his left, was running navigation and comm. Once the sim kicked in and our HUDs created the illusion of being on a real artifact carrier, we were spaced a little farther apart, but I was happy to see our positions remained more or less the same, particularly since I was not next to Tamret. She was still angry I'd considered Nayana's offer, if only for a second.

As soon as we dropped in, Steve worked the console and angled us up hard as he hit the throttle. I felt a slight pressure as the inertial compensators kicked in, knowing they were the only reason we were not jelly on the backs of our seats—or would be if this were real rather than simulated. Steve then turned us hard to port and gave it more speed. "I love how these things handle," he said dreamily. I had a sudden and clear vision of Steve the reptilian car thief.

"Oh, and check for the enemy," he said as he dipped suddenly downward, moving us dangerously close to an ice moon's gravity well.

"Let's see where they're hiding," Tamret said as she worked her console, searching for Nayana's ship.

"You want to take it easy?" I said as Steve suddenly banked hard to port. "I'm not going to be much use to you if I'm puking."

"I'm sure even puking you can thump those tossers," he said, and then pulled up fast at an uncomfortably steep angle.

"Found them," Tamret said. "Sending coordinates to your consoles."

An outline image came up at once of Nayana's ship, which was still a good fifteen thousand miles distant. We were down near the gas giant's south pole; they were circling above the north.

"If we see them, they see us," I said. I checked my data bracelet. "The clock's ticking, and if this ends up a tie, it will be a waste of time for everyone."

"Right," Steve said. "Tamret, can you check that sun for unusual activity?"

"Sure." Then, after a minute, she said, "Yeah, this star is really flaring. How'd you know?"

"Thought I recognized that planet," Steve said. "I ran this exact sim with Dr. Roop a few days ago. He showed me a little trick. How long until the next radiation spike?"

"Two minutes, seventeen seconds," she said.

"Zeke, have we got missiles?"

"No," I said. "They're not standard on artifact carriers. This ship is made for speed and safety, not fighting back."

"Too bad," he said. "Maybe this won't work." He smacked the console. "Except it will if we have a plasma lance."

I checked. "Yeah, but it's designed for minimal cabling. Six miles in vacuum."

"Not nearly enough," he said.

"Enough for what?"

"Hold on," Steve said, ignoring me. "You know how the cables on plasma lances work, right?"

"Sure," I said. I'd tried to learn as much as I could about ship weaponry after being branded a war criminal and all. "It's some kind of quantum effect. They convert the ambient atoms floating in space into solid matter."

"If we were on a physical surface, like one of these moons, would we be able to produce more than six miles of cable?"

I checked the calculations. "Yeah," I said. "With enough engine power, we could produce hundreds of miles of cable, no problem."

"We won't need hundreds, but we'll need quite a bit," he said. "Here's my idea. We're going to go to the far side of that icy moon here, and the instant the solar energy spikes, we're going to drop straight down. With a little luck, the radiation will conceal us, and to them we'll have simply vanished. They'll likely need a minute or so to figure out what we've done, but by then we'll be on the moon's surface, and we'll have cut power."

"If we cut power, we'll die," I noted.

"Not really, because this is a simulation suite, not an airless moon," he said with a grin. "Anyhow, we should have at least enough breathable air in this ship to last an hour, so the sim won't declare us dead."

"Nayana may not be as smart as she thinks she is," Tamret said, "but even she can figure out that if we drop off sensors as we pass a moon, we're probably on that moon. She'll come looking for us."

"She'd better," Steve said. "Otherwise this plan is total pants."

"Wouldn't want that," I mumbled.

We positioned ourselves so that the moon was between us and Nayana, and when Tamret signaled the crest of the radiation wave, Steve pointed us toward the surface and throttled hard.

The nanites must have been messing with my brain chemistry, because my stomach felt like it was coming out my nose, and my eyes were being pushed into my brain. It was horrible, and I had no doubt that if we were trying this in real life, it would be a whole lot worse.

We dropped like a stone toward the blue menthol surface, and then, with lightning reflexes, Steve leveled us. I felt another violent, nauseating jerk, and he must have felt it too, but he remained calm and in control. He carefully set us down, and he killed the ship's power.

We were in complete darkness. Pure blackness. I sat there, listening to the three of us breathe.

"Here's a question," I said, keeping my voice low as if somehow Nayana and the others might hear me. "How are we going to know when they're in lance range if we have no power?"

Steve, I couldn't help but notice, did not answer.

"You do have a plan, right?" Tamret asked. "Because if I have to kill you, I'm going to feel bad about myself."

"Why is it I have to think of everything?" he asked.

"Oh, my glob!" I shouted. "You just lost this for us."

"This plan," Tamret observed, "is total pants."

"Look at it this way," Steve said. "At worst it will be a tie. They'll never find us."

We were silent for a few minutes. I was irritated, not really angry. Steve's plan had been good up to this point. The problem was that there was no way to track Nayana's ship. If only we had some means of following their movements that wouldn't register on their sensors.

Except we had exactly that.

"Okay, guys," I said. "How do you feel about working maybe a little bit outside the rules?"

"Cheating? I feel fine," Tamret said.

"Prefer it, if you want to know the truth," Steve said.

I turned on my data bracelet. "You can follow the sim from an outside channel, right? We saw Ms. Price doing it. So, we'll be spectators." I found the sim and called up a three-dimensional representation of the contest. There we were, on the surface of the moon. And there was Nayana, making her way toward us.

"Brilliant," Steve said. "As soon as they're in range, we power up."

Suddenly I felt bad about bending the rules. "I know it was my idea, but maybe we shouldn't do this. When you think about it, it's not really fair."

"Sure it is. We're using the resources we have available." I could tell from Tamret's voice that she was grinning.

"Absolutely," Steve agreed. "Besides, she's welcome to use her bracelet, same as us. Nothing unfair about it."

"Except she's hunting for us with her ship's sensors, not her bracelet," I said.

"Her mistake," Steve said. "Let's wait until she's about thirty miles out, and then we'll power up and strike."

"I love this!" Tamret shouted. "We're going to totally destroy her."

We sat there for ten minutes, watching Nayana's slow

progress on a three-dimensional grid projected from Steve's bracelet. She was being thorough, performing slow and deep scans, but she was circling slowly into our range. A couple of times she tried to send messages to us, as if we would forget we were hiding and answer. I suppose I couldn't fault her for trying.

"She should be within thirty miles in less than thirty seconds," Tamret said.

"Let's wait for twenty, just to be safe," Steve told me. "I'd hate to get this close and blow it because the cable isn't up to spec."

We waited until she was within range and powered up the ship. The lights turned on, and our consoles chimed as they instantly came to life. I went to work, and it took me another twenty seconds, which felt endless, to get a confident lock on her ship. There was no messing around here. We had one chance to get this right.

I found my target, locked it in, and fired.

The plasma lance is incredible technology. Both the lance and the cable itself are made entirely out of ionized particles, the lance composed essentially from the same stuff as lightning. In space, where there is no sound, it would make no noise, but the moon had some kind of unbeatable atmosphere, and we set off a deafening sonic boom as the lance flew free.

As soon as the forward tip of the lance came in contact with the energy shields surrounding Nayana's ship, it sensed the resistance, and its own nanoparticles instantly began to restructure its atomic makeup, deionizing and turning the lance and its cable into a superstrong metal alloy. It passed effortlessly through the shields and affixed itself to their hull, bonding with the metal so that there was, for all practical purposes, no way to detect where the hull ended and the lance began.

Meanwhile the nanoparticles were generating gravitons that caused Nayana's ship to be drawn to ours, as if caught in a gravity well. Nayana could not pull away. She could only resist or be pulled down to the planet's surface. She chose to resist, and her ship came to a full stop.

The technology was powerful, but it had its limitations. All Nayana had to do now was reconfigure her shields, just for a moment, to protect against physical impacts. The cable would then be severed on the atomic level. That was precisely what she did. The cable fell away.

That was the moment our victory was assured, because I'd been waiting for her to switch shield frequencies, and the instant she did, I unleashed a steady stream of PPB bursts. She had been at full stop, and we were at full stop, so her systems were easy to target. My first blast took out her shields. Then I took out her engines, and then the weapons. In a matter of seconds, she was dead in space, drifting and powerless to defend herself.

Nayana signaled us, and Tamret put her on speaker. "Fine," she said. "We surrender. Whatever."

Before Steve could say anything, Tamret stepped around to my console, and began to fire PPB blasts. Her fingertip danced happily on the console, sending out blast after blast, until Nayana's ship exploded.

"Hey!" Nayana shouted over the comm.

"Even when she's dead," Tamret said, "she won't stop talking."

"You cheated," Nayana said as we met out in the hallway. She had her data bracelet streaming three-dimensional data. Clearly, she was smart enough to figure out how we had pulled it off.

"We didn't cheat," I told her. "We won."

"You went outside the sim to monitor us," Nayana said. "This is supposed to simulate real-world conditions. In the real world, you can't go outside reality to watch your enemy."

"In the real world," Steve observed, "you use whatever you can to defeat your opponent. And we did."

"Just admit we won," Tamret said.

"You didn't win honestly," Nayana snapped.

"There is no honest," Tamret said. "You either get the enemy or the enemy gets you."

"There are rules of engagement," Mi Sun said, "and you violated them. I know your boyfriend likes to just shoot things out of the sky, but that's not how we do things in the Confederation."

"Someone is all high and mighty," Tamret said. I noticed she was not denying I was her boyfriend, and I wondered if that meant anything, but it seemed like a bad time to raise this question. "Tell me how many points you racked up in there so I can relieve you of them."

"I refuse," Nayana said, folding her arms. "And I am disappointed with you, Zeke, betraying your own kind for these aliens."

"His own kind who won't have anything to do with him?" Tamret asked.

"I'm not going to argue with an animal." Nayana lifted her chin imperiously. "And I am absolutely not giving you any experience points. If you try to take them, I won't hesitate to report you."

"We did promise," Charles said.

"I didn't promise to be cheated."

"It does seem like a bad idea to take Earth experience

points and hand them over to another planet," Mi Sun said.

"Except that you lot agreed to it," Steve said. "Not quite cricket to back out now, seeing as you suggested this wager in the first place."

"And now I'm suggesting you forget it," Nayana said.

Tamret stepped forward. I knew that look, and it meant nothing good. "You cheating she-[*pig*]."

"At least I don't look like I pee in a litter box," Nayana answered.

I wedged myself between them. "This bet was a bad idea to begin with, so why don't we move on. We played the game, we learned some things, and we all got XP. Everyone wins."

Tamret's ears shot back. "I don't believe this. You're taking her side."

"I am not taking her side," I said. "I'm taking *your* side. I don't want you to get caught doing something that will ruin everything for you."

"You're not thinking about me. You're too busy trying to win over the people who treat you like dirt to worry about your real friends."

"That is not true," I told her.

"I'm so done," Nayana said. "You two can have your little master-pet argument on your own time."

She headed toward the door, and Charles and Mi Sun followed.

The three of us stood there, me feeling ashamed and angry and nervous from the adrenaline and hormones and who knew what else bouncing around in my system. Tamret seemed to be firing on pure rage. Steve tasted the air, and I could tell he didn't like what he was getting.

"Yours are emotional species," he said.

Tamret growled and actually stomped her foot. "How's this for emotion? I hate her. I don't care if I get in trouble. I am going to get even with her."

"Tamret, please don't. Just leave it alone." I knew I was in dangerous territory, but I couldn't let her self-destruct. "Just give yourself a day to cool off. See how you feel tomorrow."

She stared at me, her disbelief hard to miss. "You really would drop me to get back in with your delegation, wouldn't you? That's why you're trying to protect Nayana."

"I'm trying to protect *you*. I don't see why you don't get that."

"I don't get it because the second she crooked her finger at you, you went running." She pulled open the door to the hall so hard I thought it might come off the hinges. And then she was gone.

Steve put a hand on my shoulder. "I want you to know," he said, "that I still love you, mate."

Steve and I went out for a snack, but I can't say I enjoyed myself. I was distracted by what had happened with Tamret, upset that she was so angry with me, and mildly heartened that she seemed to be jealous of Nayana. I was also worried. I hated how ready she had been to hack into secure Confederation files with an enemy's full knowledge. The thought that she might get caught, might get kicked off the station, filled me with dread. She represented a full third of the beings I fully trusted on the station, and as much as I liked Steve and Dr. Roop, I had never held hands with either of them and, frankly, never intended to.

Steve and I called it quits shortly before curfew. I dropped him off at his room and was heading down the hall to my own, hoping that Charles would be either asleep or, preferably, still out, when I saw Ms. Price coming toward me.

"Well, look who it is," she said, flashing an unexpected smile at me. "Ezekiel Reynolds, scourge of the Phandic Empire. The Butcher of Ganar. Destroyer of worlds."

"Uh, hey there." I said.

"You're up kind of late, aren't you?" she asked.

There was something about her mood that I couldn't quite make sense of. She was upbeat, but it didn't feel natural to me, like she was trying to convince me, all of a sudden, that she was my buddy.

I shrugged. "I was just hanging out with—" I stopped myself. She didn't want me hanging out with Steve.

"I know who you're spending time with." She shook her head, not quite able to fathom my foolishness. "I recall telling you to spend less time with those aliens."

"I don't see the humans lining up to hang out with me," I said.

"Hmm." She put a finger theatrically to her chin, pantomiming contemplation. "Maybe we should do something about that."

Or maybe we should run away screaming, I thought. I said, "Sure. I guess."

"What do you say I take you out for a bite to eat. I think you and I have a great deal to discuss. You have this idea that I'm not looking out for you, and I suppose I can see things from your perspective, so in the best interests of our delegation and our planet, maybe we should get to know each other better. There's this place that serves amazing plant sushi in Nebula Heights. You know that neighborhood?"

I checked the chronometer on my data bracelet, hoping the time would get me out of this conversation. "It's like five minutes before curfew."

She waved her hand. "You don't need to worry about that if you're with me."

I didn't know if that was true or not, but I had the strangest feeling that it wasn't, and that Ms. Price was trying to get me into trouble. Not that it mattered. Even if I was entirely sure she was right and I was allowed to go out and have vegetable sushi with her, the last thing I wanted to do was make conversation with her in the middle of the night in a strange part of the city about how I needed to abandon my friends.

"You know, I'm really tired," I told her. "Maybe another time."

"Of course." She smiled with all the warmth of a vampire. "I think it's time for the two of us to become friends. To trust each other."

I felt sure that was never going to happen. "Okay," I managed to say. "You betcha."

"I look forward to it." She put out her hand. "Friends?"

I wanted to walk away, to tell her I did not trust her and I never would. She'd proven she was my enemy, and now she was trying to separate me from the beings I most cared about on the station. I was never going to trust her, but I could not tell her so.

"Sure," I managed, and I shook her hand, which was colder than Steve's reptilian grip.

She seemed pleased with herself. "Good night."

I stood there, in shock, watching her walk away and disappear into her room. What had that been all about? Why was she suddenly trying to get me to trust her? I had no idea how I could make sense of it, but I knew I didn't believe it.

I sighed and then turned in the other direction, and there—close enough to have seen everything but far enough away not to have heard a word of it—was Tamret. The universe had taken the time and trouble to position her in exactly the spot where she could most effectively misread what had transpired between me and Ms. Price. Tamret's eyes were wide with disbelief or anger or confusion. She had seen me shaking hands with Ms. Price, my enemy and hers. I was once again, in Tamret's eyes, putting the members of my own species first and being chummy with the woman who wanted me to avoid the other randoms.

"Tamret," I started to say, but her name caught in my throat and came out like a cough.

She turned and ran in the other direction.

I hurried after her, but by the time I reached the main junction, she was long gone, so I went back to my room before any more insanity could track me down.

CHAPTER TWENTY-ONE

I wanted to hide from everyone and everything, but since that wasn't really an option, I hid from everyone and everything until after breakfast and then went off to the classroom. I showed up exactly on time, hoping the others would already be inside and seated so I could avoid conversation, but Ms. Price was waiting for me outside.

"Good morning, Zeke." Her smiled was crooked and almost endearing in a reptilian sort of way. No, I take that back. Steve was endearing in a reptilian sort of way. Ms. Price was something else. I would settle for insectoid—at least until I had an insect friend.

"Hey," I said, dazzling her with my linguistic charm.

I tried to walk past her, but she stood in front of the door. "I'm glad we had a chance to talk last night. I want to be sure you understand that I have a job to do, Zeke, and it isn't always easy."

"I get it," I said, cutting her off. I didn't want to hear her speeches. "You think I'm swell, but you don't want me having friends. Oh, and if it should prove to be in the best interests of the planet Earth to ship me off to be tortured and killed, you'll be first in line with the packing tape."

"Not first in line," she said.

"You big softie," I said, and made my way into the classroom.

• • •

Things with Tamret were not so easily resolved. She barely looked at me during class, and she sat with me and Steve for lunch, but she didn't say more than three words. Steve, somewhat oblivious to mammalian moods, talked cheerfully about our victory over the other humans the night before.

After she finished picking at her food, Tamret excused herself and began to walk away. I hurried after her. "I want to talk to you about what you saw, or what you think you saw, last night. Ms. Price and I aren't friends. She just kind of came up to me."

She did not slow her pace. She may have quickened it. "It's not my business what you do with the members of your own species. I know how important they are to you."

I put a hand on Tamret's arm, and she shrugged me off, but at least she stopped. "I get that it looked like we were being all chummy, but we weren't."

"I'll tell you what it looked like," Tamret said. "It looked like there is no amount of abuse you won't take from someone as long as they come from your own world. That woman wants nothing more than to throw you to the Phands, and she wants to keep you away from the only beings who care what happens to you. But even after all that, you're still trying to get on her good side."

"I was not," I insisted. "I don't want anything to do with her."

"And what about Nayana, who's so beautiful? Are you still ready to run off with her?"

"You asked me if she was pretty for our species, and I told you. But so what? Some people are pretty, but I still don't like her, because she's unpleasant."

"*I'm* unpleasant!" she snapped.

"Not to me, you're not," I said quietly.

That seemed to have some effect on her. She lowered her defenses, if only slightly.

"I like you, Tamret," I told her. I wasn't admitting to anything, but I was still saying I liked her, and that admission made the rest of it somehow easier. The words just came out of my mouth before I could stop them. "I don't know how to be any clearer about it. I don't know why you're so angry with me."

She took a step back, and she looked sad, which was not the reaction I'd been hoping for. "I don't think you know what you feel. What I do know is this—you never miss a chance to try and get closer to the people who treat you like you're garbage. You are so desperate to belong with them that you don't care how they treat you or how they treat us."

"Of course I care, but you don't understand what it's like to be totally shut out."

"Don't I?" she asked.

Okay, that was stupid. "Maybe," I attempted, "it's not the same with your kind, but human beings are social creatures. On my world, cats don't live in groups, so maybe—"

Her eyes went wide, and I could see that the word "cat" had produced some kind of unflattering translation. "Is that what I am to you? Some kind of domesticated animal?"

"That's not what I'm saying. It's just that we need to be part of a group, and I don't think it's so terrible that I want to be part of my group."

She took a step back, like she didn't trust herself not to hurt me. Her jaw jutted out, her whiskers twitched, and her eyes tightened to narrow little slits. "That's your problem, Zeke. That's why I'm so angry with you. You *are* part of a group. Steve and I are your group, but to you it's just a temporary arrangement until the beings from your planet take you back."

"That's not true," I said, but I wasn't sure now. Was she right? Would I have dropped the randoms if the rest of the humans had invited me in? Would I have lost interest in Tamret if Nayana had liked me? I honestly didn't know how I would have felt in that first week on the station, but now things were different. There was no way I could ever imagine choosing to spend time with the other humans over Steve and Tamret, who had proved themselves the best friends I'd ever had. I knew that was true, but I wished the other humans would accept me as one of them. I didn't want to choose one group over the other. I didn't want to be rejected by any of them.

I was certain that was how I felt, but Tamret had seen my face, my moment of indecision. She was walking away, and once again, I wanted to go after her but there was nothing I could say that would make a bit of difference.

Over the next few days, I continued to log as many hours as I could in the flight sims and the game room. I knew that Tamret was also spending time in the computer lab, working on programming and, I hoped, nothing illegal. I continued to gain XP, and now had enough points to move up to level thirteen, though I kept myself at level nine so I wouldn't freak out the other humans, who were all tens. I was tempted to put points in strength, but I stuck with the starship-pilot track and continued with agility, intellect, and vision, with a couple of points in health. Steve and Tamret were also at nines, but I knew Steve was an actual twelve, well above the rest of the Ish-hi. Tamret refused to tell us how many XP she'd racked up.

About a week after the disastrous incident in the flight simulator, Tamret showed up in the cafeteria just as Steve and I were finishing breakfast. She looked tired. Her fur was a little matted, and her hair was unkempt. Her clothes were wrinkled, like she'd slept in them, or hadn't slept at all, and her eyes were streaked with red.

"Are you okay?" I asked.

"I was up all night working on something," she said, "and I don't think any of us are okay. You both need to come with me."

We followed her outside to a courtyard, where Hluh was sitting on a bench by a fountain, waiting for us. She had her data-bracelet keyboard materialized, and she was busy typing away. "You might as well sit down, not that it matters. You're all pretty much doomed."

Under the circumstances, sitting seemed liked good advice. Tamret and I sat on the bench, on opposite sides of Hluh. There had been room next to me, and I'd been hoping she would sit near me. If I were doomed, I'd rather be doomed next to her.

"Since when are the two of you friends?" I asked.

"Oh, we're not friends," Hluh said. "I don't much like Tamret. She's too moody."

"But I'm useful, apparently," Tamret added.

"Yes, she has some remarkable computer skills, and she's been helping me look into these matters." Hluh's fingers skittered over her virtual keyboard and called up a file on the selection committee. It was just a bunch of names in their indigenous alphabets or pictograms or whatever. If I looked at them for another few seconds, they would transliterate, but I couldn't be bothered. The names of a bunch of dead aliens, no matter how important they'd been in choosing me, wouldn't much matter.

"What do you know about them?" Hluh asked.

"The selection committee usually oversees the initiation process," Steve said. He was still standing, but leaning back slightly on his tail. "This time they're not around."

"And do you know why they aren't around?"

"They were killed," I said. "Some kind of space attack or accident."

"Are you sure about that?" Hluh asked.

I tried to think what Dr. Roop had said, but I couldn't remember exactly. "What are you trying to tell us?"

"I checked out the official news stories. I sent copies of some articles and video feeds to your data accounts if you want to take a look, but they're vague. The committee was on its way from scouting out a small world when their ship was attacked. The articles don't say by whom. It's implied that pirates got them."

"Wouldn't that be unusual?" I asked.

"Unusual, but it is possible." Hluh said. "Confederation space is well patrolled, but there is the occasional renegade or desperate refugee from Phandic space. The point is, what happened to the committee is left unclear."

"Maybe no one knows," Steve said. "Space is big. You can't know everything that happens, right?"

Hluh continued to type, and the holographic image was suddenly flashing with warnings about security and restricted access. "That's true, but my point is that everything to do with all five of these beings has since been buried or classified. Sure, I can find public information about them, articles about their elections, opinion pieces they wrote, images and interviews and whatever, but if you go deeper, into the government records, everything has been taken out of the public domain and seriously encrypted. I can't gain access, but I know who is blocking the way: the Xeno-Affairs Judicial Council. Chief Justice Junup has made it impossible for anyone to learn anything about what happened to the selection committee."

"Which is why Hluh messaged me," Tamret said.

"I suspected Tamret would have no problem breaking every law there is protecting the privacy of information," Hluh said. "She is both skilled and immoral."

"And awesome," Tamret concurred. "But I couldn't gain access to any of the secret files concerning the selection committee. It was all too encrypted."

"Too encrypted for you, ducky?" Steve asked.

This earned Steve a smile. I wished it had been mine. "You have to understand how these Confederation types think," Tamret explained. "To them a sign that says 'do not enter' has the same effect as a high-security fence. That's already all they need, but this time they actually put safeguards on their files. The truth is, I could get around the encryption and gain access to the files without too much effort, but I would set off a zillion alarms, and they'd trace the hack to me within a few hours. I want to know what's in those files, but not enough to get kicked out of the Confederation."

"Can I point out that you're not supposed to be hacking?" I said. "Hluh, you can't let her do this for you."

"It was her choice," Hluh said.

"After you asked her," I snapped. "You're taking advantage of her, and you don't care if she gets caught. It won't bother you."

"Should it?" Hluh asked.

"The point," said Tamret, "is that there is information out there the judicial council doesn't want known, and whatever it is, it's under the absolute highest level of government secrecy."

"I don't think any of you are here by accident," Hluh said. "And I don't think the committee disappeared because of a chance act of aggression."

"That's not good," Steve said.

"What?" I asked.

"Think about it," he said. "These blokes have an open and free society, so why conceal information?"

"They're obviously trying to hide some sort of blunder," Hluh said.

"How could the selection committee be a blunder?" I asked.

"Oh no." Genuine worry clouded Tamret's face.

"Will you guys tell me what's going on? I don't get it."

"This is bad," Steve said. "The committee chooses its randoms not randomly, and except in your case, we are all fairly shady characters. Then the committee is attacked, and the government classifies and encrypts its own records about the committee. I can't help but think that maybe the Confederation itself took them out."

"But why?" I asked. Then the answer occurred to me. "Oh no," I added to the chorus. "They were Phandic spies, weren't they?"

Steve nodded. "That's what I'm thinking. It makes sense."

"Then that means we weren't chosen to help our worlds join the Confederation," I said. "We were recruited to help the Phands."

"And the Confederation knows that," Tamret said.

"I think you are drawing unwarranted conclusions," Hluh

said. "You have been here for weeks. Has anyone from the Phandic Empire tried to contact you or recruit you?"

"No," I said, but I was thinking that maybe the Phands had been keeping an eye on Earth for a while. Their ships were flying saucers, after all, which were what most people reported when they claimed to have had contact with aliens. Maybe just like the Confederation had been seeding its culture in Earth's science fiction, the Phands had been scouting my home world as well. Did the Confederation know that? If they were to find out, would that make them suspect me?

"Any of the rest of you?" Hluh asked. "Have you had any contact with the Phands?"

"No," Steve said, "but if they had been planning on recruiting us, it could be that Zeke's destruction of their ship may have made them rethink their approach."

"I am not convinced," Hluh said. "Even if Zeke angered them by destroying that ship, it would not alter their position if they had invested time and agents in putting you in place. You may have been chosen to serve the Phands, but you may have been chosen for some other, less menacing reason. Either way, it doesn't change the fundamental truth about your situation."

"Which is what?" I asked.

"The selection committee was up to something illegal," Hluh said, "and clearly the Confederation doesn't want this discovered. It seems to me that the only thing the two greatest political forces in the galaxy have in common is that they would rather you were not around."

CHAPTER TWENTY-TWO

Were we originally recruited to be enemy agents? I didn't want to work for the Phandic Empire. I liked the Confederation. I liked being on the side of peaceful exploration and expansion. But if a Phandic agent had come to me and asked me to spy for them, I'm sure they wouldn't have taken no for an answer. They would have had leverage, and whatever it was, it would have made it impossible for me to do anything but obey.

Except if Steve was right and the Confederation knew about the committee's betrayal, then it would have known we were going to be recruited as spies. Would we have become double agents? Not likely, because if the Confederation had wanted us as double agents, they'd never have tipped off the Phandic Empire by getting rid of the committee.

It was easy to get lost in a maze of partial information, but the truth was we had no idea what these discoveries meant. Hluh said she would keep digging, and I begged her to leave Tamret out of it, but I don't think I made much of an impression. I had to hope that Tamret would not get caught, and I had to hope that whatever mysteries swirled all around us would not interfere with our ability to do what we had come to do. Whatever the reason we'd been chosen, no matter how devious the plan, we were part of our delegations now, and the only thing that mattered was helping our worlds get into the Confederation. We couldn't control what people thought of us. We could only change those things that were in our power.

So that was how we lived for another ten days. Then things got worse, as they are inclined to do.

Dr. Roop came to see me as I was sitting on my bed, reading that night's homework. His suit looked rumpled, and when he walked into my room, he sat on my bed and buried his giraffe face in his furry hands.

"This can't be good," I said.

He looked up. "There's a hearing in three days regarding your actions on the *Dependable*. In addition to the Xeno-Affairs Judicial Council, a member of the Phandic governmental advisory council will be there."

I needed a moment to process this. "That's definitely not good." Apparently, I had taken skill points in understatement.

"It's worse than not good. This particular Phandic representative was the brother of the captain of the ship you destroyed."

I was on my feet. I believe I was pulling at my hair. "His brother? You've got to be kidding me! Is the judicial council going to give me up?"

He took a deep breath. "They may try, Zeke. I have to tell you some things now, and they are secret. You can't repeat them to anyone—not even to your friends. I'm only telling you because they now affect you, and you need to understand."

I nodded. I did not like how this was going, and just in case I fainted, I sat back down.

"You know that we've been in a state of conflict with the Phandic Empire for a long time. They believe in conquest; we believe in self-determination. Those two things can never coexist peacefully."

"Yeah, that's pretty much the first thing we learned about them."

"You know that the détente has been maintained because their skills with weapons are countered by our skills with defensive technologies."

"Yes," I said, drawing out the word. I had a feeling that what I thought I knew was going to turn out not to be the truth.

"That stalemate ended about twenty years ago," Dr. Roop said. "Their weapons have improved faster than our ability to defend against them. We've been losing engagement after engagement. The truth, the terrible and secret truth, is that if the balance of power does not change, the Confederation is going to fall within another fifty years, possibly even much sooner. Hundreds of worlds will be overcome by the Phandic Empire, which will become the sole galactic superpower."

"I agree that this is terrible, but I don't see why you're telling me. What does this have to do with my destroying that ship?"

"You embarrassed the Phands," Dr. Roop was saying. "They want to punish you for that, and the Confederation may not be in a position to say no. If the empire offers some kind of truce, even if it's just a small and temporary one, the leadership may feel compelled to take it. Anything to buy time may be too tempting to resist."

All the pieces were coming together, forming a full picture, and I did not like what I saw. "So the Confederation may violate its own principles and hand me over in the hope that inevitable collapse might be put off for a few more years."

"Time is the only thing the Confederation has," Dr. Roop

said. "It's the only thing that stands between trillions of inno-cent lives and Phandic conquest."

"What are you saying?" I asked Dr. Roop. "That I have to sacrifice myself for the good of the Confederation?"

"No," he said. "I am going to do everything in my power to prevent that. Ms. Price and I will try to use all legal means to keep you safe."

"Ms. Price won't help me!" I was starting to sound a little hysterical, even to my own ears, but maybe hysteria was called for. "She'll wrap me in a bow and hand-deliver me if she thinks it will help Earth."

"Not this time," Dr. Roop said. "I've made it clear that the Confederation does not look favorably upon those who do not defend their own citizens, who sacrifice the innocent in the hopes of advancement."

"And yet that's exactly what the Confederation is planning."

"It's not our best showing," he admitted. "But please under-stand that you have friends."

"Not a whole lot," I said bitterly.

"Nevertheless, the ones you have are powerful. I've spoken with Bliauk. She is coming in to testify at the hearing, and if things don't go our way, she is prepared to smuggle you off the station and put you in hiding until the crisis is over."

I felt panic rising, ready to overflow. How could there be players involved I'd never even heard of? "Who is Bliauk?" I demanded.

"Captain Qwlessl," he said, his eyes widening for an instant. "She does have a first name, you know."

I could not believe this was happening. "She can't help me. Won't she get in trouble?"

"She would likely lose her commission," Dr. Roop agreed.

"She loves captaining a starship," I said. "I can't ask her to sacrifice her career for me."

Dr. Roop lowered his neck. "You have not asked her to do anything."

"I don't see how they can get away with this," I said. "People think I'm a war criminal because they don't really understand how close we were to being destroyed. If this is a hearing, then the truth about what happened on that ship will get out. Isn't the judicial council worried they'll look corrupt if they hand me over once all the facts are known? Won't it look like they're in league with the empire?"

"The hearing won't be public," Dr. Roop said. "Technically, it should be open, but they will find a way to keep it a secret."

"Doesn't that sort of thing make it hard to tell the good guys from the bad guys?" I asked.

"That is most definitely part of the problem." Dr. Roop stood up. "I hope the council will have the courage to uphold the principles of the Confederation. I believe it will, but no matter the outcome, I will not allow you to be handed over to the enemy."

"You'd sacrifice the Confederation for me?"

"Delivering you to our enemies will not help the Confederation," he said. "It will only allow some frightened beings to believe they've put off the inevitable, and I won't surrender you so that cowards can be, for a little while longer, a little less afraid."

"You've got to get off-station now," Steve said.

As soon as Dr. Roop left, I called Steve and Tamret to my

room. I didn't tell them the super-secret stuff, but they didn't need to know all the details. They were both from flawed worlds, like my own, and they understood that governments sometimes do bad things for what people convince themselves are the right reasons.

"I can't just go," I told him. "I have like thirty-seven credits left in my account."

"I can get you the money," Tamret said. "Credits are just data, which means I can hack them. I can have as much as you need in your account in an hour."

"If I leave, the Earth is out of the running. I can't do that to my world." *Or to my mother.*

"If you're handed over to the Phands," Tamret pointed out, "your group is short a delegate, anyhow. Maybe the time has come to think about saving yourself."

"But where would I go? There aren't any public transports to Earth, and I don't know anyplace else. What kind of life would that be, on the run, entirely alone?"

Tamret looked at me, and for a minute I thought she was going to offer to go with me. I wouldn't have let her. I wouldn't have allowed her to sacrifice her future and her world's future so that I would be less lonely, but it would have been nice if she had offered.

"I guess the question is, how much do you trust Dr. Roop?" Steve said.

"I trust him."

"Me too," Steve agreed.

Tamret nodded. "If he says he'll protect you, riding it out may be your safest bet."

• • •

I had no choice but to wait, and the waiting was excruciating. I had three more days, and then I would be sitting in a closed room with the brother of a man I had killed. Me. I had somehow, along the way, killed a guy—a bunch of guys, really. And yes, that guy had just killed a bunch of kids, and we all know the rest, but even so. There was no denying that this was all very serious.

In three days this might all be resolved for good, and I would never have to worry about it again. Or in three days I might be smuggled onto a spaceship and on the run with a renegade maternal alien. If that happened, would I ever get home again? And where was home now? I'd seen the stars, I'd met incredible aliens, and I had become more than what I had been before. I had molecule-sized machines coursing through my veins that made me faster and smarter than I used to be. If and when I got back to Earth, would it seem too small, too limited?

And what of Earth? If I ran off with Captain Qwlessl, the rest of the Earth's team would never reach eighty levels. We would be out. The Earth would be left behind, and my mother would die. The bottom line was that the hearing had to go my way, and I needed to do everything in my power to make sure it did. I trusted Dr. Roop. He was a good guy, a good friend to want to protect me, but I needed to protect more than myself. I needed to protect my mother and the world where I had been born.

At lunch the next day I was picking at my food, too nervous to eat. Across from me, Steve was not having the same problem. He had an extra-large goldfish bowl of his rat things, and they were dripping with hot sauce. I was too distracted to even turn away as he popped one in his mouth.

Tamret was suddenly there. She threw herself down in a seat and turned to Steve. "Beat it," she said to him.

"What? I'm having my lunch."

"We've got mammal business here. Find a rock and go sun yourself."

He pointed at her with a hot-sauce-covered rodent. "That's not very nice."

"We'll do sensitivity training later. Scram."

Steve cocked his head and looked at Tamret. He tasted the air with his tongue. "Oh," he said. *"That."* He picked up his gold-fish bowl, cradled it under one arm, and went in search of a table at the far end of the room. I wasn't quite sure what emotional stew he had caught wind of, but he had clearly decided that there was nothing to be gained by arguing with Hurricane Tamret.

She put her hands on the table, leaned forward, and trapped me in the unstoppable cosmic power of her lavender gaze. "You need to get off the station before the hearing tomorrow."

"I can't, remember?" I didn't have the energy to rehearse all the reasons why, at least not in detail. "The Earth. My mom. I've got to try to see things through."

She grabbed my hand, and there was nothing soft, nothing tender about it. Her grip was hard and urgent, and for all that, I still felt the thrill of her touch. "Zeke, you need to go. As soon as possible."

I had that inside-out feeling, as though I'd just dropped into my own personal tunnel aperture. "What are you talking about? Has something happened to make you not trust Dr. Roop?"

She shook her head. Her eyes were getting moist. "I think he believes he can protect you, but I'm not sure he can. It's Ms. Price. She is working against you."

"Dr. Roop says she knows she has to back me," I told her.

"Dr. Roop doesn't know everything," she said. "I've accessed her data account and—"

"Tamret, you can't do that!"

She leaned back and ran her fingers through her hair. She looked wild and slightly terrifying, but no less riveting for all that. "Stop telling me what I can't do. I can do anything I want. You need to understand that. They will never catch me."

"You've already been caught," I pointed out.

"You are such an idiot!" Her voice was so low it was almost a growl. "I *let* them catch me. They knew I hacked, so I hacked, and they felt all great about how they found me out, so now they think they know how to keep an eye on me. Trust me. I'm smarter than they are."

"And smarter than I am, apparently," I said, genuinely impressed.

"We've already established that. Listen, your buddy Ms. Price is not what she appears."

"I told you, she's not my friend."

"I don't care about that!" she snapped. Her ears shifted back and forth, like a nervous twitch. "What I'm trying to tell you is that her account has levels of encryption that go way beyond what we have, and certainly beyond what an observer from an unaffiliated world should have. I managed to get in and have a look around. Almost everything nonactive has been erased and shredded, but I was able to pick up some data fragments."

She opened up a screen on her data bracelet that projected a wall of text in front of me, a series of isolated message fragments. Most of them were too short or too vague to be of value, but then Tamret highlighted and enlarged the one she was looking for: . . . *corridor, pretended to want to make amends with him and that I was on his side. He's not very smart, so . . .*

So, indeed.

"Why does everyone think I'm not smart?" I asked.

"Because you're a moron," Tamret said, but her voice had become soft and low, and it sounded almost like an endearment.

"Can you figure out who she was sending this to?"

"No, that was completely corrupted. It could be anyone, but if I had to guess, I'd say she's working with the chief justice or someone on the judicial council, trying to make sure this embarrassing incident ends quickly. Who knows? Maybe they struck a deal in which if she helps them, they help your planet try again. Whatever the reason, she's out to get you, and that's why you need to get off this station."

"Not yet," I said. "Dr. Roop thinks he can get me through this, and I mean to give him the chance."

"If he is wrong, it will be too late." Tamret took my hand in her vice grip again. "You have to listen to me. You are too stupid to make this decision yourself. I'll go with you. Give me an hour to hack some credits, and we'll leave on the next ship off-station. I don't care where it's going."

Everything was spinning. I couldn't think straight anymore. "You would leave with me?"

She nodded.

"Even though I'm a moron?"

Tamret was now meeting my gaze. "*Because* you're a moron. You need me. You won't be able to survive on your own."

We were at a table, in the middle of a governmental cafeteria. Maybe beings were staring at us. Maybe no one cared. I was oblivious. All I knew was that Tamret was willing to give up everything to help me. So what if Ms. Price wanted to feed me to the wolves? Who cared that the Confederation was willing to trade my life for the illusion of safety? All of that seemed meaningless compared to what Tamret had offered.

I closed my eyes, savoring the feel of her hand in mine, wanting to memorize the sensation. "The trial isn't my last chance," I said quietly. "If it fails, Captain Qwlessl from the *Dependable* is going to get me off-station, so I don't need to run. Not yet."

She nodded. "If you have to go, I'm going with you."

Why was she willing to go on the run with me? I wanted to ask her, but I didn't, because I was afraid the answer would disappoint me—that it would be about her debt to me or Rarel honor or a revenge-deity oath.

"Okay," I said. "Thank you."

I barely understood the first thing about the conflict in which I was now caught up, but I was determined to win. I was going to outwit the evil of the Phandic Empire and the cowardice of the Confederation. I would beat the odds and dodge the betrayals and knock down anything else that stood in my way. I was going to do it for my planet, and for my mother, and now I was going to do it for Tamret, because if things went bad and I was on the run, my life would be in danger. No matter how much I wanted her with me, and despite what I'd told her, I was not going to let her come along. If I wanted to protect and preserve the things I cared about, that hearing had to go my way.

I was no longer willing to sit back and hope for the best. It was time to take action.

CHAPTER TWENTY-THREE

The hearing was to be held in the Judicial Building, across the government compound from our residence. Not anticipating I'd be on trial for my life, my mother hadn't bothered to pack a suit for me. She was, by nature, an optimist. I wore a long-sleeved shirt tucked into my khakis, and I hoped I didn't look too disrespectful.

Dr. Roop walked me over, but none of my friends were permitted to come along. The whole way there, he kept describing what he and Ms. Price thought was best. I made it clear I didn't trust her, but he insisted I was wrong, and that whatever I thought of her, I had to believe she would not act against the interests of her own world. I couldn't tell him what I knew, not without exposing what Tamret had been up to, so I would have to hope that if Ms. Price tried to stab me in the back, Dr. Roop would be able to step in before it was too late. I had taken some precautions of my own, and I hoped he would understand when he found out I'd been plotting behind his back. Ms. Price was far more devious than Dr. Roop, and I thought the situation required something a little stronger than the herbivore touch.

We entered what looked like a standard courtroom or government chamber. The far wall was a huge viewing screen on which was projected the gas-giant insignia of the Confederation. In front of that stood a central bench, large enough to seat perhaps twenty beings, though far fewer, as I understood it, would be present. In front of that was a series of tables where interested parties could sit, and then a large area for the public, large enough to hold perhaps a few hundred beings, though the judicial council intended that no one would observe the proceedings.

Ms. Price was already present, sitting at our designated table, looking crisp and polished in her perfectly pressed gray suit, her severely bunned red hair, and her freshly applied redder nail polish. She sat next to me and smiled her bright red lips. "You are going to be fine," she said. She even sounded like she meant it, but I couldn't find it in me to trust her. Maybe she wanted to protect me. Maybe the Confederation and the Earth were done trying to sell me out. I hoped so, but I wasn't counting on it.

Chief Justice Junup, he of the cape and goat-turtlish appearance, entered the room, followed by the rest of the council: a quadruped with a featureless and triangular face; a being who looked like a fat and clownish Darth Maul; an oozing ten-legged octopus or, I guess, decapus; and six more beings of various shapes, sizes, and colors. I hoped they were as just as they were diverse.

There was also a being of a species I had not seen before. He was almost seven feet tall, a broad and imposing-looking beast of a creature with thick skin the color of a green olive. His head was spectacularly long, rectangular, and big-jawed, with a pronounced underbite. He wore an almost skin-tight military uniform, with a narrow blade, like a fencing weapon, at his side, and he gave the general impression of a being made for war. Actually, he looked like a space orc—any Warhammer 40K fans in the house?—crossed with Frankenstein's monster.

The effect was almost funny, except that he regarded me with yellow eyes filled with unmistakable hatred. I was not laughing.

There was something else about the creature that looked familiar, something I couldn't put my finger on. The one thing I was sure of was that it had to be a Phand. This was the being who wanted me dead. He didn't simply dislike me or find me a pain or wish me not as much success as he might wish other people. He wanted me to die. I'd never seen anyone who I knew, with absolutely certainty, wanted me, Zeke Reynolds, as a particular individual, to be no longer alive. I don't recommend the experience.

I felt despair wash over me, and it was not because this alien hated me, or because Ms. Price or Junup or anyone else wished me ill. It was because it seemed to me that I was playing a rigged game.

There's a scene in the original *Star Wars* movie when Han Solo is ferrying Luke and Obi-Wan to the doomed world of Alderon, and to pass the time, R2D2 and Chewbacca play a kind of futuristic hologram chess game. When R2D2 captures a piece and Chewie lets out an indignant roar, C3PO says there's no point in complaining; it was a fair move. Score one for justice, right? Except then Han warns them that Wookiees are known to pull people's arms out of their sockets when they lose. "I suggest a new strategy, R2," C3PO says in a stage whisper. "Let the Wookiee win." Score one for brute force.

It's a moment played for laughs, and I thought it was hilarious when I was little, but thinking about it later, I found myself considering what the movie never shows: R2D2 and Chewbacca playing through a pointless game in which the outcome is already determined, and the only goal is to reach the cheerless end. There can be nothing compelling in the match for R2D2, nothing satisfying for Chewbacca. All that's left is the pantomime of an honest contest between two contestants who feel somehow obligated to finish what they've started.

That was exactly what this hearing felt like. It was play-acting, the pretense of justice, with the outcome already written. I hoped I was wrong, that things would be fair, but I wasn't willing to sit there and take it if my enemies truly meant to stack the deck against me. Better to win the game now, I decided, and worry about keeping my arms in my sockets later.

"I believe we are ready to proceed," Junup said in his deep voice. He, the Phand, and the rest of the council had taken their seats at the elevated bench in the front of the room. "Mr. Reynolds, you are not a citizen of this Confederation, and so we realize you likely will not understand all the details of our legal system. Therefore, you may inquire if the proceedings are not clear to you. To begin with, you should know that biofunctions are being monitored against their stable base. Your data bracelet will inform us if you appear to be lying. Are you ready to begin?"

"Yes, sir," I said.

"Unable to confirm veracity of statement" came a calm, gender-neutral voice.

"Perhaps," the chief justice said, "it would be better to inquire if you wish to ask any questions as this point."

"No, sir." And because I am my own worst enemy, I added, "I have every faith in these proceedings."

"Unable to confirm veracity of statement."

Honestly, I just wanted to say the polite thing, but now Junup was looking at me like he couldn't hand me over to the

Phands soon enough. Ms. Price glowered at me, as if to tell me it was probably not a good idea to embarrass the chief justice. I had already figured that out by myself. I'm sure they were both taking some comfort in the fact that there were no data collectors in the room.

That was when the data collectors entered the room, which, and not by coincidence, is probably when Chief Justice Junup decided he hated my guts.

After my conversation with Tamret, I'd understood that I couldn't just hope the hearing was fair; I had to make sure it was. I'd contacted Hluh and suggested she come to report on the proceedings and keep things honest. I'd asked her to bring a small number of her professional friends with her. When she'd told me she did not have any friends, professional or otherwise, I suggested she bring some colleagues. She seemed to think this was a workable alternative.

There were about twenty of them, some of species I'd seen before, some totally unfamiliar. Some wore the colors or insignias or logos or holographic tattoos of their various news outputs. Hluh wore a bright orange jumpsuit. All of them had activated their data bracelets, and recording devices hovered over them, taking in everything.

Junup bounded out of his chair. You wouldn't think a goat-turtle could move that fast. "What is this? This hearing is closed to the public."

"No, it's not," Hluh said in her clipped voice. And having exhausted that topic, she took a seat in the front row. Her recording device was already rolling, but she now called up her keyboard and began to type away.

"You can either leave of your own volition, or I can call the peace officers," Junup told them. "All judicial councils have the right to close proceedings at their discretion. It's clearly stated in the Guidelines of Judicial Ethics."

"You are mistaken," said one of the data collectors. He was a giraffe guy, like Dr. Roop, and he was also a snappy dresser. Maybe it was a species thing. "The guidelines clearly state you can close a hearing when a citizen is charged with a crime deemed to present a threat to the security of the Confederation. Mr. Reynolds is not a citizen, and so you have no legal right to bar us. As I'm sure you know, you can close a proceeding of this sort, but only if you have a sufficient number of citizens of good reputation present to verify a fair and open procedure. I see no witnesses at all, so you have no choice but to let us stay."

Junup worked his jaw in fury as he realized that if he had only loaded the empty seats with a few dozen of his cronies, he would have avoided this problem altogether.

"If you wish to limit the number and identity of witnesses," the giraffey data collector continued, "their names must be made available to the public for review. Unless you choose to postpone this proceeding by several weeks, you must permit us to stay."

"I have no interest in your bureaucratic niceties," the Phand said, his voice low and terrifyingly calm. "I have traveled far in search of justice. I will not be delayed by weeks."

Junup's hand was forced, just as I had intended. I had hoped that the Phandic representative would be just as happy to both embarrass the Confederation and get what he wanted. As it turned out, I was right. Junup told the data collectors to remain, but warned them not to disrupt the proceedings.

Once they had taken their seats, the Phandic representative began to make a humming noise, and he locked his eyes upon me once more. After a moment of humming and glowering, he stood and came out from behind the bench to face the board. Then he turned in my direction and studied me as though trying to take in every detail, to memorize my features, but I did not look away. I wished I had, because after he had glowered at me for a good minute, the Phand began to wiggle his jaw, moving it back and forth, up and down. Then he dropped it almost six inches, his mouth spreading open, big and black and wide, like one of those *Scream* Halloween masks. While his eyes bore down on me with the full fury of his malice, he began to vomit forth at least a gallon of a brown and chunky liquid, which pooled on the floor and, quite literally, steamed. He then reconnected his jaw and walked regally to the other side of the bench and resumed his seat.

Dr. Roop leaned toward me. "Allow me to explain," he whispered. "In his culture, disgorging is a sign of contempt."

"Yeah. Thanks for helping me interpret that," I said. "Is anyone going to clean up the puke?"

"Cleaning it would be rude," Dr. Roop said. "So watch your step when you testify."

"This council welcomes Vondik Ghandilud Vusio-om of the Phandic Empire," said Chief Justice Junup. "Though our peoples often do not agree, let this council be a place of peaceful discussion."

"It is easy to speak of peace," said Vusio-om, in a deep and menacing voice. "It is more challenging to pursue it. Our government is outraged that you harbor a war criminal among your kind, and yet you refuse to allow him to be brought to justice."

"That he is a war criminal is yet to be determined," Junup said. "It is the purpose of this meeting to uncover the truth. In accordance with our laws, you are given a voice in making that determination. Would you like to begin, sir?"

"I begin by outlining the events. On the seventh day of the Month of Holy Blindness, the seventy-second year of the Empress Donatruitu-ia, our ship was engaged in legal operations when the Confederation vessel fired upon it, using excessive and deadly force. It was destroyed, with all hands, including my own brother, before evacuations could be attempted."

"The legal operations you speak of were the destruction of a Confederation shuttle containing nonaligned citizens and firing upon the *Dependable*, sir," said the triangular-headed quadruped.

"It does not violate our treaties if our ships attack nonaligned beings in neutral space. As for firing on your vessel, it was meant as a mere warning. Your shielding, as is well known, was more than adequate protection."

"The Ganari on board that shuttle may have been nonaligned, but the shuttle was Confederation property," said the clownish Darth Maul.

"Then I propose that you give us the war criminal in exchange for reparations for the lost equipment." Vusio-om smirked at his own cleverness. "We can end this proceeding now."

"That is unlikely," Junup said. "Perhaps, if you wish to make your case, you can begin to call your witnesses."

Vusio-om called Captain Qwlessl to the stand. I knew from Dr. Roop that she would be returning to the station for the hearing, but even so, seeing her was a huge relief. There was one more person in my corner, a starship captain, a respected person in the Confederation.

She strode into the chamber, using the same side entrance from which the justices had emerged. She was a large and lumbering being, but her gait was steady and purposeful, with her huge eyes dead ahead, her trunk partially raised in a gesture of something, I was sure. She stood facing the council. She made a point of not looking at me, I suppose so it would not seem like we were in league, but I have to admit I felt better just seeing her there. Her eyes, briefly, flickered toward the pile of still-steaming Phandic puke on the floor. She was a trained professional, however, and did not pronounce it yucky.

The captain explained in compelling detail how the Phandic vessel fired on the shuttle and then, as we fled, fired on the *Dependable*. In both instances, she made it clear, the Phandic ship attacked without cause or provocation. She detailed the loss of gravity that led to substantial injuries among the bridge crew, and finally how, in a moment of desperation, she called upon an untrained civilian to stand in as weapons officer in an effort to save the ship.

"To save your ship from what?" inquired Vusio-om.

"From destruction or capture," answered the captain, her trunk held high.

"Those are different things," Vusio-om told her. "One involves loss of life, the other loss of pride."

"They are both undesirable, and we have the right to use force to prevent either."

"Perhaps even deadly force," agreed Vusio-om. "But, by definition, there is never a cause for *excessive* force. And you cannot know that your ship or your lives were truly in danger. That is speculation."

"Perhaps so," conceded the captain, "but given that the only way to find out was to let your vessel continue to fire on us, I was not prepared to make that discovery."

"You would rather destroy a ship than discover its intentions?" Vusio-om asked.

"You are twisting my words," the captain said. "My ship was being attacked with deadly force. I believe I sufficiently understood my adversary's intentions."

"But the captain of the Phandic vessel, my brother Uio-om, told you if you surrendered, you would not be harmed. You had no cause to fear, let alone place a juvenile in charge of your ship's deadly arsenal."

"Frankly, I had a difficult time believing the words of a captain who had already murdered innocent beings and fired upon my ship without provocation."

"If you presume someone is a liar, without just cause, then trust becomes impossible," Vusio-om mused.

"I consider the captain's actions the most accurate indication of his intent. We had no choice but to defend ourselves."

"Defending yourself is, perhaps, understandable," the Phand allowed. "But did it never occur to you to worry what an untested civilian might do when presented with the incredible destructive power of a Confederation starship?"

"Certainly," said the captain. "I knew that Mr. Reynolds had logged only a few hours with simulated systems, and I was indeed worried that he would not possess the skills to defend my ship and crew. Given that the assault of the Phandic ship had left most of my bridge officers incapacitated, I had no alternative."

Vusio-om snorted at this. "One final question," he said. "Do you believe that ten dark-matter missiles, fired at a single Phandic vessel, is excessive?"

"I do," said the captain. "I also believe that Mr. Reynolds had no way of knowing that."

The captain was told to step down, and next the Phand called Urch, who came in through the side door with the same professional stride as the captain. I supposed they learned it in their starfleet academy, or wherever it was they trained. I had not seen any of Urch's species on the station, and with his tusks and warthog face and long ropes of hair, he appeared a terrifying thing. He was *my* terrifying thing, however, and I was glad to see him.

He stood before the council, made a genuflection that I imagined to be a gesture of respect, and then jutted his jaw forward, showing his teeth and tusks. Vusio-om asked a series of questions to bring out that Urch had been impressed with my weapons skills, and that he had trained with me the night before.

"Did you consider the possibility that Ezekiel Reynolds had handled weapons before?"

"He did not say that he had," Urch answered.

"Simulated weapons?"

"He indicated that on his world there are games that simulate space combat."

"So, even if he had not trained specifically with Confederation weaponry, he had trained with simulated weaponry, and he had trained for simulated space combat."

"In the context of a game," Urch said. "When youths from such worlds play these games, they do so understanding them to be fantasy."

"You speak from experience, I believe, coming from such a primitive world."

"Perhaps," Urch suggested, "you would like to come visit. You would be well treated."

"Unable to confirm veracity of statement," said the monitoring system.

Urch showed his teeth again.

"Yes, I see," said the Phand. "These games you mentioned. Do they not desensitize a youth to the prospect of destroying real ships harboring living beings?"

Urch hissed out a laugh. "Zeke did not strike me as being unable to distinguish reality from simulation. I find it absurd that you are attempting to turn his efforts to save the *Dependable* into a war crime. Your brother was a murderer, not a victim."

"That is quite enough, Mr. Urch," said Junup.

"We are not the ones who have violated the treaty," Vusio-om told him. It was a mistake, as Urch had pointed out in the past, to read my own species body language onto another species, but the Phand gave every impression of shaking with anger.

"The weak and the deceitful hide behind legal niceties," Urch said. "If your [*parasitic insect, known for its horrific odor*] brother hadn't launched his cowardly assault, then no one would have been harmed."

"This is an outrage!" cried the Phand. "I insist that this being be tortured at once!"

"It is not our custom to respond quite so forcefully to rudeness," Junup said, "but your point is well taken. Mr. Urch, please answer the questions, and no more."

Urch hissed, which might have been the equivalent of a nod. Or maybe it was just a hiss.

Vusio-om appeared to regain control of himself. His huge hands relaxed and he folded them before himself on the table. "Let us return to your training session with Ezekiel Reynolds. Did you explain to him the destructive power of the dark-matter missile?"

"Not using specific metrics," he said.

"But you made it clear they were powerful?"

"Yes."

"Did you advise him to fire multiple missiles at a target?"

"No," he admitted.

"Did you advise him that it was policy to wait after firing a missile to assess damage before firing another?"

"Yes," said Urch, "but—"

"So when your captain claims that Mr. Reynolds could not know firing multiple missiles to be against your codes of conduct, she is either ignorant or deliberately deceiving us."

Urch hissed again, this time, I believe, in frustration. "You attempt to twist words, but although I had explained basic rules of engagement to Zeke, I do not believe that—"

"Yes or no!" the Phand shouted.

"You must answer," Junup said after Urch remained silent for several painful seconds.

"Yes," he said at last.

"Thank you, Mr. Urch. That will be all."

Then came the moment I'd been dreading. Vusio-om called me to stand before the council. I stepped in front of our table, moved all the way to the end of the row, and then headed forward to face the council.

"You take a most circuitous route to stand before us," Vusio-om said when I stood before the council. "Perhaps you do not wish to speak of what happened on the Confederation vessel."

"No," I said. "I took the long way around to avoid the upchuck."

This earned me a glower, and so I considered it a job well done. Vusio-om then began his interrogation. "What was your state of mind when operating the weapons console?"

I considered my words carefully, not wanting to be called out for a lie. "I was scared."

"For your life?"

"Yes," I said. "And I was scared that I would make a mistake. Captain Qwlessl gave me a job to do, and I didn't want to fail her."

"Were you concerned for the lives of the people on the Phandic ship?"

"No," I admitted. "I'd just watched them murder civilians, my peers, and they were in the process of trying to murder us." Okay, no objection from the truth-o-meter. Maybe I could stop second-guessing myself.

"So you claim to believe. Tell me, Ezekiel Reynolds. When you fired those missiles, were you trying to disable the Phandic ship so it could do no more harm? Or, rather, were you trying to destroy it? Did you hope it would explode in a big ball of fire?"

"I did not think I had the skill to disable it, and I did not know how many more hits the *Dependable* could take before it was destroyed. It didn't really seem like the time for nuance."

"Such as the nuance of allowing survivors to escape once the vessel was nonfunctional?"

"Like I said, I did not think of that at the time." I was doing a poor job of concealing my frustration, and I took a breath, trying to calm myself.

"So it was your hope that you might kill everyone on board?"

I paused to consider my answer. "I didn't think about the people on board until it was all over. All I cared about was saving the *Dependable*. I believed it was us or them, and it wasn't until the battle was done that I even thought of the Phandic ship as containing beings. Until then, the ship was an *it* that would destroy us if I didn't stop it."

"Do you now wish you had considered the matter more thoughtfully?"

"At the time, I did not have the knowledge or the skills to behave other than I did," I told him. I'd practiced that line in my room. I thought it was pretty good.

"Do you consider yourself a criminal?" Vusio-om asked.

"No," I told him.

"Do you admire criminals or seek out their company?"

"Of course not."

"I call your attention to these images." He waved his hand, and several pictures of me with Steve and Tamret appeared on the screen. They had been taken in public places throughout the compound. I could only assume Junup had provided them. "Do you know these beings?"

"Yes," I said, my stomach sinking as I realized where he was going with this.

"And do you know they have criminal records on their home worlds?"

"Yes," I said.

He waved his hand again. A picture appeared of me and Tamret. We sat at the table in the commons, and she held her hand in mine. It was all in stunning high definition. She looked really pretty, I thought. I looked like a total dork, but despite being on trial for my life, I took some pleasure in that that everyone could see that it was me sitting with that beautiful girl.

"You are clearly associated with this being," he said. "This touching of hands is a ritualistic expression of affection, is it not?"

Yes, that was me turning beet red before my sworn enemy, the council, and, with the data collectors there, the billions of good beings across the Confederation watching this fiasco. "We're friends."

"Did you know that this being was caught breaking into secure computer systems on this station?"

"Yes," I admitted.

"Do you approve of her actions?"

"I keep telling her that she should follow the rules." No squawking from the computer.

This seemed to surprise him. "But you were involved in a wager, were you not, that would have required her to break into the point-allocation system and redistribute points?"

A bolt of anger shot through me. How did he know about that? Who was feeding information to the Phands? Charles? Nayana? Mi Sun? One of them had ratted us out, and not over some minor infraction. Tamret could get kicked off the station for this, and that would cause her whole delegation to fail. The future of an entire world, a species, was in the balance, and someone from my own world had completely betrayed everything that mattered. There was going to be a reckoning, I decided. Someone had tried to hurt Tamret, and when I found out who it was, I would hurt them back.

"Ezekiel Reynolds?" the Phand said. "We are waiting."

"I was against that bet," I said at last. "I said it was a mistake."

"So, to clarify," the Phand said, "despite your wishes, your friend, this fur-covered creature, encouraged actions that could result in her exile from the Confederation?"

I sat there, saying nothing, trying to think of an answer that would be both honest and help Tamret. Nothing came to mind.

"Please answer," Junup said.

"The details are hazy," I attempted.

"Unable to verify veracity of response," the computer said. I was not surprised.

"We shall read your silence as affirmation of this creature's guilt," the Phand said, "as well as an indication of your unwillingness to tell us the truth. Now, as to this wager, you did not approve, but you did participate. Is that correct?"

"I agreed to the contest, but no one did anything illegal. We talked about messing with the point system, but we didn't do it. Tempers were flaring. Kids say all kinds of things."

"'Kids say all kinds of things,'" he repeated. "And did you believe the 'kid' Tamret when she said she intended to hack the system and reallocate points?"

I did not want to answer this. "I can't know what she intended."

"What is your guess?"

"My guess does not matter. She never broke the law."

"But you must have an opinion."

The clownish Darth Maul seemed to lose patience. "He does not wish to answer, and I don't see that he should have to speculate regarding another being's thoughts, nor, frankly, how their little competition has anything to do with the purpose of this hearing. Please move on, sir."

"Very well," Vusio-om said. "Whether or not she broke the law on this occasion, she indicated a willingness to do so. And you choose to associate with her knowing that she has broken the law and speaks of doing so again. Is that not so?"

"Yes."

"Why do you associate with her?"

"Why shouldn't I? She's an initiate, like I am. The selection committee chose her."

"No other reason?"

I was not going to sell out Tamret, and I was not going to apologize for her, but I needed to put her in context. The entire Confederation was watching, and I would not let them turn Tamret into some kind of criminal reprobate. "A being is the sum of many qualities, not simply the product of one action selected from a lifetime of actions. I choose to associate with her because I like and admire her."

"She is a random selection," he said.

"Yes."

"As are you."

"Yes."

"And to the best of your knowledge, you have no particular skills that would qualify you to be here."

"Yes," I admitted.

"Do you think you are worthy of being here with the rest of the delegates from your world? Do you believe yourself a strong representative of your planet?" Vusio-om asked.

"Yes," I said.

"Unable to confirm veracity of response."

"Those are all the questions I have for you."

I turned to head back to my seat, but then shot back. In the confusion that had naturally sprung from my public humiliation, I'd almost forgotten about my ace in the hole. I had better use it now, before it was too late.

"May I ask you a question?" I said to the Phand.

"No," answered Vusio-om. "I will not be made to answer anything put forth by my brother's killer."

"Counterquestioning is permitted," said the clownish Darth Maul.

"I do not choose to permit it," answered Vusio-om.

"Chief Justice," I said to Junup, "on my world, failure to grant the accused their rights disqualifies the findings of any judicial proceeding. How do you guys do things here?"

"The applicant is correct," said the quadruped to the Phand. "You must answer, or this hearing is not valid."

"That is an insult," the Phand said in his low voice. Then he worked his jaw side to side for a moment and glared at me. "You may ask what you will."

I took a deep breath. I knew in my heart that I had saved the *Dependable* that day. If I had been better trained, perhaps I wouldn't have destroyed the Phandic ship, but at the time I did the best I could with the little knowledge I had. I didn't have a lot of great moments in my life, but that was one of them. Even so, I believed the hearing was not going my way. Vusio-om was doing a pretty good job of making my actions look rash and my character appear shady. I had one play remaining, and it was time I made it.

My heart pounded in my chest as I began to speak. "When the Phandic ship attacked the *Dependable*, it cut through the shields much more quickly than the bridge crew expected. I later learned that it was using new weapons technology, which the Confederation would be able to learn how to counter.

So my question is this: If the Phandic ship did not intend to destroy the *Dependable*, why waste a one-time advantage on the attack?"

The Phand slammed his hands down on his table. "I have no idea!" he shouted.

"Unable to verify veracity of response."

Vusio-om snorted. "Then I shall say that information is classified, and I need not reveal more than that."

"That is true," Junup said. "He need not be made to provide information regarding military secrets."

He didn't have to answer. The facts were now out. "That's all I wanted to ask," I said, and I sat down, knowing I had done what I could, and hoping it would be enough.

I returned to my seat, and Vusio-om called his final witness: Nora Price.

She stood and stepped forward to face the council.

"How well do you know Zeke Reynolds?" asked Vusio-om.

"I met him only when his name was provided to my government," she said.

"Other than the day he destroyed a Phandic cruiser, have you ever seen him engage in criminal activity?"

"I have not witnessed such activity."

"What about morally dubious activity?"

"The day I met him, he attempted to extort special favors from the leader of my nation in exchange for his listening to the proposal from the Confederation representative."

She was talking about my asking the president to help my mother with her insurance.

"Are you saying," Vusio-om asked, "that Ezekiel Reynolds would not entertain the possibility of helping his world advance into a technologically superior civilization unless special favors were granted to his family?"

"Essentially, yes."

"And did this surprise you?"

"I thought it lamentable that he did not appreciate the opportunity presented to him."

I looked at Dr. Roop, who was busy rubbing his horns nervously. Ms. Price had sold me out, just as I thought she would, just as Tamret had warned me. The woman from my own world, my own country, who was supposed to be looking out for me, was trying to make certain I was delivered over to the enemy.

"You participated in a debriefing session immediately after the destruction of that ship?"

"Yes."

"Did he say he regretted his actions?"

"No. Quite the opposite. He said he was glad he had destroyed the ship."

"Did Ezekiel Reynolds inquire how many beings were aboard the ship he destroyed?"

"No. He was mainly interested in defending what he had done."

"And as far as his associating with the criminal delegates from other species, did you have any objections to that?"

"I did," Ms. Price said. "In fact, I told him to stop spending time with those beings, but Zeke would not follow my instructions. He refused to listen to me."

"Even though you are in a position of authority?"

"Correct," Ms. Price said.

"Thank you, Nora Price. I have no further questions or witnesses."

She returned to her seat and smiled at me and Dr. Roop as though we could not have objected to anything she said. Dr. Roop would not meet her gaze, but I felt myself trying to bore a hole in her face with my eyes.

Vusio-om now told the council he wished to make a summary statement, and he was given permission to do so.

"Members of the council, I believe what has been made clear here today is that Ezekiel Reynolds had an understanding of the destructive power of dark-matter missiles, was familiar with your rules of engagement, and in spite of this knowledge, fired ten of the most terrible weapons you possess . . . at a single ship. There is no possible interpretation of this act but a clear desire to kill. Given that he has expressed pride at what he did, a willingness to do it again, and has shown no regret for his actions, I believe we must conclude that Ezekiel Reynolds is an unrepentant killer.

"His species, the humans, are guilty on their home world of the most monstrous atrocities: murder, slavery, genocide, the deployment of weapons of mass destruction against civilian populations. The same is true of the Rarels, the Ish-hi, and the Ganari. I believe that the deaths of my comrades are the direct result of the selection committee's deliberately choosing to recruit barbarian species out of recognition of the Confederation's fading power."

"With all due respect," said the quadruped, "you have no idea what the selection committee intended. None of us do."

"That is where you are wrong," said Vusio-om. "As is known to your chief justice, as well as to other high-ranking members of your government, the ship carrying your selection committee was detained when entering Phandic space illegally. Your leaders have been briefed as to their location and condition. We have had the leisure to learn much from your selection committee about this group of initiates."

The data collectors, in their tight little cluster, began to speak excitedly among themselves. Three bombshells had been dropped: first, that the selection committee had been intentionally recruiting species with a tendency toward violence; second, that the members of the committee were alive and held prisoner by the Phands; and third, that members of the government knew all this and had kept the whole debacle a secret.

"I cannot comment on classified information," said an embarrassed-looking Junup, "but if you are holding our citizens hostage, then I ask you to release them."

"They are not hostages; they are criminals," said Vusio-om. "However, should we find ourselves in a situation in which relations between our two cultures are more amicable, I believe we would be inclined to free those prisoners as an act of goodwill."

And there was bombshell number four. If the council voted to hand me over, the Phandic Empire would free the committee members. Great. These guys were all politicians. They were probably friends, ate at one another's houses. Who would the judicial council want to protect more—their colleagues or an alien troublemaker?

Junup looked flustered, but once he had returned the room to order, he announced that it was time to call for a vote.

Dr. Roop had explained to me that the council would cast their votes using their bracelets, and that once all votes were in, the results would be displayed on the screen behind the bench.

I watched as each member appeared to lose focus and then nod to him- or her- or itself. The entire process took less than thirty seconds. No one seemed to take much time to deliberate, and yet I think I felt every heartbeat in those seconds. Dr. Roop whispered something in my ear, and I was unable to concentrate enough to listen, but I nodded. What happened now would seal my fate on this station, maybe the fate of my entire planet.

Finally the insignia of the Confederation broke apart, and the screen began to assemble the tally. Letters and numbers presented themselves, and though my nanites translated them, they were still nothing but gibberish. I couldn't make myself see them. Then, all at once, they snapped into place.

Six members of the council had voted to refuse extradition; four had voted to approve. I slumped in my chair as the meaning of this information hit me. I was safe.

Vusio-om launched himself to his feet. "I was promised justice, not a farce!"

Dr. Roop was hugging me, and then he was shaking my hand, Earth-style. The data collectors were busy talking and recording and typing excitedly. Somewhere in all this, Ms. Price had excused herself, and she was nowhere to be seen.

Junup, for his part, looked furious. Had he expected things to go the other way? Had he been sure they would? I had no idea, but in that moment I felt absolutely certain that Junup had wanted me to be sent to the Phands.

Vusio-om rose from his chair and stormed down the aisle. He then turned to face the council, dropped his jaw, and vomited prodigiously once again. Once again it was disgusting, and once again no one needed to tell me that this was a gesture of contempt.

"I see now I was wrong to place my faith in Confederation

justice," he said, slurring the last word. "You ask me to prance about for your amusement, but you never intended this to be a fair hearing. I now say, for all to hear, that Zeke Reynolds is a criminal, and his very world is an abomination. We shall take steps to cleanse the galaxy of its contagion. As for you of the Confederation, you claim you seek peace, but you offer up insult. Understand me when I say that there will be no peace while Ezekiel Reynolds lives."

So saying, he left the court.

Vusio-om's words stung me because I understood them for the threat they were. The Phandic Empire did not consider this matter resolved, and their beef was not with the Confederation, but with *me*. More than that, Vusio-om had uttered almost the exact words used by the Klingon ambassador about James Kirk in *Star Trek IV*. That was bad news, because if the parallels continued, I would find myself living in *Star Trek V*, without doubt the worst *Star Trek* movie of them all.

CHAPTER TWENTY-FOUR

The data collectors swarmed around me as I left the hearing room, but Dr. Roop made a serviceable bodyguard, and soon we were past the press of cameras and camera things and hovering recording devices and shouted questions. A secure area had been set off to the side, and Dr. Roop took my arm and gently steered me in there to wait out the chaos.

Tamret was waiting for me, and the instant I stepped through the doors she ran over and threw her arms around me. I knew she had been watching on the news outputs, and that meant she'd seen that I'd been forced to talk about the things she'd done. I only hoped she didn't hate me for it.

"I'm sorry I gave you up," I said softly, feeling dizzy in the wake of all that had happened.

"You tried not to," she said. "You did everything you could to protect me."

"I'm glad you know that."

I saw her face grow dark with rage, and I thought my inexperience with females of any species had led me to make a huge error. Then I realized Tamret was reacting to something else entirely. Charles, Nayana, and Mi Sun had just walked into the room.

Tamret walked toward them, fast and steady, swaggering like a predator. One of her fingers jabbed the air, her claws out. Her expression was dark, and her mouth was open, exposing her sharp canines. "You have a lot of nerve coming here."

"I know," Mi Sun said, holding up her hands. "Dr. Roop messaged us when he found out the data collectors were going to broadcast the hearing, and we saw the whole thing. I'm really sorry, okay? I'm so sorry to both of you. I didn't know she was going to use it against you."

The apology seemed to confuse Tamret. "What, so now you care what happens to me? To Zeke?"

Charles was about to answer the question, but he was distracted by Ms. Price, who entered the room. Mi Sun strode up to her, looking every bit as dangerous as Tamret had looked just moments before.

"Before anyone gets angry, you need to understand something," Ms. Price said.

"I understand you're a liar," Mi Sun said, her voice cold and full of contempt, "and I'm sick of it! You told me you weren't going to do anything to hurt her, and then you used what you tricked me into telling you against Tamret *and* Zeke? A member of our own delegation? What is wrong with you?"

"I am doing everything I can to protect our *world*, which is a lot more important than any one person." Ms. Price spoke slowly, her voice thick with constrained fury.

"That's what you tell us," Charles said, "but I begin to wonder. I am through cooperating with you. We have discussed this, and we are all in agreement."

"I don't think you know what you're saying," Ms. Price told him.

"And I don't think you know what you're doing," Mi Sun said. "You've been against Zeke from the beginning. You're the one who made us box him out."

"I advised you how best to advance to eighty levels," Ms. Price clarified. "I'll remind you that the Rarels and Ish-hi have ostracized their randoms as well."

"The Ish-hi and Rarels don't have a random who saved an entire starship," Charles said. "After that, you still ordered us to turn our backs on Zeke."

"Wait, what?" I said, but they were not listening to my insightful commentary.

"It is a historically valid practice," she told them. "I knew he would bring down the team scores. Look at him. He's level nine."

"You don't really believe that, do you?" Mi Sun was now shouting. "He logs every possible hour in the flight sims. He destroyed a Phandic cruiser. He's constantly playing and winning those stupid Former games. Do you honestly think he's only level nine? He's holding back on his leveling to fly under the radar—for all the good it's done him."

Ms. Price stared at me, her expression dark and murderous. "Is this true?"

"Initiates are under no obligation to use skill points as they achieve them," Dr. Roop told her. "Frankly, I wonder why this possibility upsets you so much."

"Quiet, Skippy," Ms. Price said. "No one's talking to you."

"Skippy," I informed her, "was a kangaroo. Not a giraffe." Someone had to take a stand for pop-culture justice.

Mi Sun turned to me. "Zeke, while we were watching the hearing, we all agreed that we were wrong in how we treated you. It would have ended a long time ago if Ms. Price hadn't told us that Earth's future depended on us not being friends with you. We're all really sorry."

Tamret took my hand and glared at Mi Sun. "He doesn't accept your apology."

I appreciated her coming to my defense, even if I would have phrased things differently.

"Thank you," I offered Mi Sun.

"Don't thank her," Tamret said coolly. "I hate her, and so do you."

Ms. Price balled up her fists and let out a groan of frustration. "You all need to grow up!" she shouted. "You think this is a game? The Phandic Empire, the most dangerous collection of beings in the known galaxy, wants Zeke dead, and you are treating this like it's a Taylor Swift song in space. Don't you understand that you are all in danger? Our entire planet is in danger. Did you not hear the ambassador just threaten the Earth? You want to think I'm the villain, but I am trying to keep as many humans alive as I can."

"Would they really attack Earth?" I asked Dr. Roop.

"I don't know," he said. "They haven't done anything like that in the past, but they're angry, and, uh, they may be willing to take more drastic steps than they have in the past."

I knew what he meant. Maybe in days gone by the Phands never would have dared to attack a planet the Confederation was evaluating, but now things might be different. Had I endangered my world by refusing to face Phandic justice?

"Do I turn myself over to them?" I asked Dr. Roop.

"Don't be an idiot!" Tamret shouted. "Dr. Roop, tell him not to be an idiot."

"Do not be an idiot," Dr. Roop said.

"But Earth might be in danger."

"The Confederation has a vast fleet," he said. "Command

understands the situation. Earth will be protected."

"Were the Ganari protected?" Ms. Price asked. "You are kidding yourself if you think the Confederation is going to inconvenience itself for our little planet. I hate the idea of having to hand Zeke over, but my duty is to my country and my world, and that will always come first. It should come first for all of you, too."

She turned around and marched out of the room. No one said anything for a long time. Every time I began to think I understood a person or a situation, it seemed the rules changed around me. I felt like I needed to get away, not least because I suddenly realized what was so familiar about the appearance of the Phandic ambassador. The shape of his head was exactly like that of the artificial fighters in the sparring room.

All this time, the Confederation had been training us to fight Phands.

A couple of minutes later, Captain Qwlessl and Urch walked into the room. I greeted them both. The captain hugged me and Urch slapped my back until I begged him to stop. Then the captain took me aside.

"I can't stay long," she said. "This hearing diverted me from an ongoing assignment, but I wanted to stop by and see you before I left."

"Dr. Roop told me what you were prepared to do," I said quietly.

"It doesn't matter now because it wasn't necessary."

"It matters to me." I looked over at Dr. Roop, who was looking at us and pretending not to. "It matters to him, too. I think he still likes you, by the way. If you're wondering."

"That was a long time ago," she assured me. "Back then, I actually considered converting for him."

"You two are from different religions?"

"No, nothing like that. It's what we call it when we change our outward appearance. Sometimes when members of two different species want to be together, it's easier if one of them changes his or her exterior."

"You can do that?"

"To a degree," she said. "You can't make yourself into an Ish-hi and have your friend's abilities, if that's what you're thinking. It's all cosmetic, but it can make for a happier relationship. But our lives got in the way, and here we are now."

There was an unmistakable tone of sadness in her voice. "I'm glad you didn't have to give up being a captain to help me," I said.

"Being a captain of a Confederation ship means it was my duty to help you," she told me. "Everyone else may forget what we're doing here, but I won't."

She gave me another hug, and I said good-bye to her and Urch, and they headed out. Then we were just standing there, recovering, and no one had anything to say.

"I'm going back to my room," I announced.

"I want to talk to you alone," Tamret said. "Come to my room."

When we got to her room, Tamret said, "Hold on. I've worked out a system so Thiel won't disturb us." She then proceeded to affix a note to the door that read *Stay out, or I'll punch you in your stupid face.* Nice system.

Once we were alone, I felt it all catch up to me. My legs grew wobbly, and I sat down on Tamret's bed and put my head in my hands. All along I had been aware of the stakes, but now I felt how close I had come to losing everything—my life, my mother, my world. It could have gone either way, all too easily. At this moment, I thought, I might be on board a Phandic ship, bracing myself to suffer torments and punishments I could only guess at. Or, if I was lucky, I'd be spirited off with Captain Qwlessl, who would have sacrificed her career to save my life. Even in that best-case scenario my mother and my planet lost out, and I would probably never see Tamret again.

"I almost lost everything," I said.

"But we had a plan, didn't we?" she said, her eyes wide. "We were going to escape together. Right?"

"Tamret," I began, and I knew uncertainty was written all over my face.

She pushed my shoulder. "You lied to me? You wouldn't want me to go with you?"

"They want to *kill* me," I told her. "I couldn't ask you to die or be imprisoned or be tortured. I couldn't ask you to give up everything, including your world's chance to join the Confederation, just so you could die on the run with me."

"That's my decision," she said. "And nothing would have happened to me. The point is that you have to do what I tell you to do because as long as you're with me, nothing is going to happen to you."

"You don't know that."

"Yes, I do. I told you. I can do anything."

I felt my muscles tense with frustration. "You say that, but saying it won't save you."

She rolled her eyes at my evident stupidity. "I saved you today."

"What do you mean?" I asked her.

She stood up, took in a long breath, and began to pace around the room. "Zeke, that hearing was not going to go your way. Everyone could see it was a big joke, which was why I decided I needed to sort of keep an eye on things."

Now I was standing too. I couldn't believe what I was hearing. "You hacked into the system?"

"Calm down," she said. "I did what I had to do. I saw the vote before anyone else. And then I changed it."

I sat down again, terror replacing my irritation with Tamret. "What was the vote? What was it really?"

She turned away. "Zeke."

"All of them?"

She nodded. "It was unanimous against you."

"They're going to find out," I said. "Tamret, they are going to catch you."

"I know how to cover my tracks." She came over and sat next to me. "They may eventually figure out the final count was hacked, especially if they talk to each other about how they voted, but they won't be able to trace it back to me."

I looked at her. "You really can do anything."

She grinned. "I keep telling you."

"Thank you," I said. "I wish you wouldn't put yourself in danger, but thank you."

"I will always help you, Zeke. You have to believe that. But I also need you to be honest with me about your plans. Can you do that?"

"Yes." It was all I could manage. Her fierce loyalty was almost more than I could bear.

"Do you believe you'll be safer if you tell me everything?" she asked.

"I think I'll either be a whole lot safer," I said, "or in a whole lot more danger."

She thought about that for a moment. "That sounds about right."

About a week after the hearing Steve, Tamret and I were walking through the commons when I was approached by a humanoid with onyx-black skin and an explosion of brilliantly white hair, all of which made her look like a drow.

"You're him, aren't you?" she said, full of bubbly enthusiasm. "You're Zeke Reynolds."

"Beat it," Tamret said. This was pretty much how she addressed most beings who came up to me, especially the female ones.

The girl turned to her and was about to say something when a collective gasp filled the space. I looked around. Everyone, for as far as the eye could see, was now turned toward their nearest video monitor or looking at a video feed on a data bracelet. We were about twenty feet from a projected public holographic screen, but people stood in the way. Steve and I muscled our way forward, and I pulled Tamret along by her hand.

When I got close enough to see, I felt a wave of nausea sweep over me. I suddenly grew cold. Tamret must have sensed it, because she wrapped her arms around me before looking at the screen. When she saw what was there, her arms went limp.

The screens were tuned to different news outputs, but they were all showing the same thing. It was shaky footage of a battle in space between a single, small Confederation ship and three massive Phandic saucers like the one I'd destroyed. The text at the bottom of the screen identified the images as having been picked up from Phandic media broadcasts. They identified the ship as the *Dependable*.

I watched as the Phandic ships surrounded the *Dependable* and opened fire. The *Dependable*'s shields held, but it did not fire back as it tried to retreat, to force its way out of the confrontation. The Phandic ships kept firing, but all the *Dependable* did was evade. Why wasn't the captain firing back? There was nowhere for her to go. She zipped and doubled back and broke hard to port, then starboard. I could imagine Captain Qwlessl on the bridge, issuing orders, that intense look in her massive eyes as she tried to reason her way out of the impossible. Maybe she didn't fire because she knew it would do no good against the Phandic ships. Maybe after everything that had happened, she wanted to show them that the Confederation did not automatically turn to violence.

Whatever her reasons, they did not help her. Two more Phandic ships emerged from tunnel apertures and blocked the *Dependable*'s path. Then the Phandic ships unleashed the missiles. I didn't have to count them, or even read the text on the screen, to know how many were fired. There were ten. And then a flash of light, and the *Dependable* was gone.

The screen was now showing images of the *Dependable*'s crew. I watched as the familiar faces flashed on the screen. My friend Urch. Ystip the gamer. Captain Qwlessl. All of them dead because they had defended me, because I had refused to stand and face the punishment the Phandic Empire was so desperate to unleash.

"We need to go, mate," Steve was saying, pulling on me.

I snapped out of my sadness and saw that it was now me on some of the screens. They were talking about me. Trillions of beings, all over the Confederation, were looking at my picture and deciding that this either was or wasn't all my fault. I had no idea which way the majority would swing, but this was one vote Tamret couldn't hack.

I let Steve and Tamret pull me away. Steve was muttering, "This is really bad," over and over again. Tamret was whispering to me, telling me she was so sorry about my friends. And then the drow girl was in front of us, and she was pointing. Maybe she was mad because Tamret had sent her packing, and maybe she was just an idiot whose opinion changed with the wind, and maybe she was outraged that a Confederation ship, full of Confederation heroes, had been destroyed because I would not give the Phandic Empire what it wanted.

"It's him!" she shouted. "It's Ezekiel Reynolds! He's the one who caused all of this!"

I let Steve and Tamret pull me along, but I felt all their eyes on me, I felt their hate, the hundreds of beings on the commons, the thousands on the ships, and from across the stars the millions and millions and millions who now blamed me for everything bad that had happened that day and everything bad that was to come.

CHAPTER TWENTY-FIVE

Steve and Tamret stayed with me for a long time, but eventually I sent them away. I wanted to be alone. I lay on my bed, staring at the ceiling, while Charles lay on his own bed, holding his data bracelet in both hands and reading news updates. Every once in a while he would tell me about some latest development or opinion, but I didn't want to hear it. My friends were dead because my enemies wanted to hurt me. If I had turned myself in, they would be alive and I would be dead. There were no should-haves, no mistakes I'd made that I wished I could undo, but I felt miserable and furious and helpless.

I heard Charles say, "Everyone thinks the Confederation has no choice but to declare open war."

"And you think it's my fault?"

"It's human nature—or sentient nature, I suppose," he said. "People want someone to blame. That doesn't make it your fault."

"Do you think I should have turned myself in to the Phandic Empire?"

"You could have. But the Phandic Empire might have chosen not to kill the Ganari and attack the *Dependable*. They did those things. Not you."

I grunted. I appreciated the pep talk, but I wasn't in the mood for it, and I was still not ready to let him off the hook for his weeks of being unpleasant.

A few hours later there was a knock at our door. Charles answered and saw Tamret and Hluh standing outside. Tamret pushed past him and came into the room. "Get out," she said to Charles. "I need to talk to Zeke."

"This is my room," he said.

"Fine. Let's go, Zeke. We need Steve anyhow."

We got Steve, and then Tamret led us all into the classroom, which was empty now. We took seats facing one another, and I waited to hear what she had to say. My heart was pounding. I knew it wasn't going to be good news.

"We've learned something," Hluh said. "Something huge. Tamret did some amazing work."

"It was your idea," Tamret told her. "I would have had no idea where to look if you hadn't suggested it."

"Wait a minute," I said, trying to shake off the grief long enough to concentrate. "Are you two actually friends for real?"

Tamret stared at me. "Is that a problem?"

I held up my hands in surrender. "No, but I officially give up trying to understand anything about anyone."

"Smart move," Tamret said. "So, Hluh had the idea of looking into how we were selected. We knew the randoms weren't random, but we still didn't know how we were chosen."

"I'm not really in the mood for this right now," I said.

"This isn't about moods," Hluh said. "It's important."

"Please listen, Zeke," Tamret said, her voice now gentle.

"It occurred to me that maybe not everyone on the selection committee was necessarily involved," Hluh said. "Maybe some of them thought you were random, and some were behind the intentional selection. I thought if I could trace the choices to a being or beings, it would tell me something."

"That is clever," Steve agreed. "And what did you find out?"

"Of the four randoms, three names were changed *after* the selection committee went missing. Three out of four of you weren't even approved by the selection committee."

"Wait," I said. "So which one of us was originally part of the list?" Then I understood. "It was the Ganari, wasn't it? That's why the shuttle was destroyed."

"Wrong again," said Hluh. "It was you."

I felt my hands gripping the side of the chair, as if I might fall over. "Me?" How could it be me? Was it really true that of all the randoms, I was the only one who really was random? And why did that make me feel so weird? Did I need to be special? Ever since leaving Earth, I'd felt like I was at the center of everything, and now it looked like I wasn't important at all. It was a stupid way to feel, but there it was.

"So, me and you," Steve said, pointing at Tamret, "and that Ganari were all picked later. You said you know who did it?"

Tamret nodded. "Yeah, and this is the insane part. The being who hacked into the system and changed the names of the original randoms—it was Dr. Roop."

I couldn't keep up with all of this. "Dr. Roop is behind some kind of conspiracy?"

"It looks that way," said Hluh. "Tell him the rest."

"Dr. Roop picked the three of us. He's the one who wanted three randoms with some kind of criminal experience. He tossed the other three, which means he made a deliberate decision to keep you, Zeke. And the crazy part is, I think he wanted us to find out. Actually, he wanted *you* to find out, Zeke."

"What?" You can always count on me to ask the really insightful questions.

"I know it sounds crazy, but the password protecting the file, which I exposed when I cracked it, was an anagram of your name in Former letters."

"Which means what?" I asked.

"It's a message," Hluh said. "From him to you. I think he's saying that this information is a secret, but he doesn't want it to be a secret to you."

"If Dr. Roop wants us to know something, why doesn't he come out and tell us?" Steve asked.

"I don't know," Tamret said.

"Maybe he can't," Hluh suggested. "Maybe he's afraid he's being monitored."

"I don't think so," I said. "We've had private conversations before."

"Maybe he wants us to figure it out for ourselves," Tamret said.

That made no sense. If there was important information we needed to have, he would tell us. Wouldn't he? I wished I could make the pieces fit together, because I was suddenly feeling like the one being in authority on Confederation Central was no longer someone I could trust.

Dr. Roop canceled our classes for the next few days. As sad as I was about the death of Captain Qwlessl, I knew he must have been devastated. During those days I tried to keep earning points, but the hostile stares I received in the game room made me uncomfortable, and I lacked the concentration I needed for the flight sim. My heart wasn't in it. Nayana said, perhaps self-servingly, that the crew of the *Dependable* would have wanted Earth to succeed, and I suspected she was right, but I was going to need some time.

There was a memorial service for the crew of the *Dependable*, and thousands of beings went. I wanted to go too, but Dr. Roop said I needed to stay away, and I knew he was right. If I was there, people would be so busy blaming me they would forget they were there to honor the beings who had died.

I found myself wishing I could talk to my mother. I don't think I understood until then just how much Captain Qwlessl's looking after me had allowed me to set aside my worries about my mom. Now the captain was gone, and my mother was impossibly far away, her condition a complete mystery to me. Maybe she had already started to deteriorate. Maybe she would be in a wheelchair, or worse, by the time I got home. I didn't want to think about it, but it started to seem less and less likely we were going to be able to get Earth into the Confederation, and that meant that all the time I was leaving her on her own was for nothing.

Mostly I spent time with Steve and Tamret, or sat by myself, or even hung out with Charles. Now that Ms. Price's mandated freeze-out was over, Charles acted like he desperately wanted to be my friend. He tried to give me space, but he also made it clear that he was ready to talk to me if I wanted.

He started to grow on me during those days, about the things that made no sense to me: the Phandic need for revenge, the plots within the Confederation, all of it. I didn't tell him about Dr. Roop—I wasn't ready to go that far—but I wanted to hear what he thought of the rest. This stuff concerned him, too. Most of all, he was smart, and he might see something that I couldn't.

"I just can't figure it out," I said, at night maybe five days after the *Dependable* was destroyed. "It's like everyone is playing a deep game, and I can't see it."

Charles sat up quickly. "You're right. You are precisely correct. That is exactly what is happening."

"Okay," I said, squinting as I tried to figure out why he was so excited about this. "I'm glad you agree. I guess."

"I do agree. Get up. We need to go."

"Go where?" I asked, not really caring.

"To the girls' room. To see Nayana. We need her."

"For what?"

"You have hit upon it exactly, Zeke. This is an elaborate game, a strategic game, and we can only see some of the board and some of the pieces. We need someone who can help us see the whole thing."

Nayana. Chess. Maybe she could help, but I wasn't quite ready to swallow my pride and ask. "I don't know."

"You can never have too many friends," Charles said.

"You can if you don't trust them."

He shook his head. "Zeke, you saved our lives, and we treated you unforgivably. Please let us make amends. Please trust us."

"Why should I?"

"If you don't believe it's because we want to do the right thing, then at least believe it is in our own best interests. The Phands now hate humans. They hate Earth. No one in the Confederation trusts us. We are in this together whether we wish it or not."

I believed he meant that. I got out of bed.

• • •

Mi Sun opened the door to her room and smiled at Charles, like they were really good friends, the kind of friends who didn't always need to say a whole lot to understand each other. Like me and Tamret, maybe. I didn't know they'd become close. I didn't know much about these people, and now they wanted me to trust them. I still wasn't sure if I should.

Nayana had been lying on her bed and looking at her data bracelet, but now she looked over at me and blinked irritably. "Why is everyone in my room?" she said by way of greeting.

"You are going to help us figure out what the Phands are up to," Charles said.

"Not with that attitude I'm not," Nayana said.

"Yes, you are," Mi Sun said. "Just stop being such a princess."

"I don't like to be ordered around," Nayana said. "My time is valuable."

"This was a bad idea," I said. "I'll figure it out on my own."

"Wait." She sighed and sat up. "Fine. I'll help you, but only because I'm nice. And because I think there'll be experience points in it. For me."

"Okay, to figure out the strategy, we need to see the pieces," Nayana said.

The four of us sat on the floor in a circle while Nayana busily typed on her projected keyboard.

"The Phandic Empire and the Confederation," I said.

She snorted. "Those are the players. The pieces, the ones that count, are us, the initiate species: humans, Ish-hi, Rarels. Let's see what they look like." She programmed in some data, and hovering in the air before us she projected a three-dimensional map of a big chunk of the galaxy, highlighting the Phandic Empire and the Confederation and the locations of our three home worlds.

The two big territories spread out in weird blobs and at sharp angles, looping in and out and spiraling off in different directions, approaching, but never touching. The map showed Phandic territory as yellow, Confederation space as green. Earth, Ish-hi, and Rarel were all in the black space between. All three were lodged snugly between borders.

"Interesting," I said. "Can we see Ganar?"

Nayana highlighted it, and we could see it much farther galactic south of Earth, much farther outside the border territory. It was easily the most distant world from the heart of either the Confederation or the Phandic Empire.

Nayana bit her lower lip. "Maybe this piece wasn't important, and that's why it was taken out of play."

"I don't think so," I said. "They tried to destroy us as well."

"Unless they didn't," Mi Sun said.

I glowered at her.

"I'm not taking their side," she said, "but what if they weren't actually looking to destroy the *Dependable*? What if they were looking to disable the ship and capture us? It's possible."

"Maybe," I said. "But why? Why would they want us alive and the Ganari dead?"

"Let's consider what was said at your hearing," Charles said. "The Phandic ambassador claimed that our worlds were chosen not because they are good fits for the Confederation, but because we are violent species, which perhaps the Confederation needs."

"What do we know about the Ganari?" I asked. "Are they

bloodthirsty barbarians like us, or are they more chill?"

"Looking it up," Mi Sun said, tapping her data bracelet to call up her own keyboard. "You guys keep going."

"If we are a more violent species than the Confederation norm," said Charles, "and our worlds are in space between the two sides, doesn't that suggest we were more apt to be annexed by the Phands than the Confederation?"

"So the Confederation grabs us first?" I said. "They want tougher citizens to help balance the scales. Maybe use us as cannon fodder since we're on the borders."

Charles nodded. "It makes sense."

"Yes it does," Mi Sun said. "According to what I'm reading about the Ganari, they are omnivores and complex thinkers. They have their history of war, but no worse than the rest of us for most of their history. Then, a few hundred years ago, during their industrial age, all major global violence ended. They started resolving conflicts with a series of extremely intricate strategy games. As a result, their national leaders are selected for their intelligence and insight."

"So they're a more traditional pick," Nayana said, "but a tactical one. They could be of real use in helping the Confederation choose a strategy, so the Phands take the Ganari out of play. They keep the rest of us because they think we're not as smart and they can recruit us to their side. So maybe they were going to capture us—to convince us to defect."

"Then Zeke destroyed their ship," Charles said, "and they replaced their strategy with a need for revenge? It is not very intelligent."

"It might be cultural," Mi Sun suggested. "Maybe honor and revenge are just really important to them."

"We're talking about beings who hurl in public to make a point," I said.

Nayana sighed. "We're still just looking at pawns."

"There are too many players we haven't seen," Charles observed.

Nayana looked up, smiling. "Maybe we can't see them because they've been captured."

"The selection committee!" I nearly shouted it. She was onto something.

"Yeah," she agreed. "Think about it. They've been captured, but they're still in play. Vusio-om tried to use them as a bargaining chip at your hearing, and that's where all of this begins. The committee picked our planets. They had a grand strategy in mind."

"But we don't know what it is," Charles said. "What can we find out about them?"

I cleared my throat. "I, uh, have it on good authority that the Confederation has buried their service files. They can't be hacked."

"Good authority," Nayana said with a sneer. "What, your pet kitty?"

"Nayana," Mi Park said. "Remember, we're all on the same side now."

"Sorry," she muttered. "It's just who I am."

"Yeah, don't be who you are in front of Tamret," I said. "It might be bad for your health."

She rolled her eyes. "Your girlfriend's hacking skills aside, did you ever consider that you don't always have to break the law? The government service files may be hidden away, but there's info on these people in the public domain. Interviews, biographies, public writings, media appearances. Did you look at any of this?"

"No," I admitted, feeling kind of foolish. I'd been so dispirited at the thought of what was being kept from us, I hadn't even bothered to look at what was readily available.

She tapped on her data bracelet for a second and then looked up, grinning, like she'd stumbled on a secret stash of goodies. "You know what? I think we're on the right track."

"Why?" I asked.

"Because," she said, "I just leveled up."

We stood looking over Nayana's shoulder as she began scrolling through data on the selection committee members. I thought that even if she was right, and we were onto something, we weren't going to make any big discoveries tonight. There were five members of the committee, and they all had long records of public service, most of the context of which was totally inscrutable to us. Duggsur Yikyik Eeee had spent four years as chairbeing of the Rimerian Lower Educational Reform Council, but really, so what? Was that an impressive position or a laughable one? Influential or pointless? None of it meant anything to us.

I could tell that Nayana was growing frustrated too. She read through a lot of data on Mr. or Ms. or whatever Eeee, but the second member got a much more cursory glance.

"Maybe we should get Dr. Roop in on this," Mi Sun suggested.

"That might not be a bad idea," Nayana conceded. "Assuming we can even trust him."

I hadn't told them what we had discovered about Dr. Roop, and I still didn't know if I wanted to. I remained silent while

Nayana summoned up the image of a third committee member.

He was a big guy, muscular and humanoid, looking different from an Earthman only in minor details. He had green skin and a large protruding brow, the same as Hluh. In the picture he stood, looking at the camera or image taker or whatever, arms crossed. He wore a theatrical cape with a high collar. He wore no shirt, but there were two red bands crossing his muscular chest.

Nayana must have seen me staring. "Yeah, I noticed him too," she said. "That's some idiotic getup, right? He's a Yionian, like your data-collector friend, but that doesn't look like a Yionian name. They always have lots of repeated sounds, like his, but they are usually longer."

"Maybe he is a convert," Charles said. "I read of this—beings who transform their appearance to look like members of other species."

"Yeah," I said, my voice distant. I was thinking that too. I looked at his face. I looked at his name. I had no doubt he was a convert. A convert was exactly what he had to be.

I sat down next to Nayana.

"Not so close." She shoved me.

I ignored her. What I saw on the screen made everything else insignificant.

The numbers on the bottom of my HUD were rolling upward at a dizzying speed as the system struggled to keep up with the torrent of experience points. It was like I'd hit the bonus level on an old-school video game. The only time I had ever racked up so many points this quickly had been when I'd saved the *Dependable* from the Phandic saucer. I was going to gain a whole bunch of levels, but I didn't care about that.

"Hey, I'm suddenly gaining a ton of experience points," said Mi Sun.

"So am I," Charles said. "I think we hit on something."

Their words were a distant noise, almost like they were speaking a language I didn't understand. It was one of those moments when everything comes together. Or maybe it was one of those moments when nothing comes together and you realize just how little you actually know. I wasn't sure which, but I knew that this was one of the most important moments of my life—and that was coming from a guy who had already gone into outer space.

I looked at Charles. He had the most influence in the trio, and he was the one whose loyalty I had to make sure of. The others would follow him.

"You said you regret how you've treated me," I told him. "Did you mean it?"

"I just picked up two levels," Charles said. "Whatever is going on is important. I am with you."

"But do you *trust* me?" I demanded.

He considered this for a moment. "Yes," he told me, his voice solemn.

"Maybe," Mi Sun said.

"Trust isn't really my thing," Nayana said.

"I'm not joking," I said. "I saved all your lives on the *Dependable*, and I've got more levels than any of you. I need to know if you are willing to do some risky things if I can convince you it's for the right reasons."

"I don't understand," Charles said.

"I need to confirm some stuff," I said, "but you have to tell me if you are in or out."

"In or out of *what*?" Nayana said irritably.

"If there's one thing Ms. Price said we can believe, it's that Earth is in danger. I don't think making our eighty is going to make a difference to Earth if the Phandic Empire and the Confederation decided to fight over our planet."

"No," Charles agreed. "It won't."

"Do you want to save our planet from the Phands?"

He nodded.

"You'll follow me?"

"Doing what?" Mi Sun asked.

"Breaking a lot of laws," I said. "Probably getting our delegation kicked off the station, unless we're really lucky. But what I have in mind might just save our world. You in?"

"Yes," Charles said.

"Yes," Mi Sun said.

"No!" Nayana nearly shouted. Then she sighed. "Fine. Okay."

"I need to check some things out. Be ready." I said. Then I ran as quickly as I could.

I pounded and pounded on the door. Finally Thiel, Tamret's roommate, answered. She looked like she'd been sleeping, which made sense because it was now pretty late at night.

"What?" she said.

"I need Tamret."

"Yeah, we all know that. The whole galaxy saw the picture of you two making lovey eyes like a couple of dopes."

A white hand landed on her shoulder and yanked her back. I heard her crash into something, breaking glass, and a loud hissing sound.

Tamret smiled at me. "What do you need?"

I pulled her out into the hallway. "You told me you could hack into the secret files on the selection committee," I said quietly. "Did you mean it?"

She set her gaze at me. "I can do anything."

"But you can do *this*?"

"Absolutely," she said. "It's easy to do, but impossible to conceal. They'll find out, and they can track it to me within a few hours."

I nodded, thinking this through. "Can you find out where they are being held prisoner?"

"The Phand said the Confederation knows, which means it's in the system. That means I can find out. But again, they'll know I've been snooping around. What's this about?"

I called up the data file on my bracelet and showed her the picture. "It's about him."

"That's one of the committee members," she said. "I remember his nutty outfit."

"Yeah," I said. I was grinning so hard my mouth hurt.

"So, what's the deal? Who is this J'onn J'onzz to you?"

"That's not actually J'onn J'onzz," I told her. "J'onn J'onzz is the real name of Martian Manhunter, a core member of the classic Justice League lineup and my favorite comic book character for as long as I can remember."

"I don't know what you are talking about. If he's not this J'onn J'onzz, then who is he?"

"He's a human," I said. "He's from Earth. He's altered his appearance, but his name, that look—it's a flag that only the right person would recognize. And I'm that person."

"And how does this selection committee member fit in?"

"He's the reason why the randoms were chosen," I said. "Sessek, the Ganari, because she could break into secure buildings. You, because you can hack. And Steve. It all makes sense now."

"I don't understand," she said. "Who is this person?"

"His name is Uriah Reynolds," I told her. "He's my father."

Tamret took hold of my hand. "Anything you need. Just say it."

I closed my eyes, basking in the warmth of her touch and her willingness to help me. "Things might get really bad."

"I don't care."

"Okay," I said, as much to myself as to her. I needed to clear my thoughts. Was I really going to go through with all this? Was I really prepared to risk so much? "I have to make sure Steve can do something. If he can, I'll need you to start looking for that prison. And then the clock will be running."

"What is Steve supposed to do?" she asked.

"Exactly what Dr. Roop brought him here to do," I told her. "He's going to steal us a spaceship."

Part Three
THE BRAVE AND THE BOLD

CHAPTER TWENTY-SIX

We moved the operation to my room so Tamret's roommate wouldn't bother us. I explained everything to Charles, Mi Sun, and Nayana—that the Phandic Empire had my father as their prisoner, and how we were planning to find him and get him out. Tamret had been reluctant to take my word for it when I told her that the other humans were on our side, and she had regarded their apologies with contempt, but in the end she had been willing to suspend her disbelief. I took a break to pack an overnight bag with at least a couple of changes of clothes and some spare underwear and I told the others to do the same. It was something to do, and it seemed like a good precaution against the interior of the ship getting too rank. I also suggested they load up on food rations and hydration packs. I had no idea how long this trip was going to take, and we needed to be prepared for anything. Afterward all we could do was sit quietly until Tamret was able to hack into the Confederation governmental system and find the location of the Phandic prison where the selection committee was being held.

For more than an hour, there was no sound but the soft tap of her pads against the glossy surface of the holographic keyboard. Then she looked up, and she was smiling. "Got it," she said. Then she activated the comm feature on her data bracelet.

"Oi!" Steve's voice came over the system.

"I've got the destination. You good on your end?"

"It's like they're asking me to take their ships. I'm sending you the location of the meet right now."

"See you in a few," she said. Then she looked up. "Are you guys ready?"

If they were half as nervous as I was, they must have been telling the most serious lies of their lives, but everyone nodded. Almost everyone.

"Wait, why are we doing this?" Nayana asked. "If he wants to go after his father, that's his business. What's it to us?"

"Because he is going to go no matter what we do," said Mi Sun. "And if he gets killed or captured, we're done."

"There will be many experience points for us if we do," Charles observed.

"Fine," Nayana said. "But I won't like it."

"There's more, too," I said. "I'll explain it on the way, but this could basically secure Earth's entry into the Confederation and its safety from the Phands."

When they were all near the door, Tamret turned to face them. "Every last one of you," she said, "is a total piece of garbage as far as I'm concerned, but Zeke says I should trust you, so I will. But if I think you're even considering betraying him, I will rip your throat out and never give it a second thought."

"Thank you," I told her, "for motivating the troops. Let's go find Steve."

When we stepped into the hall, Ms. Price was there, waiting for us. Her arms were folded. "Something is going on with all of you," she said.

"Uh, no," I said. "Why do you think that?"

"Four humans and the cat hanging out."

"We're just chilling," I offered.

"You all seem to be chilling with overnight bags," she observed. "I don't like it."

"I'm way past caring what you like and what you don't," I told her.

"Tamret, go back to your quarters. The four of you, I think you'd better follow me."

I didn't know what to do. We couldn't follow her, and we certainly couldn't get separated from Tamret. On the other hand, if we ran, Ms. Price would alert the authorities.

Fortunately, Mi Sun had a solution I hadn't through of. She pivoted to her side, and her right leg shot up lightning fast. She didn't so much kick Ms. Price as smack her in the face with the top of her foot. Ms. Price was lifted off the floor and crashed into the wall. Her eyes rolled back, and she fell, limp as a sack of laundry.

Mi Sun's face was totally blank. Tamret indulged in the smallest and most menacing of all possible smiles.

"I'm sure that was satisfying," I said, "but her sudden injury will alert a medical team. We should get out of here."

We ran.

With public transport, it took almost a quarter hour to reach the docking port where Steve had asked us to meet him. I kept expecting some kind of security to catch us, but if they'd found Ms. Price, they hadn't awakened her and gotten the details about us yet. It was also possible she hadn't chosen to turn us in. However angry she was, and I had no doubt she was steaming, she was probably reluctant to sink Earth's chances of joining the Confederation just for the pleasure of seeing Mi Sun get in trouble.

We had to go through a public terminal, sort of like an airport, and then to the docks housing private ships. These were in what looked like a huge warehousing system of cubicles stretching more than a mile along one side of the station's lower section. It rose up for fifty levels of cubes, and each individual cube was about the size of a basketball court. The interior section of each was open, except when a ship was entering or exiting. Then bulkhead doors would close, and an internal plasma field, as a secondary precaution, would seal the chamber before the outer plasma field went down and the bulkhead opened.

We passed several signs that announced only beings with legitimate business were permitted in the docking area, and that seemed to represent the extent of the security. We traveled to the section Steve had indicated, and then took an open lift up twelve levels to get to the right docking bay. Steve was standing outside, leaning against the wall, arms folded, and looking like he was posing for the cover of *Spaceship Thievery* magazine.

"Artifact carrier," Steve said. "Fast, decent weaponry, excellent shielding. Best of all, the owner's off-station on a commercial venture. By the time he finds out about an unauthorized launch and asks the peace officers to investigate, we'll be long gone."

"Nice," I said. "How'd you find it?"

"I helped him." It was Dr. Roop. He emerged from inside the hangar. Given the context, his dark, boxy Confederation suit made him almost appear like a crime lord—albeit one with an unusually long neck.

The other humans looked nervous, like they had been busted. I hadn't told them about Dr. Roop's involvement in all this. I hadn't been entirely sure I understood it all until now.

"This is what you wanted all along, isn't it?" I said. "It's why you picked the other randoms. You needed Tamret to get all the data and Steve to steal a ship. Sessek, the Ganari, was supposed to help us break in once we got there."

"You'll have to make do without her," Dr. Roop said, widening his eyes. "I wasn't counting on the rest of the human delegation joining you, and I think with all your skills, you should do well."

"Why didn't you just tell us?" I asked.

"Because if you'd known your father was being held prisoner, you would have wanted to go before you were ready."

"How do you know we're ready now?" I asked.

"I don't," he told me. "I've gambled that your having discovered what you need to know indicates that you are now ready. Waiting for you to discover the truth gave you time to train, learn ship operations, and hopefully gain the skills you needed to succeed. I've sent everything we know about the prison and about Phandic security protocols to your data bracelets. I've examined the data extensively, and I believe this is something you can do."

"I don't understand," Nayana said. "Why do we have to do this? Don't you have trained people to take care of this sort of thing?"

"We do, but they won't," Dr. Roop said. "The councils are too timid to risk Phandic anger. But that is your greatest advantage: Whatever the Phands think will happen, the last thing they will expect is a brazen rescue attempt. In the Confederation, we simply don't do that sort of thing, and they know it. But your kind—you are daring and reckless, and you have all been training. I know you can do what needs to be done."

I swallowed hard. We were really going to do this, then. It was so insane, so unbelievably stupid, and we were going to do it. "You chose the three others after my father was captured," I said.

"Yes," Dr. Roop agreed.

"And me?"

"He had already tinkered with the system by choosing you," Dr. Roop said. "I was not so much breaking the law as continuing to work with a law that had already been broken."

I had no idea how my father had come to be here on Confederation Central. I had no idea why he'd left his family, why he'd left Earth. I would have to ask him when I rescued him.

"He's a good friend," Dr. Roop said. His data bracelet beeped, and he looked down. "Apparently, someone assaulted Ms. Price, and the peace officers have been asked to apprehend all of you. Perhaps it is best you be on your way."

I nodded.

Dr. Roop awkwardly offered me his hand. "Your father taught me this."

I shook his hand. "I want to know everything when I get back."

"And I will tell you. We both will." He leaned forward. "Before you go, you should level up. We're past the point of being discreet, and you'll need every advantage you can use."

I nodded. It was sound advice.

"Good luck, Zeke," he said. Then he left.

We headed inside the hangar and toward the artifact carrier. It looked much like a shuttle on the outside, and I recognized the configuration of the interior from the many sims

I'd run. This would be just like a sim, I told myself, except we might all get killed.

"I need a minute to level up before I go," I said to Tamret. "Can you get everyone settled?"

"Of course." She began tapping on her data bracelet as she walked into the ship.

I checked my numbers and I now had enough points to reach level sixteen, which meant I had six points to assign, and I put them all in various piloting-track skills. Again, I was tempted to add some points to strength, but I resisted. More than ever, I would need to make sure my piloting skills were strong. Steve and Tamret and Mi Sun were great fighters. Making myself a little stronger would not matter. Making myself a little better at the helm might make all the difference. Two points went into agility, two to intellect, one to constitution, and one to vision.

I'd leveled up before, and was always kind of disappointed that my new skills didn't make me feel any different. I wanted my heart to race, my senses to come alive, but I always felt like the same old me. I knew the added abilities were slight and subtle, but I hoped they would be enough to help us.

When I got on board, Steve had taken helm. I took navigation. Everyone was already strapped in and sitting still—except Tamret, who had her keyboard out and was typing furiously. "Don't mind me," she said. "I can do this while we move."

We shut the ship doors and sealed the inner bulkhead, and as soon as we were properly depressurized, we opened the outer bulkhead. A message came in over the ship's comm from the station's traffic server. It appeared, it said, that we were making an unscheduled departure. We didn't answer. We simply departed, unscheduled. Steve eased the artifact carrier forward, and I watched on the reverse viewscreen as the station fell away.

Just like that we were gone, in our stolen ship, heading away from the station. I felt a sudden jolt, almost as though we had tunneled. My senses tingled. The world instantly felt sharper, more defined, more vivid. I could feel my mind churning, purring like an engine. I wondered if it was the new skill points kicking in, but I doubted it. Even my hearing, which I hadn't touched, seemed improved. I knew it had to be my imagination, or maybe nerves, but I didn't care. I felt good. I felt strangely ready to take on this absurdly dangerous mission.

This is what it feels like, I thought, *to be an outlaw.*

The station's traffic server continued to send inquiries at us, imploring us to return, and then asking if we required assistance. Finally, we sent back that we did not need help, and that seemed to satisfy them. As soon as we reached the regulation distance, we plotted our tunnel and opened an aperture. We dropped out of the universe and were on our way. It would take the better part of two days to reach our destination. There was nothing to do but wait.

I did a lot of waiting. The excitement I'd felt turned to fear, and finally to worry. Steve went in the back to nap, and I sat at the helm and watched panels that required no attention from me. I tried not to imagine getting my friends killed in a pointless and reckless exercise. I didn't know what I was doing, and if I did, I would never have done it. A rescue mission on a prison planet? It was pure lunacy.

I still felt strange, like there were bugs crawling on my skin, like every sound was magnified a hundredfold. I supposed being hyperaware was the price you paid for being a criminal.

Better to be overly sensitive, I told myself, than to be oblivious.

I sat there, thinking about what we were doing, what we had done, and despite the confidence I'd felt when we left the station, I was suddenly full of dread. What we were attempting was foolish and reckless. Dr. Roop had said we could do it, but that didn't make it true.

Charles came and sat next to me, and I didn't notice he was there until he asked what was on my mind. I wasn't really in the mood to tell him my problems, but I figured I had nothing to lose. He had followed me this far.

"At the hearing," I told him, "when the Phandic Ambassador said there would be no peace while I lived, I was thinking that it was exactly like *Star Trek IV*, and how bad it would be if things became like *Star Trek V*. Now here we are. Does that make you Spock? Tamret is Uhura? The girls are like Sulu and Chekov or something? Steve is Dr. McCoy? We're all old and lame. This is going to be a disaster."

"I have not seen that film," Charles said, "but I do recall another American space adventure in which the heroes must force their way into an alien fortress. I believe in that one it was to rescue a princess. Do you know this story?"

"Uh, yeah," I said, sitting up, because I did see it. "The space adventure you refer to is called *Star Wars Episode Four: A New Hope*. I think I've seen that one. And you're right. This totally works. I'm Luke and Steve is Han Solo. I mean, think about it. The original Han Solo was a lizard guy. This is too perfect. Tamret is Chewbacca in so many ways it's not even funny. You're Obi-Wan, so you are going to get struck down but then become more powerful than we can possibly imagine. Which I guess means you'll become a disembodied voice that gives pretty good advice."

"And the girls?"

"They're the droids." I told him.

"Which one is which?" he asked.

I shook my head. "Charles, if you have to ask, you're not in the game."

Talking to Charles did cheer me up, but even if I could convince myself that our mission might succeed, I could not help but worry about why we were going on this mission in the first place. Why did my father look like Martian Manhunter? How had he ended up masquerading as a citizen of the Confederation?

"You look glum." Tamret came to sit next to me. "Something's bothering you."

I nodded. There were many things bothering me, but one thing more than anything else. I didn't want to talk about it. It was hard stuff, and it brought me back to places I didn't want to go. I was terrified that if I talked about it, I would cry, and I sure as hell didn't want to cry in front of her. But I cared about her, and she'd asked, and I owed it to her to tell her what was on my mind.

"It's about my father," I said. "I mean, he obviously at some point learned about the Confederation and the wider galaxy. He ended up out here. He wrote about it. I can understand that he wanted to be part of it, but he left us. He left me and he left my mother. How can I forgive him for that?"

She took my hand and squeezed it. "Oh, Zeke."

"He was a good dad," I said. "We played together and he was funny and fun and he introduced me to all these things I loved. From the moment I met Dr. Roop, from then on, every time there was something new, I would think, 'Dad would have loved this. I wish Dad could have seen this.'"

She gave my hand another squeeze.

"And I know he loved my mom. I remember them together, and they were happy. I know it wasn't an act."

"You don't know what I would give to see my father again," she said quietly. "Either of my parents. I'm not sure I understand why you're so sad."

"Because he went away," I said. "There was no explanation, no good-bye. He faked his death and flew off to the Confederation. I understand why he would be tempted, but he still left us. How can I forgive that?"

"Maybe he had no choice," she said. "Maybe he was taken against his will. Maybe he understood about the danger Earth was in, about the threat of Phandic annexation, and he decided that saving his planet was the best way to save his family."

"Whatever his reasons for leaving, he made us think he was dead."

She took my hand and put it to her soft cheek. I watched her do it, and I watched her looking at me with those big lavender eyes.

"Would you like to know what I think?" she asked.

I nodded.

"You don't know why he left," she said. "You don't know if he had a choice in leaving or if he was prevented from returning to you. But here's what you do know: Your father somehow created a new identity for himself in the Confederation, one that would pass all scrutiny. That meant he could have made any kind of life for himself that he wanted, but instead he worked as a public servant. Then he got himself elected to one of the most important committees in the government. There are trillions of beings in the Confederation, and they voted for him to be on the selection committee. And when he was on that committee, he moved the members in directions they'd never gone before so that your planet would be among the new initiates. And then he risked everything he had accomplished and broke the law so that from all the people who might have been the random member of the delegation, it would be his own son. I don't know whether or not he could have returned to you, Zeke, but I do know he went to incredible lengths to bring you to him."

I couldn't speak for a long time. I sat there, swallowing, feeling the moisture in my eyes but not daring to say anything. Then, when I felt like I could keep myself under control, I finally looked at her. "You are, without doubt, the most amazing girl in the history of girlkind."

"Like you would know," she said, but the look on her face told me that however little I knew, it was good enough for her. "He loves you, Zeke. From a distance of millions of miles, it's plain as day."

"Thanks," I whispered.

"Okay," Tamret said. "I've finished reviewing the files Dr. Roop gave us, and we need to talk about the prison and the mission in general. We've got a little less than a day until we get there at current speed. Crazy as it sounds, this might be doable."

We were all sitting toward the front of the artifact carrier. Everyone was getting a little stir-crazy, which made it a great time for a briefing.

"I'm not done going through the files," Mi Sun said. "Honestly, I've just started. It's hard to make sense of it all."

"Good thing you've got me to break it down for you," Tamret said.

"If Tamret's got a plan," I told the group, "I want to hear it."

"How are we going to save Earth?" Nayana asked. "That was the bargain as I recall."

"One thing at a time," I said. "Let's hear about where we're going."

Tamret sucked in a deep breath, as though she were about to take a dive. "The planet is largely uninhabited except for a relatively small prison," she said, "consisting almost exclusively of political prisoners, who are forced to work archaeological sites that contain Former artifacts. There's security, but not much of it is planetside. Mainly their defenses are designed to keep ships from coming out, less because they're worried about escaping prisoners than because they don't want anyone stealing artifacts. According to the military surveys Dr. Roop provided, it may be possible to land without being detected, but it will be pretty much impossible to leave the surface without the orbiting ship knowing."

I had my own thoughts about that problem. "Let's say we're able to land safely and quietly. What then?"

"Then we make our way to the main Phandic outpost, hack into their system, and find our prisoners. Once we have Zeke's father, our best option is to try to steal a Phandic ship and hope to slip out undetected."

"That's the worst plan I've ever heard," Nayana said. "What makes you think you'll even be able to hack a Phandic computer?"

"I can do anything," Tamret said.

"She can do anything," I agreed.

"You can't simply take that as your motto and expect people to act as though it were true."

"I got us this far, didn't I?"

"This far," Nayana observed, "is on a stolen ship on the way to Phandic prison while we just happen to have on board a person they'd really like to imprison. I'm not terribly impressed. And let's get back to the business about saving the Earth. How are we doing that?"

"Tamret just told you," I said. "Our carrier will be detected if we try to leave, so we'll be grabbing a Phandic ship on the way out. We deliver that to the Confederation; they reverse engineer it and end the technological advantage the Phands have. We change the balance of power in the galaxy, the Confederation becomes dominant, the Phands retreat, and Earth is safe."

"If it's so easy, why hasn't anyone done it before?" demanded Nayana.

"Because they haven't had us before?" Steve ventured.

Nayana was nearly ready to scream in frustration. "Uhhh! I suppose you can do anything too?"

"Not quite anything," he admitted, "but I'm not so bad at a few things. And you see, ducky, that's the point, isn't it? I like the Confederation. They're good blokes, but they're cowardly custard, if you haven't noticed. They don't like to get their hands dirty. They wet their nappies when Zeke here fires a few extra missiles at a ship that attacked first. They have big brains and big ideas, but they don't have a ton of nerve. Now, you get some of us hooligans together, and you've got another story."

"This is so stupid," Nayana said. "Don't you see what's going on? Dr. Roop admitted that this is what he intended all along.

We're not rebels and we're not heroes. We're pawns."

"No," said Charles. "I don't think Dr. Roop is that deceptive. If we were pawns, it would mean we were sacrificing ourselves in the service of another, more meaningful assault, and from what we have seen of the Confederation, I think we know that is not the case. They've maintained equilibrium for so long that they've forgotten how to fight. That's what we're for."

"So if we're not pawns," Nayana asked, "what are we?"

Mi Sun met her gaze. "The whole game is riding on us. That makes us kings."

We came out of our tunnel about ten thousand miles from the planet and went to work. If everything we'd learned was true, then our sensors were vastly superior to what the Phands' have, which meant we were close enough to watch them safely, and as long as no one tunneled out close enough to pick us up, the enemy would never know we were there.

We monitored and recorded Phandic activity for a complete twenty-six-hour cycle, and then I handed the data over to Charles and Nayana. "Let's assume every rotation is like this rotation. Study it, find a weakness, and we'll figure out our next move." Meanwhile, Tamret had been trying to work her way into their computer system, which she explained was much more sophisticated and had far more safeguards than anything she'd seen in the Confederation.

"I can overlay a private network onto their planetary grid," she told me. "That means we'll be able to communicate through our data bracelets, and they won't know about it. Unless they are specifically looking for it. But if they're looking for us, we'll have bigger problems."

I nodded. "Anything else?"

"Yeah, actually, some good news." She called up a three-dimensional map of the main compound. "Okay, so this big building here is the main prison. I was able to retrieve their personnel specs, and I think we should be able to take them. But that's not the best part, which is that the only projectile weapons on the planet are in this other building, the main command bunker. I guess they don't want to risk harming the artifacts, because all their firearms are locked up, and they're only for emergencies. If we take the bunker, we take the weapons, and we have more or less an insurmountable tactical advantage."

"How do they manage a prison if they're unarmed?" I asked.

"They're not exactly unarmed. They have plasma wands, which are essentially high-powered energy sticks. They can be deadly, but on the low setting they're just meant to hurt—to provide incentive for cooperation. A few guys with plasma wands can control a large prison population, but if we have the PPB pistols and they don't, they've got no chance."

Six hours later, after Charles and Nayana had reviewed the planetary security data, we had a plan. We sat down, and they called up a hologram of the planet.

"That trick you used to cheat us when we did that sim," Nayana said to Steve. "Did you come up with it by yourself?"

"I wish I were so clever," he said. "Dr. Roop wanted to run through a couple of sims together. He taught me that one."

"Figures," she said. "The sun in this system just happens to be extremely active, and there is a great deal of radiation bursting out in regular intervals, just like in that sim. Dr. Roop taught you that little maneuver for when you came here."

I lightly smacked Mi Sun's arm. "I told you. *Ender's Game.*"

"Don't touch me," she said. "But yeah."

"So here's how it will work," Nayana said. "The patrolling ship's orbit is not geosynchronous. It's not hovering above the prison, but regularly moving all around the planet. That makes things tougher, but just a little. When the cruiser is on the far side of the planet, we wait for the sun to be at the part of its cycle when flares are most active, and then we beeline for the planet. The solar radiation will conceal our ion trail, so we'll be invisible to the Phands' sensors. As soon as we hit atmosphere, we do what Steve did in the sim: We cut the engines to drop down hard and fast to the surface so if they notice us at all, we'll look like a meteor. Once we've dropped as far as we can, we fire up the engines and skim under their detection net to a landing site about ten miles from the main prison compound."

"That sounds too easy," Mi Sun said.

"She is leaving out the most significant problem," Charles said. "Steve learned how to execute that maneuver on a fairly small moon, which didn't have nearly as strong a gravity well as an Earth-size planet. This ship's g-force inhibitors won't be able to compensate for our approach speed. Have any of you allocated skill points in constitution or endurance?"

Steve, Tamret, and I all said we had. They were standard spaceflight skills.

"Who has the most?"

"Zeke and I," Tamret said.

I had no idea how she had applied her skill points, and I had never told her about how I had applied mine, but respect for privacy was not one of her many fine attributes.

"Our nanites will keep the rest of us from actually dying," Charles said, "but we will likely pass out. You two have the greatest chance of remaining awake long enough to prevent us from crashing into the surface of the planet and being killed in a fiery explosion."

"We'll be fine," Tamret said.

I was less confident, however. "What's plan B?"

"Plan B," Nayana said, "is that we give up and head back to the station. I like plan B, just in case you were wondering."

Tamret smiled at me like we were sharing a secret. "Zeke and I can do this."

"You know that for sure?" I asked.

"I know it for sure." She met my gaze. This was no joke and no boast. She meant it.

"Alternatively," I proposed, "we could try to slingshot around the sun to generate enough speed to produce a time warp, and then rescue the prisoners before they were ever taken."

"Is that from a movie?" Mi Sun asked. "I hope you are being a dork, because if you're not, then you're a total idiot."

"I'm being a dork," I assured her.

Once they had finished with their briefing, and we had calculated the time and coordinates for our approach, Tamret walked us through the prison terrain itself. She called up the map of the compound, pointing out the main building and the bunker. The bunker contained a huge underground complex, and it served as the barracks, the armory, and the warehouse for storing Former artifacts.

Our sensors told us that there were exactly 203 sentient beings on the surface. Based on their movement patterns, which we were able to get the computer to analyze, it seemed that only forty-seven of these were guards. The rest appeared to be prisoners.

"The real problem will be once we've found Zeke's father,"

Steve said. "We can conceal our descent using gravity and radiation, but there's no way they're going to miss us when we take off. This whole plan depends on figuring something out once we're past the point of no return. Otherwise, that Phandic cruiser in orbit is going to stop us before we get anywhere."

"We've come all this way," I said, "and it hasn't been an accident. Dr. Roop picked us for this, and he's been training us for this. I don't believe he would have led us here if he didn't think we could do it, but I have to be honest and say I don't love going in if I can't tell you how we're getting out. You guys have been great, but I can't force you to do this. If you want to turn around and go home, we will. You can drop me off somewhere first. I'll find another way back here. But I'm not going to make you take this risk."

"Good idea," Nayana said. "Let's go back."

"For what?" Mi Sun asked. "To be arrested for theft and kicked out of the Confederation? If we don't come back with that Phandic ship, we've done all this for nothing. I say we keep going."

Charles tapped my arm excitedly and then pointed at Nayana. "She is the prim, golden robot, and Mi Sun is the beeping, competent, silver robot."

I gave him a fist bump. "You have learned much, my friend."

"We've already done the impossible," Charles said to Nayana, "and we have been led to it. We may as well see where our streak ends."

"Fine," Nayana said. "But I am going to complain the whole time."

She was as good as her word.

The more Nayana thought about it, the more she seemed

to hate the idea of coming at a straight dive and plummeting toward a planet at a speed that would render some of us, possibly all of us, unconscious. Admittedly, I could understand her concerns.

"What makes you think you can pilot a ship well enough to pull this off?" she asked.

"Look at me," I said. "What do you see?"

"A guy who needs a shower?" she suggested. "A twelve-year-old in a stolen spaceship?"

"Look higher, like above my head."

She did, and her eyes went wide. "What? Sixteen? That's not possible." The rest of the humans were elevens, proud of it, and had been stuck there for a long time.

"I applied my unused points before we left the station. I'm level sixteen, and I've put every single skill point I have into the piloting track. That means I have the endurance, constitution, and agility to do this."

Nayana's reaction surprised me. She burst into tears.

Charles moved toward her to comfort her, but she waved him away. "Leave me alone. I want to go home."

"You want to go back to the station?" Mi Sun asked irritably. "We already decided this."

"Not to the station. Home. Earth. My room. I want my bed and my things and my mother and father and my pet ca—my pet. I don't want to be here anymore. You're all brave and crazy, but I'm not. I'm not one of you."

Tamret let out a long sigh and sat down next to Nayana. "As much as I hate to say it, you *are* one of us. And you *do* belong here."

Nayana looked up at her.

Tamret rolled her eyes. "I don't like you, Nayana. In fact, I kind of hate you and would like to stick my claws in your eyes."

"Focus," I said.

"But," Tamret continued, "you're the one who realized we needed to be looking at the selection committee. You figured out what was important and what was noise when it came to what we already knew. And that gigantic brain of yours cut through the Phandic patrol patterns like a hot knife through [*congealed animal fat*]. I don't know anything about this game you're supposed to be so good at, but as near as I can tell, it means you're able to see patterns and figure out strategies, and we need that."

Nayana shook her head. "You don't get it. You're not afraid of anything, but I'm scared, okay? I am afraid I'm going to die, and I'm totally freaked out."

Tamret rolled her eyes. "I won't let anything happen to you. I'll look out for you or whatever."

All the lip biting and hand wringing told me Nayana wasn't buying it. "You say that, but, how do I know you mean it?"

Tamret sighed, like she was getting ready to jump off a cliff. "Fine. You want a guarantee. How's this. I invoke the ritual of bonding, and declare before [*the first tier deity of family*] that you are now my sister. Okay, we're like family now, so I will have your back. I pretty much have no choice, so have your big-baby cry and get it out of your system, because in about ten minutes we're going to be falling out of the sky so fast there's almost no way you're not going to pee all over yourself while blood vessels burst until you black out."

Nayana sniffed and wiped her nose with the back of her hands. "Thanks."

"Sure thing," Tamret said, and walked away to give Nayana some time.

I followed her and put a hand on her shoulder. "Hey," I said. "That was great. I know that sort of thing isn't easy for you."

"The part about clawing her eyes out was pretty easy."

"I know. But that's a big step, isn't it? Making her your sister?"

Tamret shrugged. "Not really. I just have to make sure nothing bad happens to her if I possibly can, which, just between us, I was probably going to do anyhow. Just on principle. But if it helps her pull herself together, then it helps you get your father."

Tamret had just made a girl she found painfully annoying a member of her family, and she'd done it to help me. There was no way to thank her, not really, so I just took her hand, and we sat quietly for a little while. Then I turned to her. "Am I completely nuts to go down there, to bring everyone with me? I'm not a soldier. I'm a kid. I have no idea what I'm doing."

She swiveled in her chair toward me. "Let me ask you something, Zeke. Is that how you feel, or how you think you should feel?"

I considered the answer to her question. "It's how I think I should feel."

"In your heart, do you believe you can do it?"

"Yeah," I said. And it was true. When I thought about what we were planning, what insanity we had lined up, I honestly believed I could pull it off. It wasn't hope or optimism; it was a weird certainty, like how when you turn on a light switch you expect the light to go on. You don't think, *I sure hope the light comes on this time.* I expected to succeed.

"Why am I so confident?" I asked her.

She shrugged. "Don't overthink it. Go with how you feel. I'll tell you a secret about yourself," she said. "It's something only I know, and now you'll know it too."

"What's that?"

"It's not just me," she whispered. "You can do anything too."

"I wish I believed that."

"I believe it," she said, "and that will have to be enough for now." She gave my hand a squeeze and then let go. "Now let's go break into this enemy prison I've heard so much about."

We kept on the far side of the planet from the Phandic flying saucer, but as we banked in, we caught a brief glimpse of it out the port-side screen. It was huge, maybe a third larger than the ship we'd fought in the *Dependable*. Its shape wasn't silly, and it didn't put me in mind of an old movie or a comic book or the countless parodies that showed laughable aliens in their absurd ships. No, the Phandic saucer was dark and looming like a predator. I felt my heart pound and my stomach flip. Then the ship was gone from my view. I wished it could be as easily gone from my mind.

Steve was our best pilot, so he was running helm, but he hadn't put extra points into constitution. Maybe his Ish-hi toughness would get him through, but we were taking no chances. I was on navigation, and Tamret was along for the ride, but on a ship like this any of the consoles could switch over to helm in an emergency. Our plan required just one of us to remain conscious on the way down. If none of us did, we'd never know, because we'd be obliterated when we hit the ground.

We were all strapped in as tightly as we could manage. I felt my own safety belts almost squeezing the air out of my lungs. The lights and buttons and icons all glared up at me, and I knew if I let my mind wander, I would be terrified by the torturous complexity of them. It was like when you board a plane and you glance into the cockpit and see those endless dense rows of identical switches and you wonder what they can all mean and how anyone could possibly understand them all. I did understand the console, though, and for better or worse, we were going through with this landing.

When I was younger, I loved the TV show *Batman: The Brave and the Bold,* which took its name from a silver-age comic book that always featured team-ups. Each episode of the animated show would have Batman joining up with some other hero or team, and the whole thing had this silly feel to it—totally different from the gloomy tone of just about every other Batman comic or movie.

I loved the program so much I went back and collected as many of the old *Brave and the Bold* comics as I could find, and when I read each issue, I went in with one question: Which one was brave and which one was bold? I spent more hours than I would like to admit trying to tease out the difference between the two terms, and what I decided was that guys like Superman and Martian Manhunter were brave. They put themselves in danger for the greater good. They were willing to take risks and make sacrifices because doing so was the moral choice. Guys like Green Lantern and the Flash were bold—they were reckless and daring, Sure, they wanted to do the right thing, but their willingness to expose themselves to harm smacked of daredevilry, like their powers filled them with the urge to take chances.

I always admired the brave heroes, and I wanted to be one of them, but I didn't have what it took to be brave. Bravery required true courage. There was a nobility in bravery. As I prepared to drop down to that planet, I knew I was not being brave. I was being bold. I was reckless. I was taking other kids, the best friend I'd ever had, and a girl I cared about, into the most dangerous situation I could possible imagine, and somehow I had convinced myself I could do it.

Steve looked at his readout panel, which he'd configured to display solar flares. "Going to be soon, mate."

"Yeah," he said.

"You feel good about this?"

I thought about it, and my answer surprised me. "I don't know why, but I do."

"Glad to hear it," he said. "Because I'm scared out of my bleeding mind. Coming up in three, two, one. Now!" He throttled the ship forward, and we all lurched back, but the g-force inhibitors kicked in like they were supposed to. We hadn't taxed them. Not yet.

The ship began to buck violently, and the engines whined. Despite being strapped in, I jerked violently in my seat. It was impossible not to feel like we were crashing, like we were doomed. Part of me wanted to panic, but part of me watched with calm dispassion, as though this were a movie, and a boring one. I began to wonder if the dread was somehow forced, like a memory of something that had once scared me as a little kid but meant nothing now.

Steve worked the panels in a state of near hypnosis. He flicked his tongue, as if the scents in the air could tell him something about the ship's system. Maybe they could, for all I knew. Maybe it was a nervous habit.

"Listen up, sentients," he said and the turbulence increased. "Tighten your sphincters." Then we pivoted toward the atmosphere and throttled hard as we made entry. The shields kicked in, and the main screen showed the heat and fire building up toward our nose, generated by the incredible friction of reentry at top and stupid speeds. The g-force inhibitors were already maxing out, and I could feel pressure in my eyes and my sinuses. We were tossed violently. The engines screamed, and I heard the disconcerting sound of metal groaning under stress.

"Turn back," I heard Nayana moan. "I can't do this."

I wanted to tell her she could, but the effort of speaking was too much. Instead I watched as Steve broke through the atmosphere and cut the engines and we became nothing more than a meteor hurtling with murderous force toward the surface of a strange world.

I thought my eyes would literally tear out of my head. I thought my spine would come out of my back. I thought I would wet my pants. None of that happened. We fell and fell and fell. Somehow I managed a glance back, and I saw that Charles, Mi Sun, and Nayana had passed out. They were all bleeding from their noses. I didn't think I was. Tamret wasn't. Steve made a weird coughing sound, like a failed attempt at speech, tried to raise his arm, and blacked out.

Tamret managed a nod at me, and I switched my console to helm while she switched hers to navigation. And we were still falling and there was nothing but pain and pressure and the feeling of being torn apart. I envied Steve his oblivion, and I longed for it, but I could not quit on my friends, and I could not ask Tamret to do what I would not. I stayed there. I made myself stay, and focus, and fly that plummeting death trap.

Then the console chimed, signaling that it was time to come out of the dive and save our lives, but I could not do it. I was too far gone. I couldn't lift my arm or make my hands move or think about anything but the incredible pain and how, if we struck the surface, it would all end. I was giving up. I was going to let us all die.

Except I wasn't. As if looking at someone else's actions through my own eyes, I saw my hands working the controls. I didn't recall making a decision, but I was already in mid-action. The engines were firing and I was trying to level out the ship.

A doubting voice in the back of my mind told me I had waited an instant too long, but somehow I knew that wasn't true, because we were turning, hard and fast, and then we were no longer vertical. I was afraid I'd overcompensated, but we leveled out, and there we were, skimming along two hundred feet above a rough and rugged landscape of unfamiliar brush and rock and sand. Alien vistas tumbled past us in a blur of color. There were great purple and pink things, like trees with vines twisting out of thick stalks, waving in the breeze like giant seaweed. And there was grass, actual green grass, but a strange shade of dark green. Herds of quadrupeds ran from us, and things like monkeys that scattered from the vine trees. And above it all, zipping along at about seven hundred miles an hour, was me. Next to me was my unconscious pal, and next to him Tamret, who looked at me and said nothing, which was just fine because her approving gaze was exactly what I needed.

Steve opened his eyes. "You step in for me, mate?"

"Yep."

"You think I'm a tosser for blacking out?"

"A little bit," I said. "How do you feel?"

"Bloody awful. But surprisingly less bloody awful than you'd suppose. Maybe because I'm not actually dead."

"Oh my God, that was the *worst*!" Nayana cried from the back. "Let's never do that again!" The adrenaline was coursing through her. I knew it because it was coursing through me. We'd lived through something no human body should be able to survive. Now we were flying really, really fast, which seemed like a good reason to be concerned.

Steve was on top of it, though, and already working his console. He wiped at his bloody snout with the back of his hand and then proceeded to call up something on one of his screens. "Veer ten degrees to the east and then straight ahead for about twelve hundred miles."

I watched as Steve made the course correction, and I felt someone's furry hand touch my neck. "Nice flying," Tamret whispered into my ear. "You *can* do anything. And you know what that means?"

"That you were right and I was wrong?"

"Correct."

Steve put the ship down about ten miles outside the prison complex. There was a copse of low purple and pink vine trees, and while we weren't terribly well hidden, I didn't think anyone who wasn't specifically looking for the ship was going to find it. It took half an hour for our nanites to repair our various broken blood vessels and muscle tears from thrashing against our restraints, and then I made sure everyone put on fresh clothes. A shower would have been nice, but the artifact carrier didn't have such amenities, and clean clothes were our only hope of keeping our enemy from smelling us from a quarter mile away.

I'd chosen these clothes deliberately before leaving the station. I put on khaki pants, held up with suspenders over my maroon shirt, and over that my authentic *Firefly* "Browncoat" coat, which was, indeed, brown. To get through this, I needed to feel like a tough guy, and if cosplay made me believe I could be a hero, I wasn't too proud to indulge. Everyone else went for the practical: jeans and long-sleeved shirts and durable shoes. Tamret wore olive-green pants, made out of some kind of flexible fabric, and a purple shirt, both clearly chosen to help her blend into the foliage.

So, with no reason to delay, I opened the shuttle doors and we stepped out onto an alien planet. My first. I had been in spaceships and I had been on Confederation Central, which felt like an actual world, but it wasn't. This was a planet, in a strange part of the galaxy. I had traveled to another world. The air had a crisp, slightly metallic scent, and it was cool and humid at the same time, with crazy purple and green and orange vegetation growing everywhere.

"This," I noted with wonder, "is another planet."

"We chose well in having you lead us, mate," Steve said. "You don't miss much."

Charles followed me out of the shuttle, and he looked around, straining his neck. He began to spin, slowly, taking it all in. He crouched down and took a handful of the gravelly soil in his hand and let it stream through his fingers.

"He's right," Charles said dreamily. "This is another planet."

"I get it," Nayana said. "It's a new and amazing experience and all that. Plant your flag and let's move on."

"Another planet," Charles said. "I wonder if this ever gets old."

"Somehow I doubt it," I said.

Even without the wonder of being on a new world, three days on the cramped artifact carrier made walking through the jungle toward an enemy prison feel like a rare treat. After about six miles, we began to see signs of habitation. No people, but abandoned excavations where I supposed Former artifacts had either been removed or never discovered. We walked on.

Two hours later we saw our first outbuildings. There was no fence around the complex—why would there be on a planet from which there was no escape?

We heard the sound of digging, of picks on stone, and we walked through the trees until we found an active dig. There were probably fifty beings at work there, swinging axes, sifting through sand. I saw all kinds of creatures, many of whom I recognized from the station, but I did not see anyone who looked like Martian Manhunter. Around them I saw ten guards, Phands like Vusio-om, with their rectangular heads and space-orc underbites. They all looked lazy and bored, in crisp white uniforms that had a strangely British-colonial feel to them. They stood along the edge of the pit, expecting no trouble and not receiving any. This was still an insane plan, but the lack of Phandic discipline would prove helpful.

I kept looking for my father, scanning each face, each body, for that shade of green. I didn't see him, but as I moved my eyes over the mass of people swinging, breaking, grunting, I came across a familiar face. I bit my lip to keep myself from crying out in surprise and happiness. There, toward the far end of the pit, swinging a pickax with skill and strength, was a large and bulky figure I had come to love.

I hit Charles on the arm and pointed.

"Oh," he said.

Oh, indeed. She looked tired and wounded. There was a bandage wrapped around one of her arms. Her eyes, huge and far apart, were half closed, and her mouth at the end of her trunk was pursed in an expression I thought was distaste. She looked broken and unspeakably sad, but I felt a thrill of excitement. It was Captain Qwlessl. She was alive. Maybe the rest of her crew was also alive.

How? Had she somehow been away from her ship when it had been destroyed? Had the Phands altered the images of its destruction to make it look like an attack? Maybe the crew had evacuated and they had destroyed the ship themselves rather than face capture.

I would find out the details later. What mattered for now was that my friend, whom I had believed dead because of me, was still alive. That was good news for more than just the obvious reasons. It meant that getting off the planet had just become a little less impossible.

We waited until sundown, when the guards rounded up the prisoners and began to lead them indoors. It was my hope that the grounds would not be well guarded at night.

They went inside and we ate our rations and drank from our canteens. Then we waited some more, watching their movements as red points on the hologram of the prison grounds. Fourteen guards were inside the prison complex. The other thirty-three were inside the barracks, and more than half of those appeared to be sleeping. They evidently worked on fourteen-man rotational shifts, with a few extra Phands here and there. Inside the barracks there were three Phands in the front control room. The other eleven not sleeping were in a central room, probably a mess or rec room.

"Cameras here and here," Steve said, pointing to the hologram. "But look at the angle. They're pointed down, so we can assume they've never had an Ish-hi prisoner."

I looked at Tamret. "Is there a constant data stream from the surface to the cruiser in orbit?"

She checked her data bracelet. "Doesn't look like it."

That meant no one on the orbiting cruiser would know what we were up to, which was good news. "This might work. Steve, you think you can get in via the roof and get the drop on them?"

"Not a problem, mate. Mi Sun, be ready near the main door, out of range of the cameras. If I need backup, that's you."

"Got it," she said.

Steve scrambled through the brush to the far side of the building and scurried up the wall like, well, a lizard. I saw his hunched form skittering over the roof, then moving a panel and dropping down.

We waited and waited for what felt like forever but could not have been more than a minute. Then the front door swung open and I heard a loud hiss. I hoped it was the Ish-hi equivalent of a whistle. We moved.

Steve was inside the control room with three unconscious Phand guards. He held a metal cylinder in his hand and was fiddling with some controls on it.

"Nicely done," I told him.

"That was the easy part," he said quietly. "If we're going to take out the other thirty Phands in here, we're going to need to figure out these plasma wands."

He pushed a few more buttons, and a narrow metal rod about three feet long emerged from the cylinder with a satisfying click. It was maybe a quarter inch in diameter, and hollow, with evenly spaced holes all over it. Steve pressed another button, and plasma began to flow upward. It sparked wildly for an instant and then settled into a tight little blue nimbus, evenly spaced around the rod, to make a glowing cylinder about two feet long.

"Oh, wow," I said, unable to believe what I was looking at. You write something off as impossible, pure fantasy, and then suddenly it's right before you, and it's real. "Oh, wow. Oh, wow. Oh, wow. Give me one of those right this instant!"

Steve picked up another wand and tossed it to me. "Okay, mate. Keep it calm. The big button on the bottom seems to activate the rod, and the one at the top turns on the plasma. You're welcome to have a go, but I'm still figuring out the rest."

I released the rod and then activated the plasma. I held the wand, looking at its bright blue glow, and I moved it through the air. It made a *whooom whooom* noise, just liked I'd hoped it would. "I can't believe it. This is so amazing."

"You're being daft," Steve said. "It's only a plasma wand."

"No it's not," I told him, as I *whooom*ed back and forth. "It's an elegant weapon for a more civilized age. This is a *light saber*."

Once I stopped annoying my friends by waving my plasma wand around and striking Jedi poses, we got down to the business of figuring out how the weapons actually worked. We got comfortable with turning them off and on and adjusting the power settings, so it was time to actually use the darn things. We all agreed that Steve and Mi Sun would lead the way, hoping their speed and skills, and the power of surprise, would be enough to take out the eleven guards in the central room before they woke the nineteen guards in their bunks.

We found some rope and what appeared to be something like alien duct tape and left Nayana and Charles in charge of binding the guards. It was time to clear out the building.

I was no fighter—my limited time in the sparring room had proved that—but I was strangely confident in my skin, like a champion boxer when he enters the ring. Maybe it was the plasma wand, which gave me my chance to play Luke Skywalker for real. I kept telling myself that this was not a game, that we could die, that beings almost certainly would die if we were to succeed, and yet I felt so sure of myself, like taking down an alien prison was no big deal. My mind was alert, and my muscles twitched with coiled readiness. I decided it had to be the adrenaline, or maybe the excitement of knowing that at least some of the crew of the *Dependable* had survived.

Steve led the way through a corridor and down a flight of stairs, and then along another corridor toward a large room with an open door. He signaled for us to stop and waved Mi Sun forward. They activated their plasma wands and rushed in.

Tamret and I were right behind them, but we weren't fast enough to see most of what they did in there. We heard the deep whoosh of the plasma wands and the Phands shouting and unconscious guards hitting the floor. As we reached the door, a Phand ran out, no doubt hoping to signal for help. I swiped at him with my wand, striking him across his midriff. He did not vanish into a pile of empty clothes. He did, however, jerk and spasm like a man who had been electrocuted, and then fell to the floor completely senseless.

When I stepped into the room, there were more unconscious Phands, looking stiff and vaguely silly in their white uniforms. We found enough cord and wire and tape to bind them, which was time-consuming, difficult, and generally less exciting than combat.

"Look at this," Steve said. He'd been propping up one of the Phands to tie his hands behind his back, when he'd found something on his belt. It was a saber—a real one, the metal kind, like a slightly curved dueling blade. "What do you make of this?"

"A couple of the others have them," Mi Sun said.

"The ambassador had one at my hearing," I told them. "It must be ceremonial or something."

"I want one for a souvenir." Steve sounded strangely enthusiastic.

"We have to get out of here first," I said.

"Fair enough."

We finished tying up the guards and moved on.

"Next stop," Steve said, "the armory."

This turned out to be a metal cage with a lock that the plasma wand, when turned up to full power, cut easily. Inside were PPB hand weapons: pistols and rifles. Steve began to pass them out and then throw extras in a bag.

"Are they deadly?" I asked.

"They have settings," Steve said. "I've practiced with them in the sparring room, though they generally don't let initiates use them. But Dr. Roop gave me a few lessons."

"Why am I not surprised?" I said.

"Yeah," he agreed. "He was definitely preparing me for this. Still, I'm not complaining. So, at the lowest setting it's like short-circuiting someone's nervous system—sort of like the low-level jolt from the plasma wand, but more sustained."

"Are they hard to fire?" I asked. "Hard to aim?"

He grinned at me. "You'll find out."

Armed, we made our way to the barracks, which was where I fired my first ray gun. There were no beams shooting through the air that you could dodge, just flashes of light that emerged from the muzzle. Like a high-powered laser rifle on Earth, it came equipped with a laser aiming aid, in the form of a bright yellow dot. There was no kick. You squeezed the trigger, you heard a satisfying and totally science-fictional whizzing noise, and the sleeping enemy was even more unconscious than he'd been before you fired your space gun at him.

In that way it took us about fifteen seconds to render the building completely pacified. In my college applications I could now include "commando" on my list of accomplishments.

Steve and Mi Sun volunteered to remain behind to bind the Phands while Tamret and I went back up to the control room. Charles and Nayana were standing, staring at the unconscious guards, and looking generally uneasy. They were happy to see us and even happier when we handed them their PPB pistols.

Tamret went to work on the computers, digging into the system for anything that would be of use. She was at it for almost half an hour, only grunting when anyone tried to talk to her. During this time Mi Sun and Steve returned, and we stood around, peering out the window, while we waited for information that could help us.

"Good news," Tamret said at last. "There are four Phandic shuttles in the hangar. They have long-range capacity, so we can use them to tunnel back to the station."

I didn't show how relieved I was that we had a way out. "How many can they hold?"

"I can't get spec information off of this, but according to the database on my bracelet, each one can hold a dozen average-size beings, maybe eighteen if necessary."

One shuttle would be enough to carry us, the selection committee, and a few of the *Dependable*'s crew. If we split up our personnel, we could get a lot of beings off this planet, but we'd have to get past that cruiser first, and that was going to be a challenge. In the meantime, at least we knew there was a way to escape, and that was more than we'd known before.

"We have other things working in our favor," Tamret continued. "The cruiser checks in only once during the night, local 0200. That means we've got four hours before we have to either make a hostage talk, try to fake our way through a check-in, or prepare ourselves for a firefight."

Four hours wasn't a lot, but it could be worse. "Location of the prisoners?"

Tamret shook her head. "Not there yet. I'm working on it."

"Work faster," Nayana said. "You said you can do anything. You didn't say you would do it slowly."

"Eyes," Tamret muttered. "Claws."

Twenty minutes later she smacked the console. "Yes! I've got it."

I hurried over to her side. She put one hand on my back and pointed with the other. A three-dimensional map of the facility appeared on the screen.

"We've caught a break," she said. "Perimeter control is done by camera. The fourteen remaining guards are all stationed inside the prison. We've got four in the main room on the first floor. Then there are two on each of the remaining five floors. Each floor does a half-hourly check-in, so if we time it right, we can take out the first floor right after a check-in and then deal with the floors rapidly. We do that, we've basically taken control of the planet."

"It can't be that easy," Charles said.

"And it's not. There's a shift change in twenty minutes. Fourteen guards from here go over there. Once they're in place, the fourteen there come back here."

"And our fourteen aren't going to show," Nayana said.

"We don't need the strategist to point that out," Tamret said. "We need the strategist to tell us what do to about it."

"There's only one option," Nayana told us, "and I think even you know it. You go now, you hit hard, and you hope for the best. If the prison contacts the cruiser, we're all dead. You just took out like thirty guards. Another fourteen shouldn't be too difficult."

The problem was that they were spaced far apart, and the chances of them all being taken out without anyone alerting the Phandic cruiser seemed remote.

On the other hand, we had no choice and a ticking clock, which helped to motivate me. I needed Steve and Mi Sun to go on this mission. They were our best fighters. After the two of them, next up would be Tamret, but I did not want her to go into something so dangerous. Then there was me. I was hated throughout the Phandic empire as a mass murderer, but I'd never been in a fight like this. The extent of my military experience, of which I had been so proud, included shooting a bunch of sleeping guards and sucker-wanding a guy fleeing in terror. At best I would be of no help, and at worst I'd be a hindrance.

Yet we were storming this building to get my father. I knew it was more complicated than that, but that was the fundamental truth. I could not ask them to go where I was unwilling to go.

I held up my pistol and took a couple of steps so my *Firefly* coat would flair dramatically. "Charles. Nayana. Can you hold this building?"

"Just us?" Nayana asked. "No!"

"Yes," Charles said. "We can do that."

"Tamret," I said, "can you temporarily block all communication from the surface to the ship? I don't want the ship's comms blocked—they might notice that—but I want to make sure the guys on the surface can't call for help."

She sat down at the console. "Yeah, that's simple. Good call." She looked up at me. "You're smarter than you used to be."

"Why, thank you."

"I'll take the credit for that."

Once she was done, we checked our pistols and got ready to dash across the courtyard.

"Message us if anything bad happens," I told Charles and Nayana. Then I looked at Steve, Mi Sun, and Tamret. "Weapons on nonlethal, everyone. We're the good guys. If it is all possible, no one dies. Least of all us."

"No one dies," Steve said, raising his pistol.

We all said it, and we touched pistols like they were glasses.

"Randoms," I said.

"Randoms," Steve and Tamret said.

Mi Sun looked irritated. "I'm not a random."

"None of us are," I said. "All of us are. Let's go."

• • •

We crossed the courtyard and then paused outside the door. I could not let anyone else be the one to open it. I had to do it myself. I was so scared, I could hardly breathe. I was doing this. I was about to lay siege to an alien prison. I was going into battle, and people die in battles. I might die. I might see my friends die. I might suffer horrible, disfiguring, and painful injuries. My arms or legs could be blown off. And it was all real. It wasn't a movie or a game. I was here, and there was a fairly good chance I could be dead in the next twenty minutes.

I threw open the door, fired my gun, and stepped back to let Steve and Mi Sun rush in. Tamret and I fired, not really aiming, while Phandic soldiers scrambled for cover. As our pistols whizzed and sparks flew, the Phands threw themselves on the floor. They yanked at plasma wands that would not come out of holsters. They'd been on this sleepy planet with their non-threatening prisoners for so long they'd allowed their discipline to grow lax.

In the end Tamret and I were only there to crank up the chaos machine. Steve and Mi Sun did the work. I thought Mi Sun had been impressive in the combat simulations, but I'd never seen such poised and beautiful violence. There were energy weapons firing all around her, but her face was a mask of calm. Nothing existed but her, her weapon, her body, her targets. She fired and kicked simultaneously, and yet each act was separate and distinct. She dodged blows. She seemed to know when she was in someone's sights and stepped effortlessly out of the way. It was like she had been born for it.

She was nothing compared to Steve, however. He was three times as fast as anything in the room. He ran up the walls and launched himself at the guards. He fired as he scurried across the ceiling, an unstoppable menace like the creature from *Alien*. I could barely follow him as he confused and terrified and shot at the enemy.

Maybe twenty seconds after I first opened the door, all the guards were down.

"That's one for the barbarian planets," I said.

"Good start, mate," Steve agreed.

I went over to the main communications console and waited thirty seconds to see if anyone would check in to ask about the noise. I had no idea what soundproofing in the building would be like. Maybe no one had heard anything. Maybe I'd have to shoot the console like Han Solo. I had no idea. But the time passed, and no one checked in.

I looked at my data bracelet. "We've got nine minutes until these guys start wondering where their replacements are. I hate to get all movie cliché, but we should probably split up."

"Check," Steve said.

"You and Mi Sun are faster than we can hope to be. You two take the bottom three floors. Tamret and I will take the top three."

Steve nodded and waved Mi Sun forward.

Even as I said it, I knew it was the wrong call. Tamret should have gone with Steve. With his fighting skills, she would have only had to provide backup and cover. The same, if less so, was true if I had gone with Mi Sun. I was no fighter, and having Tamret with me was selfish. I had no business assigning her to someone as inexperienced as myself; I was afraid that if she went with one of the others I would never see her again.

We headed down the stairs, and we paused at the first door, giving Steve and Mi Sun a few extra seconds to get to their floor.

It still isn't too late, I thought. *I could call them back.* I was in charge. I could do the right thing. But I didn't. I was making a bad decision and I was fully aware of it, but I did it anyhow.

If I was going to be a bad leader, then I was determined not to be a coward. "Cover me," I told her, and I went through the first door. The guards were at their stations, and they looked up. I fired. Once. Twice. They were down.

Tamret grinned at me. She was enjoying this.

Maybe I was too. It was so easy, and that's why I became overconfident. I thought we could take care of the next two rooms just like I'd taken care of the first one. Two shots. Bad guys down. Tamret doesn't even need to fire her weapon. That was how it was going to be.

We went down to the next floor to take out the next set of Phands. I opened the door and fired at the guard. One guard. He went down. He was out. But he was alone. I scanned the room, looking for another Phand, afraid he might be hiding and would pop out and fire at me, not on nonlethal. I would feel a bolt of energy, and I would be dead.

Maybe if I hadn't been so preoccupied with these details, I would have been thinking about Tamret, worrying about her safety. When I was sure there was no one else in the room, I turned around, and I saw him, behind Tamret. I had no idea why he hadn't been at his post when we came in. Maybe he had been on a bathroom break. Who knows? He had clearly heard us, and had decided to approach quietly.

When I looked up, the guard we'd missed was already in motion. He had moved silently behind her, careful, taking his time. I suppose he knew our weapons were set to nonlethal, so there was no rush. He had all the time in the world. He also had one of those curved ceremonial blades. His arms were raised, coming down, with the tip of the blade pointed at Tamret.

I turned just in time to see him plunge it into her back. The needlelike blade poked out of the left side of her chest, directly through her heart. Blood blossomed out of the neckline of her shirt, spreading over her white fur like wine spilled on a table-cloth. Blood trickled out of her mouth, and her lavender eyes went dark. She fell to her knees and then pitched forward. The blade clattered against the hard surface as the pool of blood spread like a shadow. Her body shook violently, just for an instant, and then she was still.

I had killed a lot of beings aboard that Phandic cruiser, but that was different. It was cold and impersonal and distant, and no matter how scared I'd been, no matter how sure I'd been that I had to kill them or be killed myself, I'd still been playing with images on a computer screen. I knew it was real, but it sure felt a lot like a game.

This was no game. This was someone, someone I cared about, dying right before my eyes. The Phandic guard let go of the sword and reached for his plasma wand, but I wasn't going to let him have it. He was fifteen feet away from me. Tamret's still body was on the floor between us, leaking blood. I met the guard's gaze. My face felt hot, and my teeth were clenched. I could see a look of fear in the Phand's eyes as he began to grasp his weapon. He was afraid of me. Without realizing what I was doing, I took two steps forward and leaped at him.

By the time I left the floor, there must have been at least ten feet between us, and then I was on him. I couldn't leap ten feet. I knew that, but I was not rational. Ideas, sensations, images were all fragmentary. I was flying through the air and coming down on him. He fell hard, his head hitting the concretelike surface. His eyes rolled back, and just like that he was unconscious. I can't say it made me happy—I was never going to feel happy again—but there was something to savor in my victory.

But it was not enough. I raised my pistol, ready to bring it down, to crush his stupid Phandic face. I knew I should stop, that he was no longer a threat, but somewhere in the back of my head I decided that it was too late for that. He had killed Tamret, and there had to be justice.

I sucked in air, stretched out my arm, and prepared to take my revenge. Then I stopped. I was full of rage beyond anything I had ever known, and I did not want to let go of the anger, because I knew if I did, I would have to face the fact that Tamret was dead, and I was not ready for that. I would never be ready for that, but I wasn't a murderer. The Phand was harmless now, and I could not strike again. I remained there for several long seconds, my pistol still raised, unable or unwilling to move. Then I heard her voice.

"Zeke," she said. "Help me."

I was off the guard in an instant. I fired a quick shot, to make sure he didn't get up, and then I was kneeling at Tamret's side. There was blood everywhere. So much blood. My knees rested in a pool of it. Her shirt was soaked through. Her fur up to her neck was bright red and horribly damp. I hated to see her like this, dying, her life leaking out of her, but I could not look away. "I'm here," I told her. I dropped the pistol and took her hand. "I'm right here."

"Don't kill him," she groaned, her voice raspy and weak. "It's not who you are."

I tried to swallow. My throat closed up on me. "Tamret," I managed, but I couldn't say anything else.

"Not as bad as it looks," she said, gasping. "I need you to pull it out." She squeezed her eyes shut then opened them again. "It hurts so much."

I would have done anything to save her. If getting her back to the station in time were a possibility, I would have turned around right then. Rescuing my father could wait. I would have blasted through Phandic blockades and braved weapons, but none of that would have made a difference. Dr. Roop had said the nanites could protect about almost anything except traumatic heart or brain injury. Even if I could steal a Phandic shuttle and somehow elude the orbiting cruiser, she would never survive the two days back to the station.

I kept trying to think of alternatives, places I could take her, things I could do, but there were no options, no surprises, no plot twists to make all this go away. Her heart had been pierced. She was going to die. The only thing I could do for her was to ease her suffering.

"I'm so sorry, Tamret." I placed both hands on the hilt of the blade and propped one knee against her back. Squeezing my eyes shut, feeling the tears stream down my face, I pulled the sword out, knowing that it would be the last thing she would ever feel.

"By [*the primary revenge goddess*] that hurts," she said. She was sitting up, pressing a hand to her chest. "This is really extremely painful. Wow." She vomited, and there was blood in what she spewed up, but not a lot. "Sorry," she said as she wiped her mouth with the back of her hand. "I'm kind of dizzy. Can you hold me? I think I might black out."

I sat down and I held her, leaning her body against mine, feeling her hot blood soak my shirt. But not that much of it. Somehow, in my confusion, I understood she should be bleeding far more than she was.

"Why aren't you dead?" I sputtered.

"It wasn't *that* bad," she said. "Just kind of, yeah, painful."

I tried several times to speak, but each effort came out as a choking sound. Finally, I was able to form actual words. "It *was* bad," I managed.

"Maybe it was a little bad, but it's getting better. So that's what a collapsed lung repairing itself feels like. Good information to have. I don't recommend trying this, but I guess it beats the alternative. The skill points into healing go a long way."

Skill points. Okay. That was an explanation, sort of. But then, not really. She was only level eleven, so there was no way her healing could be so significantly augmented. "You can't have put everything into healing. You've obviously put a lot into other things."

"I've spread things around pretty well," she said.

"But your heart," I said. I couldn't get a handle on how she had come through this. I thought she was dead, and now she seemed almost fully recovered. "It went right through. Dr. Roop said that it was one of the few injuries the nanites couldn't fix."

"Boys don't pay attention to anything," she said, shaking her head at my foolishness. She took my hand and put it on the right side of her chest. Her fur was sopping wet with her blood. "Can't you feel that?" she asked. "I'm a Rarel, Zeke. My heart is on the right side."

I buried my face against her soft, soft neck. I didn't care

that it was covered with blood. I only cared that it was her, that she was alive. Tamret was alive.

After a second, she said, "I saw you go after him. You were angry."

"I was," I admitted.

"That was some leap. You were practically flying."

I thought I had imagined that. I looked at her, smiling at me in that knowing way of hers. There was something she wasn't telling me. "I really did that?"

She nodded. "I told you. You can do anything. We both can."

I suddenly felt like there was something more to her words than Tamret's bravado. I had done things I ought not to have been able to do. Tamret was healing incredibly rapidly on her own. "When you say you can do anything, what exactly do you mean?"

She winced in pain, but then managed to grin at me, a full-on wicked Tamret grin, and I knew she'd been up to something clever and unexpected and almost certainly against the rules.

"I hacked your account," she said. "Just before we left. After you leveled up yourself, since I thought that way you wouldn't notice. I did it with my account right after the fight with Ardov. At that point I'd already added a few points here and there, but after he almost killed me, there was no way I was about to let anyone mess with me like that again. And now no one is going to mess with you. Zeke, you are maxed out in all the branches of the skill tree, even the final, theoretical skills. Just like I am. You're the skill equivalent of level ninety-seven. You have Former skills in all categories."

I quickly called up my personal skill tree on my HUD. She was right. My experience points had gone up since I'd last looked—raiding an enemy prison will do that—but I had no empty skill slots. "But I'm still only level sixteen."

"I had to decouple your skill points from your experience points, otherwise everyone would see your real level and we'd be caught. This way you can still gain experience like you normally would, but you won't gain skill points because there's no place left to apply them."

I shook my head. "I don't believe this. I'm a superhero."

"Almost as much as I am. Your brain isn't wired to sense electromagnetic fields the way mine is. I'm an equivalent level one hundred and eight."

Incredible powers. Incredible disregard for the Confederation's most sacred rules. I couldn't process this. "Why didn't you tell me?"

"I thought you might get mad at me for tinkering with the system."

"This is totally illegal!" I protested. "They'll kick us out for this!"

"See? That's why I didn't tell you." She rubbed her hands together. "Time to move on."

"What are you doing? You can't get up. You almost died."

She lashed out, slicing the back of my hand with an extended claw. There was a moment of pain, and then blood pooled across my skin.

"What is wrong with you?" I shouted.

"Nothing is wrong with me. I just knew there was no way you'd believe me if you didn't see it for yourself. Look at your hand."

The blood was still copious and warm, but the wound she'd given me just seconds before was gone. No scab, no raised flesh, just gone.

"Next time, maybe give me the chance to believe you," I said as I wiped my hand against my shirt. "Are you sure you're okay?"

"I'm fine."

Then I realized what I'd forgotten, what had gone out of my mind the instant I saw the point of the sword emerge from her chest. We hadn't cleared our third floor.

"We need to go," I said.

We ran down the stairs and entered the third control post. It was empty.

Anything might have happened. The guards might have run past us while I was considering beating the life out of the man who had stabbed Tamret. He might have signaled the Phandic cruiser in orbit right now. I stood there, still and terrified and furious with myself. The entire mission could be blown right now, because of me.

Then I heard the whizzing sound of weapons fire coming from farther down. Maybe, just maybe, it wasn't the worst news possible.

We ran down the stairs, and now that I was aware of my augmentations, I knew immediately how to exploit them, like I had always been this strong, this perceptive, this agile. I was leaping six or seven stairs at once, and it was easy. It was easier than taking them one at a time. I vaulted over the last fifteen stairs and landed on the final level, illuminated by the intermittent flash of weapons fire. Steve and Mi Sun were crouched behind a bulkhead, firing down a long corridor at a Phand, or maybe several. I couldn't see because they were taking cover behind a corner where the hall branched off.

"I think you might have missed a couple, mate," Steve called out to me.

"We ran into some trouble," I said.

"I know the feeling," he said. "Also, just so you know, the armory is not the only place on the planet where they store PPB pistols. These two took some from a strongbox. Live and learn." He glanced around to see Tamret, still dripping with her own blood. "Everyone all right? You don't look too good, love."

"I'm fine now," she said. "But thanks."

As first I thought the hallway was completely silent; then I realized there was a sound, just on the periphery of my perception. I understood at once that it was something I could never have heard before Tamret had hacked my skill tree. It was the low, rhythmic rasping of the two Phands breathing. Almost the instant I understood what I was hearing, the sound changed to distant footsteps, boots hissing against the hard floor.

"They're taking off," I said.

"I hear it too." Tamret was checking something on her data bracelet. "That corridor isn't on the schematic. Zeke, this is bad. We can't let those guys get away."

"Why?"

"Because, if my sense of direction is right, that corridor leads right back to the bunker where we started. If they get back there, they've got a straight shot to the shuttle hangar, and I don't have a whole lot of faith in Charles and Nayana being able to stop them."

This was my mess, and I was going to clean it up. "I'm going after them," I told Steve and Mi Sun. "You guys go find Captain

Qwlessl. Get her, anyone from the *Dependable*, and whoever else she vouches for."

Steve cocked his head at me. "You sure you have this? I don't want to hurt your feelings, mate, but me and Mi Sun are both faster, stronger, have surer aim, and are generally so much better at this sort of thing than you that it's silly for you to even think of going."

"Thanks for soft-pedaling it," I said as I reviewed my new skill tree on my HUD, "but we've got this."

They looked at each other, and Mi Sun shrugged as if to say it was my funeral. Then they ran off.

Tamret gave my hand a quick squeeze. "Let's be careful," she said.

"Yeah," I said. "Cover me."

I ran out, pistols firing.

I don't tend to think of myself as a terribly frightening person, but my team had taken out virtually every other Phand in the compound, and here I was, running at impossible speeds, legs bounding off the floor, as I erased the distance separating us from the fleeing Phands. I had enhanced strength, enhanced speed, enhanced endurance. I moved more quickly than I would have thought possible, and each step, each bound, was pure joy. The two Phands saw me coming, and they fled.

You can't dodge a PPB blast the way you can dodge a blaster bolt in *Star Wars*. You can, however, evade the yellow laser light. If the light isn't on you, you can't be hit. It's as simple as that.

Before Tamret had turned me into Captain America, I probably could not have run at top speeds, fired my own weapon, and kept an eye on two laser dots to make certain neither of us was about to be hit. I don't want to suggest it was effortless, because it required all my concentration, but I could do it. PPB lights flashed ahead, and Tamret and I dodged and ducked and evaded and fired. It was nearly impossible to hit the enemies, who were moving as erratically as we were. Our shots were suppressing fire, nothing more, but they did the job of keeping the Phands off balance and, best of all, slowing them down. We were faster than they were. In fact we were much faster, though I suspected that Tamret was slowing herself to keep pace with me.

We ran and closed the gap, racing past dark junctions in the hall, but the guards never wavered. Neither did we. My legs pumped and my lungs filled with air, and I sidestepped one of the yellow laser sights as the guard turned and fired, and I heard the sound of the rubber of his boot skidding sideways on the floor as he lost his balance, just for a second. I saw it all happen, not in slow motion, but clearly, as he stumbled and righted himself. He held his breath as the pistol began to slip from his fingers, and he reached out to catch it in midair. It all happened over the space of a second, but it left him vulnerable. I raised my PPB pistol, placed my laser aim at the center of his mass, and fired.

One of the guards was neutralized. That's right. Neutralized. Because that was how I was rolling. I had my space pistol, my space coat, my space nanite augmentations. It was a bad idea to mess with me.

Without missing a beat, I aimed at the other one. He threw himself against the wall, which was not going to save him. However, he must have pushed a button or activated a panel, because a metal bulkhead shot up from the floor, completely cutting him off.

Being separated from us, and having access to a shuttle, was going to save him. It might also be the end of us.

We turned to run back to the last junction. We had no map, no idea of where it might lead, but I had to hope there was some kind of alternate route and that I had a chance of cutting him off. Tamret, who seemed to have a directional sense that humans lacked, said she was sure we were going the right way. That was good, but if it took us to a dead end, the right direction would be of limited value.

The next junction seemed to loop around to head toward where we wanted to go. The bad news was that we were sloping downward. I didn't like it, but I liked the idea of backtracking and trying to find another path even less.

After about maybe a quarter mile of running, we came to an open circular ditch maybe sixty feet across. It was illuminated with floodlights and littered with excavation tools: scaffolding, ropes, ladders, and a few workstations covered with a heavy coat of dust. This was clearly an archeological dig, a deep one, and seemingly long abandoned. I couldn't see the bottom, and I had no interest in finding out how far down it went.

Tamret shoved me against the wall, pushing me out of the way of the laser aim. The wall exploded with dust as it was struck with PPB fire. She'd probably just saved my life. I'd have to thank her later.

I looked up. There was a makeshift bridge about thirty feet above us. The guard had used it to cross the chasm and was now standing at a doorway, firing at us. He was talking into his data bracelet.

"Not good," I said. "Who is he talking to? Can he communicate with the Phandic cruiser?"

Tamret checked her own data bracelet. "No way. The comm is still jammed, and I set up an alarm to let me know if someone undid my lock. He might be trying to get help from someone on the surface."

"There's no one here to help him," I said.

"I don't know," Tamret said. "It sounds like someone is talking back."

I tried to concentrate on what they were saying. Before, I would not have been able to hear anything. Now, though I couldn't make out the words, I detected a distinct voice coming over the bracelet. He was definitely talking to someone, and if the shore-to-ship comm wasn't working, it meant there were more Phands on the surface.

While Tamret reviewed the schematics on her data bracelet, I returned the guard's fire and tried to find some way to get across. There was a doorway at our level, but we had no means to get from one side of the pit to the other. I sensed that even with my augmented strength and power and agility I could not leap across, and I wasn't up for falling to my doom.

I searched around for something, anything. Surely my enhanced brainpower ought to be able to come up with an idea. I looked up. There was a cluster of ropes toward the ceiling, retracted, held together by a thick metal cable. Before, I would never have believed I could do this, but my aim, my strength, and my stamina were all improved. It was possible, maybe even probable, and it was too perfect.

I looked at Tamret, who was done checking her bracelet. "You want to try something really stupid?"

Her eyes widened, and her lips turned up at the corners. "Absolutely."

I didn't dare fire a PPB blast at the cable holding the rope. It was too powerful and might damage the rope itself. Instead I took out my plasma wand and fired it up. The ejection of the metal rod prior to the glow of energy almost ruined the coolness of the effect. Almost.

I held it in my left hand, which was now much stronger and more accurate than my right hand had ever been before. With my pistol in my right hand, I fired off five quick shots at the guard above us. Then I aimed carefully at the metal cable high above us and tossed my plasma wand. It flew, spiraling in a perfect arc as it cut through the binding cable, leaving the rope unharmed. The wand landed against a far wall and tumbled into the pit below while the rope uncoiled and fell three feet in front of me. I reached out and grabbed it and pulled it tight, at a sharp angle.

Tamret was firing at the guard as I did this, giving me room to maneuver. I pulled harder on the rope, getting an even steeper angle and making certain it was securely anchored. I could feel the tension in it, feel the strength of its base. It would hold us.

I fired at the guard and moved over to Tamret. I put one arm around her waist and she put one around my shoulder. She looked at me and grinned, not for a second fazed by the insanity of what I intended. I could tell she loved the idea. Somehow, impossibly, she knew exactly what to do and precisely what to say. Of all her amazing powers, that was the most remarkable one of all.

"Good luck," she said, and she kissed me on the cheek.

If she turns out to be my long-lost sister, I thought, *I'm going to be extremely angry.* And then I pulled on the rope and jumped in the air. Tamret and I were flying.

Once we hit the other side, we ran. Now I was hoping we might be able to circle around the guard entirely. Our corridor was sloping upward, which was a good sign, and ahead it merged with another corridor from the general direction the guard had been going. Also good. Farther beyond that was the hangar, which was only good if we got there first.

We didn't. I pumped my legs, tearing up the ground in a dizzying whir, but I wasn't going to make it in time. I could see the form of the guard approaching a shuttle, keying the access into the shuttle's exterior panel. He was going to get inside in about three seconds. Once he was in, he would be on an independent comm line, and I knew without Tamret telling me that it would take maybe fifteen seconds for him to signal the cruiser. He didn't have to explain the details. He didn't have to explain anything. An unexpected communication from one of the shuttles would be enough to alert them.

I had one chance now. I threw myself forward and down. I wanted a static shot. I hit the floor and raised my pistol, feeling myself skimming fast across the floor. I didn't care about the pain. I needed a good shot. And then I had it. The yellow light was at the center of his chest, but before I could squeeze the trigger, there was a flash, and the guard went down.

There, beyond him, was Charles. He was too far away for me to see the expression on his face, but I was sure he was smiling.

. . .

We tied up the guard, and then I checked the time. Just less than three hours until the check-in. With the hangar secured, Tamret, Charles, and I headed back to the main control room, where Nayana had her eye on the courtyard.

"No activity," she said. Then she caught sight of Tamret. "You look totally disgusting."

"You too," Tamret said.

"Whatever," Nayana opined. "I don't even want to know what you were doing to get all that blood on you. The point is that everything has been quiet here."

That was good. I was still worried about surprises, but so far there had been none. A few hiccups, like Tamret being impaled and a couple of guards almost escaping, but otherwise, smooth sailing.

Then, through the window, I saw the door to the prison facility open. Steve and Mi Sun walked out, hands over their heads. Behind them were eight Phands marching them toward us.

"Where did they come from?"

"I don't know," Tamret said. "We accounted for everyone in the database. There must have been guards in the compound who weren't assigned here. Maybe they had another function."

I tried to think, focus on what was important now. "Could they have contacted the cruiser?"

"Not unless they have a shuttle outside the hangar," Tamret said. "I think we can assume, for now, that the cruiser still doesn't know about us."

"This is still bad," Nayana said.

"Yeah," I agreed, "but it could be a whole lot worse. We have the element of surprise. They may not know we're in here."

"Unless Steve and Mi Sun told them," Nayana said.

"Which one of those two do you think gave us up?" I asked.

Her face went dark. I realized that maybe it had never occurred to her that our friends might not betray us to save themselves.

"What is the plan?" Charles asked.

I looked out across the courtyard. Steve and Mi Sun were about two hundred feet away and getting closer. There was no plan but a showdown. "Tamret and I have pretty good aim," I said, underselling the matter somewhat. With our maxed-out skills, either of us could both probably pick off a flea at two hundred yards. "And we're quick. I think we can take out the guards without hitting our friends."

"With these pistols?" Nayana asked. "No way. They're not that fast."

"In the right hands they are," Tamret said.

"I am so sick of your arrogance," Nayana snapped.

"Tell me about it some other time when I'm not busy saving you." Tamret began to walk toward the door. I followed her. This was going to be tight, even with our skills. We had to open the door and fire off eight perfect shots before any one of those guards decided to take aim at Steve or Mi Sun. I didn't like the odds, but I could not take the chance of these Phands communicating with the cruiser.

Just as I threw open the door, I saw a flash of light. Several flashes, and the guards went down. They were all down. Every last Phandic guard on the planet—I hoped—was down. And behind Steve and Mi Sun, walking toward us, were the people who had taken these last Phands out: Captain Qwlessl, Urch, Ystip, Wimlo, and a dozen more of the crew of the *Dependable*.

. . .

"For the record," Steve said, "we let ourselves get caught so Captain Qwlessl could blindside them."

"Absolutely true," Mi Sun said. "We let them catch us as soon as they showed up from nowhere and took our weapons."

"My story is better," Steve said.

I threw myself at the captain and gave her a hug. "It's good to see you," I said. "They made us think you were dead."

"I thought they might do something like that," she told me. "They likely fabricated the images. I'm sorry about that, Zeke. I also know you're here for your father, but first things first. What's the operational status?"

"Our plan," I told her, "is to take one of the shuttles and fake our way past the cruiser. We then deliver a Phandic shuttle to the Confederation and have them reverse engineer it."

"That's not such a great plan," Captain Qwlessl said, pointing at me with her trunk. "Do you really think you can simply slip past them?"

I felt a little foolish. "I was hoping that by the time they realized we were making a break for it, we'd have enough of a jump on them to tunnel to Confederation space."

She shook her head. "Too many variables. You've been lucky so far, but you can't count on luck holding. I have a plan that should allow us to deliver the cruiser to the Confederation, which is a better prize than a shuttle, don't you think?"

"Um, yeah. But how does it work?"

"First, I can get us past the 0200 check-in."

That was good news. "How?"

"We've been working on our escape since we got here. We've had the plan, just not the opportunity to execute it.

Now you've given us that opportunity. I know the codes for the check-in, so that won't be a problem. Then, the daily supply shuttle comes at 0400. We surprise them, load up the shuttle with a shock team of twelve or so, and take the cruiser."

"How many on that ship?"

She shrugged. "It's bigger than the one we faced at Ganar. I'd say eighty? Eighty-five?"

"And you think you can take it with a dozen soldiers?"

She looked at me with her huge eyes going wide, and her trunk jabbed in my direction with good humor as she spoke. "Zeke, you just led five alien teenagers, most of whom have had no training with hand weapons, to conquer an entire planet. I'm the captain of a Confederation starship. I think my trained officers can perform as well as you have."

"Point taken," I said. "Fortune favors the bold."

"Yes, it does," she agreed. "Do you want to be part of the team? We could use you, if you think you have the weapons skills. I don't know how you've been using your points."

"Take Steve and Mi Sun if they want to go. They're very good. I'd love to help, but we're not done here."

"Right. The selection committee."

I nodded. "Do you know where they are housed?"

"They're in the lower level," she said. "They've always been kept separate, so I haven't seen where they're confined." She put a hand on my arm. "I do know he's very proud of you."

"You've talked to him?" I asked.

"A few times," she said. "They never let us talk for long."

"How does he seem?" I asked. "Is he okay?"

"He's fine. They haven't hurt him. Not seriously. You go find him, Zeke. You and your friends have performed brilliantly, but I'll handle things for you now."

I was thrilled to turn the mission over to Captain Qwlessl. I'd messed things up along the way, but I liked to think not all that badly. Still, I didn't want to have to make decisions if there was someone around I trusted who actually knew what she was doing.

"Do you want me to go with you?" Tamret asked.

I nodded. "Do you mind?"

"Do I mind?" She rolled her eyes. "All those skill points in intellect, and you are still a complete moron."

For a brief moment I believed everything was going to be okay.

CHAPTER TWENTY-SEVEN

T
he members of the selection committee were housed together, away from the general population. To reach them, Tamret and I walked down a corridor lined with cells holding other prisoners—mostly Phands, but lots of other species I had never seen. They stared at us through their bars. Maybe they had heard the PPB fire; maybe they'd noticed that there had been no regular patrols. Maybe they realized that pistol-packing alien kids, one of whom was drenched with blood, did not usually walk down the corridor.

Captain Qwlessl had told me that a lot of these people were political prisoners, but many were genuine criminals—the kind that knock off alien liquor stores or pull off alien bank heists. Other than her crew and the selection committee, none were from the Confederation, so their loyalties were unknown. We couldn't risk taking any of them with us. Our plan was to open the gates just before we left so the prisoners would have access to the planet, which meant food and water as well as any shuttles we left behind. What they did with all of that was their business, but this was a habitable planet and they wouldn't starve. We were doing nothing unethical, and we hoped we would create the biggest possible mess for the Phandic Empire to clean up.

Soon the enemy shuttle would land to deliver supplies. Then our guys would capture it, and then the captain would lead her team to take over an entire Phandic vessel. That seemed much riskier to me, but she thought she could do it, and she understood that fortune favored the bold. The captain was both brave and bold, which was a pretty good combination.

Then we were at the gate. Tamret had rigged the system so we could control it from our data bracelets, but I stood there, doing nothing. I wasn't ready for this. I had been fatherless for five years. My mother had been without a husband when she learned she was going to die slowly and horribly. I missed my father, and I loved him, but I was afraid that when I saw him I would feel nothing but anger.

"There's so much you don't know," Tamret said, as if reading my mind. "Why don't you find out?"

I nodded, activated the controls on my bracelet, and opened the doors. We stepped into a new section of the prison. Five prisoners, one per cell, each a member of the selection committee. I recognized them from the data files. As we passed each cell, the being inside nodded or waved or bowed. None of them spoke. They all seemed to understand what was happening and to respect it. I figured that their time in prison had given my father plenty of opportunities to tell them the story of who he really was.

I passed them, hardly glancing at the beings who had changed my life, changed all our lives. I walked down the corridor and Tamret squeezed my hand.

Then we were in front of his cell. He wasn't wearing the cape or the ridiculous crossed red suspenders. He wore plain pants and a plain long-sleeved shirt. He was green and muscular and had a protruding brow, but under it all he was my father. He was smiling at me, and his eyes were glistening.

"Hi, Zeke," he said.

"Hi." It was all I could manage.

He shook his head slightly. "You look more like Mal Reynolds than Zeke Reynolds."

"And you look like Martian Manhunter." I couldn't even guess what I felt—relief, pride, love, rage. All of them mixed together in a pot of boiling soup, each feeling taking its turn rising to the surface. I had no idea how my tone sounded. I didn't want to know.

He let out a breathy half laugh. "Yeah, I do. That's sort of a long story." He looked at Tamret, at the two of us holding hands. "You're one of the Rarel girls, aren't you?"

She nodded.

"I hope that's not your blood."

She shrugged. "It's fine. I'm a quick healer."

His eyes narrowed. "I guess so. Are you going to let us out of here?"

"In a minute," I told him. "I need to know why you left us."

"This may not be the best time to catch up," he said.

"I think it's a pretty good time," I told him. Maybe it was the adrenaline, the experience of being in combat, of thinking Tamret was dead, of having broken into the prison. Maybe I wasn't myself, but I was now furious. He had left his family and gone off to the stars and turned himself into a superhero. I needed to know why, and I needed to know now.

"Zeke," he said gently, "I will tell you everything, the whole story, when we're safe. For now, what you need to know is that I didn't plan to leave or choose to leave Earth. That wasn't a decision I made. I would never have done that to you and your mom."

"And you never had a chance to come back?"

He looked away. "After I'd been gone a few years, I was in a position where I possibly could have returned to Earth, though getting there was always going to be a risk. But by then I knew our world was in trouble, in danger of being conquered by the Phandic Empire, and I couldn't go home just to wait for the end. I had to choose whether I wanted to be with the people I loved or to save them. Can you understand that?"

I did understand it. I knew it was the most terrible sort of decision a person could have to make, because it was the same decision I had been forced to make with my mother. I understood he had done what he had to do, and yet I was so angry with him for doing it.

He gestured toward the four other beings from the selection committee, each in their cells, each watching me. It was a menagerie of strange beings, a variety of forms, but they all looked like they understood every nuance of this unfolding drama.

"Zeke," my father said, "I know you would do anything to keep your friends safe. Captain Qwlessl told me about you, how you saved that ship. Well, these beings are my friends. Help me get them to safety."

Tamret shoved me. "Open your father's cell and give him a hug, you idiot."

I did. I felt like I was in a trance, but I called up the command console, and told the system to open the doors. The bars slid away. My father, my big green father, stepped out of his prison cell, his arms wide, and pulled me to him. It was so weird to embrace him again, not least because he was now insanely buff. Yet as I felt his strangely massive green arms wrap around me, I knew it was him, my father, and I understood he had suffered for the choices that had been forced upon him. He had tried to do the right thing, and it had cost him.

"Can you forgive me?" he asked.

"I'm going to try," I said.

He hugged me again. "Is your mom okay?"

I nodded. I didn't have the heart to tell him the truth just yet.

"I bet she misses you," he said.

"She misses you too, Dad," I told him. "All the time. Every day."

He looked away, and there seemed to be tears in those hooded Martian eyes.

Just then a message came in over my data bracelet. "Mr. Reynolds, please acknowledge." It was Captain Qwlessl.

I tapped my bracelet. "I'm here."

"Mr. Reynolds, we have taken command of the Phandic cruiser in orbit. Our mission is accomplished. Can I suggest you finish your business on the surface so we can depart before any more surprises come our way?"

"Agreed, Captain."

"Oh, and your friend Steve thought you should have the honor of renaming our commandeered ship—perhaps in reference to one of those fictions you enjoy."

My father looked at me, and he was grinning a broad, geeky grin. It was the kind of grin he'd flash when we were watching TV or a movie and he had some especially geeky observation to make—something he was really proud of. "An enemy ship captured while escaping imprisonment. How about *Reliant*?" It was the stolen Federation ship from *Star Trek II*.

"It's a good suggestion," I told him, "but I have a better one." I spoke into my bracelet. "Ma'am, can we call her *Dependable*?"

There was a brief moment of silence; then she said, "It's a good name."

"I think so."

"How soon can you rendezvous?" she asked.

I told her to hold a minute; then I turned to my father. "The Phands were obviously looking for something here. Did they find it, or can we take it from them?"

"They found it," he said, "and that's a whole other story. There are still artifacts here, but none that are worth delaying our departure over."

I contacted the captain. "We're finishing up down here. I hope to be on board within half an hour."

"Be quick and be careful," Captain Qwlcssl said, and signed off.

It was time to snap out of it. My father was right. For now it was time to close up shop. I worked the security console to free the rest of the selection committee, and I ushered everyone back to the bunker.

As we walked, my father kept close to my side. Tamret walked ahead of us, her steps cautious and careful and pretty much catlike. I watched her ears bounce as she moved.

"Is she your girlfriend?" my father asked.

"I'm not sure," I said. "Maybe. I think so. I hope so."

"The beautiful alien girl," he said, shaking his head, smiling. "That is so old-school."

Only a skeleton crew—Charles and Nayana—had remained behind, so we loaded up the shuttle and set the console to release the prisoners in an hour, and I sat down at the helm, Tamret by my side. I had Charles and Nayana sitting behind me, and I directed the members of the selection committee to buckle up toward the back. I wanted them far enough away that I would not have to make conversation. I was not up for it, not least because the controls were totally unfamiliar to me and I didn't want them to see how clueless we were. Fortunately, it occurred to Tamret to overlay a holographic projection from her data bracelet, so in about five minutes we had figured out how to operate the shuttle—at least well enough to get us to the cruiser.

"Let's get out of here," I said, trying to sound confident. With me working secondary stations, Tamret took the helm and eased the shuttle out of the hangar. We hovered for a moment and then pointed it toward the sky. She handled it nicely considering she'd never operated a Phandic ship before.

It was only thirty seconds after we took off when my data bracelet chirped to indicate an incoming message. "Zeke, what's your status?" It was Captain Qwlessl.

"Just departed," I told her.

"Our sensors have picked up a Phandic cruiser, we think a much larger one, tunneling in. We're about a hundred seconds from aperture."

"We need six minutes to rendezvous," Tamret informed me.

I swore more loudly and more vividly than I meant to in front of my father and the captain.

"We can try to hold them off," Tamret asked.

"No," I said. I'd already reviewed the weapons and shields, and I knew there was no way a shuttle like this could last for more than a few seconds against a fully armed cruiser.

I held up my hand. I needed a moment to think. I had to figure out how we could get that stolen cruiser back to the Confederation without using ourselves as a distraction. I wanted to get the ship to the good guys, but I didn't want to be left behind for that to happen. I was not going to let Tamret fall into their hands, and there was no way I was going to let my father be recaptured less than an hour after his escape. Yet no matter how I thought about it, I knew we were expendable. Nothing mattered as much as getting the new *Dependable* back to Confederation space. That was what was going to turn everything around for the good guys. But I didn't want to have to fall into enemy hands to make it happen.

How could I do it? I had almost no training and less experience. All those nanite improvements weren't going to help me when I was so drastically outgunned. What did I possibly have that was going to tip the balance here? Tamret had tweaked the game, but I wasn't in god mode. I could still be killed. In the end, despite all the improved abilities, I was still just a dork who liked science fiction.

And that was what was going to save me.

"You're grinning," Tamret said.

"Yes, I am."

I cut the line on my data bracelet and opened a channel to the *Dependable* via the shuttle's comm system. "Captain, you need to get that ship to the Confederation, but I think I have a way we can do that without you leaving us behind. Tunnel out now, but don't go far. Make them think you are heading for home. Then turn around and come back here in exactly four minutes. Return to exactly the same place where you depart, so I'll know where to find you. By the time you pop back in, they will have gone after you in the hopes of overtaking you when you come out near the station."

"You think they'll attack us in Confederation space?" the captain asked.

"All they're going to care about at that point is making sure the Confederation doesn't get its hands on a fully functioning cruiser. They won't be worrying about surviving or ramifications."

"That could work," the captain said. "Executing now. Good luck, Zeke."

I looked back at the passengers.

"It is a good plan," my father said, speaking very slowly, "but I wonder if you've considered regulation 46-A."

That was my father, the man I remembered, the man I had come to rescue. Whatever anger I'd felt toward him for leaving us had now vanished. He had just watched me make what he believed to be a colossal blunder, but even though he was sure I'd just placed all our lives in jeopardy, he wasn't willing to embarrass me in front of the rest of the committee and my friends. He was more worried about my feelings than his own life, and I knew, at that moment, that whatever he had done he had done for the right reasons, and that his decisions had cost him more than I could easily imagine.

Regulation 46A, like his proposed name for the stolen ship, came from *Star Trek II: The Wrath of Khan*, his favorite science-fiction film of all time. The regulation was little more than a plot device to trick both Kirk's enemies, and the audience, into thinking the *Enterprise* was more seriously damaged than it actually was. Now, in command of this stolen vessel, the only audience I needed to deceive was the enemy.

I turned to my father and quoted, which was no problem since we had watched that movie together like a dozen times, "'If transmissions are being monitored during battle, no uncoded messages on an open channel.' Dad, not only did I not forget regulation 46-A, I'm counting on it. Our lives, at this point, depend on a scheme I'm stealing from *Star Trek Two*."

"If you are going to put us in a *Trek* movie's hands, it might as well be *Two*," he said. "Or *Four*. Have you considered a slingshot around the sun to take us back in time?"

We both laughed a little hysterically, and then I activated my data bracelet. It was time to tell the captain the real plan.

We broke atmosphere and settled into orbit. I knew what, I hoped, the Phands did not—that the *Dependable* was not going be returning in four minutes. That meant we were going to have to spend several minutes convincing the enemy not to destroy us. It was going to be dicey, particularly since the cruiser's weapons could easily tear us to shreds.

The limited range of the shuttle's sensors didn't pick up anything. I looked at my data bracelet. Three minutes since last communication. If all went according to plan, the *Dependable* should be back within another six minutes. If we were lucky. This was going to be tight. Quietly, so our passengers wouldn't hear my plan—and know how much of a gamble it was—I explained to Tamret what I was really up to. Tamret could find about a hundred things wrong with me when I was eating breakfast, but now she simply listened and nodded as though my scheme were the most reasonable thing in the world.

"Sounds good," she pronounced when I finished.

"It's insane," I whispered.

She shrugged. "It's pretty solid given the circumstances."

I checked my sensor readings again and saw nothing, but then, a few seconds later, I picked up a radiation spike. An instant after that it seemed as though a scalpel had slashed a line across the starscape. A wound opened in regular space and a massive Phandic cruiser came out of its tunnel. From looking at it I couldn't tell if it was the *Dependable* or the enemy ship, but I assumed the latter. Once they sent the text-only message *Surrender or be destroyed*, I was even more certain.

Tamret broke orbit and began to accelerate, heading away from the planet. The cruiser pursued, slowly overtaking us, but it had not fired weapons thus far. I could tell because we hadn't exploded in a fiery ball.

The cruiser signaled again, this time with a video communication. I put it on the shuttle's screen. If we were talking, it seemed to me, we weren't exploding, so I was in favor of talking. I was ready to negotiate. I was ready to do anything I had to in order to buy more time for Tamret and my father. I was not ready for the face that appeared on that screen.

"Zeke," Ms. Price said. She stood with her arms folded, the blood-red fingernails of her right hand tapping against her arm. She wore a humorless business suit, and she looked ready for some corporate action. "I picked up on your little trick, and we're ready for Qwlessl when she emerges from her tunnel. Her ship can take a few hits before it is destroyed. Yours can't. I don't want to hurt you, but I can't let you get away."

Okay, I thought. *This is something, isn't it?* Since leaving Earth I'd wondered what Ms. Price's deal was. Considering she was issuing ultimatums from the bridge of an enemy cruiser, it seemed likely that she was, in fact, a Phandic agent. *That* was her deal.

I typed furiously on my data-bracelet keyboard, but I did it by feel, keeping my eye on the screen camera as I hacked out a message to Captain Qwlessl. I hoped the Phands hadn't picked up on Tamret's improvised closed network, because if they had, we were as good as dead.

"They gave you your own ship?" I said to Ms. Price. "That's pretty cool. If I betray everything that's good and right, can I get my own ship too?"

"Ambassador Vusio-om is in command of this vessel," she said. "He thought you might be more willing to negotiate with me than with him."

"Really, it's six of one, half dozen of the other," I told her. "I find you both equally charming."

"Your sarcasm is less amusing than it used to be," she said. "And it was always annoying. Now please surrender. If you don't, you will be destroyed."

"Ms. Price," I said, doing my best to sound like someone who was not, in fact, facing destruction, "I think you know I won't hand over this shuttle."

"I'll tell you what I know. I know you have your father and your girlfriend on the ship with you. Maybe you have some grand plan to be a hero, but do you really want to get them killed?"

I glanced over at Tamret, who was pretending to be completely absorbed in the operation of the shuttle. Everyone was so sure she was my girlfriend. We were going to have to talk when this was all over.

"We'll take our chances."

Ms. Price had to think we were hers for the taking. She thought she knew exactly where the *Dependable* was going to manifest and when. A ship was at its most vulnerable for a few seconds after emerging from a tunnel. The sensors scattered and the shielding was unreliable. An enemy lying in wait had a huge tactical advantage, but usually an enemy had no way of knowing precisely where and when a ship would appear. My plan depended upon the Phandic ship seizing this rare opportunity.

There was again the slash against the sky as a hole ripped in regular space. I watched on our screen as the cruiser pointed toward that rip and fired.

There was nothing there. And then there was something, a tiny ship where the Phands had been expecting a larger one. The *Dependable* hadn't emerged from the tunnel. A shuttle had. This was the plan that I had sent to the *Dependable* via Tamret's data-bracelet network. My enemies had set their sights on a cruiser, and they now had to search for a target that was almost too small to hit with their blind firing. By now they would have realized their mistake, seen the shuttle, and begun to target it. I hoped they would be at least a few seconds too late.

They were. Before they could lock on to the shuttle, it deployed a plasma lance, which cut through the shields, attached itself to the cruiser's hull, and pulled, but just for a second. Then, as I had instructed, it reversed direction, so instead of pulling the cruiser toward the shuttle, it pulled the shuttle toward the cruiser. They were firing PPB blasts at it manically, but the shuttle was closing in fast and flying erratically, making it almost impossible to target.

With a plasma lance embedded in its hull and a shuttle hurtling toward it at top speed, the Phandic cruiser would want to switch shield polarity to sever the lance cable and protect against collision with the shuttle. I'm sure that was precisely what they intended to do until another slash ripped across the horizon and the *Dependable* emerged.

I could imagine the bridge of the Phandic ship, its commander countering the order to switch shield frequencies. If they protected themselves against collision with the shuttle, they would make themselves vulnerable to attack by the cruiser. My plan had been to put them in a situation where they had to choose between two evils: damage from the shuttle impact or certain destruction from another cruiser.

They opted to let the shuttle hit, which must have seemed like the smart choice. The impact would likely tear a small hole in the hull, and then there would be some brief decompression before the plasma fields kicked in. Nasty, but far less dangerous than a barrage of PPB blasts against an unshielded cruiser. Of course, they didn't know that I had advised Captain Qwlessl to place a dark-matter missile on the shuttle.

The shuttle smacked against the hull of the cruiser, midway along its port side. There was a vortex in space as the missile released its negative energy and then unleashed the volatile dark matter into the deficit. It was as if space had been sucked in and then blown out. The shuttle exploded, and a hole was ripped into the side of the cruiser, appearing amid the bright orange burst of flame as the escaping oxygen burned. The puncture ran almost the height of the ship, and nearly half its length. The entire vessel lurched violently and pointed upward and to the side, then simply hung there like an insect in amber.

From a distance I watched furniture and equipment being

sucked into space. Then, all along the breach, a flickering blue light appeared as the Phandic cruiser patched the hull breach with a plasma field, instantly dousing the fire.

I saw now that we had scored a good hit, though not a decisive one. The ship had suffered considerable damage, but it was still functional. Its ability to move or defend itself had been limited but not destroyed. I'd angered them and bought us some time, but no more than that.

I used my data bracelet to signal the *Dependable* as I programmed a course change. "I don't think major systems are damaged. Open the shuttle bay doors and give us cover. We're going to have to come in hot."

I accelerated as we moved toward the *Dependable*. It was a big, ugly Phandic saucer, but it was the most beautiful thing I had ever seen. I changed course and sped toward it, flying erratically as I tried to avoid the energy weapons the Phands had begun firing at us.

"Zeke," Ms. Price said over the video feed. "You are not making this easy for me."

"Wasn't really hoping to," I said as Tamret banked us sharply.

"I'd rather take you alive," she said. "But I will destroy you if there's no other choice."

Tamret reached over and cut off communication. She then signaled Captain Qwlessl on the private channel. "Captain, this is Tamret. You don't know me, but the short version is I'm pretty amazing. And I have an idea."

"Yes, you're Zeke's girlfriend. Go ahead."

"I want you to accelerate to ten percent below maximum speed," she said. "Keep the shuttle bay doors open. I'll come in at five percent above your speed, then match, and dock. Once I'm latched down, I want you to brake hard. We then turn and fire."

The captain said nothing as she thought this over.

"It's not going to work." It was Urch speaking. "I've tried maneuvers like this in sim, and sharp movements at accelerated speeds radically alter your ability to target. You won't be able to get any kind of weapons lock for several seconds. Meanwhile, you're stationary, and an easy target for your enemy, whose position is comparatively stable."

I had, as I recalled, tried this maneuver several times, including in that first match with the humans against the Rarels and Ish-hi, and I knew what Urch meant. It had been impossible to find a target when moving so fast. If it had been possible, we might have won that sim, but every time I'd tried this trick, it had failed.

"Maybe *you* can't do it," she said. "Zeke can. Transfer weapons control to his console here."

"Wait a second," I said, but Tamret held up a hand, letting me know it was time to be quiet.

"What makes you think you'll be able to lock from your location if we can't lock from ours?" the captain asked.

"He's picked up a few tricks," she said.

And I had. My speed, my agility, and my perception were all beyond anything they'd been before. I could do it. Maybe.

"Tamret's right," I said to the captain. "This will work."

"Zeke," she said. "I can't risk my crew on your hunch."

"It's not a hunch," I assured her. "If you've got another idea, I'm listening, but we've got to do something. Captain, please trust us. Tamret can handle the shuttle, and I can get a lock."

She paused for a moment. "How sure are you? One hundred percent?"

"It'll be a hundred percent after we do it," I said. "Maybe ninety percent now."

Another pause. "I don't like it, but I don't see any other way we're getting out of this. Keep in mind that if this doesn't work, recapture is our best possible outcome."

"It will work," I told her.

She sighed. "I'll have helm transfer our coordinates."

"Everything via data bracelet, not directly to the shuttle," I cautioned.

"Understood," she said, and broke the connection.

We received the data and then banked hard to port to follow the *Dependable*'s vector. Flashes from PPB fire flashed past the starboard viewer. We accelerated hard, and we all began to feel it. We were at almost a quarter light speed, and things were getting a little strange.

Ms. Price was on the screen again. "Zeke, please remember that I was watching that battle sim. I know what you are going to try, and I know it didn't work then. It's not going to work in real life. Let's face it. You're competent, but you're not an innovator."

"That big hole in the side of your ship says I'm kind of an innovator."

"Listen to me," she said. "I'm not bluffing when I say I know what you are planning. You are going to land hard in the shuttle bay; Qwlessl is going to hit full stop. She will then turn and fire, and she'll miss because weapons can't lock under that kind of stress—which you know. We won't take a hit, but you'll end up dead. This is your last chance to surrender."

"Let me ask you this," I said as I picked up speed. "What made you betray your world, your people? Money? Power?"

She shook her head. "I'm standing on the bridge of a starship," she said. "I'm a central player in intergalactic events. I'd think you, of all people, would understand."

"I understand that part, just not the evil."

"The Confederation isn't what you think," she said. "They only showed you what they want you to see. You have enemies in the empire, but they can be swayed. You're a talented kid. You could make friends and rise. You and the Rarel and your father could all join us."

"Good-bye, Ms. Price," I said. "I've learned a few things since I obliterated that last Phandic ship. I will try not to blow you up."

We were coming up hard on the *Dependable*. The cruiser wasn't even bothering to target us. They were saving their weapons, securing the lock.

Meanwhile, on our viewscreen, the *Dependable* grew larger as we zeroed in on it. The shuttle bay doors were open; the blue plasma shield had vanished. It was a tiny target, and we were coming so fast. Part of me looked at the shuttle bay and thought it was impossible. Tamret was working the controls, her face a mask of concentration—not panic. She had this. No matter how impossible it looked, she was in control.

We bucked and bounced and everything vibrated. Lights flashed as the ship's systems warned us we were approaching, and then exceeding, the shuttle's maximum safe speed. I glanced behind me and saw the horror on every face back there—Nayana and Charles and the members of the selection committee. Everyone but my father, whose face betrayed nothing but a proud calm, like he somehow knew I could do this thing that no one should be able to do.

I turned back to the consoles and the screens. The *Dependable* was getting closer, but was still miles away. Ten seconds later it was upon us. It was like we were falling toward it, like we were a missile bent on its destruction. There was no way to control our approach at speeds like this, but Tamret did it anyhow. She matched speed and let the shuttle bay swallow us as we came to a full stop. The g-force compensators kicked in, but there was only so much they could do, and the passengers were tossed around violently. I tried to ignore it all. My one chance to save us was coming up. That was all that mattered. I heard a couple of the passengers cry out as we set down on the shuttle bay floor, somehow without crashing. Barely. We braked hard as we came screeching to a halt across the length of the bay. In the limited atmosphere, I heard the ripping of metal on metal, and on the viewscreen I saw the sparks flying. It was ugly and frightening, and I had caused a lot of property damage, but I knew at once, even before we came to a full stop, that Tamret had landed us.

Urch came in over the comm. "That was the most messed-up landing I've ever seen!" I could tell he meant that in a good way.

"You've got weapons," Captain Qwlessl told me. "I'm turning the ship. I hope you know what you're doing."

"He does," Tamret said.

I hit my console and pulled up the weapons screen. It was time to win this.

The *Dependable* was already reducing its forward speed and pivoting to face our pursuers. It was exactly like that moment at Ganar when the gravity had cut out. It was like when we dropped to the planet's surface. We were thrown back, hard and fast. I felt my stomach drop, and my head buzzed. I thought I would vomit, I thought I would black out, but I stared at the console and forced myself to concentrate.

Then, suddenly, there was no spin, no loss of gravity, no nausea. I was in the moment, clear and precise, seeing exactly what I had to do. I tapped the screen, focused on the engines, and locked in. There was, just for a second, a moment of hesitation. I thought of giving Ms. Price exactly what she had promised me, death and destruction, but that wasn't the person I wanted to be. It wasn't the person Tamret wanted me to be. Or my father. I was better than that. I'd destroyed a ship once before, but I hadn't known what I was doing. Now I knew exactly what I wanted to do and exactly how to do it.

I chose my target, locked on to their weapons array, and fired a single missile. Once it was away, I refocused and targeted the engines with PPBs. Those I kept on firing. The missiles were slower than energy weapons, and the particle beams struck first, and there was a flash as the enemy saucer's engines burst into flame. Chunks of metal and exploding fuel plumed from the cruiser. Atmosphere hissed into the void. And then the missile struck, and there was another explosion, this one near the primary weapons array.

In an instant the ship lay dead in space, an overturned saucer, bobbing like a dead fish in the water. Air and fuel bubbled out into space. The cracked hull of the cruiser spit fire and vented plasma. In places the hull was so hot it glowed red. In other places I watched the metal warp and wave like a flag in the wind. The saucer was damaged beyond repair, and I knew beings had died—they were dead because of my decisions, and

I hated that. I was still alive, however, and so were my father and Tamret and my friends and the beings we'd rescued. I never asked for that bargain, but I would happily take it.

Captain Qwlessl's voice came over the speaker. "Mr. Reynolds, the Phandic cruiser is signaling surrender. Your recommendation?"

I let out a sigh. I felt something warm and wonderful. It was Tamret, taking my hand. Only then did I realize that I was shaking.

I swallowed, not quite sure I was up for speaking, but when I tried, my voice sounded almost calm. "Ma'am, it's your command. I'm just along for the ride."

"Let's treat it like a training exercise. Recommended course of action?"

I closed my eyes and thought for a moment. "Accept surrender. Secure ship with lances and tow it back to Confederation Central?" I ventured. "Send boarding parties via shuttle and secure personnel in the brig. I assume a Phandic cruiser has a brig."

"It does, indeed," the captain said. "Well done, Mr. Reynolds."

I looked at Tamret. She was beaming at me. "You did it. You rescued your father. You captured a ship. You got us out of there alive. You did everything."

"*We* did everything." I said.

"Yeah," she said. "And don't you forget it."

CHAPTER TWENTY-EIGHT

When all the excitement was over, I checked my HUD and leveled. Apparently daring rescues and space battles score well. My hacked skills aside, the number of experience points I had logged brought me to level twenty-four. We'd all racked up experience: Mi Sun was twenty-one, Charles nineteen, and Nayana eighteen. With most of our year yet before us, the human delegation had already exceeded eighty levels. Together, Steve and Tamret and the humans had rescued my father, the members of the selection committee, and the crew of the *Dependable*, whom everyone had thought dead. We had uncovered a traitor to Earth and the Confederation. We were also returning to Confederation Central with not one but two captured Phandic ships, prizes that would turn the tide of the war, maybe even end it. I hated to be so self-congratulatory, but there was no getting around it. We were heroes.

As soon as we were safely aboard *Dependable* and the captain had thoroughly debriefed us, we all retreated to separate cabins. Having not washed in many days, I was relieved to discover that the Phands, despite their habit of public vomiting, believed in cleanliness, and there was something like a shower in the bathroom. The water shot upward, and in streams hard enough to poke out your eye, but I wasn't complaining. I no longer stank, and that was a relief to me. It would have been a relief to others if I'd been around anyone, but as soon as I was out of the shower/torture device, I plopped down on the bed and slept ten hours.

When I emerged, we were still the better part of a day out from Confederation Central. My head was clearer, but I was starving. I checked my bracelet and saw that someone had thoughtfully already uploaded a limited schematic for the Phandic ship, so I followed the directions to the mess. No one else was in there, but I soon discovered that the *Dependable*'s crew had again shown great wisdom, this time in converting the food production units to Confederation-standard fare. I was never so happy to have bland grain porridge.

I'd finished my first bowl and was seriously considering a second when Tamret came into the room and sat down across from me. She had also changed and showered, but her clothes had obviously been ruined. She wore some kind of workman's coveralls, and while they were not the most flattering clothes in the world, Tamret made them look stylish.

"How did you know I'd be in here?" I asked.

She placed her elbow on the table and rested her chin on her palm. "I programmed my bracelet to let me know when you woke up and to keep me updated about your movements."

"Are you supposed to do that?" I asked.

She shook her head very slowly and smiled.

Thoughts of bland porridge now vanished. My heart pounded, and I could feel my face growing hot. All this time I had wanted to say something to Tamret, to tell her how I felt about her, but I'd always been afraid, or I'd decided that there was too much going on to risk it. Now we were alone, and the danger was behind us. I had nothing to lose, because I had already gained so much. I had taken on soldiers, outwitted my enemies, broken into a prison, and bested a flying saucer in a space battle, but none of that felt to me as terrifying as the prospect of telling Tamret just how much I liked her.

She breathed in deeply and sat up. "I need to tell you something."

No conversation that began that way ever ended well. My heart felt like it was ready to explode. She was going to tell me that she liked me, but not in that way, that she knew I wanted something else, but she only wanted to be friends. I could feel it. I closed my eyes and braced myself.

She looked down and away, as if ashamed. Tamret was always so brash, so confident, but not now. "On my world, there are illustrated stories, both books and moving images—do you know what I mean?"

Comics and anime. She had definitely come to the right person with this. "Sure," I told her, thinking this was a strange way to begin the *I like you but* . . . talk.

"There's a kind of character," she said, her voice trembling. "A regular Rarel boy, but with [*monkey*] features too. They're always really attractive, and, I guess, what I'm trying to say is that that's what you look like to me."

I sat in stunned silence, knowing I should say something, but I was too blindsided by this revelation to remember how to communicate. I was her version of a neko. That was what she was telling me. I was some kind of animated, romanticized object. I felt a little insulted and objectified, but I also figured that if it worked in my favor, I could live with it.

She was looking down now, unable to meet my eye. "When I first saw you, that night in the restaurant with Steve, I couldn't believe it. I'd always had a thing for [*monkey*] boys, and I knew it was stupid, because you are what your species looks like and it didn't seem right to like you because of that. But I know now that I like you because of you, Zeke. After everything we've been through, I thought it was important that you know that you're more to me than some weird space creature who looks like he's from an illustrated book."

"Thank you for telling me," I said, reaching out and taking her hand. "I wanted to talk to you, too. I didn't know if you liked me the way I like you."

"That's because you're not so bright."

She was looking at me, smiling, and she appeared as happy as I'd ever seen her. I felt like I would do anything to keep her looking that way.

Ever since I'd arrived on the station I had been circling around in Tamret's orbit, and now I understood that she had been circling in mine. We had been bound together from the beginning. We were entangled, and I was not going to wait or to think or to wonder. I'd once told myself that I had a year to try to make sense of things, but I had far less time than that, and the time for waiting was over.

Tamret leaned toward me. "I should probably warn you that I can be a little intense."

"There may have been hints of that," I told her. "No one's perfect."

She cocked her head to one side. "No, but you're pretty good."

I looked at her, really looked at her, and saw her in all her incredible alien and slightly insane beauty. She was the most confounding and beguiling girl I had ever met, and all it had taken to find her was crossing vast expanses of space. All I'd had to do to keep her was fend off an evil empire that wanted me dead. No one had ever said these things would be easy.

Tamret and I walked out into the hall, holding hands, and nearly bumped into my father. He had changed his clothes and now wore one of the same utility outfits as Tamret. He looked like a green bodybuilder.

Tamret immediately let go of my hand and stood nervously.

"Dang, Dad," I said. "You've been hitting the iron."

"It's all for show," he said with an embarrassed grin. "Part of the conversion process. I'm not actually any stronger than I was before, but I figured if I was going to make myself look like a superhero, I might as well go all the way."

"I can't argue with that," I said.

He now turned to Tamret. "I don't think I ever thanked you for helping me to escape."

"It was my honor, sir," she said.

Tamret seemed nervous, and she was actually showing respect for my father. I'd never seen her be deferent with anyone. I felt so touched I wanted to hug her.

"I should go," she said. "Let you two catch up."

She hurried down the hallway, and we watched her leave.

"I like her," my father said, "but you need to be careful."

"She can be a little out there," I said, "but she's not dangerous." As soon as I said that, I knew it was a flat-out lie. She was probably the most dangerous being I'd ever known. Or was that Steve? She was easily top two, but they were both on my side, so that made it okay.

"I don't mean that," he said. "I mean your feelings. You two are only on the station for the year. It's probably not a good idea to get too attached."

I did not want to think about that. "But Earth's admission is a lock," I said.

"It will be a long time before Earth citizens are going to be traveling throughout the Confederation."

"I don't know," I said. "You seem to have managed."

It came out more cruelly than I'd intended. I wanted to take it back, but I let it hang there.

My father glanced away, embarrassed. "I know we have a lot to talk about. I know you're angry with me for leaving, and I don't blame you."

"I'm not angry," I said, and I found, as I spoke the words, that they were true. Maybe I would have been if he hadn't been right there, next to me, looking impossibly green, but we were back together. I understood what he had told me in the prison, and I believed him. He had been faced with an impossible choice, and he'd made the better decision.

"It's just that it was hard without you," I told him.

"I know it was," he said. "But that's done. We're going to have to figure out what comes next."

"Do you think you'll be coming back to Earth?"

He looked down at himself. "I'll need to be converted again, but yeah. The truth is, I'm not going to get such a warm reception back at the station. I broke a lot of laws to do what I did."

I gestured all around us. "But you did it for a good reason. You're bringing this ship back. You've saved the Confederation."

He shrugged. "I think that was you and your friends. And yes, things worked out about as well as I could have hoped, but that doesn't change the basic fact that I'm now a criminal. That's okay, though. I did what I had to do. If the Confederation is no longer in danger, then Earth is also safe, and I don't need to be here anymore. As long as no one is too angry, they'll go for exile rather than imprisonment, and I can go back to you and your mom."

At some point I'd have to tell him about Mom being sick, but I didn't want to upset him now. Besides, it didn't matter. With our eighty levels in the bag, we would enter into the Confederation, which would begin with their giving us the technology that would cure my mother. She was only a few months away from being disease-free. The whole world was. I couldn't believe that I'd played a role in changing everyone's lives, in making the entire world a better place, but there was no denying it, and there was no denying that my father had made it all possible. The quality of life of every single person on Earth was going to improve because of what my father had set in motion. I was proud to be his son.

"Listen," he said, "would you like to come with me?"

"To do what?"

"To talk to your friend Nora Price. I have some questions, and I thought you might too."

I nodded. "I'm game."

She sat on her cot, the only piece of furniture in the brig, behind a blue force field. She still wore her tight skirt suit, but her hair had been mussed and her face had been cut in the attack on her ship. Her hands were dirty, and her eyes were red, but she didn't look like she'd admitted defeat. Not quite yet.

"What do you want?" she asked neither of us in particular.

"Where's the tech?" my father asked.

She almost smiled at that. "What tech is that?"

"I know what your friends were looking for on that planet,"

my father said, "and I have a pretty good idea that they found it, or found part of it."

"You know I'm not going to tell you. I don't want to, and your Confederation friends aren't as good at getting information out of prisoners. Do you think I'm going to experience anything like what you did?"

My father's face darkened. "You deserve it. You deserve worse."

She shrugged. "Oh well."

My father tried several more times to get her to talk, but she wasn't going to say anything, and he left in frustration. I stayed.

"How long have you been working for the Phands?" I asked.

She smiled. "Years. They helped me rise to my position in the State Department. They wanted me on the station, but when you went rogue and threatened the security of the empire, they decided it was more important that I stop you. There are other well-placed agents throughout the Confederation, and on Earth, for that matter. While idiots like Dr. Roop were trying to influence TV shows, the Phands were exerting real influence. You can't change how things are going to turn out, Zeke."

"I think these captured ships will make a difference."

"We'll see," she said smugly.

"Why would you do it?" I asked. "Why would you betray your home world?"

"I'm not betraying anything," she said. "I'm trying to put Earth in the best possible position to succeed in the bigger galaxy. You're just too brainwashed by Confederation propaganda to see that."

"Are you honestly saying you think the Phandic Empire is good for Earth?"

"Do you think the Confederation is? Zeke, you and I have had some rough history, but I respect you, and I know you're not as clueless as people think."

"Thanks?" I proposed.

"I'm sure you've done some digging around. You've at least looked at a map. You know what these worlds are—they're all border planets. The Confederation is recruiting expendable soldiers for their losing war."

"And why do the Phands want us?"

"To fight," she admitted. "But humans would have the same chance as any non-Phands to rise within the empire. They don't want to bring in species as second-class citizens so their privileged, nonviolent members can continue to stick their heads in the sand."

"I'd rather be on the side that doesn't go around conquering planets," I said. "And I know we can prove our value to the Confederation. I think maybe we just did."

"Don't be so sure about that," she said. "You may not get the reception you imagine."

"What is that supposed to mean?" I asked.

"You think the Confederation is like the United States but with much more diversity. It's not. Where we come from, when you go out and risk everything for your country and come back a hero, you expect the people, the government you serve, to honor your courage and sacrifice. You may not like how you're treated when you return to the station."

I saw my father waiting in the hall, looking worried. His protruding brow was wrinkled.

"What were they looking for on that planet?"

"Software," he said. "A former military application that

added an additional skill tree, one that would allow soldiers to develop some pretty incredible powers. Telekinesis, mind control, supernormal strength."

"Wow," I said. "Those would be cool."

"Unless someone evil is using them against you and your world."

"Yeah," I said. "Then it becomes uncool."

"Extremely uncool," my green father said. "If they've found a way to unlock that skill tree, we may be in serious trouble."

"And they found it?" I asked.

"I wasn't sure, which is why I wanted to talk to Ms. Price. I'm pretty sure they have it, but I'm also pretty sure they didn't know that someone managed to escape with the bio codes."

"Who?" I asked.

He grinned. "Me. I was able to make a copy before they removed the main artifact containing the software off-world about two months ago. That's one of the reasons you were able to take the prison so easily. The things they were most interested in protecting were off-world by the time you showed up."

"And they never caught you with it?" I asked.

"There was nothing to catch. I uploaded it to my HUD."

"You mean you can . . ." I trailed off.

"No, I haven't activated it. We don't know what it can do yet. But at least I can get it back to the Confederation and they'll be able to analyze the data and match anything the Phands can throw at them."

One more reason for the Confederation to be grateful to my father, I thought. At least, I hoped they would be grateful. I hadn't liked what Ms. Price had been implying. "What about the rest of what she was saying? She told me the Confederation isn't what I think it is?"

"I don't know," he said. "You were able to find me because there are some good beings like Dr. Roop out there, but they had to act in secret because there are some less good beings as well. The bottom line is I don't know what to expect when we return."

As we docked at the station, all I could think was what it would be like for a Confederation citizen to look out one of the viewscreens and see a Phandic cruiser towing another Phandic cruiser. The news outputs would be covering nothing else by now. Zeke Reynolds the war criminal would become Zeke Reynolds the hero, the guy who helped save the Confederation. There would be a ceremony, like at the end of *Star Wars*, and we would all get medals like Han and Luke—there would be no Chewbacca sitting on the sidelines.

The biggest story, I had no doubt, would be the capture of two Phandic ships, but there were other stories too. J'onn J'onzz of the selection committee was really the father of the supposed war criminal. The human chaperone was a Phandic spy. The crew of the *Dependable* was still alive, and its destruction in battle had been merely Phandic trickery.

We took a shuttle to the docking bay, where we walked out into the commons, a large open space sort of like an airport terminal. Honestly, I expected to hear cheering. Here we were, the beings who had managed to turn everything around for the Confederation.

When we stepped out into the common area, however, I knew at once that something was wrong. The space had been cleared of civilians. There were peace officers everywhere, with pistols out, pointed at us. Facing us were Chief Justice Junup and the rest of the Xeno-Affairs Judicial Council. Other government officials, some of whom I recognized from the compound, were gathered around. This was no hero's welcome.

I felt Tamret take hold of my hand, and I pulled her toward me, as if someone were about to separate us. I was not about to let that happen.

"Captain Qwlessl, you and your crew are most welcome in your return." Chief Justice Junup strode toward us, his stupid cape billowing behind him. "Unfortunately, I'm afraid everyone else involved in this reckless adventure is in serious trouble."

A hush fell upon the space. There were perhaps twenty officers, and almost as many government officials facing us. By my side was my father, and next to him Captain Qwlessl. Behind us stood Steve and the other humans, then the refugees from the *Dependable* and the members of the selection committee. We all remained still, and no one said a word. I think, on our side, we were too stunned.

Finally Captain Qwlessl stepped forward. "I beg your pardon, Mr. Chief Justice," she said. "These beings are heroes of the Confederation."

"These *children* stole a ship," Junup responded, "which, as I don't see it, I presume is lost or destroyed. They created an intercultural incident, worsening an already volatile situation. We are going to have to return those cruisers and pay for the damages. And *that* being," he said, pointing to my father, "is guilty of impersonating a Confederation citizen and corrupting the process by which worlds and delegates are selected."

"This is a load of rubbish," Steve said, striding forward. "You're worrying about the little details, you shelled git. We've just risked our lives to bring you the answer to all your problems, and you want to send it back? Are you daft?"

I tapped Steve with my free hand, doing my best to wordlessly convey the idea that Captain Qwlessl might be a better person to state our case.

The captain spread her hands wide, trying to look reasonable. "The Ish-hi may be a bit excitable, but he's essentially correct," she told Junup.

"You're bloody well right I'm correct," Steve said. "I've never been more correct in my life."

I glared at him, and he half shrugged.

"Chief Justice," the captain continued, "please consider what has been accomplished here. We have two Phandic cruisers, one of which is entirely undamaged. This is the war prize we've always dreamed of. These children, as you call them, not only rescued me and my crew, but they obtained these ships, which will teach us everything we need to know about Phandic weaponry. I don't understand why you are taking such a hard line here."

"The law is the law," the chief justice said.

My head pounded with outrage. After all we had done, after all we had risked to save the Confederation, this absurd goat-turtle was willing to throw away the chance to make everyone safe. I was starting to think that maybe my old principal had been right about me. Maybe I was a troublemaker. I'd certainly made a lot of trouble since leaving Earth. I wasn't proud of all of it, but I was plenty proud of those two Phandic ships and what they represented. This was not the time to quietly accept the decision of someone in authority. This was the time to speak up and to act.

"Even if you wanted to arrest us for intergalactic jaywalking or whatever," I said, "you can't return those ships. You'd have to be insane."

"And when a Phandic armada shows up at the station, demanding their ships back, how insane will I look then?"

"He'll still be a bloody [*goat-turtle*]," Steve said under his breath, "so fairly insane, yeah?"

"Then you get your own ships to defend the station," I said. "If eliminating the Phandic threat isn't worth fighting for, I don't know what is."

"Perhaps you don't care about how many lives are lost in battle," Junup said, "but I will not allow a crisis to escalate when I know it will result in the deaths of hundreds, maybe thousands, of beings."

"How many have already died?" Captain Qwlessl asked. "How many will die in the future? How many formerly free worlds are now under Phandic dominion? Those captured ships represent an end to the violence, not an escalation."

"That is your own shortsightedness," Junup said. "I choose to preserve life where I can." He waved at the peace officers. "Take them to detention."

Captain Qwlessl stepped out in front of us, as if to shield us from arrest. "Chief Justice!" she cried. "Do you really think the public will be happy with this treatment? Do you think the public wants you to surrender the greatest tactical advantage we've had in centuries?"

"I've already managed a stationwide closure of viewing screens and quarantined the dock zone," Junup said. "This entire incident has been classified. No one knows about the Phandic ships, and they aren't going to find out."

I held up my data bracelet, feeling myself smile with grim

triumph. "Except they do know. I've already sent details of our rescue mission to my data collector contact, and I've been recording this whole exchange. The fact that we secured those ships, and that you plan to send them back, is already public knowledge."

Junup turned toward me. "How dare you?" he snapped, jabbing a hairy finger at me. "You insolent little child. Do you know what you've done?"

"Not let you get away with being a coward?" I proposed. "Not let you undo everything we just risked our lives to accomplish? If you want to return those ships, then you are a total weenie, and it's my duty to stop you."

He appeared puzzled. I supposed he must have gotten some brackets with the weenie comment.

"Sir," Captain Qwlessl said, "I think the citizenry will have some very serious questions about why these beings are being treated as criminals, and why the judicial council would give up a chance to understand Phandic weaponry."

At the far end of the chamber I saw a series of data collectors— led by Hluh, in a lemon-yellow jumpsuit—trying to force their way past a security blockade and into the terminal. Peace officers were keeping them back, but the data collectors were holding up recording devices, taking in as much as they could from a distance.

"We may be creating scandal at this point," the clownish Darth Maul told the chief justice.

Junup nodded and spoke into his data bracelet. The peace officers parted, and Hluh, along with her data collector cronies, came into the room. Following them, Dr. Roop strode in and crossed the space to stand near us.

The chief justice's goaty face was twisted with anger, but he managed to pull himself together and turn toward the data collectors. "Perhaps I was hasty in my initial outburst, but we must not act outside the law. Mr. J'onzz is under arrest. And these children are in violation of their agreements as well. They are all to be detained at once."

I looked at the peace officers, and I looked at Tamret. She looked back at me, and I knew what she was thinking. I was thinking the same thing. They could not stop us if we ran.

Why shouldn't we run? Everything I wanted and cared for and hoped for was being sucked into a vortex. In the blink of an eye, all we had accomplished had vanished. My father was going back to prison. The delegation was on the verge of being kicked out, the cure for my mother was gone, and they were going to separate me from Tamret. Going along with their wishes would get me nothing. If I were free, however, I would be able to fix things. I'd rescued my father once before; I could do it again. Maybe I could figure out how to get a cure for my mom. I could steal a ship and bring it to her. If I had to choose between being a prisoner or a space pirate, it was an easy decision.

Tamret and I were strong and fast and agile. If we made a break for it, they would never be able to stop us. We could hide on the station until we could get a ship, and then we would figure out where to go. It wouldn't matter, because we would be together, and we could do anything.

The plan, if it could be called that, was completely insane, but I'd done crazier things already, and it beat letting them lock us up. No one, I decided, was going to put Tamret behind bars.

"Are you ready?" I asked her, my voice very low, but I knew with her Former enhancements she would be able to hear me.

"I'm ready," she said.

When I glanced up at Tamret, I felt my entire body tense. My heart, which had been pounding with excitement, now fluttered with misery. Her face was covered with yellow dots— laser sights. I glanced up and saw peace officers leveling PPB rifles at us. If we moved, we would be shot.

It was all the hesitation they needed. I felt my arms jerked behind me and secured. Peace officers grabbed Tamret's arms and roughly secured her. There was not going to be any escape.

We were all separated, and I was sent to some kind of holding cell within the terminal facility. It was the whitest room I'd ever seen: white walls, white floor, a white table with several white chairs. Nothing else. A peace officer brought me in, told me to wait, and released my wrist restraints before he locked the door behind him.

I tried contacting Tamret on my data bracelet, but I was barred from sending or receiving data. With nothing to do, I sat there and watched the minutes tick by. Finally, after more than three hours, the door opened and Junup entered the room, flanked by Captain Qwlessl and Dr. Roop.

Junup sat across from me, Captain Qwlessl and Dr. Roop to either side of me.

"Your friends," the chief justice said, "insisted on being present when I speak to you."

"Where's Tamret?" I said. "Where are Steve and the others? Where's my father?"

"I've just spoken with your father," Dr. Roop assured me. "He's fine."

"No one has been harmed," Junup said. "You will get a chance to see them before you leave."

"Leave for where?" I demanded.

"Zeke, you're going home," Captain Qwlessl said softly. "It was the best we could do for you."

"This situation has spiraled out of control," Dr. Roop said. "Beings are worried about protecting their reputations. No one is looking at the larger picture. There are those who wanted to put you on trial."

I had no doubt that some of those included the goat-turtle sitting across from me.

"What about the other delegations?" I asked. "Steve and Tamret?"

"Like your delegation," Junup said, "they are to return to their home worlds at once, and their species may not be considered for membership for a period not less than sixty standard years."

"No!" I stood up. Dr. Roop tried to get me to sit, but I shook him off. "You can't send Tamret back. She'll be treated like a criminal. The rest of the delegation hates her, and they'll make sure she gets blamed. You must have"—I waved my hand as I tried to think of the term—"political asylum here, right?"

"We are under no obligation to grant asylum to nonaligned species," Junup said. He remained seated, his hairy hands folded, completely undisturbed by my seething rage. "Such decisions fall to me as head of my committee, and I will not accept an application from an unrepentant criminal. I'm afraid your Rarel friend set out on this path when she chose to violate our laws. Now she must pay the price."

"I want to see her," I said. "Now."

"Zeke," Dr. Roop cautioned.

"You are in no position to make demands," Junup said. "In a

few minutes a technician will neutralize your nanites, and your skills will be returned to their baseline settings at the time of your arrival."

"I thought you didn't alter the skill system," I said. "I thought that was against your principles."

"You put yourself outside that code when you became a criminal," Junup said. "Soon your translator will cease to function, so I need to explain our decisions now. You and your friends are through here. I've already arranged for your possessions to be packed and brought to your transports. You and the other initiates shall be cast from this station, and your father will go to prison, where he belongs."

"Send him back with us!" I demanded.

"He is to be regarded as a war criminal, and exile is no longer an option."

I slowly returned to my seat, but I leveled my gaze at the chief justice. The cure of my mother, which I had considered as good as in my hands, had now vanished. I thought I had saved her, but by saving my father, I'd condemned my mother to death.

I considered more extreme options. I could, I knew, knock Junup down before the peace officers by the door could stop me, but that would get me nothing. "Before you touch me, I want to see my father, I want to see Steve, and I want to see Tamret." My voice was slow and, I hoped, a little dangerous.

Junup rewarded my efforts by looking a little uneasy, but in the end that counted for little. "No," he said.

Captain Qwlessl jabbed her trunk at him. "You are being cruel and vindictive," she said. "Let him speak to his father and his friends."

"I don't have to," Junup said, "and I don't want to, so I won't. This being has caused me nothing but trouble since he left his world, and I don't see that I owe him any favors."

Dr. Roop leaned forward and whispered something to Junup. The chief justice's goaty eyes widened, and he scowled at Dr. Roop. Then he rose to his feet.

"Very well," Junup said. "I'll arrange it."

I watched the chief justice leave the room.

"What did you say to him?" Captain Qwlessl asked.

Dr. Roop's eyes widened. "I simply reminded him that all politicians have secrets they would prefer not to be revealed."

I looked up at him. "You made an enemy of him for my sake."

"It was no great sacrifice," Dr. Roop said. "He'd already made an enemy of me. I just made things mutual."

A little while later, a peace officer opened the door and led me out. He would, he explained, take me to see my father. Then I would go back to the main terminal, where I could say good-bye to my other friends. Then I would have my nanites neutralized, and I would board a shuttle.

As I walked down the hall, a voice inside my head kept saying that this was real, it was actually happening. I was going back to Earth without anything to help my mother. Tamret was going back to her world. My father was going to prison. I tried to silence the voice. I had beaten the odds so many times before; I would do so again. I would get us all out of this. I just needed an opportunity. I would know it when I saw it. I kept saying that, but the other voice, the one that said it was all over, would not be shouted down.

The captain and Dr. Roop waited in the hall when the peace officer opened the door to my father's holding cell. It looked just like the one I had been in—pure white—and my father had been sitting, staring at the nothingness, as I had been for so many hours.

He stood up and hugged me, holding me close for a long time. Then he let me go, but he kept his hands on my shoulders and looked at me.

"Why are they doing this?" I asked him.

"I don't know," he said. "It won't stand. I promise you, Zeke. The truth will get out, and there will be questions. We can fix this." He let go and sat down in his chair. "We can fix this," he said again.

"I don't see how."

"I don't either," he admitted. "Not yet."

"What can I do?" I asked. "How can I help you?"

"How much do you trust Qwlessl?" he asked.

"Completely," I told him.

He nodded. "Make sure she is aware of the Former skill system. Someone needs to make sure they don't completely blindside the Confederation. In the meantime I'll work on my own legal problems. These people are amazing, Zeke, and they are brilliant, but they're not devious and they don't really understand crime. The fact that I've watched a lot of *Law and Order* reruns makes me one of the top legal minds in the Confederation."

I couldn't help but laugh.

"I'll get you back here," he said. "I can work the system. Just hang tight."

I nodded. "What should I tell Mom?"

"The truth," he said. "As much as you know. I wanted to have more time to tell you everything, about how it all happened, but I guess that will have to wait. But she hasn't remarried or anything? You're not just saying that to spare my feelings?"

I was withholding things to spare his feelings, but this wasn't one of them. "No," I said. "She dated a few times, but I think because she felt like she ought to. No one ever interested her. No one but you."

He looked away for a moment. "It will be hard, won't it?" he asked. "Going back to ordinary life, knowing all of this is out here?"

"Yeah," I said. "But it's not the world and the technology and wonders I'll miss. It's the people."

He nodded. "It's always the people."

The peace officers came back. My father and I hugged once more and that was it. They led me out and closed the door, and he was gone. My father, the man I'd thought dead, who was alive, whom I had freed, had been taken away from me again.

They brought me back to the terminal. There were still lots of peace officers and data collectors and government officials, but though I looked everywhere, there was no sign of Tamret. I saw Steve, however, standing with the Ish-hi delegation. I hurried over to him.

He put a hand on my arm. "I'm sorry, mate. It should have worked out better."

I didn't know if his kind hugged, and I didn't want to do anything culturally weird, so we just stood like that for a minute. "I'm sorry too. I got you into this, ruined your chances for your world. I never should have asked for your help."

"Rubbish," he said. "You did what you were supposed to do. We all did. Now they want to cover their tracks and protect themselves by punishing us. You've got no reason to be sorry."

"Thanks," I said.

"But," he added, "if it makes you feel better, we'll say you owe me one, yeah?"

"I owe you one," I agreed.

He jabbed a finger at me. "Don't you forget it, either. I mean to collect."

"Do you think we'll get a chance?"

"I don't know, mate. I just don't know."

And then there were peace officers between us, leading Steve and the rest of the Ish-hi to a gate that would take them to a shuttle, which would take them to a ship. And they would go back to their home world.

I watched him go, sadness and rage and helplessness pulsing through me. Then I heard someone call my name. It was Tamret, and she was running toward me. She threw herself against me, and if it weren't for the enhancements that she herself had given me, she would have knocked me over.

She pressed her face against my neck, and I could feel she was crying. "I can't go back there," she said. "You don't know what it's like. You don't know how much we needed to join the Confederation."

I thought again about making a break for it, the two of us, together, but there were yellow dots on her shoulders, probably on my back and hers. The thought of being shot wasn't what stopped me—it was the thought of her being shot. I'd seen Tamret struck down once already. I couldn't see it again. Even so, if I'd believed there was a chance, even a slight chance, I would have taken it, but the peace officers were not letting their guard down for a second.

I could not save her, so I held her and let her cry. Her body shuddered, and the bravest, most reckless being I had ever met convulsed with fear.

"I can't go back," she said. "They'll put me in prison, Zeke. They may hurt me. I'll never see you again."

"Shh," I said. I stroked the back of her head. I was trying to think, trying to find the words, trying to find my way out of this. Nothing came to me. All I could do was to try to comfort her. I was powerless to do anything else. "I won't let them do this."

The data collectors were pressed in now, all around us, recording us, capturing holograms of Tamret's misery, but I didn't care. I was seething with rage and frustration. I was stronger than any of these beings, I was faster and I could process information better, but what good did that do me? We were still being separated and shipped off, and no matter how I tried, I could not think of a way around this.

"We can't do anything," Tamret said. "Once we're back on our worlds, we won't ever be able to reach each other. We'll be stuck there, apart."

"We can do anything," I told her.

"Not this," she said. "We can't do this."

I lifted up her chin to look into her lavender eyes. "Tamret, I have done things I would never have thought possible, and I did them because of you. I did them *for* you. I swear, I'm not going to leave you there."

She wiped at her tears with the back of her hand. "Don't say it if you don't mean it."

"I mean it." And I did. I didn't know how I would do it, but I swore at that moment that I would not rest until I was sure she was safe. All I knew was that the universe could not be this cruel. I wouldn't let it be. I would not have everything taken away from me.

"Don't worry, Snowflake. I'll take care of you."

It was Ardov. He and Thiel and Semj walked by, holding their bags. The other two looked dour, but Ardov looked grimly satisfied.

"As soon as we leave this station," Ardov said to her, his face split open with a grin, "I am released from my vow."

As he walked away, I seriously considered going after him and killing him. I could do it, I had the strength and the power and the skills to do it, but I knew that wouldn't protect Tamret. Not really. The others in her delegation would report what had happened, and I could not help her if I was in prison.

"Hey," I said to him. "You don't want to make me your enemy."

He laughed and didn't even break his stride. "I can't see how it will matter."

"Ardov!" I shouted.

He turned around and looked at me, his expression a mask of bored contempt.

"Don't think any distance between us will protect you. I've beaten you before, and I'll do it again."

He opened his mouth to say something, but then he changed his mind. He turned away and walked toward his gate. Then he stopped as a being approached him. It was Junup. He whispered something into Ardov's ear, and the Rarel nodded. Ardov continued toward the gate, and Junup walked away, looking pleased with himself.

"I like that young being," he said to me. "He's got a real future."

A peace officer came up to us. He was one of the bull-headed ones, and he, at least, had the decency to look ashamed of what he had to do. "I'm sorry, but it's time for her to go."

Impossibly, unbelievably, I had to say good-bye to Tamret. I knew it, but I couldn't make myself accept it. *They can't make me,* I thought crazily. I did not want to waste what little time I had to talk to her, but how could I say what I had to say? How did I choose my words when they were all so pathetic? We were going to be torn apart, cast to our impossibly distant corners of the universe, and the cruelty and injustice of it filled me with rage as much as it numbed my mind.

I stepped in front of her again and took her hands and looked into her painfully sad lavender eyes. "Don't you dare give up," I said.

She threw her arms around me and hugged me until it hurt, and I hugged her back. I didn't know what else to do but bury my face in the cool of her neck and wish that the moment could never end. How could it be? I thought. How could they do this? But there was no answer. No explanation. They were doing it, and I was powerless to stop it.

"I'm so sorry I let you down," she said.

"You never let me down," I told her. "Never."

"I did," she said. "I failed you."

She let go of me, and then the black-clad peace officers were holding her arms, trying to lead her away. She fought them at first, but they gripped harder, and I think Tamret did not want to be bound or shocked, so she stopped struggling. She looked up at me.

"I'm so scared," she said.

I watched, powerless, as the peace officers led her across the expanse of the terminal and through a gate. Then the gate door sealed and she was gone.

There was so much left unsaid between us, and that her last words to me were about her fear filled me with sadness and anger and the searing, almost unendurable, pain of helplessness. I thought that she was right. I really never was going to see her again.

Dr. Roop now approached me, with Charles, Nayana, and Mi Sun trailing him. They looked like they were in shock, and when I went to meet Charles's gaze, he turned away.

They held back, but Dr. Roop walked up to me holding a black box, about the size of a hardcover book, made out of something like stiff cardboard. "As you *know*, this is yours," he said. "I forgot to pack it up and put it in your bags."

I had never seen it before, but I could tell by how he looked at me that he wanted me to have it, and that he was afraid if we said anything else, the peace officers might notice. So I took the box and held it with both hands.

"Thanks," I muttered, too distracted to make sense of what the box meant.

"I am very sorry, Zeke. You did everything I could have asked of you. All of you were what we hoped for, and that this should be your reward is so unjust. I will do what I can to reverse things from here."

"Do you think you can?"

"I don't know anymore. I just don't know. But I can promise you I will help your father."

Hands were on me now, leading me and Charles and Mi Sun

and Nayana toward our own shuttle. Everyone's eyes were cast down. We were sad and angry. Maybe they were angry with me. Maybe they had every right to be.

A quartet of peace officers approached us, each of them holding a black injector cylinder. This was it, then. They were going to neutralize our improvements. They were going to turn us back into ordinary people.

The three other humans presented their hands for injection, but Dr. Roop blocked the peace officer heading to me. "He's my friend," he said. "Please allow me to do it."

The peace officer nodded and handed him the cylinder.

Dr. Roop then gestured, waving someone over. It was Captain Qwlessl, followed by Urch. The two of them came over.

"Excuse us, Captain," said one of the peace officers. "He needs to be injected and removed from the premises."

"Will you prevent me from saying good-bye to my friend?" she asked.

"Briefly, then," the peace officer said. "There is a schedule."

I looked at the captain. "Don't you let them return those Phandic ships."

"No, I won't."

Urch reached out and took the black box from my hand. My first instinct was to snatch it back, and he must have seen my alarm, so he met my gaze as if to steady me. Then he gestured toward the captain with his head, as if I should continue the conversation. He, meanwhile, was running one of his sharp fingernails along the bottom of the box. Carving something? I had no idea.

I looked at the captain. "My father's worried about the Phands looking for Former tech. He thinks it might be some kind of specialized military skill tree. Talk to him about it."

She nodded. "I will."

I said, "Thank you for everything. When I get home, I'm going to tell my mother about you, and she's going to be so glad you were here to look after me."

"I think I'm the one who should be glad there was someone looking after me," she said, and she took me in her arms and gave me a huge hug, She felt warm and safe, but I knew it was all being taken away.

"Can you help her?" I asked. "Tamret?"

She looked over at the data collectors, who were recording all of this, every word we spoke.

"I'm sorry," she told me. "She's outside Confederation space. There's nothing I can do." The words were harsh and cold, but there was something about her gaze when she spoke that made me wonder if she was trying to tell me something. Was that too much to hope?

"Time to go," the peace officer said.

Urch handed the box back to me and then put a hand on my shoulder. "Safe travels, my friend."

The two of them walked away. Dr. Roop shook my hand, human-style. He looked down at me with his big yellow giraffe eyes, and I felt sure he was trying to tell me something, just like the captain had been, but I could not read it. Then he put one of his hands to my face, a curiously tender gesture, one I hadn't anticipated. "Remember," he said.

I wanted to ask what it was I was supposed to remember, but I couldn't make the words come out.

"I need your hand," Dr. Roop said.

I held it out.

"Your father used to say that there are always possibilities."

"Yeah," I croaked. "He would say that, wouldn't he?"

"Have a safe journey." Then he pressed the injector to the back of my hand, and I began the process of turning back into someone of absolutely no importance.

Wordlessly, Dr. Roop shook my hand again, and then the four of us were led to our gate. We passed through the door, and then through a tunnel, and then onto a shuttle. When it launched, we would leave Confederation Central, and we were never to return again.

A peace officer stood by the shuttle door, making sure we strapped in. "In a few minutes your nanites will dissolve into harmless organic matter that will pass safely through your system. This means that your translators will not function. The crew on the ship taking you home know this, and they will do their best to communicate to you what you need to know." He then held out his hand. "I need your data bracelets."

Once he had them in hand, he stepped outside, and the shuttle door whined closed.

My three companions sat, all of them looking down. I wanted to say something, but what was there to say? I looked at the rest. Charles's face was set in stony resolve. Nayana was crying. Mi Sun looked like she wanted to kill someone.

My fellow humans said nothing during the voyage. I sat still, not looking out the window, feeling myself diminish, become something less. My sight and hearing were the most obvious, but I had less power, less energy. My muscles seemed to work differently. I was like a deflating balloon. I was now simply Zeke Reynolds. Nothing more.

When we reached the ship, a stick-insect alien led us to our quarters with a series of gestures. It made an eating gesture and pointed to a door down the hall. And then it left. It had nothing more to say to us.

I turned to go into my room.

"No one blames you."

It was Mi Sun. She stood there, still looking furious, with her arms folded. Her English was heavily accented but quite good. "We are all angry, but not with you. We chose to go with you because it was the right thing. We all did the right things."

"Thanks," I told her. "I appreciate you saying so."

"They punished us," she said, "but that doesn't change the fact that we did something important. We made a difference for trillions of beings. Thank you for letting us do that with you."

I was too stunned to speak, and so I simply nodded.

"You probably wish to be alone," Charles said. "I understand that, but if you want company, we'll be in the common room. If it's the same layout as the other ship, it should be that one there." He pointed.

"Thanks," I said again. "But I'll just lie down for a little while."

"If you change your mind, you know where to find us," he said.

Nayana, who had said nothing, now gave me a very quick and awkward hug.

I turned away from them and went into my cabin.

I sat alone, looking out the viewscreen, holding the dark cardboard box in my hand. I could not bring myself to lower my eyes, and so the station receded and I watched the swirling clouds of the great gas giant, their beautiful hues as they wound their slow way across the planet's vast surface. The station grew smaller until it was hard to see the details, until the dome was indistinguishable from the metal, until it was no more than a tiny disk, a slim coin cast against the vastness of nothing and everything.

Finally I found the nerve to face the black box Dr. Roop had given me. I took off the lid and saw that the box contained two pieces of paper—one small and one large—and a black cylinder, like the one that they used to inject nanites.

The small paper contained a series of blocky hieroglyphs, all straight lines and right angles, printed by hand with a thick red ink. I shook my head and squeezed my eyes shut. What was the point of giving me a note to read when I was not going to be able to read it? Still, the script was beautiful, and it was a message from my friend, even if I could not read it.

I opened my eyes to look at it again, but this time the sharp script was gone. It had changed, in those few seconds, to English. I didn't know how, but for the moment I didn't care. It said, *This was in Tamret's room, addressed to you. Your friend, Klhkkkloplkkkuiv Roop.*

One last message from Tamret. I held the paper in my hands for a long time, fearing what it might say, savoring the thought of one more communication from her, and dreading the knowledge that it would be the last. Most of all, I feared I would be unable to read it. Finally, I summoned my courage, and I unfolded it and saw that my translator was still working.

Zeke,

If you are reading this, things have gone badly, and I am sorry for that. I wanted, more than anything else, for us to be together, but if you are looking at these words, then it means we won't be. If you need what the box contains, then your planet has not made its way into the Confederation. If I am not giving it to you myself, it means that I am dead or gone against my will.

You probably never noticed that the locket your mother gave you disappeared one night. I needed the genetic information in her hair to hack into the medical database and make what is inside this injector—the nunites that will repair her cells and cure her disease. It was so easy to do, it's shameful they did not offer to do it themselves, but they have their rules. I have mine.

I did not tell you I was doing it because I care so much for you, and I want you to care for me—for who I am, not because I did something for you. Maybe that makes me selfish, since I could give this to you anytime and ease your mind. I am sorry for that, and I hope you will forgive me.

I'm crying as I write this. It's crazy, I know. Nothing bad has happened. Maybe nothing bad will happen, but I've seen too much to believe that. If you ever read these words, and I pray by the [coalition of revenge deities] you don't, please know how much you have meant to me. If I am dead, my ghost will haunt you, and if you even look at another girl, I will make you miserable, and I will torment that girl until she throws herself off the nearest cliff.

Tamret

I was crying now, and I was not trying to hide the tears, nor did they fill me with shame. I was crying because of what they had done to Tamret. They had taken her fearlessness and made her afraid. They had taken her unbreakable spirit, and they had broken it. Tamret was the most daring and dauntless being I had ever known, and they had condemned her to prison and torture and perhaps death, and the vastness of space made me powerless to prevent it. Yet she had found a way to cross that distance and give to me the thing I'd been seeking most when I left the Earth.

I sat there like that, tears running onto my lap, my shirt, not bothering to wipe them, and then I remembered what Urch had done. I turned over the box and looked at the bottom. There, in its papery softness, Urch's predator's fingernail had carved nine simple words: *It was fun. We should do it again. Soon.*

Something escaped from my throat. Not laughter, but something grimly like it. I studied the words until they became like an icon, like a symbol of all I had been and so desperately wanted to be again. Urch's words were not a promise, and they were not a plan, but they were a cause for hope where there had been none before. My friends, the friends I had always longed for, had not forgotten me. That was reason enough to take comfort, but there was something else, too. I *read* the words. They had neutralized my nanites, and my translator had vanished, but now it was back. Was that why Dr. Roop had insisted on injecting me himself? Had he switched cylinders? Had he hinted at some plan? Was that what he had wanted me to remember?

I didn't care how it had happened, only that it had. I understood these messages, written in scripts I could not have imagined in languages I could not comprehend. I could feel that my strength and agility and hearing and sight and all the rest were no more than when I had first come to the station, but I could still translate. Maybe other skills would return. Maybe I could somehow unlock them. Maybe I could go back to leveling up once I got home. Perhaps I was not as powerless as they had intended to leave me.

I looked out the viewscreen again, and the great ringed planet was now itself a tiny disc against an endless canvas of blinking stars and swirling gases. I kept my eye on it until it was nothing but a memory, and I continued looking as if somehow I could have one last glimpse of the place from which I had been exiled. I was not ready to let it go. Not yet.

Then came a recorded announcement—in words I could understand—telling me to prepare to exit normal space. This was soon followed by that familiar disorientation, and up became down and in became out and I was flying and falling and spinning, but it was only an instant before the sensation was gone. The window, too, was gone, and my eyes fell upon the blank wall of my cabin, bland and gray and meaningless. The ship had begun to tunnel through space, and though I could feel no movement, I knew we sped past stars and planets and across the infinite emptiness between them. We had ripped a hole in the fabric of the universe, and we tumbled down its great and impossible slide, racing toward a world that once, not so very long ago, had been the place I called home.